Praise for the novels of
bestselling author Lynn Kurland

With Every Breath

"As always, [Kurland] delivers a delightful read." —*Romantic Times*

"Kurland is a skilled enchantress . . . *With Every Breath* is breathtaking in its magnificent scope; a true invitation to the delights of romance." —*Night Owl Romance*

When I Fall in Love

"Kurland infuses her polished writing with a deliciously dry wit, and her latest time-travel love story is sweetly romantic and thoroughly satisfying." —*Booklist*

"The continuation of a wonderful series, this story can also be read alone. It's an extremely good book." —*Affaire de Coeur*

"One of the best romances that this reviewer has ever had the pleasure of reading! It is enough to make even nonbelievers believe in the power of love." —*Love Romances & More*

"Lynn Kurland has surpassed even her personal best with *When I Fall in Love*. This is a book that will haunt you long after the final page is turned." —*Kwips and Kritiques*

"A sweet story of love across time. There's plenty of humor and romance to entertain . . . a splendid way to escape reality, even if it's just for a few hours. Highly recommended."
—*MyShelf*

"Revisiting Ms. Kurland's world is always a joy . . . a cheerful, positive, feel-good romance that will make your heart glad." —*The Eternal Night*

"Delightful . . . Ms. Kurland knows how to deliver a heart-warming romance and remarkable characters."
—*Romance Reviews Today*

continued . . .

Much Ado in the Moonlight

"A pure delight."   —*Huntress Book Reviews*

"A consummate storyteller . . . will keep the reader on the edge of their seat, unable to put the book down until the very last word."   —*ParaNormal Romance*

"No one melds ghosts and time travel better than the awesome Kurland."   —*Romantic Times*

Dreams of Stardust

"Kurland weaves another fabulous read with just the right amounts of laughter, romance, and fantasy."
                    —*Affaire de Coeur*

"Kurland crafts some of the most ingenious time-travel romances readers can find . . . wonderfully clever and completely enchanting."   —*Romantic Times*

A Garden in the Rain

"Kurland laces her exquisitely romantic, utterly bewitching blend of contemporary romance and time travel with a delectable touch of tart wit, leaving readers savoring every word of this superbly written romance."   —*Booklist*

"Kurland is clearly one of romance's finest writers—she consistently delivers the kind of stories readers dream about. Don't miss this one."   —*The Oakland Press*

From This Moment On

"A disarming blend of romance, suspense, and heartwarming humor, this book is romantic comedy at its best."
                    —*Publishers Weekly*

"A deftly plotted delight, seasoned with a wonderfully wry sense of humor and graced with endearing, unforgettable characters."   —*Booklist*

My Heart Stood Still

"Written with poetic grace and a wickedly subtle sense of humor . . . the essence of pure romance. Sweet, poignant, and truly magical, this is a rare treat: romance with characters readers will come to care about and a love story they will cherish." *—Booklist*

"A totally enchanting tale, sensual and breathtaking . . . an absolute must-read." *—Rendezvous*

If I Had You

"Kurland brings history to life . . . . in this tender medieval romance." *—Booklist*

"A passionate story filled with danger, intrigue, and sparkling dialogue." *—Rendezvous*

The More I See You

"The superlative Ms. Kurland once again wows her readers with her formidable talent as she weaves a tale of enchantment that blends history with spellbinding passion and impressive characterization, not to mention a magnificent plot."
—Rendezvous

Another Chance to Dream

"Kurland creates a special romance between a memorable knight and his lady." *—Publishers Weekly*

The Very Thought of You

"A masterpiece . . . this fabulous tale will enchant anyone who reads it." *—Painted Rock Reviews*

This Is All I Ask

"An exceptional read." *—The Atlanta Journal-Constitution*

"Both powerful and sensitive . . . a wonderfully rich and rewarding book." *—Susan Wiggs*

TILL THERE WAS YOU

LYNN KURLAND

THE BERKLEY PUBLISHING GROUP
Published by the Penguin Group
Penguin Group (USA) Inc.
375 Hudson Street, New York, New York 10014, USA
Penguin Group (Canada), 90 Eglinton Avenue East, Suite 700, Toronto, Ontario M4P 2Y3, Canada
(a division of Pearson Penguin Canada Inc.)
Penguin Books Ltd., 80 Strand, London WC2R 0RL, England
Penguin Group Ireland, 25 St. Stephen's Green, Dublin 2, Ireland (a division of Penguin Books Ltd.)
Penguin Group (Australia), 250 Camberwell Road, Camberwell, Victoria 3124, Australia
(a division of Pearson Australia Group Pty. Ltd.)
Penguin Books India Pvt. Ltd., 11 Community Centre, Panchsheel Park, New Delhi—110 017, India
Penguin Group (NZ), 67 Apollo Drive, Rosedale, North Shore 0632, New Zealand
(a division of Pearson New Zealand Ltd.)
Penguin Books (South Africa) (Pty.) Ltd., 24 Sturdee Avenue, Rosebank, Johannesburg 2196,
South Africa

Penguin Books Ltd., Registered Offices: 80 Strand, London WC2R 0RL, England

This is a work of fiction. Names, characters, places, and incidents either are the product of the author's imagination or are used fictitiously, and any resemblance to actual persons, living or dead, business establishments, events, or locales is entirely coincidental. The publisher does not have any control over and does not assume any responsibility for author or third-party websites or their content.

TILL THERE WAS YOU

A Jove Book / published by arrangement with the author

PRINTING HISTORY
Jove mass-market edition / May 2009

Copyright © 2009 by Lynn Curland.
Cover art by Jim Griffin.
Cover handlettering by Ron Zinn.
Cover design by George Long.

ISBN: 978-0-515-14624-0

JOVE®
Jove Books are published by The Berkley Publishing Group,
a division of Penguin Group (USA) Inc.,
375 Hudson Street, New York, New York 10014.
JOVE® is a registered trademark of Penguin Group (USA) Inc.
The "J" design is a trademark of Penguin Group (USA) Inc.

PRINTED IN THE UNITED STATES OF AMERICA

10 9 8 7 6 5 4 3 2 1

*To the ladies who thought Mary
needed a story . . . They know who they are.*

Cast of Characters*

Zachary Smith

Alexander Smith, *Zachary's brother*
   Margaret, *his wife*

Elizabeth Smith, *Zachary's sister*
   Jamie, *Elizabeth's husband*
     Patrick, *Jamie's brother*
      Madelyn, *Patrick's wife*
        Sunshine Cameron, *Madelyn's sister*
         Robert Cameron, *Sunshine's husband*

Robin de Piaget
   Anne, *his wife*
     Mary

Jackson Kilchurn
   Amanda, *his wife*
     Jackson
     Thaddeus

Nicholas de Piaget
   Jennifer, *his wife*
     Connor
     Theophilus
     Samuel

Isabelle de Piaget de Seger
   Parsival, *her son*

Geoffrey of Styrr
   Suzanna, *his mother*

* *Only a partial list of those who appear in this book. For more details, please see www.LynnKurland.com.*

Prologue

T*he* last rays of sunlight sparkled against a ruined castle that stood in the midst of rolling hills, sweetly singing streams, and roads still dusted with the last of a winter's snow.

A lone man strode through the castle gates as the sun set. He wasn't unused to the chill of a long winter, yet still he shivered under the heavy cloak he wore fastened over his shoulder with an enormous brooch. His kilt swung about his knees and a great sword slapped against his thigh as he walked without haste but with definite purpose. He had business that night.

He crossed the courtyard and climbed the well-worn stairs. There were no front doors left to the great hall, but that was to be expected. The place was ripe for not only a bit of mischief but a decent remodel as well.

Fortunately, he knew just who could see to both.

He walked into the hall, spared the place a bit of a look, then continued over to the hearth. It likely hadn't seen a fire in a pair of centuries, but that was no deterrent. He created a roaring fire with a negligent flick of his wrist, then chose a likely spot and placed a comfortable chair there.

He paused for quite a while, wrestling with a decision he didn't particularly want to make. He considered, frowned, and then, with a sigh, surrendered.

And then Ambrose MacLeod, laird of the clan MacLeod during the flowering of the Renaissance—which hadn't exactly been yesterday—placed a Tudor-rose-patterned cushion upon the seat.

He didn't particularly care to indulge in such luxuries, but he wasn't as young as he used to be—never mind that he was no longer troubled by the aches and pains of a mortal frame. The castle surrounding him was austere enough. If a body couldn't enjoy at least the sight of a few creature comforts now and again, what pleasures could he reasonably take?

He sat with a contented sigh, plucked a hefty tankard of ale out of thin air, then settled back to anticipate what he was certain would be a robust and entertaining evening of conversation. At least he might enjoy it without being stalked like a hapless rabbit across the moor by a woman who had no business casting her steely eye his way, but that was perhaps an observation better left unmade at present.

He savored the crackle and pop of the fire in the hearth for quite some time before he put his hand to his ear. Hark, was that a curse? And a stomp? He was certain he'd heard the reassuring sound of both. He looked to his left and watched a man stride through what had once been the sturdy doors of the great hall in which he now sat. That man continued to grumble his way across the hall before he, after much ado and many more complaints, settled down in his own chair with his own bit of comfort in a mug. Ambrose nodded politely.

"Fulbert."

Fulbert de Piaget, second son of a very illustrious earl of Artane and, to everyone's continued surprise, Ambrose's own brother-in-law, grunted. "I'll dispense with pleasantries. You're mad."

Ambrose lifted an eyebrow in surprise. "Am I? Why do you say that?"

"We do better when we're not inviting unknowns into our midst," Fulbert said. "This new plan of yours is a mistake. Mark my words."

Ambrose marked them, but unfortunately he couldn't discount them as easily as he might have liked. Fulbert had a point. He, Fulbert, and the third of their number had been about their work for quite some time now without any outside aid, and they were quite used to each other's methods. Bringing in someone new, someone untested and unused to the particular delicacies necessary for their usual business . . . well, it might spell disaster.

"I also don't know why we're here in this wreck," Fulbert muttered. He looked up at the night sky that was quite visible thanks to the lack of a proper roof. "Wyckham? Lovely in its time, perhaps, but surely not now." He shot Ambrose a disgruntled look. "We could have been quite comfortably ensconced at the Boar's Head Inn."

"I thought a change of venue might be refreshing," Ambrose said brightly.

Fulbert leaned forward and looked at him intently. "I imagine you do, my cowardly friend. Perhaps we would be well served by discussing what your reasons for that thought might be—"

"Ah, look," Ambrose said suddenly, gesturing with his mug toward the door. "There's Hugh."

"Run as long as you like, Ambrose," Fulbert said knowingly. "Your doom is waiting for you back at the inn. Garbed, I imagine, in pink."

Ambrose had no doubt that was the case, but that was something to think on later. Business, as always, came first.

Hugh McKinnon, laird of the clan McKinnon in the distant memory of Scottish glory, crossed the floor, frowning furiously and paying not a shred of attention to where he was going. That might have had to do with the fact that he was concentrating very seriously on something that looked remarkably like a clipboard. Ambrose was past being surprised by what tangles Hugh became embroiled in, so he merely waited until Hugh stopped tapping his chin with his pencil and muttering things about *microfiche* and *census records.*

"Hugh?" Ambrose prodded.

Hugh looked up, cross-eyed. "By the saints, Ambrose, 'tis a dodgy business, this genealogy. I can scarce read my own writin', not to mention what those friars managed to scribble in their records. How is a body to possibly find a bleedin' ancestor for the soul in question?"

"Are you telling me you haven't managed the feat?"

Hugh drew himself up. "Of course, I managed," he said with a sniff. He paused. "Eventually. After a bit of a tussle."

"Hugh," Ambrose said sternly, "what have you done?"

Hugh scrunched up his face and looked back defiantly. "I did nothin' untoward. Them genealogy librarians can be a mite testy, I'll tell ye that. They're there to help, not do for ye." He scowled. "I daresay I gave more than one feisty biddy the vapors before I found one willing to do instead of lecture."

Ambrose could only imagine. "And what did all your labors yield?"

Hugh straightened his clothes, adjusted the cap on his head, then stepped back and gestured with a flourish toward where the hall doors had once been.

In stumbled a gentleman of advanced years and very salty tongue, looking equal parts dazed and annoyed. He made his way over to the fire, then looked at them and took their measure.

"England," he said with distaste. "Thought I'd left the damp behind for good."

Ambrose fashioned another chair, then leaned over and handed the newcomer a mug of ale. "Please, sit and be comfortable. If I might inquire who—"

"You might, or you might not," the man said, taking his drink and sitting down with a grunt. "No need to introduce yourselves. I've been favored with all manner of tales concerning your exploits all the way here." He shot Fulbert a look. "I'm not accustomed to associating with Brits—"

Ambrose put his hand out and stopped Fulbert from drawing an as-yet-nonexistent sword. He couldn't stop Fulbert's growl, but he supposed their new addition deserved what he got. Ambrose sat back slowly and wondered if Fulbert had it aright. Perhaps they had made an error in bringing in someone new.

He revisited his reasons, just to see where a flaw might have been found. They had as their victim—er, *subject*, rather—a man who was not unused to things of a paranormal nature. He was also, as it happened, not unused to things of a dating nature. Ambrose had lost count over the years of the women the lad had squired about. Short ones, tall ones, plump ones, far-too-skinny ones, beautiful ones, not-so-beautiful ones. Unfortunately, there hadn't been a lassie to suit. Ambrose had decided that 'twas past time to take matters into his own hands.

The only trouble was that the soul in question was powerfully stubborn and wouldn't be sent in the direction of a truly fine match without a goodly nudge. Hence the thought of bringing in fresh blood, as it were, to potentially convince the recalcitrant descendant that ancestors on both sides of the family were very interested in seeing him well settled.

Ambrose put on his most charming smile. "We all must associate at times where we're less than eager, but we endure it as best we may. Now, if you wouldn't mind telling us a bit about yourself . . . ?"

The newcomer looked around with a resigned air, then fortified himself with a hefty swig of ale. "Drummond," he said. "Laird John Drummond, if we're to be exact—"

"Drummond?" Ambrose interrupted in surprise. He looked at Hugh, startled. "I thought we were looking for a Mackintosh."

"Depends on what part of the tree ye'd be wantin' to sit in," Hugh said darkly. "He was the best I could find. And he didn't want to be found."

"Why should I?" John Drummond demanded. "There I was, happily dividin' my time between a very nice perch atop the Space Needle and, when the rain vexed me overmuch, lurking belowdecks in the Underground—"

"In Seattle?" Ambrose asked.

Laird Drummond shot him a look. "I thought a bit of distance was needful after my own brother murdered me in my own bed!"

Ambrose looked at Hugh, who only shrugged helplessly.

"As I said," the Drummond continued with a scowl, "there I was, minding my own afterlife affairs, when I was accosted—simply accosted, I tell ye!—by that red-haired madman, who waved a clipboard at me and almost stabbed me in the eye with a pencil—"

"I did not almost stab ye," Hugh said hotly.

"You certainly did!"

"Did not!"

"Did, too!"

Ambrose broke in before swords could be drawn. "Whatever the particulars might be, you're here and we're glad of your company."

"The McKinnon said there'd be bloodshed." The Drummond shot Ambrose a look. " 'Tis the only reason I came."

Ambrose sent Hugh a look that had him shifting uncomfortably in his seat.

"Well," Hugh said defensively, "there might be."

Ambrose wasn't completely certain Hugh didn't have that aright, but he thought it best not to say as much. He turned back to their new addition. "I can't guarantee there won't be a bit, but in this venture we'll try to keep it to a minimum. The noble task laid before us is of a different nature than a full-on battle, though no less exciting."

Drummond leaned forward, his ears perking up. "Are we moving the border again? Southward this time? I'm a Highlander myself and I've generally no use for those feeble Lowlanders, but if work can be done for Scotland's glory, then count me in."

Fulbert set his cup on the floor, then looked at Ambrose expectantly. "Aye, what specifically are we doing, Ambrose? War? Mayhem? Foul deeds wrought in the middle of the night? Do tell."

Ambrose ignored him. It was either that or pull the dirk free of his boot and stab Fulbert through the heart. The thought had occurred to him before, true, but he resisted it now as admirably as he had for the past four hundred years.

"Our business is of a more, shall we say, *timeless* nature."

The Drummond's eyebrows went up immediately. "The abolition of taxes on whisky?"

Even Hugh made approving noises about that.

"Nay," Ambrose began slowly.

"Death?" the Drummond asked, looking no less enthusiastic. "You know, death and taxes are the only two things that are final." He shot Fulbert a look. "An *American* said that."

Fulbert only rolled his eyes.

"Nay, not death, either," Ambrose said.

"But there is nothing else—"

"Love, man," Fulbert exclaimed. "We're speaking of *love!*"

The Drummond recoiled as if he'd been bitten. "Love?"

"Aye," Ambrose said. "Our task is to shepherd a certain lad in the proper direction, then see to any additional details—if there are any of those sorts of details—after that proper direction has been taken."

The Drummond looked at the three of them as if they'd suddenly announced they were carrying the plague. "You three are *matchmakers?*"

"I'm not," Fulbert said, holding up his hands quickly. "I'm the Voice of Reason."

Hugh shot Fulbert a glare. "Ye're as deep into this as we are, ye bloody Brit."

Fulbert started to balk, then shrugged, picked up his cup, and applied himself to its contents.

Ambrose applied the full potency of his most convincing look on the Drummond. "We have taken it upon ourselves, as guardians of our respective lines, to assure that those lines are continued on in the best fashion possible. No matter the danger, or the delicacy required, we press on, boldly going where no shade has gone before—"

"Aye, straight to Bedlam," Fulbert whispered loudly.

Ambrose glared at him, then turned back to their temporary helper. "We can see to this on our own, of course, but we thought that since we are looking at a particularly difficult case, we wouldn't spurn aid from a new source. And so I asked Hugh to take his life in his hands and cross the Pond with the hope of finding an American ancestor willing to cast his lot in with us and give our charge the appropriate nudge if necessary."

The Drummond was speechless.

"And who is the lad again?" Fulbert asked, looking at Ambrose over the top of his cup. "I forgot."

"Zachary Smith," Ambrose said, sending him a warning look.

"Isn't he James MacLeod's doorman?"

"He isn't, which you well know," Ambrose said shortly. "He's the lady of the keep's brother, her youngest, though he is a score and eleven himself."

Fulbert sighed. "I do know what it is not to be the eldest. A burden, that's what it is."

"He seems to have borne it fairly well," Ambrose said, "and he's made a great success of himself." He turned to John Drummond. "You would be proud of him. He started university very young and had his degrees by a score and two. He's had quite a successful career over here where his particular feel for old structures has come in useful. Not only that, he's full of proper Scottish virtues that he no doubt inherited from ancestors hailing from north of the border."

Fulbert grunted, but said nothing.

"But I don't think he wants to wed," Hugh ventured. "You know, Ambrose, he's dated scores of women and not found a one to love."

"He's looking in the wrong place," Ambrose said firmly. "'Tis our job to make certain he looks in the right place."

"And where would that be?" the Drummond asked with a snort. "In a nunnery? In a pub? Surely not here in *England*?"

"He could do worse," Fulbert said, throwing the other man a dark look.

"I'm not certain he could," the Drummond said archly.

Fulbert growled.

The Drummond rubbed his hands together and suddenly a very snazzy purple gym bag materialized at his feet. He drew forth an eminently authentic-looking dirk and flipped it into the air a time or two, catching it expertly each time.

"I think I might have a bit to say about where this lad begins his search," the Drummond said pointedly, "seeing that he's *my* descendant."

Fulbert looked down his nose at the blade. "And I think I'll be offering my opinion quite loudly until I see a bit of steel that impresses me."

The Drummond flipped the knife back up into the air, then stood and caught it as it fell back to earth in the shape of a mighty Claymore.

Fulbert stood and twitched aside his velvet cape to reveal a very lethal-looking sword bearing a handful of large jewels in the hilt. "Outside, then. We'll settle this before young Zachary arrives and is forced to watch me humiliate his wee grandpa. Hugh, care to come learn by observation?"

"Aye, if ye mean learn what *not* to do."

Insults ensued, mingled with grumbles, slurs, and other mottos and slogans appropriate to the significance of the moment. Ambrose watched the trio troop across the floor flexing limbs and tongues equally.

He stroked his chin thoughtfully. Perhaps it had been a mistake after all to bring in someone new. It wasn't as if he, Fulbert, and Hugh didn't have a vested interest in Zachary's happiness. Zachary was brother-in-law to a MacLeod, and he had certainly spent enough time in Scotland to have earned a place in the clan.

Still, when embarking on a difficult quest, it helped to have family about.

"Damn you, McKinnon, if you poke me one more time with that bloody pencil—"

Their voices faded, to be replaced in good time with the reassuring sound of steel against steel. Ambrose turned back to his contemplation of the fire. Aye, family was a fine thing indeed to have about. But better still was finding a love that would outlast both death and taxes.

And given the difficulty of the match he intended to make, he supposed he might be wise to bet on the last two.

Chapter 1

Zachary William Smith lay on his back, stared up into the flat gray sky, and came to a conclusion.

He was finished with doors.

Answering them, knocking on them, being shoved back through them, and subsequently rolling down the stairs away from them; it was time to give them up altogether.

In fact, it was past time to give up quite a few things. He shifted to escape a bit of sharp gravel digging into the spot just inside his shoulder blade, then settled his head a bit more comfortably to consider what those things might be.

Architectural drawings sailed suddenly over his head and fluttered to the ground behind him. *Change jobs* was obviously going to be first on the list.

Well, perhaps *finish up with current unreasonable client* was closer to the mark. He had already parted company with his former employer on very good terms, and the next chapter in his life was waiting for him up the road that afternoon— assuming he could get there before he found himself tossed in the local jail for assaulting the man who had just shoved him down the stairs.

"I wanted the addition paneled," a voice bellowed, "not papered in zinnias!"

Zachary sat up and looked at the originator of that shout. A man stood at the top of the steps, glaring as if everything wrong in his life could be laid at Zachary's feet. Zachary winced as he rubbed a spot on his lower back where he hadn't been able to avoid an encounter with an unpleasantly large piece of driveway, then heaved himself up. He gathered up the blueprints out of habit—no sense in having them ruined by any potential sleet—and wondered if three sheets of architectural renderings were sufficient to bear up under the strain of being shoved down an obnoxious client's throat or if they would require additional underpinnings.

It was tempting to find out.

But he was nothing if not self-disciplined, so he walked over to his car, tossed the plans into the front seat, then closed the door. He brushed himself off, then walked back over to look up at Michael Smythe-Gordon, Viscount Franbury, the one who thought nothing of pushing innocent architects down half a dozen very nicely preserved Regency-era stairs. Zachary supposed he was fortunate he was so light on his feet or else he wouldn't have been back up on them so quickly.

His lordship was a very unattractive shade of red. In fact, the red was now deepening into an alarming shade of something Zachary supposed might have been called crimson. Or maybe vermilion. Whatever it was, it seemed like Franbury might be on the verge of a stroke. Obviously, the polite thing to do would be to head off the tantrum at the pass.

He shoved his hands in his pockets and propped a booted foot up on one of Franbury's very well-maintained steps. "I told you before, Michael, that I'm an architect, not an interior decorator."

"You're responsible for all phases of construction, from beginning to end," Franbury said in a garbled tone. "And that includes the decorating!"

"No," Zachary said firmly, "it doesn't."

"Your firm—"

"Our firm's contract states very specifically what I am and am not responsible for, and hanging wallpaper isn't on the list."

"I didn't want wallpaper!"

"I'm sure you didn't," Zachary conceded, "but that isn't my problem. The Lambeth Group always stands ready to recommend talented, reputable interior designers, which, if you'll remember, we did for you. You will also perhaps remember that you were uninterested in our suggestions."

"Candy Selzter is a fine decorator," Franbury said stiffly.

Zachary supposed it would be impolite to point out that the BBC had fired the dazzling Miss Selzter from her job as the assistant's assistant of a very cheesy DIY show because she couldn't tell chartreuse from candy-apple red. In Michael's case, she had probably misread panel as petunia and decided that zinnias would be more showy.

"You know, I didn't want you for this job," Franbury said stiffly. "I was convinced to take you on by one whose judgment I never should have trusted."

Zachary sighed, then looked to Michael's left and came to his second unavoidable decision of the day.

Give up women.

It was bad enough when they were just hard on his heart. Given that the lady Beatrice Smythe-Gordon had joined in the shoving along with her brother, Zachary began to suspect they were hard on his body as well. Yes, swearing off women for a few years was probably a very wise thing to do. Especially titled ones in expensive cashmere sweaters, plaid skirts, and very smart boots.

He supposed he wouldn't have to work very hard to avoid dating nobility. The fact that he'd even spoken to Michael's sister could probably be considered something of a miracle. He'd first seen her at a party he hadn't wanted to be at but had attended just the same as a favor to his sister-in-law. He'd flirted with Beatrice much like a man might flirt with a Lamborghini— by walking past the showroom window a time or two, lusting after but never intending to buy.

He'd been surprised that his first words to her had included a dinner invitation. He'd been even more surprised to listen to her accept.

It had taken approximately six minutes into an overpriced salad to realize that Beatrice wasn't an airhead; she was profoundly nasty and quite cunning. And she liked him very much, though he hadn't had a clue why. He'd spent the next month trying to very gracefully extricate himself from the pseudo relationship—unfortunately only after she'd succeeded in talking him into taking over her brother's little project from the third set of architects he'd fired.

He had agreed to do the work in direct violation of his first rule of survival, which was never to mix business with pleasure. He never dated clients, he never met with clients' wives alone, and he never designed anything for anyone for free unless it was for family where he was sure any differences in opinions on the execution of the plans could be settled over swords.

Unfortunately, he'd been too stupid to take his own advice, all of which left him where he was, standing at the feet of a very lovely manor, still short of his very reasonable fee, and wondering if Beatrice had actually broken something when she'd punched him before she and Michael both had shoved him back out the door. He wiggled his jaw a time or two and was rather relieved to find it still worked. The woman had an impressive right hook.

"I never want to see you again!" Beatrice screeched, stomping her trendy little boots, then spinning on her heel and stalking back into the house.

Zachary didn't bother to tell her the feeling was mutual. He was too busy watching Michael and wondering what the man intended to do next. His hands were very busy clenching and unclenching, but at least they were empty. That was reassuring.

"This is retaliation," Michael said through gritted teeth. "Retaliation for Bea dropping you."

"Don't be ridiculous, Michael," Zachary said shortly. "This has nothing to do with her and you know it. You approved the plans. You watched me go the extra mile for you time and time again. What you chose to do with the inside of your new addition—"

"I didn't want flowers!"

"Panel over them."

"I'll see you ruined," Michael said hotly. "Completely."

"Go ahead and try," Zachary said, before he thought better of it.

Franbury's features hardened. "You don't want to start a war with me."

Zachary suppressed the urge to roll his eyes. He knew several very good lawyers, his brother included, who would have been more than happy to take the fool in front of him down a notch or two. As for any conflicts of a more physical, personal nature, he thought he might be able to manage those himself.

But he wasn't going to say as much. Ten years ago, he might

have forged ahead without considering the odds. Now he knew very well how to spot the signs of a battle that wasn't worth the trouble of fighting.

"And you don't want anything adding to your murky reputation."

Zachary blinked. "My what?"

Michael stuck out his chin stubbornly. "You heard me."

Zachary knew he should have walked away, but that little slander was something he just couldn't ignore, especially since he actually had a very good reputation. He'd been working in England for almost a decade, making his way as a Yank in an industry full of born-and-bred Englishmen. He'd been a part of the Lambeth Group almost since he'd made the UK his home and never had anyone complain about him. In fact, most of his clients said he had an uncanny feel for what a property had looked like in the past.

He himself never commented on those comments.

Too murky.

"And I'm not talking about your pitiful drawing skills," Michael added. "I'm talking about *you*."

"What about me?" Zachary asked before he could stop himself.

"I've heard tell that you spend far more time than is reasonable with those mad reenactment types," Franbury said, looking down his nose from the great height of his illustrious title. "I understand there are swords involved. Costumes. All manner of silly Scottish things."

Zachary decided that it was perhaps best to cut his losses before he provided any more grist for Franbury's rumor mill. He merely inclined his head slightly in as close to a bow as he could muster.

"I'll have someone send you a list of people who can undo what Candy did."

"I wouldn't trust any of them."

"I don't think you can go anywhere but up from here, my lord."

"You'll regret this." Michael turned and strode back into the house, slamming the door behind him.

And, like clockwork, it began to sleet.

Zachary wasn't surprised. He cast a baleful glance heavenward, then trudged over to his car. It was a fitting end to a very unpleasant pair of months. The job had been a nightmare from the start, with Michael changing his mind about basic structural issues every two days. Zachary had finally taken to camping in the man's garden just to be there to humor those changes. Now, all he wanted to do was get into his car, hope the heater was having one of its good days, and get the hell out of Dodge.

He found that the heater was indeed functioning as it should, then drove away before Michael could come out and use his tires for target practice. He picked up his cell phone and dialed his former boss. Garrett Lambeth would need to be warned about what was coming his way, as Zachary had no doubt Michael would go immediately into his zinnia-papered den and dial his attorney. He would give Garrett the heads-up, thank him for almost nine years' worth of wonderful opportunities, and tell him again how much he'd appreciated the flexibility in his hours.

That flexibility was directly connected to the last thing in his life he needed to change. It was the most difficult, but perhaps the most important.

But that could wait until later. For now he was finished with his business in the south and he had nothing to do but get on with the rest of his life. He drove out the gates and headed happily into his future.

He pulled into a car park at sunset.

It wasn't a particularly good car park, as car parks went. It was more a suggestion as to where someone might leave his little runabout if absolutely necessary, as if the owner of the castle wasn't particularly interested in providing space for that sort of thing but felt, grudgingly, as if he didn't have much choice.

Zachary heaved himself out of his car and stretched with a groan. Getting out of London was never a pleasant experience, but today the misery had been compounded by aches he'd acquired on his trip down Michael Smythe-Gordon's front steps. At least his car hadn't given him any trouble. It could have been much worse.

He took a deep breath, then looked up. The castle in front of him was, to put it politely, a complete wreck.

It was perfect.

He walked up the way and through Wyckham's missing front gates. He could easily imagine how those gates might have looked in their heyday, with a forbidding barbican surrounding them and a heavy portcullis hanging over the way through. Now, the barbican was gone and only a hint remained of the towers on either side. It was probably just as well, for it allowed him to walk inside as if he had every right to.

He wandered around the inner bailey, considering where the outbuildings had been and admiring the path that still wandered through what had once surely been the garden but was now just grass. An ancient tree stood in a corner of that garden, but Zachary couldn't tell if it were alive or not. It was still just March, too early in the year for any sort of springtime activity. Maybe he would wait a month and see what happened. If he dawdled, it would take him that long to complete the remodel on the cottage just outside Wyckham's walls. He would have ample time to camp out and enjoy a castle that most certainly didn't belong to him.

He stopped in the middle of the inner bailey and looked at the keep itself. It had, apparently at some point in its past, been plastered on the outside and whitewashed. When the sun hit it just right, as it was doing now, it stained the remaining hints of plaster with a sort of pinkish hue that made the place look as if it belonged in a very pleasant fairy tale.

Or another century.

Zachary walked over to the hall and put his hand on the doorway with its stone unforgivingly cold and solid to the touch and grounded himself in the current year. He looked around. There were no outbuildings, no garden, no men-at-arms. Just a ruined castle surrounded by its equally ruined outer walls, a castle he wanted so badly he could taste it. A castle that found itself firmly planted in the twenty-first century.

Change weekend and holiday habits.

The last of his resolves came to his mind without any coaxing on his part. He was going to, from that point on, live an unremarkable life. No more jaunts with his brother-in-law James MacLeod to places where no sensible soul would go. No more hiding what he did on the weekends, no more narrow brushes with plague and other medieval maladies, no more going out for little hikes on MacLeod soil with map in hand and his wild-eyed brother-in-law leading the charge. He wanted prepackaged food instead of whatever critter had been caught earlier that afternoon and plunked down into a pot. He wanted to put gas in his car instead of hay into his horse. He wanted to draft plans with AutoCAD, not with quill and parchment.

And he wanted absolutely nothing of a paranormal nature that would add anything else to his already questionable reputation. His brothers and sister were married with families of their own. It was past time he at least started thinking about heading in that direction himself.

He loped down the handful of steps to the courtyard, then strode across to where the gates should have been. He grabbed a sleeping bag and backpack from his trunk, then walked back to the great hall. He shivered, wondering if he dared make a fire or if that would bring attention to him that he wasn't going to want.

He paused just inside the missing doors and realized the decision wasn't going to be up to him. A fire was already burning cheerily. Unfortunately, it wasn't the sort of blaze that would generate enough heat to fire up anything but a decent imagination.

He frowned as he walked over to the cluster of chairs sitting in front of that useless fire, chairs that hadn't been there five minutes ago. Those chairs were being used by three souls he knew from previous encounters, hale and hearty gentlemen who weren't exactly of this world.

Damn it anyway.

Obviously, the ban on paranormal activity in his life would have to wait another day.

He set his gear down next to the hearth, took a deep breath, then made a bow to the leader of the little group.

"Laird Ambrose," he said, straightening. "What a surprise."

Ambrose MacLeod lifted a mug in salute. "We're just here to keep you company, lad. Thought you might like that on such a chilly night."

"Don't believe him," Fulbert de Piaget grumbled. "He's just avoiding the Boar's Head Inn. Mrs. Pruitt's gone shopping, you know."

Zachary had been to the inn before and was well acquainted with the proprietress's military bearing. Mrs. Pruitt would have made the entire British navy snap to attention with just a look.

She also had set her cap for the less-than-corporeal Scot sitting there squirming. He smiled at Ambrose in sympathy, then turned to Fulbert. "I hesitate to ask this, but what sorts of things did Mrs. Pruitt go looking for?"

"Frillies."

"Frillies," Zachary repeated. "Really."

"That can only mean one thing," Fulbert said with a knowing nod.

Zachary smiled in spite of himself. "Our good laird MacLeod is being wooed."

"The saints preserve me, not if I can help it," Ambrose said faintly. "And as interesting a topic as that is, Zachary lad, we find ourselves here tonight for other reasons. To enjoy the brisk night air is one."

Zachary thought he might rather have been enjoying a roaring fire, but he'd slept in far worse conditions than his current one, so he would just make do. At least the ghosts in front of him didn't seem to have him in their sights, though he supposed if he didn't do something about his own marital state soon, they would.

"Are you keeping an eye on the remodel?" Zachary asked, bending down to arrange his gear so he could sit and eat.

"Nay."

"Then you're expecting a descendant of yours to show up soon?"

"You never know."

Zachary looked around for a log or a chunk of stone to use as a seat, but found nothing useful. He shrugged, then reached for the sack containing his dinner. Of course half of it needed to be nuked, but he'd made do with cold food more than once and survived. "I'm not sure who would bother," he said absently, fishing for a fork, "given the condition of the keep—"

"Ach, by the saints," said another voice suddenly. "He's not too quick on the uptake, is he?"

Zachary watched in surprise as another Scot of indeterminate vintage but undeniably incorporeal status strode into the light from the fire. The ghost created a quite lovely Charles Rennie Mackintosh–style chair, then sat himself down on it without delay.

Then he looked at Zachary pointedly.

Zachary wished quite suddenly for a chair of any design, but since there were none to be had, he simply set his supper back on the ground, planted his feet a comfortable distance apart, and shoved his hands in his pockets. "And who are you? If I might ask."

"Drummond," the man said. "*The* Drummond, you disrespectful boy. I was your grandpa way back into the far reaches of Scotland's glorious past—"

"But we're Mackintoshes," Zachary interrupted gingerly.

"Your family tree has an extra fork or two," Laird Drummond growled, "and I found myself unhappily sitting on one of them. I was peacefully dividing my time between reclining atop the Space Needle with a nice, glowing red fire and stirring up mischief in the Underground when I was assaulted—assaulted, I tell ye!—by that pencil poker over there." He gestured accusingly at Hugh McKinnon.

Hugh only smiled and waved.

"They want me here in case they need me," the Drummond finished, glowering. "But if you ask *my* opinion, romance is verra, verra silly stuff indeed."

Zachary felt his mouth fall open. He supposed he shouldn't have been surprised. Ambrose had been eyeing him purposefully for half a dozen years now, but Zachary had always managed to decamp before the geriatric plotter could broach any uncomfortable subjects, such as romance, marriage, or when they might be arranging either for Zachary before he could protest.

"Ah," he began, hoping something useful would follow without his having to think too hard.

No such luck.

The Drummond shot Ambrose a displeased look. "Perhaps you were too hasty in choosing him."

"Choosing me?" Zachary echoed, trying to make it sound as if he didn't have a clue what they were talking about. "Choosing me for what?"

Ambrose wasn't buying what he was selling. "For the coveted spot on my list," he said smoothly.

"But—"

Fulbert looked at him from under his bushy eyebrows. "Just take your turn, lad, and have it over with. It'll all go down painlessly if you don't struggle too much."

"But I have a list of my own," Zachary protested, "and romance isn't on it. In fact, I purposely put *no romance* on it this morning. Along with a few other necessary things."

Hugh plucked a clipboard out of thin air, then pulled a pencil from behind his ear, almost stabbing the Drummond with it. Laird John shot Zachary a pointed look, then got up and moved his chair a safer distance away. Hugh looked up expectantly, his pencil at the ready.

Zachary didn't wait for Hugh to take down the particulars of what he'd decided. He turned to Ambrose instead.

"It isn't that I don't appreciate your potential efforts on my behalf," he began, "it's just that this doesn't fit in with my plans. I'm starting a new chapter of my life tomorrow. The one in which I run the preservation trust for Cameron and Gideon."

"Of course," Ambrose said with a smile. "A fitting task for you, but one that will only be enhanced by your seeing to other aspects of your life, namely—"

"Getting rid of all paranormal activities," Zachary finished for him. "Exactly my thought. I've hinted as much to Jamie, but he ignored me. I trust you three won't do the same thing."

"Ignore you?" Ambrose said, lifting one eyebrow. "Now, Zachary, why would we ignore you?"

Zachary put away all pretense of not knowing exactly what Ambrose was capable of. "Because I've seen you all in action—you in particular, my laird. And while I appreciate the thought, I'll tell you once more that I'm not interested."

"Told you he'd be a problem," Fulbert grumbled. "He's seen too much."

"I have," Zachary agreed, "which is why I know exactly what I'm not interested in."

"Ah," Ambrose said, pouncing on the opening, "but I contend you haven't been looking for the right girl in the right place."

"I can imagine the places you think I should look," Zachary said evenly, "and they won't be an improvement. Once any woman finds out whom I'm related to, she doesn't understand why I don't drive a Porsche and have a valet to iron my jeans. The ambitious ones don't understand why I don't work more and the unambitious ones . . . well, they don't understand that, either. And it isn't as if I can tell them what I do with my weekends, can I?"

"Well, I suppose you do have a secret or two to keep," Ambrose conceded.

That was an understatement. Zachary scowled with a bit more vigor. After all, how was he supposed to even begin to broach the subject? *Oh, hi, I'm Zachary Smith. I'm an architect during the week, but on most weekends I run around Scotland with my insane brother-in-law looking for little patches of ground that have something special that always takes us somewhere else. Sometimes it's just to a different century; other times it's to a different location. Sometimes we get a bonus and hit both. That's the reason I don't have any money. Because I'm basically working part-time and time traveling part-time. Wanna go see a movie?*

It was actually amazing he managed to get anyone to go out with him at all.

"But perhaps there might be a girl out there who wouldn't care about what you do," Ambrose suggested.

"No," Zachary said firmly, "there isn't. I might rethink my decision if I could find an ordinary, untitled, low-maintenance girl who doesn't care how much money I have or what I do for a living, but I seriously doubt she exists."

"I wouldn't be so sure," Ambrose said enigmatically.

Zachary was thoroughly dissatisfied with that answer, though he felt somewhat vindicated when Laird Drummond nodded his head in dour agreement. That was still two against three, though, and those odds weren't good.

Zachary considered for a moment, then looked at Ambrose. "Why is Laird Drummond here?"

"Moral support."

"In case I didn't cooperate?"

"Well," Ambrose said with a very small smile, "that possibility did occur to me."

Zachary pursed his lips. He might have smiled, but his jaw ached from where Beatrice had punched him that morning and his back ached from where he'd reclined on her brother's driveway. Reason enough to stick to his earlier decisions. He shook his head.

"Again, my laird, I appreciate the thought, but I'm not interested. I'm going to check into the Boar's Head Inn tomorrow morning, then get to work. I don't have time for anything else right now."

Hugh, Fulbert, and John Drummond were exchanging

knowing glances. Ambrose was only watching, silent and calculating.

Damn him.

The former laird of the clan MacLeod pressed his fingers together, then rested his chin atop them. "You know, Zachary lad, ofttimes you find what you were looking for where you didn't expect to."

"Yes, castles to be remodeled and manor houses to be restored," Zachary said firmly. "I couldn't agree more. Now, if you gentlemen would excuse me?"

He made them all a brief bow, then turned to make himself at home for the night before any of them could say anything else. He rolled out his sleeping bag, helped himself to the comforts of the cottage's bathroom, ate his deliciously modern food, then lay down and hoped for sleep.

"No matchmaking," he announced, on the off chance that he hadn't made that clear enough before.

His only answer was the sound of someone puffing vigorously on a pipe. He squinted back over his head and saw that Laird John was enthusiastically working on filling the great hall with smoke. Ambrose and Fulbert were studying various vistas provided by the lack of roof. Hugh was industriously scribbling on paper held by his clipboard.

"No more paranormal activity, either," Zachary muttered under his breath, just in case Hugh wanted to add that to his list.

He could have sworn the last thing he heard before he fell asleep was indulgent laughter.

Chapter 2

Mary de Piaget closed her eyes and flew.

The exertion was nothing to the powerful horse beneath her. He was the fastest in her father's stables, bred from equally speedy beasts along lines she herself had overseen, bred to want to run. It wasn't always possible to predict what a horse would have the heart for, but in this case she had been amply rewarded for her care and attention. If ever there had been a horse born to fly, it was the black beneath her. Her father called him Lucifer, she called him Rex Diabolus, and they both agreed that he was quite possibly the best stallion Artane's illustrious stables had ever produced. Her father had forbidden her to ride him, which she had of course assumed was an edict ripe for a bit of negotiation. The fact that she was riding him now and had been the one to break him before was proof enough of that.

She suspected her father might just have a weak spot where she was concerned.

She was thankful for that because she wanted to fly and Rex was the horse to allow her to. The day was perfect for it. The ground was hard and flat, the sky was overcast, and there was no wind. The only thing that might have improved the day would have been a bit of warmth, but when a body had freedom it was unwise to be choosey about how that freedom was enjoyed. The only sounds around her were the pounding of her mount's hooves against the hard ground and the wind rushing past her ears. It was enough. Nay, it was more than that.

It was glorious.

She was content to give Rex his head, something her father would have been less than pleased with. If the beast wanted to run, then she would allow it for as long as he liked, even though there was some peril associated with it. One of her uncles had found himself thrown more than once from Rex's great-grandsire's back, but he readily admitted that she was a better rider than he. It was likely sinful to take pleasure in such an admission, but she couldn't help herself. She and her mother were the two lone women in a houseful of men. Being included in their talk was a pleasant thing, but besting them at one of their own games was better still.

She closed her eyes for a moment and relished again the perfection of the day, the magnificence of her steed, and the fact that she had recently avoided a very unsavory betrothal. Truly, things could not be any—

Rex slowed to a trot so suddenly that she almost bounced out of the saddle. She opened her eyes in surprise, then pulled him back into a walk without thinking.

"Hell," she said, to no one in particular.

That wasn't a curse, it was an accurate description of what, based on the size of the company she could see in the distance, would be the state of her life during the next pair of fortnights.

Damnation, those were the colors of Geoffrey of Styrr! Hadn't she managed to be rid of his annoying self but a month ago? That she should see his company coming up the road to Artane could only mean one of two things: her father had decided to agree to a betrothal and hadn't had the courage to tell her, or Styrr was making good on his promise to assault the tender, delicate walls of her heart with every chivalrous weapon in his arsenal until she swooned into his arms in artful surrender.

Why he didn't just stab her and have done, she couldn't have said. Perhaps he didn't think himself equal to the task of catching her gold as it fell from her cold, dead fingers.

She pursed her lips. It wasn't that she was opposed to marriage. The thought of engaging in it had occurred to her now and again over the years.

It had also occurred to her to dress as a lad, steal one of her father's fastest steeds, and escape the fools who had come to offer for her. She hadn't been forced to do that, though, because her father had done the distasteful work of shooing off all her would-be suitors, having found them lacking for one reason or another.

Well, he'd mostly been unimpressed by their swordplay, but given that her father was who he was, perhaps that was understandable.

He'd hastened Geoffrey of Styrr on his way a month ago after Styrr had made very loud noises about being needed at court. Apparently he was an ornament there that the king simply couldn't do without. Mary was fairly convinced Styrr was imagining his importance in Henry's circle, but she couldn't deny that he certainly dressed the part of an important courtier. He also knew how to clutter up a supper table, which was one of the other reasons her father had been so willing to see him sent on his way.

Mary had feared that neither her father's abrupt invitation to leave nor the required visit to court would keep Styrr forever from Artane's hallowed hall. She just hadn't thought he would return so soon.

Obviously, there was nothing to do about it save what she'd done in the past. She would hide in the stables until Styrr tired of waiting for her and went away, disappointed and empty-handed. Maybe this time he would finally realize that she was serious about her unwillingness to wed him and turn his greedy eye in another direction.

She turned Rex around and touched her heels to his side. He was just as swift on the way back to Artane as he had been galloping away from it, but that didn't surprise her. He would outpace any other stallion in England, of that she was certain. She raced past a pair of her cousins littering the side of the road and continued on in spite of their shouts that she stop. She wouldn't have, not for any amount of gold. Not with what was following her.

She slowed Rex to a trot as she reached the village, then walked him up the way to her father's gates. She dismounted in time to hear more shouts coming from behind her. She looked over her shoulder and cursed at the sight of a new set of lads calling for her to stop. They were a pair of her cousins from

Raventhorpe who had neglected to go home with their parents earlier that morning.

It actually wasn't unusual for any of her aunts and uncles—of which she had several—to leave a selection of their offspring behind at Artane. Mary suspected it was so those lads could combine mischief where their parents wouldn't be forced to watch, but she'd never heard any of her aunts or uncles admit as much. For herself, she couldn't say she minded. Despite the fact that the lads so left to linger seemed determined to shadow her at all costs, she had to admit that she loved them all.

But she didn't have to admit that to them presently, nor was she of any mind to discuss anything that might or might not be coming to lay siege to her heart, so she would see to her own business and leave the lads to speculate however they cared to.

She snatched up a bit of dirt along the way and rubbed it artistically onto her cheeks. She would pull her hood close round her face and hide either in the lists or the stables for the day. 'Twas a certainty that Geoffrey wouldn't spend any time in either place looking for her. Such lingering might force him to become overly acquainted with substances that would perhaps remain on his clothes or in his hair—

"Maryanne de Piaget, what in the hell were you doing riding that demon horse that way?" a voice demanded suddenly from behind her.

"What way?" she said, not looking back over her shoulder. "In a way you only dream you might?"

Laughter and curses from two different males greeted her ears. She looked behind her briefly to see Jackson and Thaddeus of Raventhorpe lurking there. Thaddeus was laughing; Jackson was not. Actually, Jackson was now shouting at his brother, who was unmoved in the face of his elder brother's considerable wrath.

Mary left them to their arguing and turned off to the left so she could walk Rex about in the lists for a bit. Her peace was short-lived, for she soon found herself joined by Jackson, who had apparently stopped shouting at his brother long enough to hand his reins over to him and command him to put both their horses away.

"If your father had seen you on the road today," Jackson said evenly, "he would forbid you to ride again."

"He wouldn't," she said placidly.

"That bloody horse could have thrown you!"

"You sound like *your* father."

"And if I had a shilling for every time he said the like to my mother, I would be building myself my own keep!"

She nudged him rather ungently out of her way. "Raventhorpe will be yours someday just the same, so don't look at me for any pity. Now, go away. I'm busy."

She said it lightly, but it was costing her quite a bit to do so. In truth, she suspected she had reason to be very nervous indeed. She had been certain Geoffrey's hopes of having her dowry had been fully and completely crushed during his previous visit. Perhaps he simply thought to wear her father down until he relented.

She caught sight of a man running up the path from the gate, then sighed as he veered toward her. He avoided Rex, then hunched over, breathing heavily.

"Did you see?" he managed.

"Of course she saw, Parsival, you fool," Jackson snapped. "Why do you think she has dirt on her face? She's trying to hide!"

Parsival de Seger straightened and looked at her seriously. "*Chérie*, Styrr has come with a full contingent of retainers. I think he intends to stay for quite some time." He held out his hand for her reins. "Let me walk Rex for you so you can take yourself elsewhere."

"But Styrr won't recognize me out here in the lists," she protested.

"He is not so stupid as you would like to believe him to be, Mary. And if the best mount in your father's stables didn't give you away, your astonishing beauty would." He reached out and brushed the dirt from one of her cheeks, then smiled and nodded toward the stables. "Go hide yourself. I'll see to Rex for you."

She wanted to protest, or make a jest, or simply ignore the potential danger of her situation, but she couldn't. It was all she could do to force a smile and hand the reins off to her cousin. She nodded her thanks and turned to walk with Jackson up the path toward the keep. He put his arm around her shoulders, but it didn't comfort her as it might have another time. And when he turned her into the mouth of the stables, she found the thought of being in such a confined space was enough to leave her breath coming in gasps.

Truly, she had to put an end to Styrr's ambitions once and for all.

If Jackson noticed her reluctance, he said nothing, but that didn't surprise her. When he had decided upon a course of action, nothing swayed him, not even the complaints of a woman bent on avoiding a betrothal she didn't want. She pitied the woman who eventually found herself shackled to *him*, for he would give no quarter.

As he was not giving to her now. He urged her along until she ran bodily into two lads who were seemingly waiting there just for such an occurrence. They were taller than she was, fair-haired, and fearless.

They were also, unsurprisingly, related to her.

Currently they looked as if they'd been rolling in the hay and fighting to see who would emerge the grubbiest, but perhaps that was a boon.

"Styrr's coming," Jackson said shortly. "Put yourselves between him and Mary."

The twins nodded as one. Mary was actually rather glad they were for her. Though they were only ten-and-six, there was something in their eyes that bespoke a ruthlessness that belied their age. Theophilus took her by the arm and pulled her behind him, whilst Samuel accompanied Jackson back to the door.

"Let's shovel manure," Theo suggested.

Mary was only too happy to agree. She walked to the very back of the stables, allowed Theo to remove a horse from its stall, then took off her cloak. She braided her hair quickly, then shoved it all up under the sort of cap most of the stable lads wore in the winter.

Within moments, she was filthy and sweating. She concentrated on what she was doing, knowing that Theo and Samuel would make certain that Geoffrey didn't come close enough to see exactly who was pitching manure out the stall door.

Or so she thought until Samuel came running toward her. He pulled her out of the stall, tore the pitchfork from her hands, and jerked his head upward.

"Hayloft. Hurry."

She didn't argue. Samuel had an uncanny ability to sense where trouble was, so she snatched up her cloak and bolted up the ladder to the loft above. She pushed herself into the darkest corner and wrapped her cloak around her before she pulled handfuls of hay over herself. It left her little to do besides lie there and listen to her blood thundering in her ears.

'Twas all madness and it had to end. She had managed to avoid wedded bliss in the past because her father hadn't pushed her toward it. Her one brief brush with a formal betrothal had ended badly. After that, she had seemed fated to simply remain happily at Artane where she might even more happily tend her father's horses.

And then Geoffrey of Styrr had presented himself at the gates and wooed everyone in sight with his very fine manners and exquisite face. She had known him long before that, disliked him for an equal amount of time, and distrusted everything that came out of his mouth.

She was the only one, though. If her cousins didn't care for him, 'twas only because they generally despised anyone who found court life preferable to an honest day's labor with the sword, and they felt duty bound to dislike whomever she did. Her parents found nothing wrong with Styrr past his failings in the lists and the unfortunate burden of his very irritating mother. She, however, saw past those things to the man himself, and what she saw unnerved her.

She waited for quite some time without hearing anything useful, so she carefully shifted until she had rolled over onto her belly and was able to peer down through the cracks in the floor of the loft. She knew she couldn't be seen, but she flinched just the same when she heard the piercing tones of Suzanna of Styrr cutting through the air. A horse whinnied in protest.

Mary understood completely.

"It smells very strongly of horse," she announced. "Something should be done."

Mary didn't dare snort, but someone else did admirably in her stead. Rolf, the stable master, shot that someone a dark look, then made Suzanna a low bow and took the reins of her horse from her servant.

"We'll see to it immediately," he said, handing off the reins to one of his lads. He gave directions for the rest of the horses to be seen to, then escorted Lady Suzanna quite firmly out of the stables.

Her son wasn't gotten rid of so easily, which was surprising. In all the years Mary had had the misfortune of knowing him, she had never once seen him inquire about anything other than when supper was set to arrive or if there might be another bottle of wine for his pleasure.

She jumped slightly as he came into her sights, but knew it wasn't possible that he could see her. As long as nothing dropped through to the floor below, she was safe. She breathed in carefully, then looked again.

Geoffrey stood there as a pair of stable lads saw to his mount. He was, as he likely would have told anyone who would listen, a very handsome man. His fair hair shined like spun gold, his visage was unmarred and exceptionally pleasing to the eye, and even his form left nothing to be desired. He wasn't nearly as tall as any of the men in her family, which likely vexed him, but he seemed to have stature enough as he was. He had never been aught but unfailingly polite to her mother, respectful to her father, and not unkind to her cousins.

If he eschewed too much time in the lists because he didn't care to sweat and turned his nose up at bread that wasn't completely free of rocks and wine that didn't pour as purely as water, who were any of them to criticize? His mother was famous for her love of fine things, insisting on only the most expensive of tapestries to line her walls and the most elegant of fabrics with which to clothe herself and her lovely second son. Mary always felt, by comparison, as if she'd just come in from the stables, grubby and in sore need of a wash.

Which, as it happened, she usually was, but her family was accustomed to it.

She supposed if she'd had any sense at all, she would have agreed to the betrothal the moment Geoffrey had suggested it. But she had grown to maturity watching horses and judging them by the slightest of movements. She had learned to take the measure of men around her in the same way. And there was something about Geoffrey of Styrr that made her very uneasy.

Her father had been putting off discussions of a betrothal between them for almost three years now. She had flattered herself that 'twas because her father just didn't want to let her go. If he had another reason, he hadn't shared it with her.

Unfortunately, she feared that the time would come when he would exhaust all his reasons and agree simply because he had no reason to refuse.

She propped her chin up on her folded hands and continued

to watch. Styrr didn't linger after his horse had been taken away. He looked about himself, sniffed delicately, then pursed his lips in distaste. He nodded regally to anyone who was looking before he strode off as if he had important business waiting for him elsewhere.

The saints pity her if he did.

She waited until he was long gone before she rolled over onto her back and heaved a huge sigh of relief. She squeaked at the sight of a face an arm's length away from her.

"How do you manage that?" she said, putting her hand over her pounding heart.

"I'm quiet," Theo whispered.

"You're terrifying."

He smiled an evil little smile that made her laugh in spite of herself. He and his brother gave their parents very foul dreams, of that she was certain. He made himself at home on the hay next to her.

"We should wait a bit longer," he advised, "just to make certain there aren't undesirables lurking nearby. Then we'll sneak into the kitchens through the secret passageway."

Mary felt her mouth fall open. "There's a secret passageway?"

"Aye."

"How did you discover it?"

"Do you truly wish an answer to that?"

Mary laughed in spite of herself. "Your poor mother."

"Aye," he agreed, "so says she. Often. At least I'm taking apart your father's keep instead of my sire's."

"I'm sure my father appreciates the attention," she said dryly.

"Surprisingly enough, I'm not sure he does," Theo said thoughtfully. "He told me he would beat me if he caught me pawing at any more seams in the foundation. I gave him my solemn word I wouldn't paw anymore."

"So you've been using your knife instead."

He elbowed her companionably. "Mary, for a gel, you're a right proper lad."

And from Theo, there was truly no higher praise.

She shouldn't have enjoyed it, but she couldn't help herself. She settled back into the hay and wished the enjoyment could have lasted. If only she could have, at some point before she'd reached her dotage, found a man who could have thought just as highly of her, a man who might have appreciated her for something besides her dowry and found fault with something besides her quite reasonable fondness for a well-turned hoof.

Geoffrey of Styrr was most definitely not that man. She wished she could have brought herself to bolt from the keep, but she couldn't. She didn't run. That wasn't to say that she hadn't made a handful of very abrupt visits to other halls over the years, but those couldn't properly be termed escaping. She had been needed to help with the tending of children. She had no fewer than a score and six cousins, so her aunts were always happy to have an extra pair of hands to help with those cousins. If she had rushed off abruptly to offer aid, who could fault her for it? Pointing out to her father the virtue of offering such a needful service had always been enough to convince him to send her off to wherever she asked to go.

She feared her sire might not be so easily convinced this time.

She considered her usual places of refuge. The contingent from Raventhorpe had already left that morning and Jackson and Thaddeus likely wouldn't be following for quite some time to come. Theophilus and Samuel's parents were in France, not at Wyckham, so there was no hope of going so far in disguise. She had family farther afield in England, but she didn't dare attempt to travel to them alone, and she didn't suppose any of her cousins would be willing to take her.

Obviously she would simply have to remain at Artane and see what Fate sent her way.

There were many places inside the keep where she could hide for extended periods of time. And if worse came to worst, she would linger for long stretches in the garderobe. She'd done it before, though she couldn't say it had been a very pleasant experience.

She thought she might be desperate enough this time for quite a few unpleasant things.

Chapter 3

Zachary wished he'd had more duct tape.

It wasn't something he wished for often, but he also didn't often find himself driving something that was smoking like a blocked chimney. He rolled down his window and swore. He'd already lost his oil cap once, and the one he'd made with the last bit of duct tape he'd had in his trunk had apparently also gone the way of all mischievous auto parts. The first loss was a suspicious one. He distinctly remembered checking the oil that morning, and he was certain he'd replaced the cap. Now, though, the results were unarguable.

Paranormal intervention or absentmindedness?

He suspected the former. He'd left Wyckham early that morning, intending to go stay at the Boar's Head Inn. As he'd started to turn onto the long road that led in that direction, his car had begun to smoke. He'd decided, as he'd sat on the side of the road and let his engine cool, that he might be better off to head for Artane and hope he didn't have to walk most of the way. A quick phone call had resulted in a freely offered room for the duration and an expression of disbelief that he'd considered anything else. He'd happily accepted the invitation, put his car back together as best he could, then continued on in a direction he hadn't expected to take. He had hoped to arrive reeking slightly less of engine smoke, but perhaps that had been too much to ask.

He hoped it wasn't an omen.

He managed now to nurse his car up onto the bluff and into the car park next to Artane. He turned off the engine, set the parking brake, then leaned his head back against the seat and took a long, slow breath.

He coughed violently. He quickly stuck his head out the window and sucked in a few restorative gulps of lovely fresh air. Once he could breathe again, he then leaned back against the seat and had his comfortable look. The view of the ocean in front of him was truly spectacular, eclipsed only by the sight of the castle to his left. He wasn't overly emotional by nature—the thought of a brace of Twinkies aside—but he would admit to getting a little worked up over the sight of a medieval castle in all its glory.

Some of it had to do with knowing what it had taken the original builders to put it together. More of it had to do with all the layers of history and living that found themselves deposited on the stones that made up any structure of any age at all. There were two things he loved and one of them was old buildings. The second was a good mystery, but he was sure he wouldn't find one of those inside the walls of Artane. The current earl's younger son, the right honorable Gideon de Piaget, had assured him numerous times in the past that Artane was devoid of any sorts of unexplained happenings. It possessed fabulous bones, boasted startlingly well-preserved artifacts, and that bedroom he was welcome to for as long as he liked. The situation couldn't have been more perfect.

He rolled up his window, unbuckled, then crawled out of his car to stretch for a moment before he locked his gear up and walked off toward the castle.

He tried to sweet-talk his way past the ticket booth, but the granny there was particularly loath to believe he might be a business associate of anyone up the way. He sighed, pulled out a ten-pound note, and handed it over without comment.

"We'll keep the remainder for a donation," the woman said, plopping the money in her till with alacrity. "Up the road and through the front door." She shot Zachary a stern look. "Don't wander off the path."

"I wouldn't dare," Zachary said honestly. He knew very well where that sort of thing led.

Again, not that it would lead him anywhere untoward here. Artane was completely free of all paranormal influences. Gideon had said so.

Why Gideon'd felt the need to repeat that so often was probably better not to know.

Zachary put any speculations about that behind him along with his smoking car and walked up the cobblestone road that led from the outer gates to the keep itself. He suspected there had been an inner bailey wall and gate as well at some point, but since the need for that had disappeared, so had the fortification. Now, there was merely a very large courtyard with a few stone outbuildings that either were original and very well kept up or were very good re-creations. He could see a smithy, a rather impressive stable that was obviously not original, and a chapel tucked into the corner of one wall. There was also a tea shop that opened its doors onto the courtyard. He wasn't sure what that had been in the past, though he assumed it wasn't the dungeon. It looked far too comfortable and too sheltered for such a thing.

It also looked to be assaulted at any moment by a little red Ford.

Zachary ran across the courtyard to try to stop the car before it backed right into the shop itself. Fortunately for the patrons, the car killed itself before it could wind up wearing any scones with clotted cream. The flower beds were, however, a complete loss.

Zachary pulled open the door and looked at the old man who sat in the front seat, white as a sheet.

"Oh, I say," the man said, "oh, look what I've done now. The earl will sack me for sure this time—"

"Let's worry about that later, shall we?" Zachary said, helping the old man out of the car. He pulled the keys from the ignition, then walked the man inside and saw him settled with a cup of tea before he went back outside to assess the damage.

Thirty minutes later, he'd moved the car, found the gardener's shed, and was in the process of resurrecting the flower bed. The few petunias that dared brave the March wind were done for, but he supposed someone else could replant those tomorrow. He concentrated on making the dirt look less like someone had been four-wheeling in it, then stood back and admired his work.

"Aren't you a little overqualified for this sort of thing?"

Zachary looked to his left to find Gideon de Piaget standing there wearing what could have been charitably called a smirk. He wiped a filthy hand on his now equally filthy jeans, then reached out to shake Gideon's hand.

"Just being useful."

"So I see," Gideon said. "We don't usually let Cedric have the keys, but someone left them in the car, apparently."

Zachary fished the offenders out of his pocket and handed them over. "All yours now. Unless you'd like to let me borrow them back so I can get to work tomorrow."

"I suppose I should, since that wreck of yours is polluting my car park." He handed the keys back. "You're off to a smashing start with this new venture, aren't you?"

"It's impressive, isn't it?"

Gideon laughed. "Very. Welcome to Artane just the same. I'll leave someone in the hall to show you to a guest room, then why don't you come find me in Father's private study. We'll discuss your plans whilst we make serious inroads into his schnapps before supper."

Zachary didn't drink, but he supposed Gideon already knew that. He merely nodded his thanks, then went to fetch his gear. With any luck, he would be able to get back inside the gates without having to make any more donations.

Several hours later, he walked back into his guest room, well fed and watered. He'd had supper and a very pleasant discussion with Gideon about potential future projects to be attempted by the Cameron/Artane Trust for Historical Preservation, assured Gideon that he wouldn't paper the cottage next to Wyckham in zinnias, then found himself with the run of the keep. He hadn't been offered any keys, but he'd been assured that the alarms were turned off for the night should he find a lock he thought he might like to pit his skills against.

He wondered just what it was that Gideon and Jamie talked about when they got together.

It was probably better not to know.

He left both sets of car keys on the nightstand, then considered the rest of his gear. He supposed his wallet would be safe enough, so he left it sitting next to the keys. He pulled his Swiss

Army knife out of his pocket and started to lay it down. He paused, then reconsidered. The knife had been custom made for him, with several additions that conventional Boy Scouts didn't need. Among other things, there were tools for unlocking all sorts of different locks of different vintages, a compass, and a soldering torch the size of a very thin pen. He didn't usually go around without it, on the off chance that he might need to cut up an apple or cut his way out of some dungeon or another, but he supposed taking it with him now was overkill.

Besides, he wasn't going to break into any of Lord Edward's glass cases. If he had tools with him, he might be tempted beyond what he could reasonably bear. Better that he be a strictly hands-off tourist for the moment. He could pick locks later in the week, when he felt more at home.

He set the knife down only to realize that he was still holding it in his hand. A wave of something whispered over him, but he immediately dismissed it as too much cheese sauce over broccoli that night for dinner. Artane was just an average, albeit spectacularly maintained, castle on the edge of the sea. He was merely going for a little walk. Nothing was going to happen that he couldn't handle with the two dirks stuck down the sides of his boots. He set his pocketknife down firmly, pulled a sweater down over his head, then left the chamber, shutting the door behind him.

He considered the wing added in the sixteenth century with its lovely wide-planked floors and cases filled with all sorts of treasures, then discarded the idea. If he were truly to allow himself to bunk at Artane for the duration as Lord Edward had insisted he should, he would have plenty of time to explore. At the moment, he wanted a fix of a more medieval sort.

He wandered through the great hall, then made his way up the circular stairs at the back. They were larger than he would have expected given the time period in which the keep had been built, but rumor had it those first Artane men had been rather large in stature. The castle had apparently been built to suit.

Zachary wandered up the stairs and down passageways, avoiding any rooms that were obviously private. He rubbed his arms suddenly as a chill ran through him. Medieval castles, no matter the century, were just plain cold. It was no wonder people had worn such heavy clothes. He gave his car's functioning heater a fond thought, then continued on with his explorations.

He walked until he found himself stopped suddenly in front of a door. He put his hand on the wood, paused, and considered. There was nothing of a paranormal nature there; he was certain of that. He was extremely familiar with that particular sort of tingle, and he felt nothing like it at present.

He let himself in and felt for a light switch. He was relieved when he found the room flooded by very modern bulbs instead of torchlight.

He stood rooted to the spot and simply stared at what was in front of him. Why the room wasn't locked, he couldn't have said. He would certainly say something to Gideon in the morning, something along the lines of "Are you out of your mind leaving the door to the mother lode without a padlock and a full-time guard?"

Fortunately for him, there was neither. He shut the door behind him, then had a very leisurely look at things he would have killed to have been able to use in a restored Wyckham.

There were chairs, a table or two, tapestries, blankets, swords, shields . . . It was hard to know where to look first. He didn't dare touch, though it seemed fairly clear that other people weren't too intimidated to at least dust.

He found himself standing suddenly in front of a small table with a lamp on it that was definitely something from the current century. He turned it on, then looked at the enormous book sitting there in a glass case. And since he was there and so was a pair of curator gloves, maybe there was no harm in seeing what the fuss was over. Besides, the case was unlocked. How could he resist?

He put the gloves on, opened the lid, then began to turn pages very gingerly. He was somehow unsurprised to find the book was a family genealogy. Hugh McKinnon would have had a field day with it.

He flipped back through history, stopping occasionally to read a bit and look at who had made up the generations of de Piagets. His family was proud of their heritage—he'd picked up more than a little Gaelic from his maternal grandfather because his granddad had been determined to keep the language alive—but his family couldn't hold a candle to Gideon's. The stories were fascinating and he felt a small twinge of envy that they had managed to hold on to their hall for so many generations. It couldn't have been easily done.

He found himself in the first few pages of the volume. He read about Rhys, the first lord of Artane, then noted the exploits of the man's children. One thing could be said for that second generation of de Piaget lads and lasses: they had reproduced prodigiously. He looked down through the generations, noting names he might or might not have recognized. He saw William de Piaget, great-great-grandson of the first lord of Artane, Rhys. He had spent a week with William in present-day fall, taking the opportunity to brush up a bit of his south-of-the-border sword skill, because he just never knew when it might come in handy.

He reached the early fourteenth century and decided he'd read enough. He wasn't sure he wanted to know who had survived the plague and who hadn't. He left the book open approximately where he'd found it, then sighed and closed the glass case. He took off the gloves, then turned off the table lamp. He had personally had more than enough of life and death in the past thanks to his jaunts with Jamie. He was more than ready for a steady stream of time in the future where he could enjoy a decent bed, food that he hadn't either gathered or killed with his own two hands, and the pleasure of shaving with a razor instead of one of his daggers.

He walked over to the window and looked out, profoundly grateful for the glass that did a decent job of keeping the sea breezes out. Perhaps with any luck, he would have the occasional day off and make use of it by jogging along that very long piece of beachfront real estate.

He took a last look around, shaking his head over the treasures there, then headed toward the door. A decent night's sleep was in order, then an early start in the morning. He reached for the latch to open the door, already thinking about where he would have the contractors start—

It took him a split second to realize that the door had been flung open so hard, it had bloodied his nose. He clutched his face and swore fluently.

The thought crossed his mind that it might have been Gideon's mother to have opened that door and he wasn't going to make a very good impression on her with his reaction, but he thought he might be excused by the extenuating circumstances. Perhaps she would realize that he was admittedly a bit distracted both by the pain and by his attempts to staunch the blood that was pouring down his face.

He felt his way out into the hallway, shut the door behind him, then came to a slow but inexorable halt.

Had that been a tingle he'd just felt on the way through that doorway?

He started to shake his head, but that made the world spin, so he avoided it in favor of continuing to hold his nose and attempting to squint past his hand.

Was that torchlight?

His eyes were watering so madly and the pain was so intense, he wasn't sure if he was seeing things or he'd just taken a very wrong turn.

No, that was definitely torchlight.

Damn it anyway.

"No," he said, shaking his head. He took a step backward. "No, this isn't supposed to happen."

He turned around, then walked back into the room he'd just come out of.

Screeches greeted him. He clutched his nose and peered at a perfectly functional solar, a solar with a decorating scheme that wouldn't have found itself in modern England unless there had been a rope separating its authentic self from overeager tourists. It definitely wouldn't have contained a serving girl standing near the fire with an iron in her hand, screaming her bloody head off.

He wished, absently, that he could see straight. He was fairly sure it would have made all the difference. He took a careful breath.

"Nope," he managed. "No. I *refuse* to accept this. Gideon *promised* me this wouldn't happen, damn him to hell!"

The girl standing near the hearth expressed her opinion of his decision with more screams.

He couldn't begin to guess exactly what time period the vignette he was looking at found itself in, but he supposed it was medieval. He couldn't go wrong with a few remarks made in Norman French.

That he knew any of *that* at all was probably something that should have bothered him, but he'd had several years to become accustomed to several things that should have bothered him.

"My apologies, ladies, I am lost," he said, using one of his standard medieval Norman French openings as he pulled the door shut. The other two were, *Nay, seigneur, I am not interested in seeing the inside of your dungeon*, and, *Yes, and while those are very pretty serving maids, I have a pressing engagement elsewhere*. He and Jamie had picked up those, plus many, many others, over several trips to places they probably shouldn't have gone. He hadn't intended to need them again.

Damned doorways.

He was tempted to simply linger where he was and see if he couldn't get what was obviously a time gate to work again, but he didn't think he would have that luxury. There wasn't even so much as a hint of magic anywhere near where he stood, and he'd had enough experience with time gates to know what he was talking about.

"I gave all this up yesterday," he announced to no one in particular.

The empty passageway didn't offer an opinion. The serving maid on the other side of the door, however, continued to offer hers. Loudly.

He began to hear shouts from a distance. He decided they were coming from his left, so he would go right. He turned and stumbled that direction, wishing he'd paid more attention to the layout of Artane when he'd had the chance. He actually hadn't intended to need the information because he hadn't intended to need to make a hasty getaway.

The shouts became louder. He found a door on his right and jerked it open. There was a gasp and a not particularly pleasant smell. The garderobe, obviously, but he didn't care. Apparently neither did the occupant. He was pulled inside and the door shut and bolted.

"My apologies, demoiselle, I am lost. I'm not interested in seeing the inside of your dungeon," he added, just to be safe.

"Oh, by the saints," a feminine voice said sharply, "will you just be silent before they find us both?"

Or words to that effect. He had spent a year in Paris on a grad school exchange and his French was actually very good. His command of the medieval Norman version of it wasn't, particularly, but he supposed adrenaline was making it better than he probably deserved. All he knew was the curses his companion was muttering weren't exactly what he'd heard on the street near Notre Dame, so maybe his year in France wasn't going to be much help after all.

He considered reaching for his dirks, but there wasn't any

room in the privy and he wasn't sure he wouldn't pass out if he bent over. Before he could determine how he was going to get his leg up where it would be useful in freeing a knife, the door splintered. He pulled his companion out of the way of the sword that thrust through the opening.

"There's a woman in here!" he shouted in what he hoped was intelligible language du jour.

The rest of the door was wrenched open suddenly and he was hauled out into the passageway. He fumbled for his erstwhile biffy mate and pulled her out with him. He had only a vague impression of a woman with long, dark hair and a face that was so stunning, he stopped to admire—and earned a fist in his gut as a reward.

He pulled her behind him where he could at least offer some protection, but that didn't last long. He was facing a passageway full of medieval guardsmen with very sharp swords, and he wasn't exactly at his best.

He managed to liberate one sword from its owner, but that didn't do much to level the playing field. He was hopelessly outnumbered, his nose was killing him, and he didn't have James MacLeod standing back-to-back with him to keep him from being skewered from behind.

He saw two of the men slip past him and reach for the girl. Before he gave it the thought he should have, he turned on them. He didn't want to leave any sort of body count behind, so he disabled them as gingerly as possible.

"Run," he shouted at the girl.

Well, that seemed to translate well enough. She looked at him with wide eyes, then backed into the shadows.

He watched her go for a moment, then addressed the matter at hand, which was getting back to the doorway and giving it no choice but to work. He used sword, hands, feet—all the things he had learned from not only Jamie but Jamie's brother, Patrick, and several of Patrick's less gentlemanly friends. While those skills bought him a bit of purchase down the passageway, they were no match for half a garrison of hardened medieval knights.

Well, them and the guy behind him who clunked him on the head with the hilt of his sword.

Zachary cursed, then slid helplessly into oblivion.

Chapter 4

Mary stood in the passageway, well out of the circle of torchlight, and gaped. She wasn't sure what surprised her more, that an unarmed man had managed to hold his own for so long against mailed knights or that he had tried to protect her.

From her own father's guardsmen.

She considered the complete improbability of that for another moment or two, then crept forward and knelt down next to the men who had been left behind. One of them had already begun to awaken from his stupor. He groaned, then squinted up at her.

"My lady, what befell me?"

"I think, Sir James, that you encountered a wall."

He sat up and clutched his head. He looked at his drooling comrade, shook him until he regained his senses, then staggered to his feet. His mate managed it a moment or two later, then they lurched down the passageway together, trying mightily to convince themselves that something dastardly had felled them from behind without their having seen it. Mary thought it would be impolite to point out it had been a stranger's feet to do the like.

She leaned against the wall and looked at the ruined garderobe door. The man had been dressed very strangely, his French had been terrible, and he'd apparently been just as willing as she to use the garderobe as a place to hide. If that wasn't curious enough, there were yet other things to question. Why had he felt the need to hide from her father's men? Why had he been in her father's keep in the first place?

And why had he put himself at risk to protect her from men who would have given their lives as readily for her as they would have for her sire?

It was tempting to find him and have an answer or two, but she didn't think she wanted to follow him to where he'd no doubt been taken. Artane's dungeon was a very unpleasant place indeed, one easily secure enough to hold a man who had disabled several of her father's fiercer lads. He likely deserved to be there for that alone, though 'twas difficult to think poorly of a man who had tried to keep her safe.

She decided she would make a discreet enquiry later, after Theo and Samuel had had the opportunity to do her investigations for her.

She made her way to the great hall to see if she might filch a bit of supper without being seen, then pulled back into the shadows of the stairwell. Supper was indeed being laid, but she decided abruptly that she had no stomach for it. And the reason for that was standing across the hall plying a very loud, noisy bit of what passed for chivalry with him on her father. She couldn't hear the exact flatteries Geoffrey was spewing, but she could tell how thickly he was layering them on.

And damn Robin of Artane if he didn't suppress a yawn or two and remain where he was instead of simply looking at Styrr as if he'd lost his wits before turning and going off to find more ale.

She watched her mother come out from the kitchens, then cross the hall to stand next to her husband. Anne of Artane was, Mary had to admit objectively, a vision of loveliness and grace, serene no matter the chaos surrounding her, always a model of everything elegant and refined. Mary always felt a little like a grubby stable boy next to her mother, but her mother never made mention of it and for that she was very grateful.

She watched her father reach for her mother's hand and tuck it into the crook of his arm. He wasn't one for overly sentimental displays, though he had been known to offer the occasional gushing flattery to his lady wife—particularly when he thought no one was listening. It was a gruff chivalry, but her mother seemed to find it to her liking.

Mary had never expected that anything akin to it might be plied on her. Indeed, she had never longed for such a thing, not even in her youth when she'd indulged in the occasional bout of dreaming in the hayloft. Or, rather, she hadn't until her twentieth autumn when she'd seen such a display of courtly gallantry that it had taken her a good year to rid herself of the aftereffects.

One of her father's former squires, Christopher of Blackmour, had brought his lady Gillian and his small son to visit at Artane. Mary had heard the rumors of the Dragon of Blackmour, of course, and been prepared to see a creature of such fierceness that even she might have stepped back a pace at his approach. He hadn't disappointed in public, for he was indeed very gruff and stern. But she had watched him a handful of times with his lady when he hadn't thought anyone marked him, and his tender care of his wife had touched her in a way she hadn't expected.

After those astonishing displays, she had found herself watching the men in her family. Her uncles, she had discovered, were rather chivalrous souls themselves. 'Twas no wonder her aunts were so content with their lives. There was something quite lovely about having some lad step up to meet harm not because it would give him reason to display his prowess with the sword, or because he might boast about it later and preen under the praise, but only because he had the means to protect a woman he loved.

A bit like that stranger had upstairs.

She realized suddenly that she wasn't nearly as well hidden as she'd thought. She caught sight of Geoffrey of Styrr looking her way with an expression of triumph on his face, and she drew back instinctively. She stepped backward up the stairs only to run bodily into something that grunted in response. She whirled around to find a cousin standing there. She let out her breath slowly.

"Cousin," she said.

Connor of Wyckham folded his arms over his chest. "Keeper," he corrected. "Yours, as it happens."

"Are you protecting me from Styrr, or myself?"

"Styrr," he echoed with a snort. "Mary, he couldn't finish an opponent if the lad were already bleeding from dozens of wounds and all he needed to do was wait. You could best him with a judiciously placed elbow."

She smiled. "Thank you. And since I'm able to fend for myself tonight, I think I'll be off now. My head begins to pain me."

Connor smirked. "I can see why it would, given that your alternative is an evening passed with that babbling woman out there. Your father has a stronger stomach than either of us does."

Mary nodded. Connor's words were nothing more than she expected but far less than she could have hoped for. He, like everyone else, had a very low opinion of Styrr's manliness, but no opinion at all about his nefarious qualities.

She was beginning to wonder if she might be imagining them herself.

That was definitely something she could reflect on at her leisure—hopefully in a keep far away. She slipped past Connor and started up the stairs, already thinking on which set of relatives might welcome a visit. Not a long visit, just one long enough to allow her father to come to his own conclusions about Styrr's potential to irritate him for the rest of his days. A pity there was no one she could ask to take her—

She came to a halt halfway up the stairs. Of course there was someone she could ask to take her. There was a man no doubt languishing in her father's dungeon who might be very willing indeed to trade a rescue for an escort. Or perhaps he could be bought. It wasn't as if she had bags of gold, but she did have enough to bribe him to take her somewhere else. At least she knew the man would be able to keep her safe.

"Mary?"

She cursed under her breath. She'd forgotten she had a shadow.

"Nothing," she said over her shoulder. "I'm thinking about horseshoes."

Connor only grunted.

She continued on up the stairs and down to her chamber. Aye, she was now thinking about horseshoes indeed and how much damage one would do to Connor if she brought it down enthusiastically on his head.

She thanked him kindly for his company, then escaped inside her chamber and waited. She would give Connor time to grow hungry and seek out supper, then she would be about a little rescuing. She tucked her braided hair down the back of her tunic and waited for far longer than she thought necessary before she opened her door and peeked out.

Connor was leaning back against the wall opposite her door. She frowned.

"What are you doing still here?"

"I thought it wise, lest Styrr wander down the passageway and find your chamber to his liking."

"I'm surprised you don't have your wee brothers here to aid you."

He shivered. "They make me nervous."

"Which makes them so desirable as guardsmen," she said. "Perhaps you should go fetch them to help you in your labors. Or at least go fetch me something to eat."

"I thought your head pained you."

"Food will ease it."

He walked over to stop in front of her. "I don't like what I see in your eye."

She sighed lightly. Jackson was pigheaded, Parsival shrewd, and Thaddeus too intelligent for his own good, but Connor de Piaget was all those things combined to unpleasant perfection. He was only a score and one, but he seemed far older than his years. Perhaps that came from having Samuel and Theo as his younger brothers. She would have difficulty in keeping anything from him.

"There's nothing in my eye," she said. "Nothing out of the ordinary."

He studied her for another moment or two. "I'd call it rebellion."

"Can you fault me for it?" she asked pointedly.

He blew his hair out of his eyes. "There is no reason to fear Styrr."

"Do you trust him?"

"Nay, but I'm suspicious by nature."

"And I'm a very good judge of men."

"You are," he agreed, "but so is your father. He won't give you to a lad who doesn't pass all his tests. He's refused enough men in the past to prove that."

"Styrr is burying him in flatteries."

"Do you think your father will be dazzled by that?" Connor asked with a snort. Then he paused, seemingly unwillingly. "I'm not sure if this will ease you or not, but he has doubled the watches whilst Styrr is here. Perhaps he is uneasy himself."

Mary suppressed the urge to curse. The more men manning the walls and roaming about the hall, the more difficult she would find it to slip out the front gates with an utter stranger.

But escape she would because she had no other choice. She looked up at Connor and manufactured a look of concern.

"With such a heavy guard below," she began slowly, "I wonder if you're sufficient here. Perhaps you should fetch another lad or two?"

Connor drew himself up. "Am I not enough?" he asked stiffly.

"Strange happenings are happening in the hall tonight," she offered. "Don't you agree?"

He shot her a look of disgust, then turned away. "As if I wasn't familiar enough already with strange happenings in my own family," he muttered as he walked away. "Bolt your door," he threw over his shoulder.

Mary had no intentions of it, but she wasn't going to tell him as much. "I changed my mind. I think I'd prefer to go to bed," she called after him. "Don't wake me, aye?"

He waved a hand without looking back at her.

Mary waited until he had disappeared into the shadows before she made a production of closing the door—with her on the outside of it. She waited until she thought Connor might have gone downstairs before she followed after him. Luck was with her, for she found the hall in an uproar thanks to something untoward Lady Suzanna had found in her stew. Connor made for the front door, which left her free to blend in with servants and go in another direction.

It was a very dodgy trip to the cellars, made all the more hazardous by a brief stop into her father's solar to filch the dungeon key she knew he kept hidden under the feet of his main coffer. She was rather more grateful than she likely should have been for all the things she had learned from Theo and Samuel.

Key in hand, she continued on to the kitchens, through them, then to the steep passageway that led down to the dungeons located in the foundations of Artane. There were no guards there. Then again, what soul with any wit at all would have wanted to be anywhere near the place? The chill was deadly. She thoroughly regretted having left her cloak behind.

She walked quickly down the passageway to the dungeon. She paused at the door and heard nothing, not even breathing. Perhaps her father had thrown the man out the front gates.

Or perhaps the man was dead.

That thought was more distressing than she'd thought it would be. If he was dead, then so were her recent hopes of an escort away from Artane. She wasn't comfortable with reducing the poor man to escort alone, but she was more desperate than she wanted to admit. Perhaps he was still senseless. She quickly fitted the key into the lock and pushed the door open.

Before she could call to the man and see if he lived, she found herself suddenly pushed into the dungeon and sent sprawling. The door behind her clanged shut and the key was turned. Booted feet ran quickly back up the passageway.

Mary crawled to her knees and felt for the metal bars that now held her captive. She shook them, called for help, then fell silent when she realized the full import of her situation.

She was locked in her father's dungeon—quite possibly with a man who might throttle her as easily as he might have looked at her.

Damnation, when would she learn to look before she leapt?

She backed away from the bars and flattened herself against the wall. There were, she could readily see, no other avenues of escape. There was a grate on the floor, but she had no hope of lifting it up. Not even her father could have managed it.

She listened frantically for the sound of another's breathing, for the sound of a footfall, for the whisper of a weapon coming from a sheath. Unfortunately, all she could hear was the endless roar of the sea, something she generally found to be quite pleasing. She was having difficulty enjoying it at present.

She jumped when she heard the scrape of a boot against the stone. She would have given much for a knife, or a sword, or the skill to use either. She took the urge to scream and ruthlessly squelched it. It wouldn't serve her to show any fear. She folded her arms over her chest—ignoring the fact that it felt more as if she were trying to comfort herself—and stuck her chin out.

"Prisoner," she said firmly, hoping she sounded much more

confident that she felt, "I can slay you with my bare hands if you try to harm me."

She saw a shape detach itself from the darkness. Her eyes were perhaps of more use than she'd hoped, for she could see his outline well enough. Aye, it was the man from the passageway. He was wearing those odd hose and a tunic that was too short. He was very tall and quite broad and she was an utter fool. If she managed to survive the next quarter hour, she just might throw herself at her father's feet and tell him that.

She saw the flash of a dagger in the stranger's hand and she screamed before she could stop herself.

She would have screamed again when his hand came out of the darkness and took hers, but she was too terrified. She could only squeak as he tugged on her. She went with him because she was apparently too pitiful to do anything else. He stopped at the door.

"Less wind here," he said, his teeth chattering.

It took a moment or two before she realized the import of his words. She gaped at him. "You aren't going to hurt me?"

He started to fumble with the lock, using a pair of daggers to their best advantage. "Nay." He worked a bit longer, then dropped one of his blades. He let out an impressive string of curses—in Gaelic, no less—then pulled away from the door. He shoved his other dagger back down his boot and began to blow on his hands.

Mary was so surprised that he wasn't going to harm her—his chivalry upstairs aside—she could only stand there and look at him stupidly. She shrank back when he reached out, then realized that all he intended was to take her hands in his and rub them to keep them warm.

She let out her breath slowly, but found nothing to say. She had fully expected harm, but instead she had found kindness. All she could do was look at the very faint outline of his form and say nothing. His hands were very cold, but that didn't seem to deter him. She let him be about his work for several minutes before she attempted to speak.

"Someone locked me in," she ventured. She said it in her tongue, even though she was able to speak his reasonably well. *Keep something in reserve* was something her father said constantly to his lads in training and he hadn't been talking about strength of arm.

"Why?" the man asked, shivering audibly.

"I have no idea," she managed. "I'm just a, um, an unimportant soul in the household."

He muttered a curse about the cold, then stomped his feet a time or two before he continued with her hands. "Will someone come?"

"Hopefully," she said, finding that the cold was now burning her throat.

"Why did you come?"

His French was indeed dreadful, as if he'd learned it from someone who had learned it from someone else who hadn't spoken it very well. But at least he was attempting it with confidence.

"Why did I come?" she asked, her teeth beginning to chatter. "To rescue you, of course."

He went still. "Why?"

"Because you protected me above. If we escape here, I will see if I can't help you out the front gates."

He bowed his head briefly. "Thank you."

Mary was pleased with that despite the difficulty she was having not weeping from the cold. If he was going out the gates, then so was she. Just exactly what she'd hoped for.

She hoped for it for a good hour before she saw what she thought might have been a faint lightening of the passageway. She was almost certain it was her imagination until she heard her father's curses coming very clearly from up the way.

"Help has arrived," she said gratefully.

Her companion said nothing, but he did stand behind her and block some of the breeze. Mary listened to her father and winced at not only his curses, but his vow to have vengeance on any and all in the area. He caught sight of her, then gestured furiously for one of his guardsmen to unlock the door.

Before she could babble anything but incoherencies—it was very cold, after all—her father had wrenched the door open and yanked her out into the passageway. She fumbled for the stranger's hand and pulled him along with her, which he seemed inclined not to fight.

Her father opened his mouth—no doubt to spew out more curses—then he froze. He stared in astonishment at the stranger for a handful of moments, then he shut his mouth with a snap.

"Leave us," he barked at his men. "Sir Ranulf, you stay."

Mary started to tell her father how kind the stranger had been to her, but before she could her father's captain had brought the hilt of his sword down against the stranger's head.

He fell to the ground with a rather unwholesome-sounding crash.

Robin looked at his captain. "Escort my daughter immediately upstairs and see she stays in her bedchamber."

"Father—"

He shot her a look of such fury that she decided she would be wise to remain silent. For the moment.

"I have been combing this keep for you for the past hour," he said in a low, tight voice. "I feared the worst. I wouldn't have thought to look here if Styrr hadn't said he'd seen you going into the kitchens, so perhaps you can look on him with a friendlier eye. And now, if you don't want me to lose my temper fully, you'll go along with Ranulf. Silently."

Not when her escort out the gates was lying senseless behind her. Mary knew that if she merely left him behind, he would be thrown back into the dungeon and then any hope of putting the sword to Styrr's plans for her would be finished. In fact, it wouldn't have surprised her to find 'twas Styrr who had locked her in just to try to bring her to her knees. But bring her to the altar?

Never.

She snatched up her Scotsman's dagger and stood over him. She knew that her father could have disarmed her without bothering to stifle a yawn, but she didn't care. She pointed the knife toward her father and stuck her chin out to give herself courage.

"Do not hurt him."

Her sire studied her for a moment, then very deliberately folded his arms over his chest and glared. It was how he often intimidated messengers from other keeps. Unfortunately for him, she'd seen him do it too many times to be terrified.

Well, perhaps that wasn't completely true. She knew she was treading on dangerous ground. There was a muscle twitching in his jaw. He was holding on to his temper, and that just barely.

"Does this pitiful whelp you've decided to champion have a name?" he asked with exaggerated politeness.

"We didn't perform introductions. We were too busy freezing."

He wiggled his jaw, once. "I don't suppose that since he neglected to tell you his name he told you where he was from, did he?"

"He didn't," she said, "though he cursed quite proficiently in Gaelic. I suspect he's a Scot, though, again, we didn't manage much speech."

"Then what, by all the bloody saints, did you do for the past hour!" he shouted.

She lifted her chin a bit more. "He worked on the lock. And he rubbed my hands to keep them warm."

Her sire's jaw went slack. "He did *what*?"

"He kept my hands warm," she repeated. She watched her father splutter in absolute fury. He was no worse than a terribly misbehaving horse—something she declined to point out—so she took a firmer grip on her fallen champion's knife and refused to back down. "I don't want you to hurt him."

"I'll kill him—"

"Then you'll kill me first."

He looked at her as if he'd never seen her before. Indeed, she had to agree with the sentiment. She had never in her life gainsaid her father in such a fashion. He hadn't been any sort of tyrant, true, but he had been impossibly stubborn and full of all sorts of expectations where she and her brothers had been concerned. She had been excused from duties in the lists, but in all else she had been expected to make the same efforts that her siblings had. And in all the years she'd lived with her sire, she had always resorted to talking in circles until he threw up his hands and gave in just to be done with listening to her. She had never in her life simply defied him.

Until now.

He scowled fiercely at her, then jerked his head toward the passageway. "Go. I won't kill him."

"Don't hurt him—"

"I won't hurt him, either!" he bellowed.

She waited for another moment or two, just as she had seen him do countless times when he'd exacted a promise from someone he wasn't quite sure would keep that promise, then nodded shortly. She handed him the dagger haft-first, then paused again.

"He was kind to me," she said simply.

He was also going to be the one who helped her get out the

front gates, but she supposed her sire didn't need to know that at present.

She walked up the passageway with her sire's captain, then paused and looked behind her. Her father had squatted down next to the man and was feeling for a heartbeat. There was no steel in his hands and he didn't look as if he planned to throttle the man anytime soon. She turned away and followed Sir Ranulf, her hands tingling.

She didn't think it was from the cold.

Chapter 5

Z*achary* woke to a pounding headache. Actually, it wasn't just a headache, it was an ache that encompassed his entire head. He wasn't quite sure how that was different from a garden-variety throbbing except that the current agony was the sort of pain that came from being clunked on the head twice with the hilt of a sword and a door caressing his nose. He didn't dare move. Just being awake was enough to make him wish he weren't. He settled for wiggling his nose briefly. It gave only a mild protest, so perhaps it hadn't been broken after all, just insulted.

It was indication enough of the day he'd had that that was good news.

He opened his eyes and looked above him. There was light streaming in from a window set high into the wall, revealing a very authentic-looking medieval ceiling. The previous night was something of a blur, but he had no trouble recalling a pair of very unpleasant hours in something that would have passed for a refrigerator in the twenty-first century. He suspected most prisoners incarcerated in that dungeon froze to death out of a sense of self-preservation.

He wondered what had happened to the girl who'd tried to rescue him. He only hoped she wasn't back in the dungeon, freezing, while he was . . . well, he was freezing, too.

Then again, that might have been because he was not wearing any clothes.

He sat up, then clutched his head until it stopped spinning long enough for him to look around. He saw a handful of kitchen lads—they couldn't have been more than nine or ten—who were watching him with grins. Another handful of kitchen maids were eyeing him with interest.

And there to his right, leaning back comfortably against the wall, was a man Zachary had no doubt was the lord of the castle.

It wasn't that he was dressed in velvets and sporting heavy rings on his fingers. He just had that look about him, as if he were in charge and needed nothing but his mere presence to make sure everyone else understood that. He was definitely the same man who had opened the dungeon door the night before. He looked no less displeased now than he had then.

Zachary studied him a bit longer. He looked, actually, a great deal like Gideon de Piaget, except for the color of his hair. Zachary considered the genealogy he'd looked at the afternoon before. Was that Rhys, Robin, or even Phillip de Piaget? Or perhaps someone farther down the line? The man was dressed in medieval gear, true, but since Artane was in the north of England, the fashions wouldn't have changed as swiftly as they might have in another location. Assuming he was still in Artane, it was conceivable that he could have been off by several decades.

That he was familiar enough with the past to know that little detail was something else contributing to his headache.

He wished he'd paid more attention to the names of those Artane lords, but he supposed it was too late for regrets now. He was facing Artane's lord, whichever one it happened to be, and that was enough to know. He cleared his throat and inclined his head carefully.

"My lord," he said.

Artane only continued to stare at him.

Zachary was profoundly grateful that at least part of him was covered by a crusty blanket. It could have been worse. He offered his most deferential smile.

"I wonder, my lord," he said in his best medieval French, "if I might have my clothes back."

Artane seemed to consider. "I suppose you might wonder that."

Zachary realized, with a start, that not only was he missing his clothes, he was missing everything else as well. That was a disaster in the making. His dirks had been made in fourteenth-century Scotland and likely wouldn't have aroused suspicion, but his Levis certainly would. Modern boots would have been the killing blow. He supposed he was fortunate he hadn't woken to find himself tied to a stake.

Well, at least he would have been warm that way.

But he wasn't precisely eager to see how warm that sort of fire might get, so he decided to see if he couldn't find a way to get out the front gates without undue effort. A little visit to the solar upstairs was, he was certain, a complete nonstarter. He wasn't accustomed to negotiating when he was less-than-adequately dressed, but, as Jamie was wont to say, there was always a new adventure around the next turn of century.

"Perhaps we could start with my boots," he said, striving to put the right amount of expectation in his tone and hoping that his accent wasn't so far off that Artane's lord would burn him just for that, "and my knives."

"I don't imagine that you're in any position to demand anything," Artane said coolly.

"I wasn't demanding," Zachary said politely. "I was asking."

Artane pushed away from the wall. "You have quite a bit of cheek for a lad with his arse bare to the wind—and one who has no good reason to be in my hall."

That was indeed the sticking point and one Zachary didn't want Artane thinking about any more than he likely had already. "I would like to be *out* of your hall as quickly as possible," he said without hesitation. "The sooner the better, I'm sure."

"And if I say you go nowhere?"

Zachary took a deep breath. "Then I'll go anyway." He'd done it before, and in more than one century.

"Oh, do you think so?" Artane asked in a very low, very dangerous voice.

"Do you think you can stop me?" was out hanging in the air in the middle of the kitchen before he realized what he'd said.

Damn it, one more thing to fix. *Engage brain before opening mouth* was definitely going to have to go on his list. Probably at the top.

He was grateful for all the things he'd learned after grad school that had nothing to do with angles and inclines and structural integrity. He leaped to his feet and yanked a long, stout knife out of a boar's carcass languishing on the work table, then snatched up a fire iron just in time to cross them above him and keep from having his head cleaved in twain as Artane brought his sword down.

It was not a pleasant skirmish. He was less interested in killing the lord of the hall than he was keeping himself alive—but he supposed he shouldn't have bothered worrying about the first. Artane had an endless supply of energy and a technique that left Zachary wishing desperately for a sword so he might at least stand a chance of not being completely humiliated.

And he was quite uncomfortable fighting in the raw, as it were.

Jamie would have been apoplectic with laughter at the sight.

"Damn you, stop your smirking," Artane snarled, almost skewering him.

Zachary didn't have time to explain what he'd been thinking because it was all he could do to keep breathing and continue to keep himself unpierced. The world was beginning to spin wildly and he thought he just might lose the very fine dinner he'd had in Artane's hall the night before. Well, he'd had that dinner several centuries in the future, actually, but who was counting?

"Robin!"

Zachary let the point of the fire iron drop to the stone floor, then collapsed against the table gratefully as Artane ceased his tortures with the sword. He looked to his left to see a very beautiful blonde standing at the entrance to the kitchen with her hands on her hips, apparently fighting her smile.

"Robin de Piaget, what, by all the blessed saints, are you doing?"

"Keeping myself occupied," the lord of Artane said with a yawn. "Barely."

"Your steward awaits you," she said, "when you're finished with your exercise here."

"This won't take much longer. Unfortunately."

Zachary watched the lady of the hall glance his way, look at her husband once more, then laugh as she turned and walked away. Zachary honestly couldn't blame her. If he hadn't been in his present condition, he might have laughed as well.

But that was apparently Robin of Artane standing there with the sword, and if he knew nothing else, he knew of Robin's reputation from tales that William had told him. He was probably lucky to still have all of himself intact. And he was under no illusions about the amount of effort Artane's lord *wasn't* putting into his morning's exercise.

But half of being a good swordsman was carrying oneself as such, so he didn't dare show any weakness. He pushed himself back to his feet and stood there with a carving knife in one hand and a fire iron in the other. He thought he might have swayed a little, but perhaps Lord Robin hadn't noticed.

Then again, perhaps he had. The man studied him for a moment or two, then resheathed his sword with a disgruntled look. He folded his arms over his chest.

"You're giving me very poor sport," he said.

"I'm better with a sword," Zachary said. "And a head that isn't killing me."

Or words to that effect, he hoped.

Robin leaned back against the wall and commenced another lengthy, silent study of things that no doubt perplexed him. "I continue to wonder," he said finally, "what it is you're doing in my hall without my permission."

"I took a wrong turn."

"Apparently." He frowned. "I have the feeling I would be better off to just kill you now and have done. You look like trouble."

Zachary supposed he could argue with Robin about the merits of leaving him alive, but in the end, it was entirely up to the lord of the keep. Fighting his way out of the keep, then managing to stay alive long enough to find another time gate— all au naturel, as it were—might just be more than he could manage in his current state. He took a deep breath, then had to wait for a minute or two until the subsequent stars cleared enough for him to see. He struggled to focus on Artane's lord.

"I would like to be trouble for a very short time, my lord."

Robin considered for another eternal moment, then pushed away from the wall. Zachary didn't want to give Robin any reason to change his mind about tossing any stray time-travelers onto the fire, but he couldn't leave his gear behind. The potential for disaster there was catastrophic. "Have a bath and wash the floor out of your hair, then we'll see where we stand."

"My lord," Zachary said quickly, "if I might ask about my clothes?"

Robin paused, then looked at him slowly. "Burned. They were crawling with vermin, or so I was told."

Zachary was very grateful for whoever had told that whopper. The less the locals thought about what he'd been wearing, the farther away from a hot fire and stake he would find himself. But there were some things that wouldn't burn so well and those were the things that troubled him the most.

"All my things, my lord?" Zachary asked.

"Your boots were beyond saving, apparently. We'll discuss your knives in my solar. Don't cause any trouble on your way there or you'll regret it."

Zachary would have nodded if he'd dared, but he didn't. "Of course, my lord," he said as deferentially as possible. He'd walked barefoot before. At least it wasn't snowing outside. It could have been much worse.

Robin stared at him for another moment, the wheels turning quite loudly, then he lifted his eyebrows briefly before he walked out of the kitchen, shaking his head. Zachary watched him go, then suppressed the urge to sigh deeply. In reality, things could have gone much worse for him. He'd already had more of a taste of Artane's dungeon than he cared to and he had no desire to revisit the place.

He laid the carving knife on the table, then walked unsteadily over to the fire to replace the iron in its place. He didn't bother with the blanket. Everyone had seen everything they were going to and they would likely think him daft for any modesty now.

"Sit by the fire, good sir," said the cook with a nod toward a stool. "We'll have a bath for ye as quick as may be."

Zachary accepted ale, then very carefully leaned his head back against the stone. Medieval England. Why wasn't he surprised?

He was going to kill Gideon de Piaget when he got home.

A n hour later, bathed, dressed, and fed, he walked unsteadily up the passageway in the care of a trio of fierce medieval knights. What he wanted was a week of vegging out in front of the TV with an endless supply of healthy snacks. Well, maybe mostly healthy snacks and a few Twinkies. After what he'd been through, he thought he just might deserve them.

He suspected lazing around uselessly wasn't going to be a part of his immediate future, as much as he might have wished for it. If he managed to finish the day without his head splitting in two from the pain, he would be doing well. If he had the chance to spend the afternoon resting, it would be a miracle. He would have preferred to be mooching dinner off his sister-in-law Sunshine and begging her for a little reflexology for dessert, but since she was hundreds of years away and he probably wasn't completely out of the woods yet with the lord of Artane, he would just press on and hope for the best.

He would have asked his escort to take him on a little detour to the lady of the keep's solar, but he didn't dare chance it. That Robin hadn't asked him any pointed questions about why he'd been loitering where he'd been found was an unexpected gift. He suspected the restraint wouldn't last long.

He was deposited in front of a doorway and told curtly to wait while one of the guardsmen knocked for him.

"Come!"

A guardsman opened the door and nodded for him to go in. He thanked them all kindly for the company, then walked inside. The door closed behind him quietly. Zachary clasped his hands behind his back and waited. Robin looked up from where he sat at his table, poring over sheets of something. Zachary made him another bow and regretted it immediately. He managed not to land on his face, but it was a near thing.

"Thank you, my lord, for the clothing," he said hoarsely, bracing himself with his hands on his thighs.

"By the saints, sit down, lad, before you fall there."

Zachary felt his way over to a chair and sat gratefully. He had to put his face in his hands for several minutes until he thought he could straighten without heaving his breakfast onto Robin's boots. His vision eventually cleared enough for him to see Robin studying him thoughtfully.

"Your French is poor," Robin commented.

"My Gaelic is better."

Robin looked at him with an inscrutable expression. "Is it, indeed?" he asked, in that tongue.

"It is, indeed," Zachary agreed, also in that tongue, rather grateful he'd had enough exposure to the medieval version of it to have acquired a decently authentic accent. "Yours, I can tell already, is excellent."

Robin lifted one eyebrow briefly. "I've had ample opportunity to learn it over the years. That doesn't answer my question, though, about why you find yourself in my hall. Did you come through the gate?"

Zachary almost flinched, then he realized that Robin was talking about the front gate. He was accustomed to inventing stories for being where he was, but he couldn't for the life of him think up one at the moment. There was, after all, no good reason for him to have found himself upstairs in Robin's keep. He could only bluster on and hope for the best.

"I became lost," he said.

"So you said before." He laid Zachary's daggers on his table and fingered them thoughtfully. "Very nice steel for a simple peasant to possess."

Zachary thought it best to allow Robin to believe what he wanted. After all, lying low and being underestimated were two of his best strategies for staying alive in times that weren't his own.

He supposed he might manage the same thing now, though that didn't help him get himself back upstairs. Maybe all he could hope for was to thank Robin for the boots and clothes, then see what he could do out in the countryside. He could immediately bring to mind two gates that were reachable without too much effort.

Of course, time gates were fickle, which he well knew, and it might take longer than he wanted to get something to work for him, but he was fresh out of quick fixes.

"Lad?"

Zachary dragged his attention back to the conversation at hand. "Aye, my lord, they are very fine blades. I befriended a blacksmith in Scotland who fashioned them for me. I feel fortunate to have them."

Robin sat back in his chair and stroked his chin. "Do you have interesting answers to any of my other questions?"

Zachary didn't imagine Robin would care for any of his answers—not that he would have given them anyway. He attempted yet another deferential smile.

"At the risk of another encounter with your spectacular swordplay, my lord, I must admit that I can offer you nothing more than the truth that I took a wrong turn and that I would like to be on my way as quickly as possible."

"Are you in any condition to be on your way?" Robin asked mildly.

"My lord, I have no choice. You've already been more generous than I deserve."

Robin shrugged. "I couldn't let you roam about my keep in your altogether, could I? My kitchen wenches won't do a decent bit of labor for the rest of the day as it is. But as for you, aye, you may be on your way as you will."

Zachary rose and carefully reached for his knives, then paused. He looked down at the blades, comfortable and familiar in his hands, then met Robin's gaze. He couldn't see him as well as he would have liked, but that would pass. His concerns, though, weren't dismissed so easily. "Speaking of serving wenches, my lord, might I ask something of you?"

"Do you want one of them?" Robin asked in disbelief.

Zachary smiled briefly. "Nay, my lord, though I would like to ask something on the behalf of one of them."

Robin frowned. "Go on."

"The lass who tried to help me last night . . . I didn't think to ask her name but understood her to be one of your serving maids. I was hoping that you might be lenient when dealing with her."

Robin's mouth fell open. "A serving maid?"

"Aye, my lord. I would be willing to work to save her any punishment."

"A serving—"

Zachary suddenly found himself sitting again without really knowing how he'd gotten there. He shoved his knives back down his boots—apparently someone else's boots—and put his hands over his eyes to keep himself from having to watch the room spin. Yes, he would have been happy to work off quite a few things if he could have just found a place to lie down for another hour or two.

"I think you're not going to be doing anything this morning besides puking into whatever corner I put you," Robin said with a sigh. "I'm short on beds at the moment. Are you opposed to a pile of hay?"

"'Tis far more than I could hope for, my lord."

Zachary heard the scrape of a chair, then the sound of

booted feet. He felt strong hands take him by the arm and pull him to his feet. He managed to stay there on his own after a moment or two. He squinted at Artane's lord.

"Thank you," he managed.

"I'll just be happy to get you out of my solar," Robin said with a grimace, "before you retch all over it. Saints, you're making *me* ill. Think you can manage the journey to the stables?"

"Absolutely."

Robin released him, then walked over to the door. Zachary followed, less steadily than he would have liked. He managed to glance at the great hall as they walked through it. He saw the shadow of the stairwell behind the lord's table, but he couldn't bring himself to even think about it. It was going to be all he could do to get himself to that luxurious pile of hay.

He hoped he wasn't making a serious mistake by agreeing to pass out in the stables without someone as a guard. Obviously, he'd become too accustomed to having Jamie to guard his back.

Then again, it wasn't as if he hadn't traveled back in time on his own more than once. The last time he'd done so was something he didn't think on often. It had been a particularly unpleasant experience, one he had no intention of repeating.

That had been five years ago, though. He was much better at blending in than he used to be.

Not exactly a skill he could put on a résumé.

He followed Robin out to the stables and waited while Robin gave instructions to his stable master. He thanked the good lord of Artane for his concessions and for his promise to leave a certain serving wench unreprimanded, had a grunt in return, then found himself led to a quiet corner.

He lay down, threw his arm over his eyes, and considered how fortunate he'd been. He wondered absently if an equal amount of good fortune had befallen that astonishingly beautiful serving girl—

He turned away from that thought sharply. She was the *last* thing he needed to think about. He was going to settle his debt with the lord of the castle for both his clothes and the girl, then he was going to get the hell back home. He would make a few additions to the master map of hot spots that James MacLeod had hanging over his desk in his office, then he was hanging up his boots. This was the very last, the positively final time he ever tripped through time. He wasn't sure if he was going to remind Jamie about that first or yell it at Ambrose. Maybe he would get Jamie on the phone and shout it while he was standing next to Ambrose.

And then he was going to punch Gideon de Piaget. Very hard. Probably in the nose.

No paranormal activity, his arse.

He took a deep breath and tried to sleep.

Chapter 6

Mary pulled her mother's solar door shut behind her and took her first decent breath of the day. She didn't panic often, but she was panicked now. She had been upstairs for the past three days and she feared she had lost any chance of an escort to anywhere besides the chapel.

She had spent the first two days after her adventure in the dungeon abed, shivering. The third, she'd found herself banished to her mother's solar. She hadn't dared ask any of the servants if a handsome Scotsman in strange clothing had been hanged and displayed outside the gates as a warning to other impudent trespassers, and she hadn't seen any of her cousins to determine the same thing. She had simply sat and stitched, which she did unwillingly at the best of times.

Fortunately for the condition of her mother's linens, today she'd been released from the tortures of the solar before noon. If she'd had to pass any more time listening to the lady Suzanna babbling about all the things that should have been going on at Artane but, to her deep disappointment, weren't, she would have taken her tapestry needle and stabbed the woman with it. Her mother had finally sent her off on an errand from which she'd had to have known Mary wouldn't return.

She hurried to her bedchamber and changed into something

more sensible for working horses, not because she intended to work horses, but because she thought if her Scottish rescuer wanted to bolt for the gates, she would want to be ready to bolt with him. Assuming he was still inside those gates.

At least she was certain her father wouldn't have hurt him. He'd given his word, and Robin of Artane never went back on his word.

She ran out of the stairwell and skidded across part of the hall floor. It was completely empty. Indeed, she might have believed she'd walked into someone else's great hall if she hadn't recognized the tapestries on the walls and the enormous hearths set into those same walls.

She wandered across the floor, feeling slightly unsteady on her feet. Had there been some sort of disaster? Had something happened to one of her cousins or, the saints forbid, her father himself? She opened the door, then came to a teetering halt. The answer was in front of her, thanks to the battle going on in her father's courtyard.

Well, perhaps calling it a battle was overstating things a bit. There was a skirmish in the offing. Part of the household was clustered on the steps, whilst the garrison and a pair of her cousins were standing on the courtyard floor. She pulled the door shut behind her silently, then saw Theo and Samuel a step or two below her. They made space for her to come stand between them, which she did without hesitation.

"You escaped," Theo said out of the side of his mouth.

"Finally," she agreed, "though I don't think my sire knows."

"He won't notice."

She saw quickly that Theo had that aright. Her sire was standing by himself in the courtyard with his arms crossed over his chest, watching the madness unfolding in front of him without any discernible expression at all—a sure sign he was very interested indeed.

Geoffrey of Styrr was there, talking to a man who had chivalry but no sword. Well, perhaps *talking* was an overstatement. Geoffrey was berating him sternly for the saints only knew what.

It was difficult to ignore the relief that rushed through her. Her Scotsman was still inside the gates and still breathing—for the moment, at least.

'Twas one thing to have seen him by torchlight, dressed in

those strange blue trews and sporting blood on his face. It was another thing entirely to see him by the pleasant light of noon, standing confidently in her father's courtyard as if he were a Scottish lord who had paused in the conquering of his neighbors long enough to examine a very loud, unpleasant trespasser whom he would subsequently dispatch lest the dolt irritate him overmuch.

He was dressed in modern clothes with his hands clasped behind his back, listening to Styrr rage at him. He still had no sword, but Mary supposed he didn't need it. She had seen what he could do with his hands and feet alone. She suspected that many men left him alone simply because of what danger his very fine form boded. The maids he no doubt bested simply with the fairness of his face.

She wondered how it was the day had become so hot so suddenly.

She wrenched her thoughts back to more useful places. "I wonder who he is," she whispered to Theo. "A Scottish lord, do you suppose?"

"Nay," he said, looking at her as if she'd lost her wits, "he's a smith."

Mary felt her mouth fall open. "He's a *what*?"

"He's not a very good one," he offered, "if that eases you any."

"How did you discover this?"

"We haunted him in the stables where Uncle Robin had him shoveling manure. Once we learned his true identity, we made immediate mention of it to Uncle, who then sent him off to the forge. I'm not certain he was completely appreciative of our aid in that, for the smithy is quite hot." He paused, then shrugged. "'Tis all very strange, in truth, for he seems not to have the skills he should."

"I wouldn't say that," Samuel disagreed. "He's very good at what Master Godric has taught him to do. He simply isn't familiar with the tasks he would know if he'd apprenticed in his youth to that sort of work, which leads me to believe that he is truly no smith—"

"Or that he's had a bump on the head and forgotten all useful bits he might have known before," Theo interrupted. "Or perhaps—"

"Does he have a name?" Mary asked, before they could

carry on their discussion of what other untoward things might have befallen that man who couldn't possibly be a worker of steel.

"Zachary," Samuel said absently. He looked at his brother. "The rest begs the question, does it not, of what he is fit for? It is no easy task to simply walk into a forge and do what's asked of you, is it?"

Mary agreed with Theo that it wasn't, but she did so silently. She left her cousins to their discussions of things that intrigued them and allowed herself to concentrate on more interesting things, such as how it was that a man who was neither smith nor stable boy—nor, apparently a Scottish lord or bespurred knight—could stand in her father's courtyard and look as if he were the equal of any of her cousins or brothers.

He also looked, she had to admit objectively, so handsome that she thought she might have felt a bit weak in the knees. She cursed under her breath. She was a score and seven, for pity's sake. Too old to be moved by the fairness of a man's face or the beauty of his form.

Still, there was no reason not to study him as dispassionately as her cousins had done. For the sake of being able to discuss the like with them intelligently at a later time, of course. Nothing more.

Zachary of the fully flowered chivalry was truly a delight to make the object of such a study. His hair was very dark, though cut short in the current style that her cousins favored. She couldn't tell the color of his eyes, but she supposed she could save that as something to be discovered later. He might not have been a smith in truth, but his arms, which were currently folded over his chest, were powerful. She knew he had calluses on those hands because she'd felt them in the dungeon. Whatever else he did, he certainly seemed to do something with his hands besides beckon for his cup to be refilled. Her father would have respected that.

Geoffrey, however, seemed not to have found anything to appreciate about Zachary the smith. He was awash in a fair bit of righteous indignation, growing louder with each accusation.

"How long has Styrr been at this?" she whispered.

"A quarter hour," Samuel said.

"What began it?"

Samuel smiled a very small smile. "I would suggest that

Styrr was suffering from an excess of envy, but I could be mistaken."

Mary smiled in return. If anything could be counted on to happen with the same regularity as the sun rising and setting each day, it was that Geoffrey of Styrr would at some point during his stay at Artane comment on his own magnificence. That someone else—and a smith, at that—should outshine him simply by breathing was something not to be tolerated.

"You look like a smith," Geoffrey announced suddenly.

"I imagine I do—"

"A smith who can't make a horseshoe!" Geoffrey shouted. He looked about him, as if he wanted to assure himself that everyone within earshot appreciated the horrors he had apparently already endured that morning. "I wanted my horse shod."

"I hadn't begun to attempt it—"

"You were doing even *that* poorly!"

Zachary took a deep breath, looking as if he would have liked nothing better than to have called Styrr fool before he turned and walked away. He said nothing in retaliation, though.

"Styrr, draw your sword and instruct him in the proper way to work with steel," Thaddeus suggested loudly.

"Aye, do," Connor agreed. "I'm certain we would all benefit from such a display."

Mary watched her cousins exchange very bland looks, which she was sure were very difficult for them to maintain. If there was one topic that found itself discussed ad nauseam at the fire in the evenings after the lord and lady had retired, it was the quality of swordsmen who had darkened Artane's hallowed gates, either in the quest for her hand or in the quest for even the most minimal training from her father. Mary had been happy to have found herself included in such discussions as the one the lads turned to for the final opinion on horsemanship.

Styrr had not fared well on any of those evenings.

She caught her breath when Geoffrey drew his sword with a flourish. Zachary had nothing in his hands, no sword at his side, no means of escape save by bolting and leaving his pride behind. She wondered if he would have the good sense to turn and run.

He didn't.

Geoffrey hadn't seemed to have noticed. She supposed, to be fair, that she couldn't say that he was completely without skill. He had managed to draw his sword, after all, and he had pointed it in the direction of his enemy, also a very good sign. But intimidate anyone with it? Not likely.

She pursed her lips. She had obviously lived with de Piaget men for too many years.

Styrr attempted to hack at Zachary the smith with wild strokes, strokes that Zachary avoided simply by stepping out of their way.

"Perhaps there is more to him than he's revealed," Theo whispered. "He might be a knight after all, one bitter from the Crusades in years past—"

"Then where is his sword?" Samuel asked.

"Perhaps he fell on hard times, or ruffians, or had a very ill sister and was forced to sell everything he owned to convince the nuns at Seakirk to take her in. I'm not completely convinced he's a Scot by birth, though his Gaelic is flawless. His French is surely better than it was since we've been working with him. Is he a scholar then, do you think?"

Samuel looked at Zachary, then shook his head. "Too much sword skill to have spent his youth only with manuscripts."

They looked at each other in a silence that was fraught with meaning.

"Intriguing," Theo said slowly.

"We must know more," Samuel said, rubbing his hands together in anticipation.

Mary agreed, and she would have bid her cousins consider silently what that *more* might involve, but listening to them speculate distracted her from the skirmish in the courtyard that she was convinced wouldn't end well. Either Geoffrey would manage to actually poke Zachary with his sword, or Zachary would allow Geoffrey to humiliate himself so thoroughly that Geoffrey would call for Zachary's death by some other means.

None of it boded well for her escort out the gates.

She looked down at her cousins who were standing in various places below her. Connor looked back at her, lifted his eyebrows briefly, then continued on with his watching. Thaddeus and Parsival were on the ground, discussing in whispers what they saw. She looked for Jackson only to find him walking over to stand next to her father. Her father acknowledged him with a slight nod.

The crowd grew. Zachary the smith was now fending off

Geoffrey's attack with a pair of long knives he'd managed to get out of his boots. She watched him catch Geoffrey's blade between them, then give Geoffrey a mighty shove backward.

"I've no quarrel with you, my lord," Zachary said, his chest heaving.

"You ruined my horse!"

"My lord, I haven't *seen* your horse," Zachary said, leaping aside to avoid a wild thrust.

"You are a liar," Geoffrey spat. "The horse is half lame and I'll see you punished for it."

Mary found herself suddenly shoved aside so forcefully, it took both Theo and Samuel to keep her from tumbling off the stairs. She regained her balance and watched as Geoffrey's mother continued down the stairs, continuing to push souls out of her way as it suited her. She came to a stop next to Robin only after shoving Jackson so hard he almost went sprawling.

"What is this!" she exclaimed. "I heard there was an injustice going on in your courtyard."

Robin looked at her gravely. "Did you indeed, Lady Suzanna?"

"This isn't even a proper fight," she protested. "I insist that you make this fair." She pointed toward her son. "Two blades to one? Absurd!"

Mary watched her father consider, then nod and walk out into the midst of his courtyard. Geoffrey seemed loath to back away, but Robin glared him into doing so. Mary couldn't imagine that Zachary would be willing to give up either of his knives, so she wondered what her father intended to ask him to do.

Robin stopped next to him and held out his hand. Mary watched Zachary exchange a very long look with her father. His expression was as inscrutable as her father's.

Lust. Mary realized at that moment that what she was feeling was lust. It was such a novel sensation that she almost had to look for somewhere to sit down.

Zachary the smith was, she would readily admit, the most handsome man she had ever seen. Her family was full of handsome men, so another one shouldn't have had any effect on her. But even standing there in borrowed clothing and what she was sure were her sire's oldest pair of boots, he was spectacular. She fanned herself surreptitiously until she looked at her hand and realized he had held it in both his own to warm it. She put her hands behind her back and clasped them there. Safer that way, no doubt.

Zachary pulled the sheath of one knife out of his boot, resheathed his knife, and put it in Robin's hand.

Her father didn't move. He simply waited. That was the first sign of any sort of surprise that Zachary had betrayed since she'd begun watching him. He stifled it soon enough, shot her sire a dark look, then pulled the sheath out of his other boot, resheathed his second knife, then handed it to Robin as well.

"Still unfair, Uncle," Connor said loudly. "Tie his hands behind his back!"

Parsival smiled at his cousin over his shoulder, then unbuckled his sword belt. "Smith!"

Zachary looked up, then caught the sword as it came flying toward him. He scarce had time to cast aside the belt and sheath before Geoffrey was coming at him in a fury.

Mary realized she was leaning on Theo only because he almost went tumbling off the stairs to his left. He smiled faintly at her, then put his arm around her shoulders. Mary leaned on him happily. She was just tired. She wasn't weak in the knees over a man who fought like no other smith she had ever seen. It was obvious that he had trained. He might have even given her father sport for an hour or so.

Geoffrey might have been a poor swordsman, but he was an excellent hurler of insults, a skill which he demonstrated to its fullest. He disparaged everything from Zachary's looks to his parentage, finally settling quite comfortably on his sword skill.

Zachary only fought without comment and without undue exertion.

The conflict went on far longer than she expected it to, with no clear winner, though 'twas obvious to her that Zachary had only made the minimum effort necessary to defend himself. Geoffrey finally made a very large production of taking a step backward.

"I've humiliated you enough for one day, *smith*."

Zachary rested Parsival's sword against his shoulder. "So you have, my lord. I appreciate the mercy."

Geoffrey resheathed his sword, accepted congratulations from any who were willing to offer them, then gathered his mother up and started up the stairs. Mary leapt off them before she could be caught. Samuel and Theo followed her, standing in front of her where she wouldn't be seen. She waited until her father had given Zachary back his knives and gone to the lists before she breathed easily.

She watched Zachary go fetch the scabbard, then walk over to Parsival. He resheathed her cousin's blade and handed it back to him. He dragged his sleeve across his forehead, then laughed uneasily at something her cousin said.

Mary had to lean back against the hall's foundation. She was, in truth, too old for this.

Parsival walked across the courtyard with Zachary, speaking with him as companionably as he might have any other lad of his own station. They shook hands in front of the forge and Zachary went back inside, presumably to go back to work doing something he didn't know how to do.

"This is a mystery," Theo said, stroking his chin thoughtfully.

"It must be solved," Samuel agreed.

"At our earliest convenience," Theo said, sealing the bargain. "Tonight after he's finished in the forge we'll lie in wait for him in the stables and hope he comes to see if Master Rolf needs aid. Though I daresay I'll need to avoid Uncle Robin today to have the liberty to be about my own affairs."

"Why is that?" Mary asked.

Theo looked at her with a wicked little smile. "Because your sire threatened to beat me if he found me either eavesdropping on him as I was this morn, or lurking purposefully near his solar. Or loitering aimlessly anywhere else in the keep. I think I startled him badly this morning, but I hardly intended to remain in the garderobe for the whole of the day."

Mary laughed in spite of herself. "Theo, you will provoke him overmuch one day and he will make good on his threats."

He looked supremely unconcerned. "I can outrun his ancient self, which I pointed out to him this morning."

"I'm surprised he didn't lie in wait for *you* so no running was involved."

"He threatened that, but I was unintimidated." He looked back at the courtyard. "I think I can outrun yon smith as well, without much trouble."

Mary pitied Zachary the smith, for he would have no peace until the twins had satisfied their curiosity. And hers, with any luck.

Though she supposed her curiosity would have been satisfied with a simple answer to a simple question and that was how soon he intended to leave Artane.

"Coming?"

She realized Theo was looking at her expectantly. She shook her head weakly. At the moment, the only thing she wanted to discover was the closest place where she might sit until her knees grew steady beneath her again. She waved the twins off to their nefarious labors, then decided that perhaps she should seek out an obliging pile of hay and cast herself down onto it until she recovered from what she'd seen that morning.

She reminded herself sternly that all she wanted Zachary the smith for was his escort away from her father's keep, not his very fair face or gentle hands. The sooner she sealed her own bargain with him, the happier she would be.

She supposed she might be reminding herself of that for most of the day.

Chapter 7

Z*achary* leaned against the door of the smithy and happily took a break. He had been enjoying his promotion from stable boy to smith for a little over two days now. He felt as if he'd been in the gym for a month without pause. It was a sad comment on the state of his life that he looked back with fondness to hours on end of trying not to puke while shoveling horse manure.

The past three days hadn't been without their bonuses, though. His headache had finally stopped; he'd had decent sleep and many hearty meals. He'd also had the pleasure of that ridiculous encounter with Geoffrey of Styrr earlier that morning, but he didn't think he could thank Lord Robin for that. He'd simply been in the wrong place at the wrong time and run afoul of a fool's ire.

Other than the fact that it had put him in Styrr's sights, he could honestly say that he enjoyed his new temporary job. It gave him work and answers both. Artane's smith, who was currently waiting for a broken arm to mend, was a very talkative soul who seemed to have his finger on the pulse of everything going on in the keep. He had also been more than happy to have even an unskilled laborer help him while he waited for the replacement of his cousin the freeman from another village. That cousin's village had been wiped out by marauders from the north, so business for him had been pretty skimpy. Zachary had thought fond thoughts about the stoutness of Artane's walls, then happily learned more about metal smithing than he'd ever thought to.

He had also learned the year: 1258. He hadn't been surprised. Once he'd resigned himself to a bit of time in the current day, he'd concentrated on soaking up as much trivia as possible. Gideon would appreciate the details, after he recovered from the broken nose he was going to have.

All things considered, life in medieval Artane was good. The work was satisfying, the company pleasant, and the food quite edible, despite the poor harvest he knew they'd had the year before. At least when it came to supper, it helped to be working in a job that was so critical to everyone's survival. If he ended up having to go all the way to Falconberg to find a working time gate, he would at least go well fed.

He'd given his plans quite a bit of thought while learning how to pound steel. He'd given up on the idea of trying the solar door. Even with as decent as Robin of Artane had been to him, he couldn't imagine that the man would simply look the other way as his pitiful smith traipsed up the stairs and loitered at the lady Anne's doorway. And if he tried without an invitation, he suspected he would make a very sudden, pointed journey back to the dungeon. He imagined he couldn't count on a second rescue.

And speaking of rescues, he hadn't seen anything of his champion. Lord Robin hadn't volunteered any information about her and he hadn't dared ask anyone else to identify who might have found herself locked in the dungeon a handful of nights ago. He had begun to wonder if he'd imagined her.

Or he did until just that moment.

As if she had materialized from his imagination, the girl walked across the courtyard. Zachary pushed away from the wall of the smithy and watched in surprise as his erstwhile rescuer led out a horse that had to have been seventeen hands high. It wasn't an enormous horse by twenty-first-century standards, but big enough for the thirteenth.

The beast was not well behaved. Zachary started to follow, then realized he had a job and couldn't just go as he pleased. He turned to talk to Godric only to find the man standing next to him, watching him with a smile.

"Have a drink, lad, then go for a walk," Godric suggested. "You've earned it."

"I think I just might."

"I suggest you watch where you're looking, though."

Zachary felt one of his eyebrows go up. "Is it impolite to look?"

Godric scrunched his face up in a look that was so reminiscent of Hugh McKinnon that Zachary did a double take. Godric considered, then shook his head.

"'Tis not my place to say anything at all. Just be careful. Things aren't always as they seem."

That was probably the understatement of the year. Zachary enjoyed the irony of it as he had a drink, then went to have his look. He walked out of the inner bailey gate and came to a stop against a wall where he could look in peace. There was a cluster of men already there, watching. He didn't join them, though he recognized the stable master Rolf, Robin's nephew Parsival, and the blond twins who seemed determined to shadow him at all costs. He'd been startled by either or both of them more than once and immediately identified them as major troublemakers. Theo had very willingly offered himself as language coach, but Sam had seemed merely interested in following him constantly in an effort to ferret out details Zachary hadn't even considered giving.

Currently they seemed to be very concerned with that serving wench masquerading as stable girl, so he forgave them the starts they'd given him. Of course, *he* wasn't interested in her. In fact, he was so uninterested in her, it was all he could do to stay awake to watch as she hooked the horse up to a long, leather line and sent him running around her in circles. He came to a rapid though no doubt obvious conclusion.

She was no servant.

He stuck his hands in his pockets only to realize he didn't have any pockets. Still. He settled for folding his arms over his chest and having a good, long look.

The girl was dressed in boy's clothes, which didn't surprise him. It would have been impractical to tend horses in a gown. That she was allowed to do so, though, much less have anything to do with a horse that made her look so slight, was another thing entirely. He only caught fleeting glimpses of her face as she continued to turn in a small circle, forcing her horse to run in a large circle around her, but those were enough to convince him his first impressions of her hadn't been wrong.

She was absolutely stunning.

It was with an effort that he dragged his attentions away from her lovely face long enough to watch what she was doing with the horse. He knew enough about the art to appreciate the skill she used in training the stallion. His brother-in-law Jamie was the best horseman he knew, but this girl had more control over her mount than he'd ever seen Jamie command.

She turned the horse in the other direction—or tried to, rather. The stallion was suddenly having none of it.

Zachary stepped forward, but found a hand on his arm. He frowned at the stable master.

"That horse is dangerous."

"He won't hurt her."

"Are you crazy?" Zachary said incredulously.

Rolf only smiled.

Zachary turned back to the mayhem in process and watched as the horse fought his mistress. The beast stepped on the line, he walked toward her, he reared. In fact, he reared up not a foot in front of her.

Zachary found there were suddenly hands on both his arms. Rolf held one side and Parsival held the other.

"If you don't calm yourself, she'll shout at you," Parsival said placidly. "I'd avoid that, were I you."

Zachary supposed Parsival had that right. If nothing else, he didn't want to do anything to startle her unnecessarily. He let out a careful breath, thanked both his keepers for their restraining hands, then folded his arms over his chest again and watched complete madness.

It took another fifteen minutes, but finally the horse gave in and went the direction the girl wanted him to. By that time, both of them were panting and Zachary felt a little queasy. Still the girl didn't release him. She continued to work him, sending him in opposite directions every now and again, until he was completely obedient.

He wondered, absently, why she'd tried to help him that night. Maybe she'd felt sorry for him, or wanted to repay him for trying to keep her safe. Maybe she'd felt a kinship with him thanks to the forty-five seconds they'd spent together in the loo. He was sure of only one thing and that was that a girl who could control a horse that size without flinching didn't do anything else without a very good reason.

He couldn't help but wonder what that reason was.

He watched for another half hour as she hopped on the stallion's back and schooled him in what apparently passed for medieval dressage. Under saddle, the horse was absolutely obedient. It was one of the most amazing displays Zachary had ever seen, and he'd spent ten years with a family full of expert horsemen.

He looked at Rolf. "I need a rest."

"Aye, lad, we all do."

"Who is she?"

Rolf slid him a look. "Don't you know?"

"Would I be asking you if I did?"

Rolf scowled at him. "You'd best watch your tongue, son, lest I have you shoveling manure tonight instead of enjoying a fine repast at my fire."

Zachary smiled. "Point taken."

"I'll tell you what you want to know," Parsival offered, "in repayment for the entertainment you provided this morning. Surely that display of self-control should be rewarded somehow."

Zachary had to agree. The temptation to put Geoffrey of Styrr in his place had been almost overwhelming. If he hadn't been so determined to get in and out of medieval Artane without drawing any more attention to himself than necessary, he would have. "Let's start with the horse." That seemed safer, somehow.

"'Tis hers," Parsival said, "though my uncle wouldn't concede that if he had a sword to his throat. He allows her to ride—indeed he first put her in a saddle as soon as she could sit up—but that was only because he didn't want her to endure what her mother had."

Zachary felt his mouth fall open. *Her mother.* Was that wannabe serving girl actually Robin of Artane's *daughter*?

"The lady Anne had her leg crushed by a poorly trained stallion when she was a girl," Parsival continued, "and limps a bit because of it to this day. I daresay my uncle thought the only way to spare Mary that was to teach her to manage a horse from an early age. 'Tis an unusual thing, though, for a woman to ride so well. My sisters certainly don't. I don't think Robin is particularly happy about it, but he hasn't forbidden her."

"Maybe she gives him well-trained horses," Zachary managed.

"I think he would prefer she give him well-trained grandchildren," Parsival said dryly, "but some of that is his own fault. He was very choosey about her suitors in her youth." He paused, then shrugged. "Now, I think her years discourage those who might otherwise have offered for her."

"Her years? But she can't be more than what, a score?"

"A score and seven," Parsival said, then he shut his mouth and frowned. "I'm not sure what it is about you that leads me to babble so."

"I don't babble to others," Zachary said without hesitation, "if that makes you feel any better."

Parsival studied him in a way that made him slightly nervous, as if he looked for something he shouldn't have. Zachary gave him his best nothing-to-see-here look, but he had the feeling that Parsival wasn't buying it.

"Zachary, my friend, you intrigue me," Parsival said, confirming Zachary's fears. "A smith without burn scars, a stable lad with sword skill. There are many things about you that simply don't fit. Perhaps you'll enlighten me over supper. I have an appointment presently with my uncle in the lists that I daren't be late for, but I would be interested in your tale later, if you've a mind to give it."

Zachary nodded, though he suspected his tale was the last thing he would be giving the knight who was now walking away from him. It was one thing to make up a history for himself and spin that lie as long as he needed to. Harder, though, was to explain to Robin's nephew how he found himself inside Robin's keep without anyone having seen him enter.

Then again, the little twins seemed to do it with regularity, so perhaps it wasn't impossible.

He allowed himself another lingering look at Mary de Piaget. He was very surprised that she hadn't been snapped up the moment she'd turned twelve. Maybe Robin had kept all the candidates at bay until it had been too late. He wouldn't have thought twice about her age had he been a medieval sort of guy with title and gold.

Then again, he had a soft spot for tomboys, so perhaps he wasn't the one to be offering an unbiased opinion.

He admired for another minute or two her skill with a horse that even he would have hesitated to ride, then shook his head. The sooner he got out of Artane, the better off he would be. And until that time, he would do well to simply stick to his business. Not that any looking or thinking he might have done mattered. That girl was farther out of his reach than even the normal women he attempted to date. Not only that, he couldn't have dated her even if he had dared to.

Leave no mar in the fabric of time.

Jamie's cardinal rule couldn't have been any more a part of him if it had been tattooed on the backs of his hands where he could see it constantly. He and Jamie had perfected the art of looking for what needed to be done in any given time period, then leaving no trace of their passing. Well, almost no trace. There were times when interactions with those in the past had been not only desirable, but necessary.

But dating a gorgeous woman was definitely not on either of those lists.

He walked off the field and made his way to the forge, where he found Godric waiting for him.

"Well?" Godric asked.

"Please give me something to do that requires my full attention."

Godric laughed at him. "Looked a bit too much, did you?"

"I'm afraid so."

Godric smiled at him knowingly, then stroked his chin with his good hand. "You've made a good start on a nail. What say you to the crafting of a dagger this afternoon?"

"It sounds hot."

"'Tis all hot, my lad. You'll simply have to work fast."

Zachary smiled and went to fetch what Godric asked for.

Three hours and several burns later, he had created something that might have resembled a knife if he'd invaded Lord Edward's stash of schnapps and was now admiring his work while completely plastered. Godric had assured him it would go better the next day and sent him off to look for supper. Zachary left the smithy, then paused and considered the possibilities. Supper could be found in the garrison hall.

It could also, as it happened, be found in the stables.

He walked there not because there was manure there that someone else couldn't shovel, or horses there that someone else couldn't groom, or food there that someone else couldn't eat.

He went because he was an idiot.

Don't do it, a nagging little voice whispered in his head.

Actually, it was less of a whisper and more of a shout, but he ignored it just the same. It was just dinner and he would probably eat it alone. After all, it was fairly late in the day. Surely Mary de Piaget had already gone inside for a comfortable seat at her father's table.

He wandered down the aisle between the stalls, then came to a halt. He glanced to his left. There was a quite lovely horse there in a stall, a mare who looked as if she were floating even as she stood perfectly still. She also had very nice manners. Zachary suspected that was because her mistress didn't give her any choice. He paused, then cast caution very deliberately to the wind and leaned on the edge of the stall door where he could watch Mary de Piaget brush the mare's tail.

The woman was, he had to concede, even more beautiful from ten feet than she had been from a hundred. He couldn't believe he'd spent an hour with her in a dungeon and hadn't bothered to introduce himself or ask her who she was. Then again, he hadn't been at his best and neither had she.

"What are you doing here?" a voice demanded from his left.

Zachary watched Mary dive for a spot just inside the stall door. He almost told her to get up before she found herself trampled, but he supposed she knew that well enough without his pointing it out. He took a fortifying breath, then turned to see Geoffrey of Styrr standing in the aisle, fighting his mount.

"My lord," Zachary said deferentially. "How may I serve you?"

Geoffrey threw reins at him. "See to my horse."

"Of course, my lord." Zachary took the reins, then soothed the beast with whispers until it was merely standing there, quivering. He wondered if Lord Robin would be angry if he tied the horse up then punched the good lord of Styrr very calmly in the face. Repeatedly. Truly, the man had no business anywhere near a horse.

"Have you seen my betrothed?"

Zachary looked at Geoffrey blankly. Who the hell would be crazy enough to get engaged to the jerk facing him?

"Your betrothed?" Zachary echoed.

"The lady Mary, you fool," Geoffrey said impatiently. His expression hardened. "I understand she was about her usual foolishness with horses today."

Zachary had absolutely no means of answering that in any useful way. He would have looked harder for something innocuous to say, but a movement near the stable entrance distracted him. He looked over Geoffrey's shoulder to find Robin de Piaget standing there, his expression inscrutable.

Geoffrey stiffened, as if he realized he had revealed just a bit too much and hoped an unintended audience hadn't been privy to it. He schooled his features into a pleasant smile before he turned to face Robin.

Interesting.

"My lord Robin," Geoffrey said smoothly. "I was hoping I would see you here. I would like to speak with you at supper tonight about a matter of *importance*."

Robin of Artane would have made a formidable poker player. His expression gave absolutely nothing away. If he'd heard what Geoffrey had said, he gave no sign of it.

"I was looking for your daughter," Geoffrey continued brightly. "Just to take a bit of her burden from her, of course. I don't mind tending a horse for a beautiful woman after she's finished with her little amusement of riding it."

"I daresay Mary's in her bedchamber," Robin said, "readying herself for supper. Shall we go await her at table?"

"Of course, my lord." Geoffrey looked back over his shoulder. "See to my horse, smith. And keep away from his shoes."

"Of course, my lord," Zachary said with a nod. "I appreciate your patience."

Geoffrey laughed politely, then walked off to join Robin. Zachary watched them go, convinced beyond all doubt that Geoffrey of Styrr was absolutely not what he wanted others to believe he was.

He turned away from the sight and the mystery with equal firmness. He didn't want to know what Styrr was hiding behind that mask. What he wanted was to get home and get on with his life. Getting thrown back into the past had been an unfortunate aberration. The sooner he got out of medieval England, the better off he would be.

He found an empty stall, tied up His Lordship's poor mount, and began to remove its tack. The horse hung its head, obviously exhausted.

"He beats his horses."

Zachary jumped in spite of himself, then turned around and found one of the twins leaning over the wall approximately three feet from him. He let out his breath slowly. "Sneak up on me again, little lad, and I can't guarantee what will be left of you. Now, which one are you?"

The lad grinned. "I'm Theo."

"For the moment, at least. Where's your brother?"

"Following Styrr."

Zachary lifted the saddle off the gelding and handed it over the wall to Theo. "Be useful and go put that away."

Theo took it, then paused. "My father is a lord, you know."

"Is he?" Zachary asked, taking off the horse's woolen pad. He turned and looked at Theo. "And?"

"You might want to show me a bit more respect."

Zachary piled the rug on top of the saddle. "My brother is an earl and my sister's husband a Scottish laird. If you want to test which of our connections makes us more worthy of respect, I'd be happy to settle the question with a wrestle."

"I'll return posthaste."

"Not in the stable," Zachary called after him, but Theo was already disappearing down the way. He shook his head, then looked for a brush of some sort.

One was being held out to him.

He met Mary de Piaget's very pale eyes and smiled. "Thank you."

She only rested her arms on top of the stall door and watched him work. He wasn't one to find himself particularly unnerved by the scrutiny of a woman, not even an excessively beautiful woman who was seemingly capable of managing males weighing in at fifteen hundred pounds, but he found he was now just the same.

He was, as he had decided earlier, an idiot.

He finished with Styrr's horse, accepting tools from Mary as needed, then he closed the door and looked at her still standing there. Before he could stop himself, he reached out and picked a stalk of hay out of her hair.

"I think you're supposed to be upstairs."

"Thank you for keeping my presence here a secret," she said quietly.

He leaned back against the door next to her, because it was safer to stare at the horses across the aisle than it was to stare at her.

He wasn't supposed to look where he couldn't have, after all.

"Styrr's not a completely unpleasant sort," he offered, when he thought he could say the words without adding a curse or a snort.

"He's also *not* my betrothed," she said sharply, "though 'tis difficult to deny that is his purpose." She scowled. "He beats his horses."

"So I saw," he agreed. He considered for a moment or two, then considered a bit longer.

No footprint.

That was somehow easier to do when the life in question didn't belong to a woman who he could see would be crushed by a man who hated what she loved the most.

"You won't have a choice," he said quietly, "will you?"

She looked at him assessingly. "I haven't given in to him yet."

"I suppose, then, being a servant might have its advantages. In allowing you to remain out of sight, perhaps."

"Unfortunately, I'm no servant."

"I know."

"And you're no smith."

He smiled. "It's a family name, not an occupation."

"Apparently."

He laughed and had the faintest of smiles as his reward.

Oh, that was bad on so many levels.

It was all he could do not to reach out and run his hand over her hair. She was particularly beautiful, true, but that wasn't what intrigued him the most. It was the fact that she had faced down a monstrous black beast that afternoon yet conceded him not so much as an inch. If that stallion had reared on him, he would have backed away and been happy to do so. Yet she had stood firm.

Astonishing.

He wondered abruptly if Styrr had any redeeming qualities.
If he'd had any sense, he would have looked for them, then
pointed them out to Mary so she would be happy in what was
no doubt going to be her life. The life he couldn't get involved
in. Her life that would end hundreds of years before his began.

The thought of that left him feeling quite suddenly as if
someone, many someones, had just punched him in the gut.

Damn it anyway.

"You should probably hurry upstairs," he managed, grasping
for the first thing that came to mind. "Just so you aren't caught
in the hall and forced to eat with someone you don't want to."

She only regarded him steadily. "I've eaten in the stables
before. And I have further business here this night."

At that moment, he knew he was taking the first step toward
a piece of colossal foolishness. What he should have done was
wished her a nice evening, then found a very cold place to go
sleep until the wind blew some sense back into his increasingly
fogged brain. She wasn't an unremarkable, plain girl from
down the road who probably wouldn't mind his questionable
reputation and car that smoked. She was the only daughter of
one of the most powerful lords of medieval England. He didn't
want to think about how much her dowry was worth or how
high the bar was for the guys who wanted to even consider
walking through Artane's massive front gates to apply to Robin
for a chance to court her.

And she had the most amazing pair of green eyes he'd ever
seen.

And freckles over her nose. Not many. Just enough that a
man might happily kiss one a day for a week, have a laugh each
of those days as his reward, then begin again the following
week just as willingly.

For all the weeks of his life.

"Let's go see what Rolf has on the fire," he heard come out
of his mouth before he could stop it.

She looked at him in surprise. "In truth?"

He could only nod. It was a terrible idea. Not only did he
owe the past a very brief, unremarkable intrusion, he owed
Robin de Piaget everything from his life to his boots. To take
liberties with his daughter, even when those liberties only included dinner, was truly beyond the pale. Not only that, he knew

firsthand how disastrous getting involved in the past could be. He *knew* it.

But he made her a small bow just the same, then waited for her to walk ahead of him.

She hesitated, then started toward the back of the stable.

Zachary took a deep breath, then took a single step. The second step toward absolute madness was easier, but not by much. It was a mistake.

It was also just dinner.

Jamie would have disagreed, but Jamie wasn't there to tell him what an absolute blockhead he was being.

So he continued to take steps toward a place he knew he shouldn't have gone.

Chapter 8

Mary sat on a pile of hay in her very favorite place in all of Artane and wondered if it were possible to be more content.

Samuel and Theo were flanking her, as was their habit. They had been flanking her since they'd come to Artane at ten, before, as they liked to boast, their father hanged them by their toes on his front gates until they rotted as warning to the rest of their siblings not to imitate their doings. She had loved them from the time they'd been wee babes, of course, and they had grown into such impossibly charming terrors that her affection had only grown.

Connor was there as well, lying in the hay with his hands behind his head, chewing on a piece of straw. He was watching the ceiling as he listened to his brothers tell impossible tales of mischief and glory. He periodically shook his head slowly, as if he couldn't quite believe what he was hearing, though Mary was certain the tales were being recounted without exaggeration.

Thaddeus was industriously applying himself to what they had left of supper. He'd arrived late, apparently having barely escaped the hall. Parsival sat apart from him, having already filled his belly whilst the filling was easily done. He wasn't watching Thaddeus reducing supper to nothing, or Connor shaking his head, or the little twins tripping over themselves to use just the right word to describe a particularly captivating piece of mischief, or even her as she sat between the twins trying to be as unobtrusive as possible.

He was watching Zachary.

She understood. She was, too.

The smith, who was not what his surname announced, was simply sitting with his back against a stall door, his legs stretched out in front of him, a mug of ale in his hands. He was listening to the twins and making noises of either appreciation or disbelief in all the right spots.

The twins adored him.

She could tell that because they couldn't seem to stop badgering him with their talk. Perhaps Theo feared he would lose track of Zachary and not have the promised wrestle. Perhaps Samuel just admired a man who seemed the equal of his father and brothers but presumably had no reason to act that way. It could have been that they were simply happy to have a man of Zachary's quality pay attention to them.

She could understand that as well.

For herself, all she could do was watch the way the torchlight flickered against Zachary's dark hair, the way half his mouth quirked up wryly when the twins attempted to top each other's boasts, the way he laughed when they had gone too far. He seemed perfectly at ease with lads that she loved as much as she did her own brothers, as if he too had grown to manhood in a house full of siblings who didn't doubt their worth. She'd heard him tell Theo of his brother the earl and his brother-in-law the laird, which left her with even more questions. If his relations were all that, then what was he?

And how willing would he be to aid her?

She was more than willing to wait out her cousins so she might have the chance to ask him in private.

"Impossible," he was saying to Theo. "You're one of *ten*?"

"It came as a vast surprise to me as well," Connor drawled. "Especially that my mother was willing to risk it twice more after these two imps were born. Perhaps my father hoped to balance out the little demons with an angel or two. My youngest sisters are that, to be sure."

"Your father, Nicholas?" Zachary asked mildly.

"Aye." Connor leaned up on his elbow and looked at Zachary in surprise. "Do you know him?"

"Of him, only," Zachary said. "And I understand your mother is a very fine musician. Where are you in line, Connor?"

"Fourth," Connor said, sitting up and shaking the hay out of his hair. "And you?"

"The baby," Zachary admitted with a chagrined look. "I have three older brothers and a sister. All of them wed with children."

"Why not you?" Parsival asked. "You're how old?"

"A score and eleven," Zachary said easily. "And I suppose the reason I'm not wed is likely the reason *you're* not wed."

"I'm but a score and three," Parsival said archly, "but aye, I haven't found a lass to suit. At least I have time. Ask Jackson if you want reasons for avoiding the happiness of a wife whilst worrying that you're sliding toward your dotage. He's Mary's age, but impossible to please."

"Mary isn't impossible to please," Theo said. "She isn't wed because we won't let her go."

Mary would have elbowed him very sharply in the ribs, but Zachary was looking at her and she didn't dare. She thought she should have perhaps blushed that the shame of her situation should come to light, but Zachary only smiled at her.

"I can see why you wouldn't want to," he said quietly. "What would you do with yourselves if you didn't have her loveliness to look at each day?"

"Go haunt her husband's hall," Samuel said firmly, "that we might make certain he didn't mistreat her. We've rid her of all her suitors, you know."

"Have you, indeed?" Zachary asked, looking at him with an unwholesome amount of interest. "How?"

Mary handed Samuel her cup of wine before he could begin. "You look thirsty," she said shortly. "Don't let your speaking distract you from attending to that."

Thaddeus took the cup away from Samuel and helped himself to its contents. "These sorts of conversations make Mary uncomfortable" he said helpfully. "I'll speak for the lads and tell you that the suitors who came for her didn't have the spine to face the horrors of Artane, namely my uncle in the lists and my wee cousins over there everywhere else."

Samuel leaned close. "Let me divulge but a few of our more noteworthy capers, Mary. They're vastly amusing."

"To you, perhaps," Parsival put in pointedly, "but perhaps not to your cousin."

"Oh, but she'll enjoy it," Theo said. "She's a right proper lad."

Mary would have bid them all be silent, but she was too busy being humiliated. Could they not simply content themselves with filling their mouths with food instead of spewing out all her worst faults?

"She might dress in boots and hose," Zachary agreed, throwing a crust of bread at Theo along with a warning look, "but she is a woman, Theophilus. You might try treating her as such now and again."

Theo blinked. "Why?"

Mary looked pointedly at Zachary. He only laughed and held up his hands in surrender.

"I tried," he said. "I don't know how I can stop them from talking short of gagging them."

"I'll survive it, I imagine." She was appalled to find that she sounded as breathless as any of her father's serving maids when Parsival gave them an especially sultry look.

Thaddeus handed her back her cup, then refilled it. "You might need that," he said solemnly.

Mary drank, then wished desperately for more, but she didn't dare help herself to any lest she choke on it thanks to something Samuel might say. She certainly didn't dare look at Zachary. She did, however, make the mistake of looking at Parsival, once.

He was watching her with an expression so thoughtful, she wanted to protest whatever was going on in that canny head of his. He smiled at her, then turned his attention to Zachary. She breathed a sigh of relief until she realized he was watching Zachary with that same sort of thoughtful look. She held on to her cup and looked for a distraction.

She found it in the person of her father.

He was standing just outside the circle of torchlight, leaning casually against a post with his arms folded over his chest, simply watching silently. She wouldn't have even marked him if she hadn't glanced his way. He didn't have a stance that bespoke anger or irritation. He was simply standing there, apparently content to be unmarked so he could listen in peace.

Unfortunately, that peace didn't last as long as she would have liked.

"By the saints, what in the *hell* is going on here?"

Jackson would have stomped right into their supper if he hadn't run into his uncle's suddenly outstretched arm first.

Mary watched her father give his nephew a slight nudge backward, then straighten and walk into the light himself. Her cousins were all on their feet as if they'd been jerked there. Even Zachary was standing. She started to rise to her feet, but found a hand suddenly extended in front of her.

She put her hand in that hand only to realize it was Zachary's. He pulled her to her feet, then took a step backward into the place where he'd been. She didn't dare look at her father to see how he'd reacted. She suspected her guilt might show too clearly in her face.

She wasn't sure what she had to feel guilty about, yet still she did. Had her father watched her looking at Zachary the smith as if she'd been a woman dying of thirst and he a cool cup of water offered by some foul fiend that would require her soul in trade?

She lifted her chin. She wasn't betrothed. It was hardly her fault that Styrr was so enamored of her dowry that he was willing to take her ancient self in the bargain. And it wasn't as if she'd been alone with Zachary. Well, she had been, but that had been in the dungeon and he had been nothing but perfectly chivalrous. And it wasn't as if she had any reason to think Zachary might have wanted to do anything untoward with her even if he'd had the chance.

The embarrassment of having thought that he might was enough to bring what she was certain was an appalling amount of color to her cheeks. She would have gladly retreated to an obliging stall until she felt more herself.

Besides, romance—a word she could hardly believe she was even thinking at such a moment—had nothing to do with what she needed Zachary for. She had agreed to dinner because she'd been hungry, and she'd wanted to have him to herself so she could ask him if he might be willing to take her with him when he left. That was all.

Robin tilted his head toward the stable entrance. "Go."

Her cousins deserted her without a backward glance. Jackson was less eager to go, which earned him the task of gathering up all the wooden trenchers and cups and carrying them to the kitchens. Mary simply stood and waited for her father to shout. She stole a look at Zachary. He looked no less guilty than she felt, which made her wonder mightily what secret it was that he strove to keep. A treacherous plot to steal Rex whilst she wasn't looking?

But her sire didn't shout. He only studied Zachary for a bit longer before he nodded toward the doorway again. "We'll settle our account tonight, Master Smith."

"Of course, my lord," Zachary said, making Robin a small bow.

Mary found herself in her father's sights.

"You'll go upstairs, daughter."

She nodded because there was no point in arguing, though she had no intention of doing as he bid. If her father intended to settle anything with Zachary, it would no doubt involve a discussion of Zachary's plans and those were plans in which she was very interested indeed.

Her father turned and walked away. Mary waited for Zachary to go ahead, but he only indicated that she should go first. She did, though she was excruciatingly aware of him walking a pace or two behind her.

Apparently her father noticed it as well. By the time they had reached the courtyard, her father was walking with Zachary, leaving her to go ahead. She frowned at her sire, had a half smile and a shrug in return, then decided the two of them were mad. She walked up the stairs in front of them, then made a production of heading toward the stairs. She waited until she saw that they were making for her father's solar before she abandoned her direction and went to the kitchens.

She wondered, as she walked, why it was her father had been out in the stables. He had reportedly passed almost the entirety of the past four days in the lists. If she hadn't known better, she would have thought he was avoiding Styrr and his company.

Then again, knowing her father, perhaps that was exactly what he'd been doing.

She went to the kitchens, procured what she needed in the way of wine and sweet things, then carried the wooden trencher back to her father's solar only to find a pair of fair-haired lads already there with their ears pressed to the wood. She nudged the twins aside with hip and foot, then balanced her tray on one hand and knocked.

"Come!"

She entered the solar before her father could rethink who might be knocking and send her away. She didn't look at him as she entered, lest she see something she wouldn't like. She merely shut the door behind her, then carried the tray over and set it down on her father's table.

"I thought you might be thirsty."

"You're a good gel," he said shortly. "Now, go up to bed."

She poured two cups of wine, then went to sit on a stool by the hearth. If he wanted her to leave, he would have to remove her bodily. "I'm cold."

"Warm yourself upstairs."

"Your fire is hotter."

"And my seats less comfortable. Go upstairs, Mary."

"In a minute, Father."

He shot her a disgruntled look, but she only returned that look steadily. He looked at her as if he'd never seen her before, then turned to Zachary.

"I've lost control of her. I'm not sure when."

"Perhaps the first time you let her sit a horse?"

Robin laughed uneasily. "My Anne has said the same thing often enough in the past, so I suppose you both have it aright. But now you see, Zachary, what I must endure. Disrespect and cheek at every turn. I thought my lads were what would put me in my grave overearly only to find 'tis my gel here instead who threatens the like."

"If it makes you feel any better, I think my father would say the same thing," Zachary said, accepting a cup of wine from Robin. "My sister gave him all his gray, or so he claimed. She is, though, the joy of his heart. As I'm sure your daughter is of yours."

Mary looked at her father and was very surprised to find that he was slightly misty-eyed. Either that, or he had swallowed amiss and was choking. With her sire, she just never knew.

He cleared his throat roughly. "Aye, she is less a burden than I'll admit to. Now, you, however, have been irritating from the moment you set foot without my leave in my hall. Demanding clothing, spoiling my horseflesh, stirring up brawls in my court-yard. What will you combine next?"

Zachary smiled. "I hate to think."

Her father set his cup on his table, then leaned back. "So do I, actually. So before you pull my hall down around my ears, consider me amply repaid for anything I've given you. You may trot freely out my gates to wherever it is you'll go."

Zachary smiled, though it somehow didn't seem to come as easily as any of his smiles in the stable had. "I think I will, my lord. I need to return home as quickly as possible."

Mary tucked her hands under her arms to hide their trembling. That was exactly what she'd been waiting to hear. Now all she had to do was wait for the time of his leave-taking and determine how to attach herself to him as he went.

She settled herself comfortably and tried to make herself unobtrusive. The sooner they forgot she was there, the sooner she would hear something interesting. 'Twas a pity she was reduced to that sort of open eavesdropping, but there it was. Her father continued to think he needed to keep things from her and she remained equally convinced he didn't.

It took two cups of wine before her father and Zachary were speaking freely. Mary sat with her elbows on her knees and her chin on her fists and simply watched them. If she hadn't known better, she would have assumed they were equals. Whatever else Zachary the smith might have been, he was not uncomfortable in the presence of powerful men. He was respectful of her father, but he didn't cower and he didn't grovel.

And he was so handsome, she could hardly look at him.

"For a smith who isn't one, you haven't done badly," Robin said. "You haven't burned down my forge yet."

"I've tried not to," Zachary said with half a laugh, "though Master Godric might have a different opinion."

"And all to save a certain serving wench a thrashing she so richly deserved for liberating you from my dungeon," Robin said, shaking his head. "There's a decent piece of chivalry for you."

Mary saw the look her father threw her way, but she didn't allow herself to react to it. She was too busy being surprised by what she'd heard. So Zachary had worked for her father to spare her pain. Geoffrey never would have considered doing the like.

Nor, as it happened, would any of the others who'd come to lust after her dowry.

"What is it you do in your life outside my gates if you aren't a smith?" Robin asked. "I'm assuming you do something besides linger at your father's table, eating through his larder."

"I have made my own way in the world," Zachary said. "I'm an ar—I mean, I am . . ." He considered for a moment. "The word escapes me, my lord. Let's just say that I design buildings for others to build."

"A master mason, then."

"Of a sort, aye."

"And where have you built things?"

"All over England. I had been preparing to begin work on a project here in the north for my brother-in-law before I, um, lost my way."

"And found yourself inside my keep."

"I took a wrong turn."

"So you've said before. A wrong turn that took you through my front gates, across my courtyard, into my great hall, and up my stairs to my wife's solar."

"It was a *very* wrong turn, my lord."

Robin grunted. "Perhaps you were distracted by thoughts of the building you were intending to do here in the north." He studied him for a moment, then spoke. "I'm a little surprised that, given the skills you possess, you were willing to shovel manure."

"You were the man with the sword, Lord Robin."

Mary watched her father laugh easily. The conversation veered off into less personal topics, politics and the like. She continued to listen happily, partly because it gave her an opportunity to watch Zachary whilst being unobserved herself and partly because she enjoyed the talk of men. Indeed, there was little not to appreciate about a lad. They were generally straightforward and economical in their speech, forthright in their opinions, and baffled by the things that went on in her mother's solar.

She understood completely.

And they weren't afeared to simply end a conversation after a subject had been discussed to their satisfaction. As her father and Zachary were doing now. They stood, shook hands like equals, then exchanged good wishes and other pleasantries.

Zachary paused, then looked at her sire. "Shall I see your daughter to her chamber?"

Her father considered. "I suppose she would be safe enough," he said slowly, "given that you'll have more escorts than you need. And given that you're leaving on the morrow."

Mary didn't dare look at her sire, lest he see something in her eye that would give her away.

Lust, perhaps.

Desperation, definitely.

She nodded to her sire, bid him a good night quietly, then allowed Zachary to open the door for her. She walked out into a cluster of cousins, but she didn't mark which ones. All she could sense was the man walking next to her with his hands clasped behind his back, the man who waited for her to precede him up the stairs. She had a hard time walking steadily. Not even a day of riding had ever rendered her so weak in the knees.

'Twas appalling.

Zachary walked down the passageway with her. He paused at the door to her mother's solar.

"What is it?" she asked.

He put his hand on the wood and was silent for a moment or two, then he smiled at her.

"Nothing. I was just curious."

She couldn't imagine why or about what, though it was near where she'd seen him first so perhaps he had memories of the place she couldn't divine. She continued on with him until she reached her own doorway. She supposed she might have felt a small twinge of regret at parting company with him if she hadn't been planning to see him in the future.

Very soon in the future.

She opened her door, walked inside, then turned and looked at him.

"Thank you."

He glanced at the cluster of cousins who were watching him, then smiled. "I think you would have been safe enough without me, but it was a pleasure just the same. A good night to you, demoiselle."

She nodded, then shut the door. She leaned back against that door, then considered what to do next. She would need clothes and food, no doubt. She also supposed she shouldn't take a horse. Her father would discover she had gone eventually, of course, but the longer she could put off that discovery, the more time she would have at her disposal to do what she had to.

She put Zachary the smith out of her mind and concentrated on what she needed to do. After her father had been dissuaded from his plans to see her wed, she could return again to her very pleasant life of enjoying the companionship of her cousins and working her father's horses.

She firmly ignored the fact that she contemplated the like with slightly less enthusiasm than she usually did. She certainly didn't give any thought to the man who was to blame for that.

Nay, no thought at all.

Chapter 9

Zachary walked through the woods near dawn and knew he should have been content. The air was still, he had a decent cloak to ward off the chill, and it looked as if the sun might actually shine at some point that day. He had no one texting him, no former clients pushing him down stairs, and no ghosts dogging his steps and trying to make a match for him he didn't want. At least he could safely say that quartet of shades weren't responsible for sending him back in time—

He came to a very sudden halt.

They weren't, were they? They hadn't actually thought to set him up with . . . Mary de Piaget?

He retrieved his jaw from where it had fallen almost all the way to his chest, shook his head firmly, then continued on. The lack of sleep was getting to him and he was starting to hallucinate. Ambrose knew very well that there wasn't any possible way for him to stay in medieval England. He had no money, no title, and no piles of gold sitting in the future that he could bring back to buy either. Robin of Artane, as great a guy as he seemed to be, wouldn't have given his daughter to anyone without a pedigree to match hers, no matter how nicely he was asked.

Of course, that wasn't to say that if he'd met Mary in his

time that he wouldn't have fallen to his knees and begged her to give him the time of day. Constantly. For the rest of his life. But the hard truth was, she was where she was and he was where he was going to get back to and never again the twain would meet. His journey to medieval England had simply been an aberration. A wrong turn, nothing more.

Unfortunately, setting his mind at ease about that didn't solve the other thing that was bothering him.

He was being followed.

He hadn't noticed it at all yesterday, which Jamie would have found completely unacceptable. In his defense, he'd been reeling from the double shot of distress he'd endured: walking past Anne de Piaget's solar door and finding it nothing but wood, and leaving that completely-out-of-his-reach Mary de Piaget at her own, unremarkable doorway. He'd been more than happy to take off from Artane at dawn and pass the day trying to forget about both.

He'd walked quickly but carefully along a road that ran south and west. He hadn't worried about thugs, though he hadn't been particularly eager to meet any lest he do damage where it hadn't been done before. Better to just avoid any encounters and hope to hell he could get all the way to Falconberg to that gate that would hopefully work just as it should.

He actually wasn't as worried about the usefulness of the gate as he probably should have been. Perhaps familiarity really did breed contempt. He and Jamie had been in several dodgy situations that had run over his weekend allotment for time traveling and left him counting on his sister to call London and explain his unexplained absence. He'd probably had more relatives die unexpectedly than any other employee in Lambeth Group history. It was amazing Garrett hadn't asked any questions. He wasn't sure he wanted to know why not.

And if he and Jamie hadn't found one gate responsive to their demands, they'd always had a backup plan. They had become uncannily able to find spots of ground that possessed that certain something that signaled a first-class return to the future. Based on reports he'd had, he was certain he would find the fairy ring at Falconberg responsive to his requests. It was worth the two weeks it would take him to get there, no matter how much raw meat he had to live on along the way.

Or so he'd thought until sometime during the middle of the

night. He'd wondered if he were imagining things until he'd heard the sound of a twig cracking twenty feet away from him.

He'd decided that instead of confronting the lad immediately, he would continue on. He was a very good tracker, thanks to countless endurance hikes with Patrick MacLeod, and he was a very silent walker, thanks to an equal number of jaunts with Jamie. He'd been fully prepared to lose his stalker quite quickly and be on his way. Or he had been until he'd listened to how clumsily he was being tailed.

He'd eliminated a peasant immediately. Artane's peasants wouldn't have had any use for a hundred-and-fifty-mile march south, not when safety lay behind Artane's substantial walls. A local thug also wouldn't have had the patience to continue to follow him without trying something a bit more aggressive long before dark.

He had run through a mental list of Mary's cousins and decided that it had to have been one of the twins, either Theo or Samuel. Why they hadn't come as a pair was a mystery, but one he would solve soon enough. And then he would deposit the errant boy at Wyckham and continue on his way.

That had been hours ago. He continued on now in the shadow of the trees lining the road until he saw that the sky was beginning to grow light in the east, then he disappeared into the shadows and doubled back.

It didn't take him long to see the cloaked and hooded figure creeping along toward him. He remained in the shadows of a tree and considered what he could do that would teach the most pointed lesson. He decided jerking the kid off his feet and slamming him firmly against a handy tree might do the trick. There was no sense in not leaving a lasting impression. He was fairly sure the current lord and lady of Wyckham would thank him for it.

He waited until the boy had crept within arm's reach, then grabbed him and did just as he'd planned—only to find that it wasn't a boy he held at all.

He was so stunned by the sight of Mary de Piaget standing there, gasping unsuccessfully for breath, that he found himself for once in his life completely at a loss for words. It matched her condition perfectly, though hers was a rather involuntary one, to be sure.

"I'm so sorry," he stammered finally. He had never in his life winded someone he hadn't intended to. "I had no idea it was you."

"A-apparently."

He helped her sit in the weeds to the side of the road, then squatted down next to her. She glared at him as she continued to struggle to breathe, which was a nice counterpoint to the tears of pain she probably didn't know were standing in her eyes. He took a deep breath for her.

"Those unkind thoughts you're thinking about me aren't helping," he said. "Instead, why don't you tell me why you were following me?"

He had another glare for his trouble.

"Or perhaps later." He reached out and rubbed her back gently before he thought better of it. He wasn't sure it would help her any, but it would certainly give him a minute or two to think.

He couldn't just leave her on the side of the road, and he couldn't just drop her off at Wyckham. Even if she had been a twenty-first-century sort of girl with a car, he probably would have at least offered to follow her home to make sure she got there safely. But the daughter of a medieval lord who didn't have a small army of her father's most skilled guardsmen to protect her? He would have to do more than wish her a nice day.

He rubbed his free hand over his face wearily. He would have to take her back to Artane, but he couldn't see it happening that day. He'd already been on his feet for the better part of twenty-four hours and she obviously had been as well. He couldn't expect either of them to make a return trip without some kind of rest first.

He looked at the surrounding countryside. Wyckham was probably the closest safe haven. He supposed he shouldn't have enjoyed the thought of that as much as he did, but Mary needed shelter and he needed a rest. Why not manage both in a keep he wouldn't be unhappy to see in its original glory?

"You attempted to slay me," Mary wheezed suddenly.

He looked back at her and smiled. "I assumed you were either Theo or Sam and thought a lesson was in order."

"Which lesson?" she managed. "Never to sneak out of the keep or never to sneak up on you?"

"Both, probably," he admitted. He looked her over critically. "Is anything broken?"

She put her hands to her back and winced. "Just bruised, I daresay." She shot him a look. "I'm ready to curse you now."

"Curse me later, when we're somewhere safe. Can you move?"

"I don't think I have a choice."

"Then let's be on our way."

He rose, then held down his hands for her. She looked at him briefly, then slowly put her hands in his. He pulled her to her feet, then looked into her face so close to his. Her eyes were still that lovely green that looked like backlit leaves on a summertime tree.

An enormous déjà vu washed over him.

And he knew déjà vu.

She looked up at him, an expression of surprise on her face that he was certain mirrored his own. He knew he should have released her hands immediately, but he couldn't bring himself to. Never mind that he had no business touching her, or looking down into her beautiful face, or wondering suddenly if she'd ever been kissed. Or why she hadn't been married to some lecher the moment she'd turned twelve.

Or why the hell he couldn't have been a medieval baron with spurs on his heels and gold in his purse.

He gave himself a hard mental shake, then let go of her. He took a step backward, for good measure.

"Tell me why you're here," he said. It came out more brusquely than he'd intended, but that was probably just as well. The more he succeeded at thinking of her as a bother and less of an angel, the better off he would be.

"I was hoping you would take me with you," she said, lifting her chin. "South."

He blinked. "South?"

She folded her arms over her chest in a pose that was so reminiscent of her father, he almost smiled. She, however, wasn't smiling at all.

"You said to my father that you were going south. I want to come with you." She nodded firmly, as if she expected him to nod right along with her. "I assure you I won't be any trouble."

He wasn't sure he could manage the response that deserved.

Trouble didn't begin to describe what she would be. A beacon to thugs, a constant reminder of what he couldn't have and shouldn't be wanting, a colossal distraction. No, she wouldn't be any trouble at all.

"And your destination?" he asked, when he thought he could say it calmly.

"Sedgwick," she said. "My uncle Montgomery's keep. I would prefer to go to France, but I didn't suppose you would be interested in a sea journey. Sedgwick is far enough for my purposes."

Zachary looked at her in astonishment. "You want me to walk you all the way to Sedgwick, then *leave* you there?"

"Aye," she said simply.

He took a step backward, because he had to do something to buy himself some space to think. If something happened to her, her father would kill him. Actually, Robin wouldn't have to commit murder because Zachary was fairly sure he would do the honors himself.

"I only need an escort there," she added. "I don't expect you to remain there with me."

Of course she wouldn't. He hadn't expected anything else and he was too damned old to have his feelings smart because a titled woman completely out of his reach wanted him only for his ability to protect her. She needed help and he was conveniently there to give it to her.

Damn it anyway.

He turned and started walking. No, he wasn't going to take her with him and he suspected he'd be lucky to make it where he was going himself once her father figured out she wasn't hiding in her chamber or whatever other excuse she'd used for giving herself a head start.

"Zachary?"

He closed his eyes briefly. She said his name with a soft sort of *ch*, as if she were a sweet French girl who'd taken just enough German to manage it properly.

It about killed him.

"I'm taking you to Wyckham," he said shortly, "where we will beg a pair of horses, and then *nay*, I am not taking you south, I'm taking you home to Artane. And then *I'm* going home—assuming your father, or your cousins, or your father's entire garrison doesn't kill me because they probably think I brought you along with me in the first place!"

He shut his mouth before he said anything else. He supposed he wouldn't have blamed her if she'd slugged him. He'd never in his life spoken that rudely to a woman, not even his sister.

Well, he might have gotten into it with Elizabeth a time or two, but he was sure she'd given back better than he'd dished out.

That Mary only walked next to him silently said something. He wasn't sure what, but it definitely said something. Maybe she was waiting for a good time to remove one of his dirks from her father's worn boots and stab him with it. He didn't feel slender hands groping his calves, though, so perhaps she didn't plan murder.

They hadn't walked far before his temper had disappeared the way it had come, to be replaced by other things. First was regret for his behavior, followed quickly by curiosity over her motives. Whatever else she might have been, Mary de Piaget wasn't a fool. She must have wanted something very badly to have risked rescuing him, a complete stranger, from her father's dungeon. If she had been willing to sneak out of her father's keep, alone, trusting that he would help her, then she must still want that thing very badly. He wasn't sure he was ready to speculate yet on what that thing might be.

He wanted even less to face the realization that his usefulness to her began and ended with that as-yet-unexamined thing.

It took another quarter mile before he'd ingested enough of a robust serving of guilt to face the uncomfortable fact that he was reacting to more than just Mary's having tailed him with more skill than he ever would have suspected her capable of. It wasn't her fault that she was intelligent and courageous and so damned beautiful that he couldn't seem to catch his breath when he looked at her.

It also wasn't her fault that he was an untitled Yank with no claim to fame or fortune except what he was related to by marriage. He wasn't one to engage in speculation about the damages to his inner child, or gaze at his navel for long stretches of time, or indulge in all sorts of other self-examinations that made him want to find a sword and do damage to someone with it, but he thought his reaction might have a bit too much to do with being reduced to guardsman by a woman he wished would see him as something else.

He should have given the whole paranormal thing up a month earlier. Obviously, he'd gone through one too many time gates and ruined whatever common sense he might have once possessed.

"Zachary?"

He took a deep breath, then stopped and looked at her. He attempted a smile. "Forgive me. I was ill-mannered."

"Nay, I have inconvenienced you. I meant to, of course," she added. "I just hoped it wouldn't be too much of an inconvenience."

He sighed. "Did you leave any sort of missive behind?"

"Aye. I said that I was going to spend the next pair of days in prayer. It will occur to my sire sometime today that I'm resigning myself to my fate too easily." She paused. "I was hoping to be farther from Artane by tonight."

He looked at the determination in her eyes and revisited his earlier opinion. Whatever had driven her from home was serious. And it wasn't a stretch to guess exactly what had sent her off on a journey she couldn't have been all that eager to take.

Damn that Geoffrey of Styrr to hell and back.

He was so busy thinking about all the ways that might happen that he didn't see trouble until he realized it had come to stand on the road in front of him.

There were four of them. Four dirty, ragged, sinewy thugs whose sunken eyes and hollow cheeks told the story of their recent years. Zachary pulled Mary behind him and backed up, keeping all the ruffians in plain sight in front of him.

"Yer gold an' yer wench," the leader suggested.

Zachary knew Jamie would have been impressed by his ability to understand that so well. Obviously paying that Cambridge tutor to walk him through excessive amounts of Anglo-Saxon poetry had been more useful than he'd dared hope it would be at the time. He continued to step backward, keeping Mary behind him.

"Nay," he said politely, "but thank you just the same."

He could see what they intended before they began it and he countered the attack without mercy. To hell with leaving no trace of his passing. If he didn't get himself and Mary free, she would be hurt and then he'd have to tell Robin de Piaget why. He jerked his knives free and threw himself into the fray.

The men were no match for a combination of Patrick MacLeod's Advanced Studies in Honorless Street Fighting and the strength of a man who'd never gone hungry in his life. Well, he'd gone hungry during college now and then, but the deprivation had been limited to junk food, so he supposed that didn't count.

He rendered two of the four immediately unconscious with a pair of roundhouse kicks, then sent the third into oblivion with the heel of his hand under the man's chin. The last man was more desperate than his fellows and Zachary had to fight him off with knives for a moment or two before he could do more modern damage to him. He wasn't entirely sure he hadn't snapped the man's neck as a result.

He spun around to look for Mary only to realize there had been five bad guys, not just four. Number five was trying to drag Mary off into the forest with one hand over her mouth and the other in her hair. She was fighting him fiercely, but without success. The man had apparently tired of it because he stopped long enough to backhand her across the face.

Zachary didn't think; he flipped his dagger so he held it by the tip of the blade, then flung it with all his strength into the man's chest. The ruffian released Mary to clutch the knife, looked up in surprise, then slowly fell backward until he was prone.

Mary looked at the man, then turned and threw up.

Zachary couldn't blame her in the slightest. He retrieved his knife, cleaned it, then shoved it back into its sheath. He knew life and death was a part of the bargain in medieval England, but he didn't like being a part of the situation. Guardsman, indeed. Well, he'd played his part and would continue to do so until Mary was safely behind her father's walls. Then he would go home and make sure he was never again faced with the choice he'd just made. He took Mary by the arm and pulled her back onto the road.

"How far to Wyckham?" he asked.

"We're near Ledenham Abbey," she said faintly, "not a place to linger. We've another hour before us if we make haste. Longer if we walk."

"Can you run?"

"Of course," she said, putting her shoulders back. "Can you?"

He would have smiled if he'd had it in him. "I'll try to keep up."

She only nodded, her face ashen, and started into a stumbling run with him.

He was actually quite grateful she'd spent the whole of her life on horseback. He wasn't sure he could have carried a delicate lady-in-waiting all the way to safety. Then again, if she'd been a delicate lady-in-waiting, she probably wouldn't have been following him in the first place.

He looked behind them periodically, but saw nothing. He wasn't going to press his luck, though, so he continued to run. He also decided that he might want to beg a sword from Robin before he attempted his next trip south. Getting killed while doing something noble was one thing; getting killed because he wasn't prepared was something else entirely.

Though he thought he'd had just about enough of death to last him a lifetime.

He ran with Mary for quite some time before he chanced a look at her. She was still white as a sheet, but he suspected by the look of concentration on her face that she was already working on plan B. It was no wonder Robin always looked a little nervous when he couldn't immediately lay his finger on his daughter's whereabouts. Obviously Mary was even less eager than he'd realized to marry Styrr.

Why Robin would have even considered forcing her to bind herself to a man she obviously didn't care for was something he probably would never understand. He felt equal parts angry that Styrr was such a jerk and devastated that Mary would probably find herself shackled to someone who couldn't possibly appreciate her.

He concentrated on the anger. It made it easier to run.

He realized suddenly that the forest had disappeared only because the road had taken a sharp turn and he found himself facing Wyckham. A perfect, functional, spectacular Wyckham. He skidded to a halt and gaped.

"Have you never been here before?" Mary asked, panting.

He considered the answers he could give, then discarded them all one by one. How could he tell her that the last time he'd seen the place, it had been missing most of its defenses and all of its roof? And that he'd parked his beater Ford just about where they were currently standing? No, he couldn't tell her any of that. He could only stare at the castle in front of him and try to come up with something intelligible to say.

"I've never seen it on such a perfect day," he managed.

And then he made the fatal mistake of looking at her. Yes, the keep was perfect, but then again, so was she. Perfect and courageous and currently looking at him as if he were the only thing able to save her.

"Please," she whispered. "Please take me with you."

Zachary took a deep breath. "Ah—"

"I wouldn't be any trouble," she said quickly. She paused. "I could tend your horses for you at your home, if it pleased you."

He felt as if he'd been kicked by one of those horses he didn't own. He wasn't one to weep, but he was dumbfounded to find that he was tempted to. The thought of that fierce, proud, bewitching woman reduced to begging was almost more than he could take. First she wanted him as her guardsman, now she was willing to be his servant?

He had to take many, many deep, even breaths before he trusted himself to speak.

"I can't," he said. "I can't take you where you need to go, and where I'm going you can't come."

Damn it all to hell.

She looked at him again, searchingly, then she sighed. "As you will," she said quietly. She gestured toward the fully functional gates. "They will give us shelter. And something to eat, with any luck. We'll have peace to rest before we start back."

Zachary nodded, though he was far less interested in a place to rest than he was in spending the remainder of the day convincing Mary of Artane that while he might have been a decent guardsman, he had suddenly realized that he would have preferred to be quite a bit more.

No footprint, no footprint, no footprint.

The words were like an annoying, incessant chant in his head. He could hardly think straight because of them. He'd already left a footprint back there in the forest; he couldn't leave another at Artane.

"Wyckham boasts a well-stocked larder," Mary continued

as they walked toward the gates, "and handsomely appointed stables full of very fast horses. My uncle is particular about his steeds."

Zachary imagined he was. He supposed, based on the tone of her voice, that the only question he had now was how long it would be before she made use of one of those particularly fast horses to go where he wouldn't take her.

It took her two hours to ditch him, which was about an hour longer than he'd expected. She'd gotten them inside the gates, charmed the cook into providing them with a meal, then convinced the steward that Zachary needed a tour of the keep. Zachary had agreed to the last without hesitation because it wasn't often he had a chance to commit to memory all the details of a keep he wanted desperately to restore seven hundred and fifty years in the future.

It wasn't until he was ogling a spectacularly fashioned Norman arch spanning the great hall that he realized he was admiring stonework all on his own. He left the steward talking to thin air and bolted from the great hall in time to catch Mary as she was trotting what looked to be a very speedy stallion toward the front gates. He managed to stop her only because she apparently didn't have the stomach to either run him over or kick him in the face to escape.

"Don't," he said seriously.

"I must," she insisted. "And I am more than capable of going alone."

He wasn't going to argue that point with her. She was certainly capable of riding to wherever she chose to go. It was what would happen when she had to stop to sleep that worried him.

"Other than the fact that Styrr's an arse," he said, "what do you have against him?"

He, of course, had a very long list, beginning and ending with the fact that the man would have the pleasure of looking at Mary de Piaget's lovely face every day while Zachary wouldn't, but he wasn't sure saying that would add anything to the conversation—even if Mary had been amenable to that kind of thing.

"You won't believe what I believe of him," she said grimly.

"I will." He held up his hands for her. "You can tell me all about it inside."

She scowled down at him. "Nay."

He paused, considered, then looked up at her seriously. "Please."

"I cannot go home."

He reached up and very carefully removed her reins from her hands. He hooked them over his arm, then held up his hands again for her. "You cannot go south, either," he said quietly. "I promise I will listen to you, believe you, and help you if I can."

He wasn't sure where the last part had come from, but now it was out there, he couldn't take it back.

She looked at him in surprise. "You will?"

He nodded solemnly.

She considered his hands, still held up toward her.

"I can get down by myself."

"I imagine you can. Let me help you anyway."

She had trouble getting her feet out of her stirrups, then even more trouble getting herself in a position where she could lean over and put her hands on his shoulders. Zachary wondered if no one had ever bothered to help her down from a horse before.

He handed her reins off to a stable boy, then clasped his hands behind his back where they wouldn't get him into any trouble. He nodded toward the hall.

"After you, my lady."

She glanced at the conspicuous collection of guardsmen clustered at the front gates, then muttered something under her breath. Zachary only nodded in the direction of the great hall. She capitulated, but she didn't look happy about it. He followed her up the steps, then found himself coming to a stop. He put his hand on the plastered and whitewashed wall to steady himself as something occurred to him that hadn't before.

What if he had been destined to walk through a doorway, run into Mary de Piaget, then help her get out of a marriage that she couldn't avoid on her own?

He thought about that for another moment or two. It was possible. It made more sense than thinking Fate had sent him back in time so he could do a free fall into something he couldn't have with a woman he shouldn't even have been looking at, a woman who apparently only thought of him as nothing but a sturdy, potential guardsman.

"Zachary?"

He shook aside his thoughts, productive and unproductive, then smiled at her gravely. "Nothing. Shall we go?"

She frowned at him, then turned and walked into the hall. Zachary ignored the feeling of déjà vu that washed over him again as he crossed the threshold behind her. He had no doubt been sent back in time to help her as he could, then be on his way.

Nothing more, nothing less.

Chapter 10

Mary leaned against the wall in her uncle's great hall, well away from any torchlight, and wondered how she was now going to carry on with her usual life after she had touched a man who made her entire world shudder to a halt.

She stood in the shadows and watched him, certain she wouldn't be noticed. For one thing, he was completely engrossed in turning very slowly in a circle and looking at Wyckham's great hall as if he sought to memorize every detail. She supposed she could understand why. Wyckham was a lovely place full of the most modern of conveniences and comforts. And it was, as she had noted before, home to a handful of very fast steeds.

Another reason Zachary wouldn't have been looking for her was that he'd sent her upstairs for a rest and instructed her to sleep away the better part of the day, which he likely assumed she was still doing. She had insisted that he rest as well, though she doubted he'd done so given that he had threatened to sit at the base of the stairs lest she decide to sneak off and filch another of her uncle's horses.

She hadn't had the stomach for that. She'd given thought to the morning's events and reconsidered her plan to escape on her own. If Zachary hadn't been there and so perfectly able to protect her . . .

She turned her mind to other things before she embarrassed herself again by any untoward physical expressions of terror. Nay, she wouldn't go alone, even if she'd been riding one of Wyckham's fastest stallions. Not now.

She watched Zachary as he continued to look around him as if he'd never seen the inside of a great hall before and wondered about him. He had killed a man to save her life without hesitation and without undue hand-wringing, just as her cousins or father would have done. He had led her on an exhausting journey away from her home, had the strength to dispatch that handful of ruffians, then continue on all the way to Wyckham. He had to have been weary, yet he had made no complaint. The more she saw of him, the more he puzzled her.

Who was he, in truth?

Samuel had told her that he wasn't wed, nor was he a knight, and he most certainly wasn't a smith. She wondered if he might be a faery. Her uncle Montgomery would have had quite a bit to say about that, but she didn't suppose she would be seeing him anytime soon if she found herself wed to Styrr, so she wouldn't have the chance to ask him.

She considered a bit longer. There were several things about Zachary she didn't understand, such as what had vexed him so thoroughly that morning. She'd assumed he would be irritated at the trouble of taking her with him, but she'd been very surprised at how angry he'd been.

Theo and Samuel wouldn't have reacted that way. They were quite normal lads of ten-and-six, interested in swordplay, mysteries, and serving wenches, in that order. Thaddeus was obsessed with having his spurs, Connor with finding something useful to do as the fourth son of a very powerful lord, and Parsival was who he was to the fullest: handsome, charming, and French. Truly, there were no worse faults combined in one man, faults that left every maid within the sound of his voice swooning. If she'd inconvenienced any of them, they would have rolled their eyes, grumbled at her loudly, then capitulated without further comment.

Jackson, she suspected, would have been as angry as Zachary had seemed to be—but he often surprised her with his reactions. He had secrets, that lad, secrets that he didn't share. He could be prickly when pushed in the wrong direction, impossibly stubborn all the rest of the time, and deeply apologetic when he realized he hadn't been as polite as he should have been. Zachary was that sort of man.

She wondered what sorts of secrets *he* kept.

She jumped suddenly when she realized he was watching her. She started to back up farther into the shadows only to realize there was no purpose in it. She had been seen and there was no point in trying to hide now.

She waited for him to walk toward her, but he merely stood in the middle of the hall with his hands clasped behind his back, silent and still. She frowned. Did he think she should be the one to cross the distance first? She folded her arms over her chest and stared back. He tilted his head to one side and studied her, as if he realized what she was doing.

She thought he might have smiled.

She watched him for another moment or two, then supposed she wasn't above giving in a bit. She didn't like to, for it was a sure sign of weakness, but Zachary was also not a horse. She unfolded her arms and took a step forward in the most commanding way possible.

He did smile then, of that she was certain. He also took a matching step toward her.

By the time she had met him halfway, she couldn't decide if she felt flushed or weak in the knees. She knew she felt foolish, so she decided to fall back on a bit of bluster.

"You're making sport of me," she accused.

"I wouldn't dare," he said seriously. "I might be teasing you, though. In the most respectful and deferential way possible, of course."

"If you'd been interested in being deferential, you would have come to escort me to this spot instead of making me cross on my own."

"Should I have?"

"It would have been the chivalrous thing to do," she said archly.

He laughed, a brief bit of humor that finished off her knees completely. "Then I apologize for causing you the exertion. I would have been willing to come to fetch you."

She felt herself smiling a bit in return. "I didn't truly mind meeting you halfway."

"I didn't, either," he said dryly.

She laughed a little in spite of herself, then felt her smile fade. He was suddenly staring at her so thoughtfully, he made her a bit nervous. "What is it?" she asked.

Zachary clasped his hands behind his back again. "You know," he began slowly, "it might be interesting to meet as equals for an evening." He smiled a very small smile. "Daughter of a powerful lord, son of a healer."

She couldn't look away from him. A handsome, gallant man unrelated to her who, for even a single day, might look and see her instead of her dowry? She took a deep breath.

"Would it be interesting or foolish?" she managed. Foolish for her, no doubt, given what would be left of her heart afterward.

"Let's choose interesting." He took a step backward and nodded toward the fire. "Come sit by the fire, and I'll go find us something to eat. Then you'll tell me your tale before we think of other things that we might do as equals."

He turned, then looked over his shoulder and offered her his arm. She hesitated, then slipped her hand into the crook of his elbow just as she'd watched her mother do hundreds of times with her father. She was fairly certain, though, that her mother's face never flamed as hers was doing presently.

"You sit," she said as they reached the hearth on the other side of the hall. She pulled away from him before she embarrassed herself further. "I'll go to the kitchens."

"I can—"

"Sit? Aye, I'm sure you can."

She walked away before she had to see his expression. She made her way without delay to the kitchens, procured things that required servants to aid her in carrying, then made her way back to the great hall. A table was fetched and set between the two chairs there, supper was laid after a fashion, and she soon found herself attempting without success to eat.

Zachary seemed to have no trouble. Then again, he was a man and she had rarely seen a man be put off his supper by anything.

He looked up. "Not good?"

"I'm nervous."

"With me?" he asked, sounding surprised.

"Daft, isn't it?"

"Completely, so stop it and eat something."

She was briefly shocked by his words, then realized that had been his intent. She smiled faintly.

"Are you seeking to deliberately provoke me?"

"I'm treating you as an equal." He filled a cup full of wine and handed it to her. "And I don't want you to faint, so drink up, then eat something . . . Mary."

"Very well . . . Zachary."

He smiled. "This shouldn't be difficult. You have cousins."

"You aren't my cousin."

"I think I'll take that as a compliment," he said wryly. "And while you're feeling so comfortable with me, why don't you tell me what you don't like about that dolt from Styrr?"

She drank, then she set her empty cup aside and looked at him. "I fear he plans to kill me."

Zachary choked. She rose and thumped him on the back until he held up his hand in surrender.

"I didn't expect that," he gasped.

She sat down with a sigh. "Nay, neither did I."

He refilled her cup and handed it back to her. "Start from the beginning. How long have you known him?"

"Almost four years. I met him when his older brother came to court me." She smiled briefly. "I was betrothed to Roger shortly thereafter."

"Were you?" he asked in surprise. "He must have been quite something for your father to have agreed to it."

"Roger had a fondness for the lists and treated his horses well."

He smiled. "Your father's sort of man."

"Well, I wouldn't go so far as that," she said. "He did frequent the lists often enough, but his swordplay never impressed my sire."

He propped his ankle up on his opposite knee. "Does anyone's swordplay impress your sire, Mary?"

"Rarely," she said, "though Roger did make a valiant effort." She shrugged. "I didn't love him, but I had long since given up on that sort of romantic foolishness."

She said it all in as offhanded a manner as she could manage, though it wasn't easily done. There was no point in telling him just how many foolish hours she had spent in the hayloft after that fateful sighting of Blackmour and his lady, dreaming of a handsome, chivalrous man who would come to her father's hall, take her by the hand, and demand that her father give him what he wanted most—which would have been her own poor self, of course. Roger hadn't done any demanding, but he had been kind in a distracted sort of way. At the time, she hadn't hoped for anything better.

"And then?"

Mary dragged herself away from her unproductive thoughts. "My father wanted to see Roger's hall before he agreed to have any banns read, on the off chance that he might find anything untoward there. We were traveling north when we were caught out in a terrible storm. When the storm passed and my sire left his tent, he found half the company dead, including Roger."

Zachary's foot hit the floor with a thump. He leaned forward and looked at her in surprise. "Was your company attacked?"

"Nay," she said. "There was just death there, with no sign of its passing. My maid woke the next morning to find me senseless beside her. My parents brought me home immediately, where I lay abed for a month, half dead. It took me several fortnights before I could ride again."

His mouth fell open. "From what you caught on that night?"

"Aye. My father insisted it was the ague, but no one else had it. Indeed, no one who had lived endured what I did."

"Was it poison?"

She shrugged helplessly. "What else am I to think?"

He didn't answer. He merely studied her thoughtfully for a moment or two, then looked out into the gloom of the hall. He was silent for several minutes, but he gave no sign that he was thinking she had lost all her wits. He finally turned back to her.

"Do you believe Geoffrey was responsible?"

"'Tis a mad thought, isn't it? He comes as close to perfection as a man might dare without sinning. He dances flawlessly, he dresses at the height of fashion, and, well, you have seen his face—"

"His eyes are crossed."

She smiled in spite of herself. "They are not."

"You obviously haven't spent enough time looking in them to know," he said, "but I have. When I was trying not to get in the way of his sword thrusting forward by accident, I had ample time to see those eyes. Very crossed. I'm sure that's a flaw."

She felt her smile fade. "I wish my father would dismiss him for something so simple."

"Oh, I imagine your father could find a dozen things wrong

with his swordplay before he even looked in his eyes." He looked down at his hands for a moment or two, then back up at her. "I can understand why he might want to kill his brother—a title would be a powerful temptation for a younger son—but why would he want to kill you?"

"What use has he for me once he has my gold?"

"He might want the pleasure of looking at your beautiful face each day," Zachary said.

She would have blushed if she'd been at ease to do so. Unfortunately, her fears exacted too terrible a price for that. She took a deep breath.

"He views me, I assure you, as a necessary evil to endure—and rid himself of with as little trouble as possible." She shrugged. "Poison administered over the course of months, or in a large dose immediately after childbirth—"

Zachary stood up suddenly, then held down his hand for her. "I want to dance."

She looked up at him in surprise.

"What?"

"Let's dance."

"Why?"

"Because your paragon of perfection doesn't deserve you and I can't think about it anymore. Were the musicians left behind, do you think?"

"The question is, would I dance with you even if they were?" she asked with a shiver. "And the answer is I think not, what with your current humors obviously so vile."

He dragged his hands through his hair, then smiled. Or attempted to, rather. He took a deep breath, then let it out slowly. "I'll stop thinking about it while we're dancing. Your toes are safe."

"Can you dance?"

"Nay, but you're going to teach me something simple." He reached for her hand and pulled her to her feet. "I see that a rather well-fed viol player has arrived, eager to do our bidding. And a man with something to blow on. Who knows who else might show up with enough time? You're going to have to tell them what to play, though. I wouldn't know what to ask for."

She started to protest—until she caught full view of his expression. He looked almost as devastated as she felt.

She understood completely. When she thought of marrying Geoffrey of Styrr, she wanted to think on something else immediately as well. Dancing, however, was generally not what first came to mind.

She walked across the hall just the same and discussed with what had became a trio of players the music she wanted to hear, then turned to find Zachary waiting for her in the middle of the floor. She walked over to stand in front of him.

"You truly know no dances."

"I know a Scottish sword dance," he said, "which I learned to humor my brother-in-law. But I'm not sure you want me to dance it for you."

She smiled at his rueful tone. "We'll start with something simple, then. A pavane, perhaps. Even Theo and Sam can manage that one."

"Your confidence in me is staggering."

She laughed, because she couldn't help it. She realized that, in spite of everything that had happened that day, she had laughed more since sunrise than she had in months. Even though she knew that her freedom to do so couldn't last longer than a single evening.

She wished quite desperately that it could.

It was a perfectly pleasant hour. Zachary watched his feet a great deal and frowned quite a bit. She didn't say anything to distract him. It gave her ample opportunity to watch how the firelight flickered against his dark hair, against his handsome features, against the pale blue green of his eyes. She found herself the recipient of his quick smiles and the beneficiary of his uncomfortable laughter when he ruined yet another set of steps. He stopped at one point and looked at her.

"You don't have anything where we just hold hands and march about in a circle, do you?"

"We need more players for that."

He shot her a knowing look. "You're purposefully trying to humiliate me."

"You made me walk across the floor to meet you."

"Halfway."

"Then I'll only humiliate you halfway."

He looked at her with a smile that was full of something she couldn't identify. She was fully aware, however, of how he took the hand he already held and laced his fingers with hers. Then he reached up slowly and tucked several stray strands of hair behind her ear.

"You are a remarkable woman, Mary de Piaget," he said, still wearing that same smile.

He opened his mouth to say something else. She didn't dare hope it would have been something to the effect that he couldn't bear the thought of her wedding Styrr and he had another plan.

Instead what she heard was a bellow from the other end of the hall.

"What in the *hell* is going on here?"

The musicians immediately scurried for higher ground. Mary found herself pulled behind Zachary. She peeked around his shoulder.

"Zachary, 'tis only the lads—"

He tightened his hand on her arm. She frowned and tried to pull away. When that didn't work, she tried to move around him.

"Woman, stay *behind* me," he whispered harshly.

"If it eases you any," she said, fairly reasonably to her mind, "I don't think 'tis me they want to kill."

"I'm not going to take that chance."

"We aren't going to lay a hand on her," Jackson snarled. "Now, you, however, I think we'll lay our hands on repeatedly."

Zachary squeezed her arm. "Go get out of the way, Mary."

Mary stepped away, then glared at Jackson. "You stop this right now—"

Jackson snarled another curse at her, which led her to believe he wasn't in the mood to be reasoned with. Connor didn't look any less forbidding. Even Thaddeus looked as though the journey had left him with rather unpleasant humors. Only Parsival was standing apart, wearing a particularly Gallic look of long-suffering. He pushed away from where he'd been leaning against the wall and walked over to take her by the arm.

"Come along, *chérie*, and we will watch the spectacle from the comfort of the fire. A cushion for me? And food? How lovely. It has been a trying journey here and I'm in sore need of a rest."

"You could instead stir yourself to pay heed to the potential slaughter in the hall," she said pointedly. "At the very least, you could give Zachary your sword. You've done it before."

Parsival sat down in her chair and looked at sheaves of

parchment he seemed to have picked up from somewhere. "Have you seen these, Mary? They're quite lovely drawings."

"Parsival!"

He looked up and blinked at her, then looked over to the midst of the hall. "If things become too unbalanced, I'll see if I feel inspired to aid him." He turned back to his study of what he'd found. "Zachary doesn't even seem to feel the need for his knives. Perhaps he thinks Jackson is even less skilled than Styrr."

"Shut up, Pars," Jackson bellowed. "I'll show him how we repay lads who take liberties with our women."

"*I* was dancing with *him*," Mary said loudly.

"Which you wouldn't have been if he hadn't been dancing with *you*!"

Mary looked at Parsival, who only shrugged.

"Logic is not Jackson's strength," he offered.

"After I finish with him, I'll see to you," Jackson snarled, pointing his sword at his cousin.

"And find Connor's father highly irritated with you that you scuffed his lovely floor with your muddy boots," Parsival said, stretching his legs out and crossing his feet at the ankles. "I'd be careful, were I you."

Jackson didn't heed the warning. Mary sank down onto a stool next to Parsival only to realize that she couldn't sit. She moved to stand behind Parsival's chair where she could lean on it if necessary.

Her cousin lashed out at Zachary suddenly. Mary found herself unequal to determining just what happened next, but when her heart started beating again, she realized that Zachary had rolled under Jackson's swing, then come up to his feet next to Connor, where he then relieved Nicholas's fourth son of his sword before Connor could blurt out a protest. He then threw himself into the fray.

He wasn't Jackson's equal, but then again, few were. Apart from her brothers, Jackson and Connor were two of the few who gave her father any decent sport at all. If Zachary managed to stand against Jackson for any length of time, it would be a miracle.

Not that he was a poor swordsman, for he wasn't. He was actually quite good for a man who apparently didn't make his living with the sword. She also knew he could be quite lethal.

There were a handful of ruffians who could have attested to that, if they'd been alive to do so. But best Jackson Kilchurn? Nay, he would never do that.

She supposed it would have gone badly for Zachary at some point, but fortunately Jackson ended the battle prematurely by catching the hilt of Zachary's sword and sending the blade flying across the hall. It snagged itself in a tapestry, making quite a rending sound as it slit the threads on its way down to the floor.

Parsival tsk-tsked loudly.

Connor walked over to the wall, liberated his sword from the remains of one of his mother's favorite wall coverings, then resheathed the blade. He shot Jackson a look as he passed him.

"Leave it, Jack."

"I will not—"

"*Leave it.* There was nothing happening."

Mary watched Zachary watch Jackson with a wary eye until her cousin put up his sword with a curse. He glared at Zachary.

"Your life is spared this time, *smith*. I won't be so lenient the next time."

"I appreciate that, my lord," Zachary said carefully.

Jackson brushed past him, cursing, and made for the kitchens. Mary started out into the hall, but Parsival caught her by the arm.

"I think, cousin," he said mildly, "that you should, as Connor advised, leave this alone."

"I was teaching him how to dance," she whispered sharply.

"He's obviously a hopeless case. And you may be on the verge of dancing with a different man for the rest of your life."

She pulled her arm away, glared at him, then walked across the great hall. She didn't dare look at Zachary, though she did shoot Thaddeus a warning look.

"Mary," Jackson warned from the back of the hall.

"I'm going to tend your horses!" she shouted before she slammed the hall door shut behind her. By the saints, was she never to know a moment's peace? All those bloody men who couldn't seem to keep their noses out of her affairs. 'Twas a wonder she hadn't been driven daft long ago.

She oversaw the care of the horses, seeing to Parsival's mount herself only because she needed something to do and his stallion was too feisty for any of the stable lads. She groomed him, then saw to his tack, polishing it far longer than she should have. At least she had peace whilst she sat on the floor in the dirt, rubbing the leather of the saddle until it gleamed by the faint light of the torch.

Once she had polished until she could polish no more, she put the saddle away, then turned to leave the stable. She squeaked in spite of herself.

Zachary was leaning against a post with his arms folded over his chest much as her father had been a pair of nights ago, simply watching her with a very grave expression.

"How long have you been there?" she asked.

"Quite a while."

"And you didn't offer to help?"

"I wasn't sure I wanted to come between you and your saddle, actually," he said with a faint smile. "You were possessed of very—how shall we say it?—vigorous humors." His smile faded. "I understand there was quite a search put on for you this morning."

"I imagine my father is angry."

He lifted one eyebrow briefly. "I don't think angry is the word I would use."

"Surely he knows this isn't your fault."

Zachary shrugged. "I imagine his only concern is one for your safety. Other things will no doubt occur to him as time passes. I'm simply hoping the thought of how attractive I would look impaled on the end of his sword isn't one of them."

"Are you coming back to Artane?" she asked in surprise.

He nodded. "I think I should tell your father what you told me."

She closed her eyes briefly. "Thank you."

"I'm not sure he'll believe me, but I'll try." He took a step backward and made her a small bow. "After you, my lady."

She didn't move. "Are we that, now?"

He hesitated, then smiled grimly. "It was a mistake to be anything else, I think. Your cousins no doubt agree."

"They're just protective," she said quietly.

"I am as well, my lady." He took a step backward, then nodded toward the hall. "I'll see you safely inside."

She walked on ahead because she suspected that if she didn't, he would simply wait for her all night. She kept her thoughts to herself until they were standing outside the hall door and Zachary was reaching for the latch.

"I don't think it was a mistake," she said, very quietly.

He was silent and still for so long, she wondered if he simply couldn't decide what terrible thing to say to her.

Then she realized she had misjudged him again.

He reached out and very gently smoothed his hand over her hair and down her braid. Then he smiled at her. "Go sleep, wench. I won't be responsible for you falling off your horse tomorrow."

"I never fall."

"So said she who was angling for a tumble." He opened the door. "After you . . . Mary."

She looked at him solemnly, then walked in front of him into the great hall. She sent Jackson a warning look as she crossed the hall floor, then climbed the stairs to sleep in her aunt's solar.

And she dreamed of dancing.

Chapter 11

Zachary decided that there were some things in life that were just better left alone. Prickly medieval knights who were very protective of their cousins. Riding for hours after not having spent any time on horseback over the winter. Swearing off certain things and actually formulating those forbidden items into some sort of list.

It was bad karma, apparently.

He traced his current situation back to that fateful day, which couldn't have been more than a week ago, when Michael Smythe-Gordon and his lovely pugilist sister, Beatrice, had helped him down their equally lovely Regency-era stairs. If he'd just dusted himself off and driven through their front gates without any resolutions, he probably wouldn't have found himself in Fate's sights. But no, he'd had to go and make a damned list. Change jobs. Change girlfriends—and avoid any with titles. Change weekend and holiday habits. And as a result, where was he?

Masquerading as a blacksmith in medieval England after time traveling to a keep where the lord's daughter just happened to be the most gorgeous, fascinating, courageous woman he'd ever had the pleasure of not being able to fall in love with. One he'd promised to try to get out of a potential marriage to the biggest jerk this side of the English Channel. One who deserved a man who would appreciate her passionate nature and untempered mouth.

Where was that nice, safe, unremarkable life?

Not within reach, apparently. He dismounted in front of the stables with the little traveling company and wondered which made more sense: pulling Mary behind his back so Robin didn't kill her, or hiding behind Mary so Robin didn't kill *him*.

The good lord of Artane looked capable of either, or both, but he wasn't a coward and neither was Mary. He walked with her, wondering if he could put in a good word for her before Jackson opened his big mouth and told Robin things that would only add fuel to the fire. He ignored that little nagging voice—Jamie's, probably—that told him he should just keep his own big mouth shut.

He ignored that voice because Mary was counting on him to at least make the effort of helping her. Besides, it was entirely possible that she might have convinced her father of Styrr's character herself even if he hadn't found himself loitering in 1258. He was only strengthening the slightest bit an event in history that would have taken place anyway.

Surely.

He stopped a few paces away from Robin. The lord of Artane was absolutely stony-faced. Jackson, however, was not only willing to let his emotions show on his face, he was happy to have them show in his voice.

"We found them *dancing* together at Wyckham."

Zachary was actually quite glad at that moment that he'd mastered Jamie's look of . . . well, nothing. He looked at Robin with what he was certain was a look as inscrutable as the one Robin was favoring him with. Robin stared at him in silence for another protracted minute, then turned back to Jackson.

"And?"

Jackson was practically spluttering with fury. "There were ruffians littering the road and *musicians* at Wyckham, Uncle. Musicians playing music!"

"My brother has more patience for all that screeching than I do," Robin said, "which is why he keeps all those lads about who are infinitely inferior to his wife in the art. But what about the ruffians?"

"Five of them," Parsival put in helpfully. "A pair of them

were actually still alive. Jackson did them the favor of wringing confessions from them before he put them to the sword. Apparently our good smith here defended Mary quite well. They were convinced he was a demon."

"I'm not sure I don't believe the same thing," Jackson growled.

Robin shot him a look, then turned back to Parsival. "And then?"

"We had a decent supper at Wyckham, sent Mary to bed, then gathered her up and brought her back this morning. Nothing else of interest."

Zachary watched Robin consider for a bit longer. He looked at the lads, then turned to look at Mary.

"Go upstairs to your mother's solar."

"Father—"

"And remain there until I give you leave to come below again," he said briskly. "And if you even so much as go near the outer gates, mistress, I'll lock you in your bedchamber. You're dismissed."

Mary stared at her father for a moment or two in silence, then walked away, her back ramrod straight. Zachary watched her go, but said nothing. He saw her pause as she stood on the top step leading into the great hall. She made no move, she simply looked at him over her shoulder, then turned away and went inside.

"I think this smith—"

"Jackson, go inside and find something to eat," Robin said shortly.

"But—"

"Then meet me in the lists," Robin said sharply. "And if you say another word, I will keep you there for the next fortnight without pause. If you think I cannot, think again."

Connor and Thaddeus slunk off without hesitation, apparently before the same invitation was extended to them. Jackson made his uncle a stiff bow, then walked away.

Well, after Zachary found himself the recipient of a look full of the promise of retribution. Zachary only smiled faintly and nodded, acknowledging the inevitability of unpleasant things to come.

Parsival made Robin a very low bow, then straightened. "I haven't said anything, you know."

Robin nodded with a jerk over his shoulder toward his hall. "Continue on with that sort of restraint and you'll find yourself remaining in my good graces."

Parsival left without comment.

Zachary clasped his hands behind his back, hoping he wasn't making an enormous mistake in leaving himself open for any stray daggers to be flung into his chest. He returned Robin's look steadily. There was nothing else to do. Robin would either do him in, or he wouldn't. He supposed there wasn't much middle ground with Mary's father.

Robin studied him for several moments in silence, then he pursed his lips. "You're here again. Inside my gates."

"I had to bring your daughter back."

"I'm assuming you didn't take her in the first place."

"Nay, my lord, I didn't."

Robin chewed on something for an extended period of time, as if he couldn't quite bring himself to spew it out. Zachary watched the man's mask slip briefly and saw just what Mary's leaving had cost him.

"I will admit," Robin said finally, "that I wondered if you had taken her with you."

Zachary shook his head slowly. "Nay, my lord. I wouldn't have repaid your generosity that way."

"Good sense did prevail eventually," Robin continued, as if he hadn't heard Zachary. "My wife's good sense, I'll concede. Once we realized Mary had gone, I suspected she would catch you eventually and you would make for Wyckham." He lifted an eyebrow. "You could have let the lads return with her."

Zachary nodded slowly. "I could have, my lord, but that wouldn't have allowed me to do what I promised to do."

"And what, pray tell, is that?" Robin asked with a snort. "Talk me to death like that damned Jackson Kilchurn? Startle me like those bloody little imps, Theophilus and Samuel? I vow if I find them hiding in another untoward place, I will throw them in the dungeon."

Zachary smiled. "I wouldn't blame you. But nay, my lord, I have a more specific purpose in mind. I promised your daughter I would speak to you."

Robin looked at him for a moment in silence, then his mouth fell open. "About what? Something to do with *you*?"

"Well, nay," Zachary said, slightly taken aback. That hadn't been his intention, of course, though he was slightly surprised to find he wished it had been. "Nay, my lord," he said, dragging himself back to the matter at hand, "I wanted to tell you of her unease about Styrr."

Robin pursed his lips. "I know all about it."

Zachary imagined that Robin had been down this path more than once with Mary already. There was no sense in traveling it again when the destination was what he needed to reach as quickly as possible. He would just have to get to the point before Robin lost all patience.

"My lord, she fears—"

"Being wed, aye, I know," Robin interrupted. "Do you know that she actually tried to convince me to hire her as a stable lad rather than resign herself to being a bride? It required almost three days in the lists to rid myself of all the shouting I wanted to do at the mere thought."

Zachary wasn't at all surprised, given that he'd had about the same reaction. He considered, then chose his words carefully. "Being willing to reduce herself to stable lad says something, does it not?"

"It says she's bloody stubborn and I never should have let her up on a horse."

"It's more than that, my lord—"

"By the saints," Robin said with a snort, "do you champion all disobedient lords' daughters by bludgeoning their fathers with endless chatter, or do you simply go about rescuing maids who seem to need it?"

Zachary winced in spite of himself. He'd certainly championed a girl or two in the past, but he couldn't say it had turned out very well. This was different. It was different because he was doing the bare minimum necessary to simply nudge along what likely would have happened anyway. No more.

No matter how much more he would have liked to do.

"Nay, my lord," Zachary said faintly, "though it seems to me that your daughter is worth championing at any cost. Especially given that she fears for her life."

"Proof?" Robin demanded.

"I just have a feeling—"

"What a womanly load of tripe," Robin grumbled. "I've known Geoffrey of Styrr for years now and found him to be, as I said, a fool. He's nothing more than he appears to be: enamored of himself and easily intimidated. I will terrorize him regularly and she will have a good life."

"If she's allowed to live to enjoy that life."

Robin shot him a look of warning. "Whilst I appreciate your enthusiasm, Master Smith, I think I've heard enough."

Zachary let out his breath slowly, then nodded. He couldn't force Mary's father to believe what he didn't care to, and he couldn't stay to be Mary's bodyguard indefinitely.

Even if he could have brought himself to watch her marry a man who didn't love her.

He made Robin a small bow, then straightened and attempted a smile. "Of course, my lord. I appreciate the time and the ear."

"I imagine you do." He frowned. "Now, what are your plans? Is there yet another concession you will seek before you go?"

Zachary shook his head. "I simply returned to see Mary safely home. I'll be on my way now."

"No horse?"

"My feet will serve me well enough."

Robin stared at him for a very long handful of minutes in silence, then nodded. "And you'll return home this time?"

"With any luck."

Robin glanced toward the lists, then back at him. "I have business with my nephew, else I would at least see you fed."

"I'll be fine without, my lord."

Robin hesitated, then held out his hand. "A safe journey to you then, lad."

Zachary shook Artane's hand, then made him another low bow. "Thank you, my lord, for all your aid."

Robin looked at him with another thoughtful frown, then lifted his eyebrows briefly and walked off toward his lists.

Zachary glanced up at the keep one last time, then turned and walked down toward the barbican. He had done what he'd said he would do. All that was left was to get himself back to where he belonged. He considered his potential destination and decided that perhaps a change of direction might be useful. He would walk up the coast and look for a particular clutch of rocks he knew could provide him with a quick trip back to the twenty-first century. Much closer than Falconberg and perhaps even free of highwaymen looking for goods he couldn't provide.

He walked out of the gates without looking back.

Not because he wanted to, but because he had no other choice.

He walked back in those gates the next morning just after sunrise, hungry, exhausted, and very discouraged. He was truly doing everything in his power to leave Artane behind. Despite those efforts, though, Artane was where he seemed to find himself more often than not.

He didn't want to know why.

He had spent the better part of the day and night running along Artane's coast, looking for that damned cluster of rocks he'd been told about. He'd found them, based on a description that he'd had from one of Jamie's relatives-in-law, Thomas Mc-Kinnon. Thomas had used those rocks to get himself and his future wife back home from medieval England, so the gate was definitely verified. He had found the rocks where Thomas had said they would be, but they were nothing but rocks. He had tried several things, ranging from sneaking up on the spot to simply sitting there in a lotus position and meditating for an extended period of time.

It had been frustratingly useless.

It had occurred to him, as he'd resigned himself to the necessity of returning to Artane for sleep and food, that the rocks weren't the only gate in the area. Thomas McKinnon's grandmother had wandered into a farmer's field and subsequently found herself in Elizabethan England. Jamie had done his own investigations of that particular patch of ground and found it mostly responsive to his desires. If worse came to worst, he could check out a Shakespearean play or two before he made his way home. He could hang out with the bard and give him something to use as a tragedy, say the story of a man who went back in time and, despite his best efforts, fell hard for a lord's daughter who would end up marrying someone else while the modern guy couldn't do a damned thing about it besides stand there and watch.

His life was, as his father would have readily agreed, very strange indeed.

All of which left him returning to Artane when he hadn't intended to and hoping Robin wouldn't bar the gates against him. He would try again the next day. There really wasn't anything else to do.

The guards only yawned at his approach and waved him on, fortunately. He found himself hailed by several on his trip up the way. He nodded to Godric, then stopped when he realized that Robin himself was standing in the middle of his courtyard, staring up at the sky. Zachary stopped several paces away and waited for the lord of Artane to acknowledge him.

"Lose your way again, lad?" Robin said, turning away from his contemplation of the heavens.

Zachary smiled, though he felt anything but cheerful. He wondered how long it might take him to work off the purchase price of one of Robin's poorest nags so he could get to new and exciting locales on something besides his own two feet.

Probably until Mary's wedding, which he most certainly didn't want to witness.

He dragged his hand through his hair. "I did," he admitted. "I was hoping I might stay for another day and work off the price of a meal or two."

Robin studied him for a moment or two. "You said you were a mason. What sorts of things do you build?"

"What sorts of things do you need built?"

"I need better accommodations for my hounds."

Zachary smiled. "I can do that."

"When are you leaving again?"

"Tomorrow morning, if possible."

"Very well," Robin said, turning for his hall. "Draw what I need for them today, then you may be off again on the morrow. I'll have my lads do the construction whilst you're away. You can inspect it when you return—as I'm assuming you'll be back."

Zachary smiled, though he supposed it hadn't been a very good attempt. He didn't want to say as much, but he sincerely hoped he didn't return. He didn't want to spend the rest of his life in medieval England, being judged by his lack of title, and living without any hope of anything with saturated fat.

Of course, those didn't touch on his real reason for wanting to get away from a place where he couldn't change events, but he supposed that was a reason better left unexamined.

He followed Robin inside the hall, where breakfast was being prepared. He didn't see Mary, but that was for the best. If he'd laid eyes on her once more, he might have been tempted to talk to her father about other things than how many hounds he required kennels for.

Robin stopped at the mouth of the passageway that led to the kitchens. "Tell cook I said to feed you well," he said, "then you're welcome to my solar for the day. I'll be interested in seeing what you can do."

Zachary nodded wearily and turned away. Robin had been more than kind to him, something he had certainly not merited by any action of his own. He hesitated, then looked behind him to find Robin standing in the same place, watching him with an inscrutable expression.

"Might I ask you something, my lord?"

Robin lifted one eyebrow. "You might."

Zachary smiled. "You've been very kind to me. I wondered why."

Robin leaned back against the wall and folded his arms over his chest. "Irony," he said distinctly.

Zachary blinked, then smiled uneasily. "Irony, my lord?"

Robin started to speak, then shook his head and pushed away from the wall. "You'll understand it, Zachary, when you have children of your own. I only wish I could be there to see the look on your visage when you understand what I mean." He shot him a look, then turned and walked off, shaking his head again.

Zachary rubbed his hands over his face, then turned and walked down the passageway. It had been a cryptic answer to a silly question and he deserved the headache that trying to unravel the meaning threatened to give him. Better that he make inroads into breakfast, then be about his work. The labor wasn't worth what he was getting in return, but he would design Robin of Artane the most luxurious dog runs he could.

He resisted the temptation to find a cousin and see if Mary might want to come offer an opinion.

It was very late by the time he climbed the stairs to the hayloft and stretched out on the hay. He let out a deep breath, then gasped in spite of himself at the faint outline of two heads he was quite certain were covered with blond hair. He let out his breath slowly.

"Don't you two have anything better to do?"

They shook their heads silently.

"If you sneak up on me again, I am going to commit grievous bodily harm on you both."

They, as one, slunk back down out of sight. Zachary smiled to himself, then closed his eyes. It had been a very long day. He'd spent all of it in Robin's solar, drawing up plans for the number of hounds Robin said he needed kennels for. He'd wished he'd had a better idea of current building codes, but since he hadn't, he'd done the best he could.

There had been a spare sheet of parchment amongst the things he'd been given to work with. He hesitated, then set to work on something else, something that he likely shouldn't have even attempted. Once it was finished, though, he couldn't deny that it had been worth the effort.

Robin had approved the five sheets of plans for his kennels. He'd then looked at the final drawing and gone completely still.

Zachary hadn't waited for an opinion. He'd thanked Robin quietly for his aid, then left the lord of Artane standing by his fire, a single sheaf of parchment in his hands.

All of which left him where he was: lying in the hay being haunted by two troublemaking teenagers and wishing that he could magically make things other than what they were.

No footprint.

He was beginning to loathe those words.

He cleared his throat. "Lads?"

"Aye?" came the chorus.

"Watch over Mary after I'm gone."

They made firm noises of assent.

Zachary supposed he could do nothing more. He *couldn't* do anything more. He'd done more than he should have, not only by dancing with her but by saying anything at all to Robin. It wasn't his life, it wasn't his time period, and he wasn't supposed to interfere. He knew better.

But just the same, he was going to have quite a bit to say to Jamie about those little flaws in the fabric of time.

And how heartbreaking it was not to create just one more.

Chapter 12

Mary stood on the battlements and looked out over the countryside. She couldn't say she enjoyed heights, as it had always seemed more sensible to her to be closer to the ground. Today, though, she wasn't sure she cared.

Zachary had left three days ago.

Worse still, she hadn't seen him at all for the day that he'd been there. She supposed she should have suspected something when her father had confined her to her mother's solar, but she'd been discouraged enough to simply comply without thinking to question the order. She'd been discouraged because Geoffrey of Styrr seemed, with each passing day, to grow more convinced he would have what he wanted.

She had finally escaped her mother's solar on the second day only to realize whom she'd missed. She'd heard tell of the marvelous plans Zachary had done for her sire, then gained her father's solar to have her own view of them. She'd looked at Zachary's drawings and had been speechless at their beauty. The kennels looked as if they existed somehow on parchment in truth. The hounds he had drawn inhabiting an opening or two were so well done, she half expected them to leap off the page as well.

And then she had looked at the last page and seen herself pictured there.

He had drawn her sitting in a chair in front of the hearth in her father's solar. Her hands were folded demurely in her lap, but she was wearing lads' clothes, as if she'd just come in from the stables. Her hair was hanging loose over her shoulders and she wore a faint smile on her face. He had, by some magic she had no name for, managed to make her look as elegant and beautiful as her mother, in spite of her clothing.

She had looked up at her father to find him watching her with an expression of pity on his face.

He'd straightened immediately and gone to fuss with things on his table, his visage reflecting nothing of what she'd seen on it but the moment before. She hadn't had to see that former expression to understand it, for the feeling that had no doubt inspired it was one she shared herself.

Regret.

Regret that Zachary the smith wasn't a nobleman himself with spurs on his heels and a castle at his back. It might have been possible, given the obvious feeling he'd poured into his portrait of her, that he might have even cared for her.

A gust of suddenly bitter wind pulled her from her thoughts as surely as if she'd been struck. Zachary was no doubt well on his way now to wherever it was he planned to go. London, Scotland; perhaps it didn't matter the direction. He would go back to his life and she would proceed with hers.

The saints pity her for it.

She rubbed her hands over her face, took a deep breath, then put her shoulders back. Of course Zachary would go back to his life, and good riddance. She certainly hoped she never saw him again. Her life was bound to improve so greatly that he would be the one to regret not having stayed to be a part of it. He had done for her what he'd agreed to do and that was that. Besides, what did she need with a man who had no title and no ability to dance? Better that she concentrate on things she understood, such as horses.

She shivered suddenly. The weather was terrible and looked to worsen very soon. She hoped Zachary had found somewhere comfortable to stay, else he would be very damp indeed.

Not that it was any of her affair, of course. He would either freeze or survive as he traveled and she wouldn't be the wiser. All she could do was turn her attentions to her future and leave him to his.

She pulled her cloak closer around herself and left the battlements. What she should have done, likely, was seek out a place in front of her mother's fire, but she was certain she wouldn't have managed to sit still. Being in her mother's solar would have also meant passing time with Styrr's mother, and she couldn't have borne that.

She couldn't bear the thought of her father's solar, either. She would have been tempted to look at what Zachary had left behind, which would only distract her from the task at hand, which was to avoid any entanglements with Geoffrey of Styrr. Nay, best that she go work her horses, then consider what could be done about that.

She made her way down through the keep. The passageways were fairly empty and she managed to skirt the company sitting in front of one of the hearths in the great hall. She put her head down and walked past them and out the hall, hoping no one would call for her to halt.

She saddled Rex quickly, then led him out into the wet. He wasn't happy with the weather, but at least he didn't fight her as she walked him across the lists.

Things changed quite abruptly when she started to work him.

A tremendous clap of thunder frightened her so badly that she lost her concentration for just a moment. Rex bolted, taking her with him until she managed to let go of the line. After she was facedown in the mud, of course.

She pushed herself back up to her knees, then dragged her muddy sleeve across her equally muddy face. That didn't do much besides clear her eyes. She tucked her face inside the neck of her tunic, which accomplished only a muddying of other parts of her.

She had certainly had better days.

A hand appeared in front of her. She looked up to find Thaddeus standing there, watching her solemnly.

"Aid?" he offered.

"Thank you," she said, allowing him to pull her to her feet.

"Falling off a horse who won't allow you to forget it the next time you ride him will do that to a gel, or so I've heard."

She scowled. "Perhaps it escaped your attention, but I hadn't gotten to the riding part yet."

"Even worse."

"Are you helping?"

He only laughed a little. She glared at him, then went to chase down her horse. By the time she managed it, she was limping badly, her hair was plastered to her face, and she was absolutely overcome by vile humors.

She put Rex away, cursing under her breath as she did so, then banged her way out of the stall and stomped down the aisle.

Right into Geoffrey of Styrr.

She realized with a start that she was alone. Her cousins she had sent scurrying half an hour before with her foul tongue. Rolf and his lads had done all their work and were no doubt comfortably ensconced in front of the fire in the garrison hall, happily downing cups of ale and relishing the fact that none of the garrison was fool enough to call for a horse in the current storm.

She was alone and the howling wind would make it so no one would hear her scream.

She swallowed her unease and took hold of more sensible emotions, such as disdain. She folded her arms over her chest in her father's favorite pose of intimidation and looked down her nose at Styrr.

"Aye?"

He brushed off the front of himself whilst wearing a look of extreme distaste. "You're filthy."

"That, my lord, tends to happen when you do more than simply stare at the lists. Now, if you'll excuse me, I have business inside."

"I'll escort you there. After we're finished here."

She wondered how it was that someone who was that handsome, with such perfectly formed features and very nice teeth, could be so profoundly unpleasant. Unpleasant in a way that was so subtle that no one seemed to mark it save her.

Well, and Zachary Smith, who thought Styrr's eyes were crossed.

They weren't, she saw, but Zachary had likely been looking for something to make her laugh. She couldn't imagine that Styrr would ever have bothered with that himself.

She didn't move when Styrr took a step closer to her, still smiling pleasantly, though she was terribly tempted. She supposed he would have simply complimented her on the quality of her screams as he slipped a knife between her ribs, then complained about the mess she might have made of his hands.

"I think we're finished now," she said, starting to walk past him.

He stepped in front of her. "I don't think we are."

She opened her mouth to call him a fool, then wrinkled her nose. If his vile self wasn't offensive enough, there was that faint hint of scent that seemed to always cling to him. It wasn't something she marked often—having always had the good fortune to be far away from him—but now the wet had augmented it far past its usual cloying sweetness. By the saints, did the man douse himself in scented water like a woman? What next? Dainty dishes at table, especially fashioned wines, soft and delicate sheets and coverings at night to protect his equally soft and delicate self?

'Twas no wonder her cousins mocked him relentlessly behind his back.

"Let us come to an understanding," he said softly, "just you and me."

"I think I understand you very well already—"

"And I daresay you don't," he said. He stretched out his first fingers and pushed into her shoulders with them.

Mary suspected he did so with equal parts a desire not to muddy himself and the intention to cause her as much pain as possible with as little effort as possible on his part.

She backed up, because she had no choice.

"Stop that," she said sharply.

He pushed her again, not so hard that she would have fallen, but hard enough that she was forced to take another step backward.

"I have no intention of stopping," he said curtly. "You, however, will accustom yourself to stopping when I tell you to. Riding, speaking your mind, dressing as a lad. All these unpleasant behaviors will be things you will stop when *I tell you to*."

"When hell freezes over—"

"And that, too," he said, with another push. "You will *not* talk to me in that manner. I am the lord of Styrr Hall and you will accord me the respect due me."

Mary rubbed her shoulders, but she couldn't get away from his very painful pokes or his continued and very relentless march forward. She shoved him suddenly, but he was, despite his unwillingness to engage in any sort of activities that her cousins would have considered manly, a very solid sort of lad. All she managed to do was dirty the front of his tunic.

His anger was truly terrifying to behold. She turned suddenly and bolted—

Into a wall.

Only it wasn't a wall. Hands pulled her out of the way and behind a very solid form that she had no trouble recognizing.

'Twas Zachary.

She let out the shakiest breath of her life. She took hold of his dripping cloak and rested her head against his back. It was literally the only thing that kept her on her feet.

"My lord Styrr," Zachary said politely.

"You have no business here, *smith*," Geoffrey snarled.

Zachary didn't move. "Actually, I do, my lord. Something to do with removing refuse from the stalls. Shall I start with you? And before you answer, perhaps I should point out that you seem to have acquired a bit of an audience. They've no doubt come to watch your tender care of the woman you hope to wed."

Mary looked around Zachary's shoulder to see Thaddeus and Connor standing at the entrance to the stables, wearing expressions of such coldness that even her father might have been impressed. Thaddeus made Styrr a very low bow.

"The smith has it aright," he said, straightening. "We missed my cousin at supper and were sent to see where she had gotten to."

"Then you've just arrived," Styrr said firmly, as if he hoped by saying it, it would make it so.

"Recently," Connor conceded. He stepped back and gestured toward the courtyard. "Allow me to be your guard back to the hall, my lord. Lord Thaddeus will make certain that my cousin arrives in an equally safe and timely manner."

Mary had to admit that Styrr had more courage than she'd given him credit for. She wouldn't have walked within arm's reach of either of her cousins for any amount of gold if she'd seen them in that mood. Connor followed Styrr, with his hands clasped behind his back—likely so he wasn't tempted to put one of them on his sword and use the hilt of that sword to carve Styrr's heart out of his chest.

Thaddeus only nodded to her, then went to stand at the opening of the stable with his back to her. Mary took a deep breath, then looked up at Zachary. He watched the stable entrance for a moment or two, then turned to her.

"Aren't you supposed to be inside?" he asked.

"I had to see to my horse." She frowned up at him. "It wasn't as though I expected to see him here." She frowned a bit more. "I didn't expect to see *you* here, either. Why are you?"

His expression was more strained than she'd ever seen it.

"I realized as I was traveling that I shouldn't have left your father with unbuilt kennels," he said quietly. "It seemed a poor precedent to set."

"You came back for dog kennels," she said in disbelief.

He pursed his lips. "Perhaps I came back to help you."

"Help me what?" she asked tartly. "Find my way to the chapel?"

"I imagine a bit of time there might serve us both," he conceded, "but I think you should have a bath first."

"Rex bolted," she said pointedly.

"Taking you with him, apparently."

She smiled in spite of herself, but she felt her smile fade all too quickly. "Did you see what Styrr did?"

"Aye."

"My father won't believe it."

"I'll tell him of it." He reached up and rubbed gently at her cheeks with the hem of his sleeve, then he looked suddenly over her head. "Here he comes. I'll tell him now, if he'll listen."

Mary turned and found her father standing twenty paces behind her. He had assumed his pose of ultimate intimidation with his arms folded over his chest and his expression one of intense disapproval. Zachary only made him a very low bow.

"My lord Artane."

"Smith," Robin said shortly. "You returned."

"Your kennels are unbuilt. And I was thinking that I should spend a bit more time with Master Godric and perfect my dagger fashioning. And, if you're willing, perhaps work off the price of a sword."

Her father seemed to unbend a little at that. He let out a deep breath, then clasped his hands behind his back. "Have a brush with unsavouries, did you?"

"Briefly," Zachary agreed.

"'Tis a dodgy world out there, lad."

"'Tis a dodgy world in here," Mary muttered.

Zachary smiled briefly at her, then looked at her father. "It is, my lord."

Robin studied him for a moment or two. "I'm beginning to think I should just give you a permanent bed here in the stables."

Zachary smiled, but Mary could see the worry in his eyes. She had no idea why he couldn't seem to get himself home, or why he thought it was so important that he return to build something to house her father's hounds, or work for Godric in the forge, or procure a sword that he most certainly didn't need to have to protect himself.

It couldn't have been that he had missed her.

"I appreciate the concession," Zachary said gravely, "but I'll be happy enough to bed down wherever there's space. If you wouldn't mind allowing me to finish what I started for you and rest a bit, then I'll be on my way again."

Her father looked at him for another moment or two in silence, then nodded. "Come inside and eat, then you can begin to work at your leisure. Actually, I think I'll eat in the kitchens with you. 'Twill be the least unappetizing meal I've had in a se'nnight, I daresay. Mary, go inside and go upstairs."

"I might want to eat," she said pointedly.

"I might have something sent up."

"I must tend my other horse first."

Her father shot her a sharp look. "I think, missy, that you've had enough adventure in the stables today."

"I'll stay with her," Thaddeus said, appearing at his uncle's elbow.

Robin pursed his lips. "Leaving the lady Anne with the enviable task of seeing to both Styrr and his mother. I have a feeling I'll be repaying this debt for quite some time to come."

Mary wanted to ask her father why, if he couldn't bear the thought of supper with Styrr, he thought she could bear the thought of life with the man, but Zachary sent her a quick look that had her biting back what she intended to say. Perhaps he had a plan.

She wanted to go along with him and see what it might be,

but she supposed that wouldn't be the way to learn what she wanted to know.

Fortunately for her, she knew what would be.

*T*wo hours later, she was lying in the hayloft with Theo discussing various things, but nothing that could possibly aid her in her current straits. She elbowed Theo when she thought she heard the sound of voices. If it was her father come to fetch her, she didn't particularly want to be found. If it was Styrr, she most definitely didn't want him to know where to find her. If it was anyone else, she wanted to hear their confidences.

"But the question is, would it matter? Your uncle wouldn't give her to anyone but a man equal to her in station, would he?"

"Of course not."

Mary turned her head to find Theo watching her with very bright eyes.

"This will be a spectacular bit of eavesdropping," he predicted.

"Then be silent and use your ears to their best advantage," she suggested.

He nodded carefully, then closed his eyes, presumably to listen more fully. Mary didn't have to. She could hear Zachary and Parsival well enough without resorting to that.

"But why not look for a man who loves her for what she is?" Zachary asked.

"Because, my naive friend, most men are looking for a bride of ten-and-two whom they can fashion into a woman who won't argue, or speak her mind, or meddle with their horseflesh. And the reason Mary doesn't gainsay her father is because she loves him and wouldn't think to bring dishonor on him by making a fool of him."

"Even if that means she'll have a life of unhappiness."

Parsival was silent for a moment or two. "Duty, Zachary."

"I don't mind duty when it applies to what I need to do, but I find myself much less enthusiastic about the word when it applies to a beautiful woman who deserves better."

Parsival laughed. "You're a romantic. A pity you aren't a romantic with a title lurking behind your tender heart."

"A pity it matters." Zachary paused. "Parsival, what would you say to a little journey?"

"I imagine it depends on the destination and what mischief might be combined there. Tantalize me with salacious possibilities and I'll see."

"I want to go north."

"North," Parsival repeated. "That is a very large destination, no?"

"I'm interested in a particular part of the north."

"To what end?"

"To solve a mystery."

Mary suppressed the urge to either weep or shout with relief. It wasn't possible that Zachary intended to go to Styrr Hall and investigate things she couldn't.

"Do you have time for such a thing?" Parsival asked. "I thought you were eager to return home."

"I am finding that my roads don't seem to lead there," he said, finally. "They seem to lead me back to Artane."

"Perhaps to solve our little puzzle?"

"I'm beginning to think so."

"Let us return to the hall and find Connor," Parsival said. "He is always ready to embark on a quest that might result in bloodshed."

"Heaven help us," Zachary said with half a laugh. "I'm hoping we might avoid that."

"We will see."

Mary continued to listen but only heard sounds receding. She sighed and rolled to her left only to squeak at the sight of Samuel looking at her from where he lay within an enormous pile of hay, between her and Theo.

"It would serve you right," she said evenly, "if someone stabbed you by mistake with a pitchfork."

He only smiled. "I don't hide here in the daylight."

"Wise."

"Aye," he agreed. He propped his head up on his hand, shaking his head briefly to remove things from his ear. "Eavesdropping," he said wisely. "It always yields interesting things."

She looked at both her cousins. "I think it yields nothing but heartache."

"I think Zachary's fond of you," Theo offered.

"Fond enough to engage in a few inquiries," Samuel agreed. "North, if memory serves."

Mary said nothing. She considered for quite some time in silence before she looked at her cousins again.

"I might need aid in the morning."

They both nodded solemnly.

"I'd best at least look as if I'm off to bed early tonight."

Theo smiled. Samuel rose to his feet and reached down to pull her to hers.

"We'll see to it," he promised.

If only all her problems could be solved so easily. She thanked the lads kindly, then made her way down to the floor. Thaddeus was waiting for her just outside the stables. He said nothing, only put his arm around her shoulders and walked with her to the hall. She thanked him very kindly for the escort once he left her in front of her bedchamber.

Aye, she would go with Zachary in the morning, simply because of the smell she'd noticed clinging to Geoffrey earlier.

She had smelled that particular scent before. It reminded her sharply of something lingering in Roger's cup of wine she'd only had a sip of the night he had died.

She went inside her chamber and began to gather up gear for a brief journey north.

Chapter 13

Zachary stood on a little bluff that straddled two medieval estates and contemplated things that perplexed him.

To his right was Styrr Hall, visible in the distance as it sat on one end of what Zachary could see were vast tracts of land, much of it arable, the rest a bit on the marshy side. It was the sort of place where an arrogant monarch might decide to take a ride just to see if he could lose all his crown jewels at once instead of over years thanks to sticky-fingered courtiers. Neither the land nor the hall was welcoming. It all gave the appearance of a place that had somehow seen better days and had no hope of them returning.

Short of an enormous influx of cash, of course.

He looked to his left and saw Meltham Keep, a rather smaller place apparently owned by Ilbert of Meltham, whom Zachary had met not an hour earlier. A friendly sort of guy that would have, in seventh grade, talked everyone out of their lunch money in return for promises of something really great and left them feeling as if they'd gotten the bargain even when he didn't deliver. His fields were currently being tilled by happy peasants, his breakfast had been served by equally happy lads and lasses, and his ample wife had presided over it all with a cheerfulness that had been infectious. The mere mention of Styrr's

name had left the wife gushing about his fine qualities and
Meltham himself wearing as much of a smirk as he likely ever
permitted himself.

Something was definitely up there.

Zachary looked at Parsival, who stood next to him wearing
an equally contemplative expression.

"Why do I have the feeling Lord Meltham is holding something over Styrr's head?"

"He smiled too much."

"And he invited us to join him in a game of chance," Connor
offered from where he stood on Zachary's left. "There is a man
who is accustomed to putting his hand into fat purses that aren't
his."

"We don't have even thin purses," Zachary said with a smile,
"though he seemed to think we might have left them behind
where we could go and get them and gamble the contents away."

"Obviously our attempt to pass ourselves off as peasants
was a failure," Parsival said with a little sigh. "I never held out
much hope for it. At least in my case it is very hard to disguise
such superior bloodlines."

Connor made a noise of disgust and walked away to swing up
into his saddle. "Let's go home. We've proven that Styrr needs
funds, but nothing else. Perhaps there is nothing else to prove."

Zachary looked at Parsival. "Is this hall worth killing an
older brother for, do you think?"

"I wouldn't kill my older brother for it," Parsival said with a
smile, "but I'm fond of him. I don't think Geoffrey bore Roger
any love." He shrugged. "Roger never cared for the trappings
of court, leaving Geoffrey free to wrap himself in them as he
wished. One would think that would have been enough to satisfy
him."

Zachary nodded and turned to get back on one of Robin's
lesser steeds. He'd hoped for a mystery that might equal Geoffrey's eagerness to indulge in wedded bliss, but he'd found
nothing. He and Mary's cousins had discussed a trip south to
London to see what sort of dirt could be dug up at court, but
they'd come to the conclusion that it wouldn't yield anything
useful, either. Zachary was convinced Geoffrey of Styrr was a
medieval Dorian Gray, presenting a youthful, perfect face to
the crowd at large while hiding all his dirty deeds on a portrait
in the attic of Styrr Hall.

He just didn't want Mary to be the one to find that painting and realize just what she'd been shackled to.

He sighed deeply. He had exhausted his options for time gates in the north and she was close to exhausting her options for getting out of marriage to a man who not only didn't deserve her but might be detrimental to her health.

And short of providing conclusive evidence of nefarious deeds, he wasn't sure how he would convince Robin of the latter.

It was afternoon before they rode up the way from Artane's gates to the stables. Zachary frowned at the sight of commotion there. Maybe commotion wasn't the right word. There wasn't any more activity in the inner bailey than usual; this just seemed more purposeful. Or maybe it was that he suddenly found himself with his hands full of a horse that didn't like the fact that two sixteen-year-olds were running his way.

He managed to keep his seat, barely, then dismount without landing on his head. He soothed his horse, then handed the reins off to one of Rolf's lads before he turned on the twins.

"Do that again and I'll take your heads and crack them together," he said shortly. "Whatever you have to tell me isn't worth it."

"The banns were read today," Theo blurted out.

"What?" Connor said in astonishment. "You're daft."

"And we're a handsbreadth from being thrust out the gates," Theo added faintly. "I think we vexed Uncle Robin overmuch this morning."

"What did you do this time?" Parsival asked in surprise.

"We tried to follow you," Samuel said, his face devoid of all color. "We didn't make it past the village."

Zachary closed his eyes briefly. "By yourselves?"

They shook their heads as one.

"I take it Lord Robin is the one to have found you?" Zachary asked grimly.

Theo nodded. Samuel simply looked ill.

"What were you thinking, you fools?" Connor exclaimed.

"Mary wanted to help," Theo said weakly. "'Tis her life, after all."

Zachary bent his head and rubbed the back of his neck, then he sighed deeply. "Where is she?"

"In her chamber. But Uncle Robin wants to see you all in the lists when you return."

"Does he indeed?" Parsival asked in surprise. "Why?"

Theo shifted. "I fear we might have blurted out something that might have resembled telling him that you three knew better than he who Mary should bind herself to." He paused. "Or words to that effect."

Connor and Parsival exchanged looks, then Connor sighed. "I'll go first. I might manage to take the edge off him."

"Thad's been trying for the past pair of hours," Samuel offered. "Unsuccessfully, I might add."

Connor shot his brother a look. "And what again were the possibilities for your punishment? I hope they were dire."

"Uncle said he would invent something appropriate when he was less likely to murder us."

"Then you'd best find some way to appease us as well," Connor growled as he walked off. "And keep your bloody mouths shut the next time!"

"We've considered that," Samuel called after him. He looked at Theo. "Haven't we?"

"If we haven't, perhaps we should."

Zachary would have smiled, but he was too sick at heart. He looked at Parsival. "I appreciate the company today."

"And just where are you scampering off to, you coward?" Connor yelled, turning around to look at him. He continued to walk backward toward the lists. "I believe my uncle wants to see us *all* in the lists."

"I'm going to the smithy," Zachary called after him. "I'm going to see if Master Godric has a sword to loan me."

He could only hope he managed to keep himself alive with it.

*I*t was sunset before the torture ended. Zachary couldn't say that he'd fared particularly well. He'd been up well before dawn and spent the bulk of the day in futile endeavors that had drained him of all his enthusiasm for anything useful. He had stood against a furious Robin of Artane for almost an hour, which was something, though he'd been last in line and perhaps all the others had managed to wear Robin out just the slightest bit. Perhaps.

The man was, he would readily admit, absolutely terrifying with a sword in his hands.

But now the joy of having been used to alleviate Robin's frustrations was over and he'd been granted the concession of dinner. He walked back across the courtyard with Parsival, wondering where he might find that dinner that didn't involve crossing swords again with Robin of Artane to have it.

He returned Master Godric's sword to him, then stood at the entrance to the forge and listened to Parsival talk to the man about things he couldn't bring himself to pay attention to. He simply looked up at the sky and considered the impossibilities of the situation.

He'd managed the barest minimum of conversation with Robin earlier, telling the lord of Artane that he was convinced that Styrr was definitely up to something. He attempted a bit of conjecture about Lord Meltham's perhaps swiping a bit of Styrr's lunch money, necessitating a hasty marriage to a very wealthy lord's daughter that Robin might know.

Robin had told him to mind his own business.

Which was, he also had to admit, what he probably should have done in the first place.

He rubbed his hands over his face. Maybe he hadn't had any part to play in Mary's life. Maybe his difficulty in getting home could be chalked up to nothing more than his failure to get himself south to Falconberg. Maybe Mary would go on to have a decent life in spite of her fears.

He continued to study the darkening sky. What if she was destined to marry Styrr, bear him half a dozen beautiful children, then live out her life in peace? For all either of them knew, Styrr would marry her, sire all those children, then fall off his horse and kill himself by bashing his head against a rock.

He wished he'd paid more attention to that book of genealogy he'd read in Anne's modern-day solar. At the time, what had impressed him had been how prodigiously that first generation of de Piaget siblings had reproduced. He hadn't intended to need the knowledge beyond being able to drop the occasional name to flatter Gideon.

He did remember that Robin hadn't been beyond repopulating the north of England himself, though he and Anne had been less busy than Robin's brothers and sisters. Robin's children hadn't put the brakes on, either, though there had been fewer of them to start with than their aunts and uncles. He frowned as he struggled to remember how many children Robin's eldest had had. His only frame of reference there was William, who was Phillip's great-grandson, and he'd never thought to ask William any questions about his progenitors.

Next after Phillip had come Kendrick, who he thought had died before his time. There had also been a Jason, who had apparently married well and produced a half dozen sons.

He shivered. He hadn't met Kendrick and he hoped he didn't. Knowing about someone's death before they met it prematurely was something he didn't think he had the stomach for.

He knew he was missing someone in those first sets of inhabitants, but he felt like he was reaching for a name in the fog. All he could think about was poor Robin and Anne who had lost a child as an adult—

Maryanne. Someone had had a daughter named Maryanne who had also died as an adult.

Maryanne.

"Zachary?"

Zachary looked at Parsival. Well, he would have, but he was having trouble seeing him.

"My friend, are you unwell?"

Zachary leaned against Godric's wall because he thought he might fall down if he didn't. Maybe he had the generations wrong. Maybe he'd been so wasted from engine smoke that day that he'd misread the de Piaget generations and misunderstood the relationships. He looked at Parsival.

"Do you have an aunt named Maryanne?"

Parsival looked at him blankly. "What?"

"Is there a woman in your family named Maryanne?" Zachary repeated impatiently.

Parsival's mouth fell open. "Are you daft, *mon ami*? We have only one Maryanne."

Zachary shook his head. He wanted to stop, but a particularly horrible sensation of déjà vu washed over him, more than once. He was standing where he was, but he was also standing in Anne's solar looking at that huge book in the glass case.

Maryanne.

He couldn't believe it could be Mary, but what did he know?

He stood there and shook his head over and over again, unable to stop. It wasn't possible. Surely.

"'Tis an old custom of these Englishmen," Parsival said, looking at Zachary as if he expected him to lose it at any moment. "In times past, the parents might take their names, toss them together, and see what emerged that was pronounceable. I suppose Mary is fortunate she wasn't called Robanne. Or Annebin. No one calls her both names together, though. Well, Jackson does, but the rest of us do not. Not often, at least. Why do you ask?"

Because suddenly, as if he were reading it afresh, the entry he'd read in Artane's solar came into focus.

Maryanne de Piaget, b. 1231, d. 1258.

April 12, 1258.

Ten days from where he stood. He knew that because Godric's cousin had sent word he'd been delayed and wouldn't arrive until the sixteenth. A fortnight from then.

"Zachary?"

Zachary leaned over with his hands on his thighs and concentrated on breathing. It was one thing to traipse through time and see things he probably shouldn't have, or be a bystander for things he would survive while others didn't. It was nothing special to pick up a few interesting historical tidbits and find himself fairly fluent in tongues that had been dead for centuries.

It was another thing entirely to look at a woman, a lovely, vibrant woman, and know she would meet her end and there was nothing he could do—*should* do—to stop it.

Actually, he knew exactly what that felt like because he'd had it happen to him before. The only difference was, he hadn't loved that poor girl who had met her end despite his efforts to save her.

He pushed himself upright and walked away, ignoring Parsival's exclamations of dismay. He bypassed the stables and walked into the lists. He ignored Mary's cousins, ignored Jackson, who stood in his way like a statue. He simply walked around him and continued on to where Robin was standing.

Robin looked at him darkly. "Back so soon for more?"

"I need a steed, my lord," Zachary said hoarsely. He didn't dare say anything else. The knowledge he had in his head was so terrible, so profoundly, devastatingly awful, he just couldn't say anything else.

Robin blinked in surprise. "Is aught amiss?"

Yes, Zachary wanted to shout. *Your daughter will marry that bastard who doesn't love her, and he is likely the one who puts her in her grave!*

But he couldn't.

For all he knew, he was wrong. Maybe Mary had had a daughter Maryanne and he'd just confused the dates. Maybe she needed to marry Styrr and have that daughter. Maybe she was killed in a riding accident. Perhaps Styrr had been killed with her. Interfering would leave Styrr alive when he should be dead and add threads to the cloth of time where they didn't belong. Maybe Robin would be so grief-stricken when Mary died that he would wipe out the entire Styrr family. Those were threads Zachary didn't dare leave in where they should have ended.

He couldn't understand why anyone ever visited a fortune-teller. Knowing the future was a terrible, dreadful, appalling thing. It was far better left shrouded in mystery.

"I am simply in haste," Zachary croaked, when he trusted himself to speak again. "I have nothing of value to give you except for my knives—"

Robin waved aside the words impatiently. "You saved my daughter's life on the way to Wyckham. I'll even concede that today your motives were pure. A horse in trade seems a very poor bargain to me."

You saved my daughter's life.

Zachary nodded briskly, because if he'd spoken, he would have shouted.

"When do you want to leave?" Robin asked.

"Now." If he didn't get out of Artane in the next ten minutes, he was going to lose it.

"As you will," Robin said, nodding toward the stables. "Let's see what I have that will suit you. I'll see the portcullis raised immediately."

Zachary nodded his thanks, then followed Robin across the lists. He said nothing to Mary's cluster of cousins who were standing in the middle of the courtyard, though he knew he should have. They were silent, so perhaps his expression told them all they needed to know.

He walked into the stables behind Artane's lord, accepted gratefully the horse Robin chose for him, then waited impatiently as it was tacked up. He held out his hand to Robin, shook his, then looked at him gratefully.

"Thank you, my lord Robin, for all your many kindnesses," he said sincerely.

"I'll think of you fondly every time I visit my hounds," Robin said seriously. He paused. "No more words to bludgeon me with? No last pleas for me to keep my daughter here to tend my steeds?"

"My lord, I wouldn't presume to interfere," Zachary said, though he almost choked on the words.

Robin pursed his lips. "You already have and more than you're likely comfortable with." He nodded toward the stable doors. "Be off with you, lad. And good fortune to you."

Zachary took the horse by the reins, then turned to walk out of the stables. He only made it five steps before he came to an ungainly halt.

Mary was standing at the entrance, watching him silently.

He hoped he hadn't made the sound of distress that was echoing in his head, but he couldn't guarantee that. He put himself on the right side of the horse and continued on. He only paused once.

At the door.

He reached for Mary's hand and held it, hard.

She held his just as tightly. She didn't say anything, nor did he. He held on to her hand as long as he dared, then he let go without speaking to her or looking at her.

He couldn't.

He did catch a partial view of the look Robin sent his daughter. It wasn't quite pity, but it was full of parental distress. The man was, after all, only a man and doing the best he could to give his children the opportunities he thought they should have.

Heaven help them all.

Robin walked with him down to the gates and commanded that the portcullis be raised. Zachary thanked him once again for the mount, then swung up into the saddle and rode beneath the spikes. The portcullis slammed home behind him with a bang.

And that was that. Zachary set his face forward and rode through the village. He supposed he might actually be able to make it to Falconberg in three or four days if he rode hard. He wasn't quite sure what he would do with the horse once he was there, but maybe one more equine addition to the future wouldn't throw things completely off.

He rode on, because he could do nothing else.

Though it about killed him to do so.

Chapter 14

Mary walked into her father's solar just before noon. He didn't look particularly displeased, but his expression wasn't welcoming, either. At least he had given up on his fury. She imagined if she were to make note of the days, she would have said that his anger had lessened for every day that Zachary had been gone. Now, he simply looked impossibly grim, as if he were just as unhappy with the entire situation as she was. Not that there was any situation to be unhappy about. Now that he had forced her hand by having the banns read, there was nothing to be done save wait for her future's relentless approach. He had given his word and if there was anything that could be said about her father, it was that he never went back on his word.

"You could have knocked," he pointed out.

"I could have, my lord," she said shortly, "but I chose not to. I have been locked in my chamber or sequestered in my mother's solar for almost a se'nnight and I refuse to bear it any longer. If I must listen to Suzanna of Styrr instruct me in the proper way to hold my work or how ladies of fashion sew their seams, I will fetch a fire iron and clout her over the head with it. I am only here to inform you that I am taking my horse for a ride. Outside the gates. If you don't care for my plan, you may put me in the dungeon."

He only pursed his lips and said nothing.

It was singularly unsatisfying. She wanted nothing more than to have him shout at her—which he had never done, but she had often imagined how shocking it might be—so she might shout back.

She shot him a glare instead, then turned on her heel and left his solar, slamming the door shut behind her. She walked swiftly through the great hall only to hear cousins scrambling to catch up with her. She ignored them and bolted for the stables.

She'd already saddled Rex before she'd gone to see her father, so she was several minutes ahead of her cousins in any sort of equine preparation. She swung up onto Rex's back whilst they were still tripping over each other to simply get themselves inside the stables, then sent him trotting right on into the press.

Lads dove out of her way.

Rex's trot was an enormous thing, but his canter was even more impressive. His gallop was, in a word, breathtaking. She didn't allow him anything but a trot until they were free of the castle and over the dunes that lay between her and the sea, but once she reached the strand, she gave him his head, and he flew.

But not fast enough to outrun her thoughts.

She didn't spare any for Styrr. She would face him when she had to and either survive or not. For now, whether it was wise or not, she intended to spend her thoughts on another man.

She remembered the day she'd first seen Zachary and what she'd been doing. She had been flying atop Rex, outrunning her ordinary life in an ordinary keep. She hadn't known that Styrr would come with whip in hand and determination to break her in his mouth. She hadn't known that she would meet a man who was in his own way as quietly dangerous and intimidating as her father was, a man who thought nothing of plying chivalry on her, or putting off his own affairs long enough to attempt to help her with hers.

How much a fortnight could change things.

Mary closed her eyes at one point because the wind in them made them tear. She wasn't weeping, of course. The wind was simply bitter and Rex's speed drove it against her face with force enough that she needed to avoid it. She didn't even dare move enough to drag her sleeve across her face. It was work enough to simply keep herself balanced in her stirrups and allow Rex to run his heart out.

She rode for a very long time.

The sun was falling quickly toward the west when she had to concede that it wasn't only the wind to make her eyes tear. Nay, 'twas a bit of sand, or perhaps something carried in from the sea. She certainly wasn't weeping over a man who couldn't decide if he were staying or leaving.

She sat atop her horse and looked out at the ocean. It took a moment for her eyes to clear enough for her to actually see it. That was well, for it gave her a moment or two to gather her thoughts into something more rational than they had been.

She had no use, she decided firmly, for a man who couldn't dance, or make a proper sword, or stop himself from pulling her behind him every time he thought there might be danger coming her way. And she most certainly didn't need to be the beneficiary of any romantic notions of chivalry demonstrated by a man who slipped her horses treats when he wasn't supposed to and had left bruises on her hand where he'd held it almost a se'nnight ago as he'd been scampering out of her father's stables.

She looked at the ocean once more, then turned away from it. Styrr's keep was on a barren, unpleasant bit of soil that held no delights whatsoever. It wasn't in the midst of lovely rolling hills like Wyckham, and it certainly wasn't on the edge of the sea like Artane or Raventhorpe. She would travel there after her wedding and likely never see anything again but bleak moors.

'Twas a certainty she would never again see her cousins, who had spent the better part of the past three hours simply huddled in a group a quarter league down the strand from her, well away from anything unpleasant she might have shouted at them.

She pursed her lips. As if she would have done something so unladylike. And why would she shout? She was on the verge of becoming a bride.

She turned Rex and sent him walking back toward her

cousins. She reined him in only to have Jackson look at her sternly.

"You shouldn't have been out here alone," he growled.

"I wasn't alone. You were here."

He blew out his breath. "You should have allowed us to ride with you," he said, his tone slightly less fierce. "Though I can't say I blame you."

She nodded, though she couldn't look at them. It reminded her sharply of what she was going to be leaving behind. She turned Rex back toward the keep. Connor rode on one side of her, Jackson on the other, and the rest of the lads followed along behind.

She wished she could have ridden forever, to a place where death didn't lurk in the shadows.

She put her shoulders back and tried to shake off the premonition, but she couldn't. She'd heard about Zachary, Connor, and Parsival's journey north and what they hadn't found, but that didn't convince her she was imagining things. And that didn't mean that those imaginings wouldn't catch her up when it was too late for her to do anything about them.

She walked Rex up the way from the gates to the stables, then continued to walk him in a circle as her cousins tended their mounts. She found, much as she might have wanted it otherwise, that she simply couldn't stop moving. If she did, those dark, terrible things would lay their hands on her and never let her go.

She wondered, absently, if she was going to lose all her wits before her doom found her.

"Mary?"

She realized Thaddeus had come to stand in the middle of her circle. She couldn't answer him. She could only stare at him, mute.

"Maryanne, shall we stay?" he asked, his expression very grave.

She could only shake her head.

"Your horse is weary," he said quietly. "Put him away, love, and come inside the hall. We'll wait."

"Nay," she croaked. She cleared her throat. "I'll be well, Thad, though I thank you for the consideration."

He smiled, pained. "As you will. But make haste. We'll come look for you else."

She nodded, then continued to walk Rex in a circle until the last of her cousins had honored her wishes and gone inside the great hall. Her father didn't come out to look for her. Her mother was likely keeping Suzanna of Styrr from causing an uprising in the kitchen with her complaints. There was no one in the courtyard but her and her horse. It was tempting to get back on him and ride until he couldn't run any longer.

Only there was nowhere for them to run to.

She sighed, then led Rex into his stall and put his tack away. She brushed him far longer than she needed to simply because it gave her something to do with her hands. She stood with him for as long as it took him to finish his grain, then resigned herself to the necessity of supper. She pulled the stall door shut behind her, then turned to leave the stables.

She ran bodily into Geoffrey of Styrr.

He said nothing. He simply looked at her with eyes that were so full of evil that she did something she never did.

She took a step backward.

A shadow loomed up behind Styrr. She would have screamed, but she realized there was no need.

"My lord," Zachary said coldly, "I think you're missing supper inside."

Styrr spun around to face him. "You, here again."

"To keep the lady Mary safe, as it happens."

Mary heard a sound escape her. She wasn't sure if it was a half sob she hadn't been able to contain or if it had been a hastily stifled sound of relief. She clapped her hand over her mouth and backed up again as Zachary walked around Styrr to put himself in front of her. He turned to face Styrr.

"Anything you care to say to her, you can say to me."

"I wouldn't spare the breath."

"Then perhaps you should retreat inside and warm yourself comfortably by the fire," Zachary suggested. "Before something untoward happens to you."

"Is that a threat?" Styrr asked with an ugly laugh. "How dare you."

Zachary said nothing, but his hands down by his side clenched briefly. If Styrr noticed, he said nothing of it. He only sniffed disdainfully.

"Toy with her now, if you can stomach it, *smith*, but I will have her in the end."

He shot Mary a look of promise, then turned and strode away. Mary watched over Zachary's shoulder until he was gone.

Zachary turned and took her by the shoulders. "Did he hurt you?"

She shook her head, but she could say nothing. And then she didn't care to say anything. Zachary gathered her against his chest and wrapped her in an embrace that left her breathless—and not simply because he was holding her tightly. She wasn't sure why he'd come back. She wasn't sure she wanted to know why he'd come back. She was simply relieved he had.

"My betrothed has no manners," she managed finally.

"He isn't."

She lifted her head and looked at him. "What?"

"He isn't."

"Don't you mean *he hasn't*? As in *any manners*?"

"No, I don't mean that at all," he said, his expression perfectly serious. "I mean he isn't your betrothed."

"But I'm going to wed him."

"When hell freezes over," he said. He pulled away and took her hand. "Let's go."

"What do you mean?" she asked as she trotted to keep up with him. "Zachary, wait!"

"I'm sorry," he said shortly, "I forgot to ask you if you were interested in wedding him."

"Of course I'm not—"

"Then let's go."

"Where?"

"To talk to your father."

"That is kind of you," she said weakly. She had no idea what had changed his mind, where he had been for the past week, or why the hell he had chosen now to return and rescue her. She supposed it was enough to know he was willing to try again.

He swore. Quite inventively, truth be told. She supposed it might be best to simply not offer any more opinions on his chivalry at the moment.

He didn't seem particularly inclined to discuss it, either. He merely strode across the courtyard, pulling her along after him.

Or at least he did for a bit. He stopped and stepped in front of her so quickly that she ran into his back. She peeked around his shoulder to see Jackson standing there in front of the steps, his arms folded over his chest, as if he'd been a bloody gate-keeper determined to see that no one but those who pleased him passed by.

"Move," Zachary said shortly.

Theo and Samuel immediately appeared to her right, their eyes alight with something akin to pleasure. Connor, Thad-deus, and Parsival came loping down the stairs, as if they'd been waiting for just such a confrontation.

Jackson's expression was stony. "Release my cousin."

"Get out of my way," Zachary growled.

Jackson drew his sword. Mary found herself pushed into Parsival's arms and pulled out of the way. She started to speak, but Parsival tightened his arms around her so quickly that she squeaked instead. She jerked away from him with a curse. By the saints, when would these louts ever treat her as a lady in-stead of just another of them?

Likely when she started wearing skirts.

She was certain Zachary would die, then she felt her mouth fall open as she watched him kick Jackson's sword out of his hand and send it flying up into the air. Zachary leapt up and caught it before Jackson could, then flung it away. In the next heartbeat, he had Jackson flat on the ground with Jackson's arm wrenched behind him, his knee in Jackson's back, and his free hand pressing Jackson's face into the dirt.

And then he told Jackson just what he could do with himself in very vile terms.

"Ohhh," Samuel said, his eyes wide.

Theo purred in satisfaction.

Parsival leaned close to her. "Ah, but he has made no friend there, *n'est-ce pas*?"

"Shut up," she whispered miserably.

Jackson had several things quite a bit more violent than that to say.

Zachary let him curse for quite some time before the fight seemed to go out of him. Zachary finally released him and leapt well out of Jackson's way. Mary thought it was best to do some-thing besides stand to the side of the battle and wring her hands. She jumped in front of Zachary just as Jackson lashed out, nar-rowly avoiding being hit as a result.

Zachary, predictably, pulled her behind him.

"If you want more of me, then you can have it," Zachary said shortly. "After I've talked to your uncle. I don't want to make it so you can't get up again, but I will if you don't *back off*."

Mary wasn't quite sure what *back off* meant, but Jackson seemed to come to terms with the meaning, if not the actual words.

"When you leave my uncle's solar, you'd best pray you have someone very skilled to guard you," Jackson said, his chest heaving. He dragged his sleeve across his mouth. "You unchivalrous whoreson."

Mary watched Zachary shrug, as if he'd heard worse. He reached for her hand and pulled her toward the steps. She looked over her shoulder in time to watch Thaddeus grin as he said something to his elder brother, who then dashed after him with murder in his eye. Connor and Parsival only smiled at each other, then trotted up the stairs behind her.

Within moments, she found herself standing in front of her father's solar. Zachary rapped smartly.

"I'm busy!"

Zachary cursed, then reached for the latch. Parsival caught his wrist.

"You shouldn't," he said mildly.

Zachary considered for a moment or two, then pulled his hand away and rapped again against the wood.

A moment or two later, Robin himself jerked the door open. His eyes widened only briefly. Mary tried to pull her hand from Zachary's before her father might note that and school his features any more than he had already, but Zachary wouldn't release her. She looked at her father helplessly.

He only stood back and allowed Zachary inside. Zachary pulled her along inside after him. Mary looked over her shoulder in time to watch her father shut the door in the faces of her cousins. No matter. They would stand there with their ears pressed against the wood anyway.

Styrr was sitting in a chair by the fire, nursing a mug of something and looking particularly comfortable. He couldn't have been there more than a handful of moments, but he gave the impression of having been there for most of the evening already. He might not have looked so comfortable had he watched what Zachary had done to her cousin not a handful of minutes earlier.

Her sire walked over to his table and leaned against it. His hands were merely curled around the edge of it, not grasping it furiously or fumbling for a blade, so perhaps that boded well.

"Well?" Robin asked. "What could possibly be so important that you need to interrupt my parley with my daughter's future *husband*? And, if I might ask, why the hell are you holding my daughter's hand?"

"I'm protesting the marriage."

Mary felt her heart stop. It took her a moment or two before she managed to take any breath at all. She looked at her sire, but he was only watching Zachary with mild curiosity.

"Are you indeed?" he asked.

"I am indeed."

"On what grounds?" Robin asked, lifting an eyebrow in challenge. "Consanguinity?"

"Incompatibility."

Styrr guffawed. Mary looked at him and thought his laughter might have sounded a bit forced. He looked at Robin lazily.

"Throw him out, my lord, and let us return to our pleasant conversings. Listening to this peasant chatter on is going to ruin my appetite."

Mary watched her father glance at Styrr, then turn back to Zachary.

"Incompatibility is not a reason to pass up a perfectly suitable marriage partner," he said slowly. "Have you any other reasons to put forth, or shall I do as Styrr suggests and throw you out?"

Mary looked up at Zachary. She had absolutely no idea what he intended next. He'd already tried to convince her father of Styrr's perfidy, but would he try again with the man sitting right there? Surely he hadn't been loitering near Styrr's hall to look for things to use against the man. She had assumed he had started for home.

Apparently she'd been mistaken.

Zachary gave no sign of what he was thinking. He simply returned her father's look evenly, as if he wanted to make certain Robin knew he was serious.

"Well?" her sire prodded. "You don't want Mary to wed with this man here. Your reason?"

Mary looked up at Zachary and watched his mouth move. It took her a moment to realize what he'd said.

And when she did, she thought she just might faint.

Chapter 15

Because I want her for myself.

Zachary knew he was really going to have to learn to keep his mouth shut. Soon. Before he got himself into a situation he wasn't going to be able to fast-talk his way out of.

He'd meant to say, *Because the man over there isn't good enough for her,* or, *Because I want your daughter to be riding your horses when she's sixty.*

Instead, he said what was the absolute truth.

He had the feeling that what had been a very long week had just gotten a lot longer.

He wished desperately for pockets and the time to shove his hands in them and think. He supposed he could take a couple of minutes and review the events leading up to his current pot of hot water. It might help him regroup.

Things actually hadn't gone so badly during his first day's travel from Artane the previous week. He'd made great time, avoided being robbed or gang-pressed into a bit of sowing on some lord's property, and enjoyed several meals that Wyckham's obliging cook had packed for him during a brief pit stop there. He'd had every intention of reaching the fairy ring, hopping inside, then clicking the heels of Robin de Piaget's oldest pair of boots together a few times to get himself back to Scotland. Modern-day Scotland.

He'd reminded himself during that first day of all the reasons he couldn't stay. He'd given himself all of Jamie's Time Travel Ethics lecture series verbatim. He'd considered the ramifications of both pulling Mary out of her time and pulling himself out of his. He'd considered them all very seriously. And at the end of each round of arguing with himself he'd arrived at the same place.

He couldn't cheat Fate in either century.

He had tried that before, with disastrous results. That wasn't an experience he relived when he could help it, but it had seemed appropriate at the time.

It had all happened on a surprise trip to what Jamie dryly referred to as Puritanical New England. They had arrived just in time to see a young woman on trial for witchcraft. They'd tried to save her.

They had failed.

The aftermath had been particularly unpleasant, resulting in a harrowing escape back to the future. He had argued with Jamie for days about the outcome, but Jamie had dug in his heels and insisted that Fate should be allowed to play her hand as she saw fit, no matter how unpleasant that hand might be. Zachary had disagreed.

And then he'd made the almost fatal decision to take matters into *his* own hands.

He'd managed to get himself back to the proper time period, but his arrival had been off by about twenty-four hours. It had been a nightmare trying to avoid being seen by his other incarnation while attempting to rescue a girl whose turn on the world's stage truly had been destined to be a brief one. He'd managed not to leave a body count behind, but he'd done so by failing to accomplish what he'd set out to. Despite his best intentions, the girl had met her fate and he'd set in motion a chain of events that had his other self and Jamie almost finding themselves burned at the stake right after her.

And he'd almost died himself in a bitter New England winter waiting almost two weeks for the time gate to decide he'd learned his lesson.

Jamie hadn't said anything at all when he'd dragged himself back into the keep, freezing and half starved. He'd only shaken his head and gone to fetch Zachary something warm to drink.

Zachary had reminded himself of all that on Day One, been resigned to the truth of it, then carried on with his plan to go to Falconberg and do what he knew he needed to.

And then Day Two had dawned, taking with it his good sense and any hope he'd had of looking at the situation rationally.

All he'd been able to see was Mary de Piaget's lovely green eyes, the way wisps of her dark hair fell along her jawbone, the way her hands looked in his as they'd danced. It was one thing to read about someone in a book and know she had died young. There was regret, surely, but it was an academic sort of regret that passed probably more quickly than it should have.

It was another thing entirely, however, to actually know the woman herself, to have seen her master an enormous horse, to know what she sounded like when she laughed.

He hadn't known that girl in seventeenth-century America, but he knew Maryanne de Piaget.

Day Three had been absolute hell. Every hoofbeat that took him farther south was like the pounding of a giant hammer with his head as the anvil. He came to the point when he'd merely stopped his horse, sat there, and cursed.

He'd thought about Styrr marrying Mary in her father's chapel. He'd thought about Styrr taking her north, to that barren bit of soil he was so proud of, to a keep that seemed to suck all the sunlight into itself. He'd thought about Styrr taking Mary into his arms, up the stairs, and into . . .

He'd had to stop there before he cracked his teeth from gritting them together too hard.

He looked at the facts, then very deliberately decided to ignore them. He had turned back and ridden the way he'd come. It had been the height of foolishness, the very depths of irresponsibility, but he couldn't any more have stopped himself than he could have managed to continue on. He had to keep Robin de Piaget from unwittingly sending his daughter to her death at what he was convinced would be Geoffrey of Styrr's hands. No matter the cost. He simply had to.

All he'd planned to do was convince the man that it was better that Mary be allowed to just live out her life in peace without out a husband.

He'd never intended to offer for her himself.

"And just what is it, *smith*," Styrr said, his tone dripping with scorn, "that *you* propose to bring to such a union? Your skill with hammer and tongs? Your ability to move large quantities of horse droppings in a short amount of time? Your exceptional prowess with the sword?"

Zachary dragged himself back to the present with an effort. He was still standing in Robin de Piaget's solar, still holding Robin's daughter's hand, still needing to make his case beyond that initial admission.

"A pile of stones that are still standing because of good fortune," he said, looking at Styrr evenly, "is not exactly an accurate measure of what a man is, my lord. Why don't we make this a bit more personal? Meet me on any field you choose and I will best you."

Styrr snorted. "I wouldn't bother."

"I would," Zachary said. "Because Mary of Artane is worth the effort."

He watched Styrr begin to calculate furiously. Maybe he was feeling Robin's gold slip through his fingers and was busy counting how much of it he'd already lost.

"I just wouldn't bother with the sword," Zachary continued. "I'd rather use the lance."

"Can you joust?" Mary whispered.

He squeezed her hand. "I'm undefeated." Never mind that he was undefeated because he'd never faced anyone over pointy trees. His skills, such as they were, lay with the sword, his knives, and his hands. He had the feeling, though, that Styrr never bothered with lances, either, and wasn't going to want to learn anytime soon.

"Jousting is for barbarians," Styrr said huffily.

Zachary watched Robin shift just the slightest bit. He imagined the good lord of Artane had spent more than his share of time on horseback, trying to knock his opponent off his with a very long stick. Styrr wasn't scoring any points presently. He glanced at Robin, then turned back to Styrr.

"Then let's choose something else," Zachary said briskly. "Name your weapon, name the day, and I'll best you. Shall it be right now with the lance? Tomorrow with the sword? The next day with my fists?"

Styrr threw back the rest of his wine. "I wouldn't stir myself to even consider such a ridiculous contest." He set the cup down on the floor next to his chair, then looked down his nose. "I am the lord of Styrr," he said, his tone slathered with hauteur, "and

I bring a castle, a garrison of fifty knights, and a hundred acres of arable land. What do you bring?"

Zachary watched Robin reach for Mary's hand and pull her over to stand next to him. Zachary released her not because he wanted to, but because he didn't miss the symbolism. Robin was taking her back and whoever was willing to sacrifice the most for her would have her.

He realized at that moment that he would have given absolutely anything to have been that man.

He took a deep breath and turned back to Styrr. "I bring the willingness to fight for her. Again, the rest could be earned, couldn't it?"

"That settles it," Robin said, pushing off his table. "I say in a se'nnight, with swords, in my lists. Geoffrey, you'd best go dig out your blade."

"You cannot mean for *me* to actually lower myself to contend in any fashion with this *peasant*," Styrr said stiffly. "I am one of Henry's most valued courtiers. You cannot expect me to sully my hands in such a fashion. You cannot be serious."

"I find, increasingly, that I am," Robin said grimly. He walked over to his door and opened it. "You'll want to find your mother and escort her to table, I'm certain."

Styrr's mouth fell open. "But, Robin—"

"That is *my lord Robin* to you," Robin said sharply. "Now, show me the courtesy due me and be on your way. You and your mother will sit on my right, of course, in the places of honor."

Zachary found himself to be the recipient of a look of absolute hatred, but it wasn't anything he hadn't seen before on Styrr's face. It bothered him far less when it was directed at him than when it was directed at Mary.

But just as quickly as it had come, the look was gone. Styrr looked at Robin and made him a slight bow.

"If it amuses you, my lord Robin," Styrr said smoothly. "I will be pleased to humiliate this creature the cesspit spewed out, but it will be at a time of *my* choosing. I will extend him the very great courtesy of four days to attend to his skills. I wouldn't want to kill him too easily."

Four days. Zachary shivered. That was the date he dreaded. He had no idea how that would factor into Mary's death, but it couldn't be coincidence. It was exactly as he'd feared. He took a deep breath, but couldn't bring himself to look at either Mary or her father.

"Generous," Robin conceded.

"I am that." Styrr sent Robin a confident smile, then left the solar, pulling the door to behind him.

Robin locked the door, then turned around and leaned back against it, his arms folded over his chest. He seemed to consider for a moment or two, then he opened the door again and exchanged a very quiet word with Parsival. Zachary turned away to find Mary watching him. Her expression gave nothing away.

He sighed deeply and walked over to stand close to her, with his back to her father. He wondered if it was possible that a fraction of his misery might be showing on his face. Perhaps Mary saw it, because her smile was pained.

"Your chivalry is showing, you know," she said quietly.

He dragged his hands through his hair. There was no possible way to tell her everything he knew. Worse yet, he wasn't sure he dared tell her what he felt. He could only smile at her wearily. "I don't deserve anything kind you can say about me."

"You're rescuing me. Is that not deserving of a kind word or two?"

Not when what he wanted to be doing was offering for her in truth. Not when he had no choice but to try to save her life, then walk away. Not when what he should have done was keep on going to Falconberg, step inside that bloody faery ring, and get back to modern-day Scotland—

Where he would have spent every moment of every day for the rest of his life wondering how he could continue to draw breath when he'd been such a callous bastard.

Necessarily callous, but that didn't make it any easier.

He was saved from having to answer by the sound of Robin coming over to sit by the fire.

"Come sit, Zachary. Mary, pour us wine."

Zachary sat. He didn't protest when Mary's hands trembled so badly that he ended up wearing part of what should have gone into the cup. He smiled up at her and ignored the pounding in his head.

You have to go, you have to go, you have to go.

He would. But not yet.

"So," Robin said slowly, "you want to challenge Geoffrey of

Styrr for my daughter. And just what do you hope to accomplish by it?"

Zachary took a deep breath and discounted what he wanted to say in favor of what he needed to say. "I want Mary to have the life she wants."

Robin pursed his lips. "And if I don't give her to Styrr after I've promised to, what will become of my honor? How will I show my sweet visage at court without being mocked relentlessly?"

"You never go to court, Father," Mary put in.

He shot Mary a dark look. "I go occasionally, when I have no choice." He turned to Zachary. "Well?"

Zachary had a sip of his wine before he thought he could manage to spin the story he needed to. "Events have been changed," he said, "because Styrr agreed to risk it all on a single fight with the winner claiming the prize. Your honor will remain intact and your daughter will remain a—" He'd started to say *alive*, but he bit off the last word just in time. "Your daughter will remain as she wishes to be, doing what she wishes to do."

"And what do you suppose that is?"

Zachary couldn't look at Mary. He didn't dare look at her. He could only take another in a long succession of deep breaths.

"I think she wants to remain at Artane, to care for your horses and live with the family she loves."

Robin studied him for several minutes in silence. "And you, Zachary? What do you want?"

Zachary felt a little winded. He looked at Robin and saw that the man knew exactly what he was asking and precisely the effect the question was having. He had to have another drink before he trusted himself to answer.

"My lord, what I want doesn't matter. I have no title, nor any means of having one, nor any means of convincing you to give your daughter to me. And even if a miracle occurred and I could have any of those things—along with the miracle of persuading your daughter to want me in the first place—the hard truth is that I cannot stay. I must return home. But before I go, I want to make certain Mary is out of danger from Styrr."

He made the mistake of glancing Mary's way as she sat on a stool next to her father. The firelight flickered against her fair skin, her dark hair, her pale eyes. It was all he could do not to look at Robin, give him the entire truth, then ask the man if there wasn't some way he would just ignore all the current medieval conventions and give him a woman so far above him in rank that in a normal household he probably would never have been allowed to do more than polish her riding boots.

He found Robin studying him. It was possible there was pity in the man's eyes.

Fortunately, the pity was soon gone. Robin set his cup aside.

"I suppose, then, we'll see how you fare in the lists, and see what is left of my honor as a result. Go have a wash before supper, children. Mary, you might sit next to your cheeky champion if you like. I imagine I should go put a guard in the kitchens, lest we all find ourselves poisoned by mistake."

"I think that would be a very wise precaution," Zachary said quietly.

Robin shot him a look, then shook his head. "You've been drinking the same water Mary has. Styrr is nothing more than what he appears. And since he is just that, you should have an easy enough time besting him. Just the same, you'll train with me tomorrow."

Zachary was very surprised by the offer. William had said that Robin had been notoriously stingy with his trade secrets. He had trained his sons and grandsons without question, his nephews when he thought they merited it, and only a very few of his squires because they were good enough—and of those only the ones who didn't crawl home begging their sires to send them somewhere else.

"Unprecedented," Zachary managed.

"Aye, it is," Robin agreed. "Yet another in a very long line of concessions I've made to you for some unfathomable reason. Perhaps I'm approaching my dotage sooner than I feared."

"I imagine you don't have to worry about that," Zachary said with a smile. He paused, then couldn't help a question he likely was a fool to ask. "And you don't think I can best him with what I know?"

Robin's eyes actually twinkled. "I never said that, did I? But we're discussing swordplay, not that other business you're so proficient at. And speaking of that, if I were you, I would be more worried what that damned Jackson Kilchurn would leave of me than I would be what damage Styrr might do. You'll want to thank me for saving your sorry neck."

"I'm very grateful."

"See how you feel tomorrow afternoon." He rose. "Best have a decent meal. It might be your last."

Zachary rose, then held out his hand to pull Mary to her feet. He didn't dare keep hold of her hand, though. He looked instead at her father.

"Thank you, my lord."

"You will leave her childless, Zachary," Robin said mildly, "and forced to endure my foul humors until the day I die."

"Better that she be alive to do so than the alternative," Zachary said quietly.

"I think you credit Styrr with too much cleverness."

"Desperation, rather."

"Foolishness, assuredly," Robin said dismissively. He walked over to his door and held it open. "You may dance with her once tonight, lad, if she'll agree to it."

Zachary nodded his thanks, then waited for Mary to leave the solar first. He watched Robin reach out and smooth his hand down her hair as she did so. The sight struck him so forcefully, he felt his eyes burn.

Damn it anyway, he had to get out of medieval England before he completely lost it.

Robin didn't farewell him as affectionately, but he also didn't boot him out the door, so it could have been worse. Robin only watched him silently, then pulled the solar door behind him and went off apparently to make sure dinner wasn't going to kill them all.

Zachary walked with Mary along the back of the great hall, then up the stairs. He had plenty of help in the endeavor, though Jackson was conspicuously absent. He was probably off somewhere sharpening all his blades so he would have a good selection to choose from when he meted out his revenge. Zachary walked with Mary down the hallway until she stopped in front of her mother's solar. He looked at her in surprise.

"What?"

"I thought you might like to linger here," she said gravely.

Heaven help him, she was too observant for her own good. He put his hand on the wood, found it to be nothing but wood, then smiled at her.

"I think your mother's solar must be a pleasant place."

"It would be, if Styrr's mother would leave us in it by ourselves."

He nodded, then continued on with her until they reached her bedroom. She smiled up at him.

"Thank you."

He took a deep breath. "What you really want is your horses."

"Of course," she said. "What else?"

He clasped his hands behind his back. It was safer that way. *No footprint, no footprint, no footprint.*

Well, he'd already screwed that up, but perhaps he could leave as few as possible.

He took a step backward and made her a low bow. "I'll save you a place at the table."

She closed her eyes briefly, then nodded. She looked at him again, then slipped inside her room and shut the door. Zachary rubbed his hands over his face, then turned to the audience to his left. Connor, Theo, and Samuel were standing there, looking like three Nordic statues with their blond hair and intimidating physiques. Well, Connor intimidated. Theo and Samuel terrified with their aura of mischievousness alone.

"And what are you three supposed to be?" he asked.

"Guardsmen," Connor said. "I'm watching after Mary."

Zachary looked at the twins. "And you two? Are you guarding her from me as well?"

Theo grinned. "Nay, we're here to keep you safe from Jackson. Thad's coming later to aid us when he's recovered from what his brother did to him in the courtyard."

Zachary laughed uneasily. "I think I might appreciate the help."

"You will," Samuel agreed promptly. "And Parsival found you a sword of your own. You might want to take it with you to supper."

Zachary imagined he probably should. He walked with them to a chamber where he found clean clothes and a sword that were apparently meant for him. More generosity from a man who had already given him more than he deserved.

He had a wash and changed his clothes, then headed for the door. Theo and Samuel were apparently taking their guard duties very seriously. They escorted him down to the great hall, pulled out his chair for him, then stood behind him against the wall as if they'd been his pages and he a great lord.

Styrr was already there, sitting to his mother's right. He looked at Zachary disdainfully, then turned back to talking at Robin over his mother's head.

Mary came running out of the stairwell only minutes later. He stood up because that's what his mother had taught him to do. Well, that and the sight of Mary de Piaget in a dress merited it.

He pulled out the chair next to him, saw her seated, then smiled over his shoulder at Theo, who had held his own chair for him. Mary moved her chair closer to his.

"We'll share a trencher, fortunately," she muttered.

"Afraid you might stab Styrr with your fork?"

"With any luck."

He smiled, then reached out to pick a piece of hay out of her hair. She looked at him quickly.

"I was in haste."

"You're absolutely perfect," he said, because she was and because he just couldn't seem to keep his mouth shut. "Don't change anything."

She looked at him as if she'd never seen him before.

No footprint.

He thought if he heard those words in his head one more time, he would come unglued. He ignored the echo of them and sat back in his chair to nurse a cup of wine he was certain didn't taste any worse than medieval wine usually did. And while he sat there, he came to a conclusion or two.

He could get hit by a bus and his life would be over. Well, he couldn't at the moment, but he could in the future. Mary could be trampled by a horse. The material point was, their lives could be over in the blink of an eye and then where would they be? And if they both might be dead in a week, what would be the harm in perhaps reaching for a bit of happiness for themselves while they were able, no matter how fleeting it might be?

He suspected they might come to regret it. He also suspected that he would never in his lifetime meet another woman like Maryanne de Piaget.

He leaned over toward her. "If you were to die tomorrow, what would you want to do this evening?"

She looked at him, startled. "Bid farewell to my horses, of course. What would you want?"

"To dance," he said quietly. "With you."

Her eyes widened briefly. "In truth?"

He nodded solemnly. "Will you?"

"Aye."

"Pick one I know."

"You only know one dance."

"See how simple that was?"

She smiled, then looked away still smiling. He watched her and saw the wheels turning, as usual. He looked over her head to see her father watching her as well, an expression of faint alarm on his face.

Zachary understood completely.

Mary turned back and looked at him in silence for a moment or two. "To meet as equals?"

He nodded slowly.

"'Twill irritate Styrr greatly."

Zachary shook his head. "Mary, I don't give a damn what Styrr thinks. I'm happy to irritate him with many things, but not anything that has to do with you. I just want to take advantage of the fact that your father has granted me one dance with you tonight."

"And tomorrow?"

"Tomorrow, I'll bargain for two."

She lifted her chin just the slightest bit. "I'll leave your heart in ruins."

He smiled. Or at least he attempted to. "You already have."

She looked almost as devastated as he felt. She turned to look out over the great hall. "Where are those bloody minstrels? We need a distraction."

He couldn't have agreed more. It was foolish to think about wooing her in any meaningful fashion, and he could think of a dozen reasons just off the top of his head why he shouldn't, but somehow when he looked at her those reasons didn't seem very important.

The voice inside his head was, for a change, silent.

He wasn't sure if that was an improvement or not.

Chapter 16

Mary stood in the lists and wished she'd had a bit of sword skill. She had aunts enough who could defend themselves if necessary. Even her mother had wielded a blade in her youth with great success. If she'd been able to do the like, she would have used a very sharp dagger on one of the men she was watching and that man wouldn't have been Zachary. It would have been Connor, for he was fighting with Zachary and he wasn't holding back.

She supposed it could have been worse. It could have been Jackson trying to reduce Zachary to tears. He'd been threatening the like for two days now, since Zachary had bested him so thoroughly in the courtyard with his bare hands alone. She supposed some of his anger was over that. The rest came from a misplaced determination to defend her.

She had discussed with him her lack of need for that in angry whispers that morning during Mass, something he never attended more than once a year. He had spent most of his time pointing out to her that Zachary was a rogue he intended to kill at his earliest opportunity. She had called him a dozen kinds of idiot. The conversation, if it could have been called such, had deteriorated from there until they'd both been asked to leave the chapel. Jackson had scowled at her, then stalked off, no doubt to visit the armory to see if there might be something there to add to his already too-large collection of sharp things.

She had retreated to the lists to see how Zachary fared. He had begun his day with Thaddeus, but soon moved on to Connor. At least her father was only watching him at present instead of offering very caustic opinions on how Zachary could improve himself.

Mary had been surprised at the way her father had from the very beginning subjected Zachary to a steady stream of criticism about where he was failing to live up to expectations. On those very rare occasions when he had actually deigned to work with someone, he always put them through several weeks of the simplest of exercises before he began to critique their technique. She had witnessed more than one man look at her father in disbelief at his harshness, then turn and walk off the field, having found Robin of Artane's requirements to be a little too demanding for his taste. Zachary, however, hadn't flinched. He had merely performed with exactness whatever her father had told him to do.

As Parsival had remarked more than once, Zachary certainly looked like a lad who wanted something very much.

She wasn't sure she wanted to know what that something might be.

She took a deep breath and looked to her right to where her father stood watching Zachary. She didn't like to disturb him in the lists, but today she was past the point of fretting over niceties. She walked over to him and slipped her hand into the crook of his elbow. He looked down at her in surprise, then turned back to the fight in front of him. He was silent for so long she would have suspected he'd forgotten she was there if it hadn't been for the fact that he was patting her hand occasionally. He patted her mother as well, when he was thinking difficult thoughts that he wasn't sure she would want to discuss.

Her father was, as her mother would have readily admitted, a very tenderhearted man under all his grumbles.

He cleared his throat suddenly. "Would you want that lad out there if he stayed?" he asked quietly.

"He won't stay, Father," she said just as quietly, "for reasons he will not name. In his own way, he's easily as stubborn as you are."

"Am I stubborn?" he asked, feigning puzzlement. "I'm sure I don't know what you're talking about."

"Father, you want me to marry Geoffrey of Styrr. Against my will, I might add."

He pursed his lips. "I think you should be a wife and mother, gel. He seems the least objectionable of all the fools who've come to look at you."

"He beats his horses and his dogs."

"Very well, he *seemed* to be the least objectionable of all the fools who came for you. He is, if you'll think about it, *still* the least objectionable."

"What does that say about the others?"

Her father only muttered something under his breath and refused to answer.

"Was Grandfather this pigheaded with you?"

"Pigheaded," he repeated soundlessly. He shot her a dark look. "I am not pigheaded."

"You also attended your wedding with a sword in your back."

His mouth moved soundlessly a bit longer, then he scowled at her. "You, Maryanne, could stand to temper your words."

She smiled up at him. "I love you, Father."

He turned her to him and put his arms around her. He held her in silence for quite some time, then he cleared his throat again. "I love you," he said gruffly. "You wee feisty wench."

She smiled against his chest. She turned her head and watched Connor and Zachary fight. She wasn't sure how long Zachary would last, but he seemed to be holding his own at present.

"Who do you think he is?" she murmured.

"Someone who loves you, I daresay."

She sighed deeply. "A pity he must leave."

"I think he believes he has no choice. And if he weren't so bloody stubborn, he might give you all the reasons why. He won't give them to me."

"Have you asked?"

"Repeatedly, whilst beating upon him with my sword."

"You like him, don't you?"

"For all the good it does either of us, love, aye, I find him tolerable enough. He might even manage to tame you with enough time, something not even I have managed." He shook his head. "My first mistake was putting you up on a horse. I see that now."

She looked up at him. "Thank you for it, Father."

He kissed her forehead, smiled, then pushed her head back against his shoulder. "Take that lad there for a ride along the strand, daughter, after Connor's finished with him. I daresay you both deserve a respite from more serious things."

"He has welcomed the training, Father."

"All for you, Mary," he said very quietly. "All for you."

Mary had to think very grim thoughts about potential injuries incurred whilst falling off her horse to keep her burning eyes from leaking.

She watched Connor put the finishing touches on Zachary, though she readily admitted that it hadn't been easily done. They were a match in size and strength, though Connor certainly had the advantage of having had a sword in his hands from the time he'd been able to hold one. It was apparent, though, that Zachary had paid attention to what her father had taught him. And whatever skill he might have lacked, he made up for through sheer determination.

Zachary finally conceded the battle. Connor put his hand on Zachary's shoulder in passing, said something that made Zachary laugh, then continued on his way to what she was certain would be one of the ale kegs in the kitchen.

Zachary stretched his arms over his head, then resheathed his sword before he came to stand in front of her sire. He smiled at her briefly, then made her father a low bow.

"My lord," he added politely. "Your thoughts?"

Robin considered with a frown. "You didn't show poorly, for as long as you managed it. We'll discuss later where you went astray. For now, I think you've earned something to eat and a very small rest."

"Very generous, my lord."

"I am that, always," Robin agreed. "Just return prepared to work very hard this afternoon—"

"Why doesn't he face me now instead?" Jackson interrupted angrily.

Mary looked over her shoulder to find Jackson standing ten paces away, a less-than-welcoming look on his face. He only had one sword, which boded well, though she could see hilts of daggers poking up from the sides of his boots. Then again, Zachary was sporting an equal number of blades, so there was no advantage there. She was tempted to remind Jackson of everything she'd already told him that morning, but she suspected he wouldn't hear any more of it now than he had then.

"He won't face you," her father said evenly, turning to his nephew, "because I said not now. Because whatever he did to you the other night is nothing more than you deserved. 'Tis passing unsporting to assault a man with your sword when he has no sword himself, especially when that man has been a guest in my hall. Something a knight of your breeding and experience should know."

"Is he afeared—"

"Jackson," Robin said sharply, "if you don't cease immediately, *I* will stir myself to remind you why I am master here. I guarantee you will not enjoy the experience."

Jackson fought with himself for a moment or two, then let out his breath slowly. He made his uncle a low bow, then turned to Zachary.

"I apologize."

"Forgiven," Zachary said without hesitation.

"I'll kill you later, when my uncle says I might."

And with that, he turned and strode away. Her father watched him go, then turned to Zachary.

"I'd suggest you watch your back, lad."

"Warning heeded, my lord."

Her father seemed to be fighting his smile. "I imagine he didn't care for your treatment of him the other night."

"I had business with you, my lord," Zachary said calmly, "and he was in my way."

Robin laughed briefly, then clapped a hand on Zachary's shoulder. "I leave my daughter in your care, then, since you appear to be quite capable of protecting her. I'll expect you back in a pair of hours, though, whether Jackson is in your way again or not." He looked at Zachary, then laughed and walked away, presumably to keep Jackson from planning a violent bit of business just the same.

Mary watched him go, then turned to Zachary. He was drenched in sweat, but so beautiful in spite of it, she could hardly draw a decent breath.

All for you, Mary.

"You worked hard," she offered.

"I have good reason to," he said. He reached out presumably

to tuck the lock of hair that was falling over her eye back behind her ear, then he paused. "I don't dare touch you in my current state. I could go have a wash and meet you somewhere though, if you like."

"The stables are comfortable," she offered.

"And so they are," he agreed. "I'll go have a wash, then meet you there." He paused, then looked over his shoulder at Thaddeus. "You'll protect her until I return?"

Thaddeus nodded solemnly.

Zachary made her a small bow, then walked out of the lists. Mary watched him go, then looked at Thaddeus, who had been leaning against the wall, silently watching the madness.

"I thought you were his guard. Or was that Connor?"

"He doesn't need either of us any longer," Thaddeus said with a smile, "but you do. Let's be about finding something edible. Your love will arrive intact, I imagine."

He isn't my love, she started to say, then she realized she was past denying it.

The saints pity her.

A quarter hour later, she was staring at food she couldn't bring herself to eat and watching Zachary as he downed things seemingly without regard to their taste. He drained his cup, then looked at her.

"Rex looks restless. He might need a run."

She felt a little breathless. "I daresay he might."

"Which is your father's second-fastest steed?"

"Bella," she said without hesitation. "And she's mine."

He smiled. "Of course she is. I imagine I don't dare ride her, though."

"Or Rex, for that matter," Jackson said flatly from where he stood at the edge of their circle, apparently unwilling to come any closer.

Mary shot him a warning look. He scowled, then folded his arms over his chest. She turned back to Zachary.

"I'll ride Bella if you think you can manage Rex. He's very obedient under saddle."

"I'll manage," he said gamely, "if you're up for a race along the beach."

"Absolutely not!" Jackson exclaimed.

Mary rose without hesitation and went to saddle Rex, leaving Bella for Zachary to see to. She could hear her cousins tripping over themselves to ready their mounts and Jackson swearing very loudly as he joined them in doing the same.

She met Zachary in front of the stables, then traded him reins.

"He'll test you," she warned.

"Is he worse than your father?"

She smiled. "I've never met my father over blades, so I'm not one to judge. If you can get yourself on his back, though, he probably won't throw you off."

He laughed uneasily. "Don't leave me behind if he does." He reached out and tucked her hair behind her ears, then pulled her hood up. "I'll race you."

"And my prize when I win?"

"Name it."

Your heart was the first thing that came to mind, followed closely by *your smile every day of my life*. But she could say neither. She let out her breath slowly.

"Whatever it is, it will come very dear indeed. But I suppose you might require the same of me."

He smiled. "You know you're inspiring me to win, Mary-anne."

She looked down at the reins in her hand, then up at him. "Why do you call me that?"

"Because it is a very beautiful name. And because it's your name." He looked at Rex, then at her. "Let's go."

She swung up onto Bella and watched him do the same with Rex. Rex was behaving fairly well so far, but she could tell he knew something was afoot. Zachary had to hold him back all the way through the village and over the dunes. She supposed her cousins were keeping up. She honestly couldn't have said.

"Be prepared to lose," he said, struggling to keep Rex in check, "and pay a very high price indeed."

Mary smiled in spite of herself, then called a fair start. She thought that Zachary might have blurted out either a prayer or a curse as Rex leapt forward. He was in a full-on gallop within half a dozen strides, but Bella matched him stride for stride.

Zachary was, she soon found, an excellent rider. He was also on the faster horse, but in the end that didn't matter. She would have liked to have said she'd won because she was more skilled, but the truth was she pulled ahead of Zachary only because he made a mistake or two that didn't allow Rex his full power. She laughed for the sheer joy of the speed, slowing Bella only when she heard Zachary plead for mercy.

Rex didn't particularly care for the cessation of his sport and made certain Zachary knew it. She rode Bella in a large circle to cool her off and watched Zachary as he struggled to convince Rex that he should do the same. She rode beside him finally, trotting back down the beach toward her cousins, who had never come close to catching them.

"I am bested," Zachary said, his chest heaving, "and flawlessly done."

"You kept up at least. And you are still atop Rex's back. I'm certain Jackson was very jealous."

He slid her an amused look. "Has Rex thrown him?"

"Half a dozen times."

Zachary laughed. "I won't remind him of that. But since you have bested me so thoroughly, what will you have? Shall I go make you a dagger and teach you to use it?"

She hesitated. "Not that the dagger you made wasn't . . . well . . ."

"Useful?" he supplied politely.

"I'm not sure I would have chosen that word."

"But since I did, you'll use it?"

"I don't think admitting that will serve me."

He laughed and swung down from Rex. "I'm under no illusions. What would you say instead to a walk along the beach?"

"If you like."

He turned to her cluster of cousins, who had come to a halt ten paces away. "Anyone care to come tend horses for us?"

Thaddeus handed his reins to Connor, then jumped off his horse to come take Rex and Bella. Mary felt herself begin to blush when Zachary held up his hands to help her from her horse, but she supposed there was no point in trying to hold on to her dignity any longer. If her cousins didn't know how she felt about the man setting her gently on the sand, they were fools.

And they weren't fools.

Jackson leaned on the pommel of his saddle and scowled at Zachary. "Divulge your plans," he said shortly, "and I'll see if I approve."

Zachary folded his arms over his chest and looked up at Jackson. "My plans are none of your business."

Jackson began to splutter.

Zachary took her hand and pulled her along with him.

"Let's hurry before he decides to come kill me."

"You vex him overmuch," she said breathlessly.

"I can't help myself. The results are so satisfying."

She smiled up at him, into his sea-colored eyes, until something occurred to her and she had to look away. She found herself suddenly overwhelmed by a feeling of loss. She looked out to sea and struggled to ignore the urge to weep.

She didn't want to ask him if vexing Jackson was his only reason for spiriting her away from her relatives. She didn't care if it was. In truth, she had no use for Zachary past his usefulness in helping her be released from a betrothal she couldn't bear the thought of.

She wasn't at all affected by the fairness of his face, or his strength of arm, or that he was purposely putting himself in harm's way for her benefit alone. She wouldn't mind if she never saw his smile again, or heard his laugh, or watched him watch her by the light of a torch with that very small smile on his face, as if she were something very precious and he feared she might vanish if he looked away.

Nay, she didn't care for him at all. In fact, she would be very happy to see the last of—

She found herself suddenly with her nose pressed against his chest and his arms around her. She felt him pull her braid from inside her cloak and smooth his hand over her hair. And then she did what she never did.

She wept.

He made a noise of distress and gathered her closer to him. He held her as tenderly as she ever could have imagined that a perfect knight would have. He didn't seem to mind that she was drenching him, or that she was not a tidy weeper, or that she couldn't keep from clutching the back of his tunic under his cloak so tightly that it was likely cutting off quite a bit of his air. He only kept one arm around her waist and one hand either brushing her hair back from her face or brushing away her tears.

And then he simply held her.

She wondered if she would ever manage to release him.

"Forgive me," she croaked, finally.

"Nay, Mary," he said, so quietly she could scarce hear him over the endless roar of the sea. "This is my fault."

She looked up at him, dragging her sleeve across her eyes before she could see him.

His eyes were full of tears.

She attempted a smile, but failed miserably. "Your arrogance is astonishing," she said with as much bluster as possible. "Surely you can't imagine I'm weeping over you."

He didn't smile in return. In fact, he didn't say anything at all. He simply looked at her for so long, she wondered if he actually believed her lie.

Then he bent his head and kissed her.

Mary clung to him as her world began to spin. She closed her eyes because she simply wasn't capable of keeping them open any longer.

It was no wonder her uncle Nicholas was forever pulling his wife into darkened corners and kissing her senseless. She understood now why his wife always looked none too steady on her feet after the kissing had ended.

Zachary was very good at it, though she was the first to admit she had nothing to compare him to. She supposed it wouldn't have mattered. The moment he'd touched her lips with his, she had been completely lost.

He kept at his goodly labor until she thought she might quite like to find somewhere to sit down. He tore his mouth away from hers finally and buried his face in her hair. Mary found that her breathing was very ragged indeed, but it seemed to match his quite well.

He eventually pulled back and looked down at her. His eyes were very red. "Let's walk," he said roughly. "Before Jackson decides to kill me truly this time."

Mary looked over her shoulder. Jackson was indeed watching them, but his expression was one, surprisingly, of pity. The rest of the lads were finding other things to look at.

She felt Zachary take her hand and tug her along with him further away from her cousins. She watched him drag his sleeve across his eyes, then look at her. She could only return his look, mute. He smiled very faintly, then released her hand and put his arm around her shoulders. He caught her free hand and pulled it around his waist, under his cloak. She walked down the strand with him as she had seen her father and mother do countless times and wished the day would either end right then or go on forever.

She finally spoke. "Zachary?"

"Aye, love?"

She swallowed her pride—and it was a great deal more difficult than she'd imagined it might be—and said the words that burned in her mouth. "Please stay."

He flinched as if she had struck him. He stopped and turned toward her. The anguish in his face was, she was certain, the same that he no doubt saw in hers. He closed his eyes and pulled her into his embrace. He held her for so long in silence, she thought he would never speak. She wouldn't have been unhappy had he chosen not to, for she knew already what he would say.

He finally sighed deeply and pulled back far enough to look at her, though he didn't release her.

"I wish," he said very quietly, "that I could."

"I don't care about titles and gold."

He smiled, but there was absolutely no humor in it. "I don't either, actually, but in the Year of Our Lord's Grace 1258, sweetheart, it means more than either of us wants." He reached up and smoothed her hair back from her face. "How am I to make a life for you here, Maryanne? Am I to carry you off to my hovel in the village? Will you sleep with both me and the chickens and swine and whatever else we need to shelter during the winter—if we're fortunate enough to be able to afford all those animals to start with? Will you spend the rest of your days scrabbling over our plot of ground that's no bigger than your father's solar while I go till the lord's? Or are we to live forever on your father's charity?"

"I've heard worse ideas," she said grimly.

"So have I, but that doesn't change the reality." He paused. "Would you trade your horses for this life of luxury I could provide for you?"

"Aye," she said simply.

He groaned, then pulled her close and held her so tightly, she thought she might never take a decent breath again.

"I love you," he whispered harshly against her ear. "I love you, Maryanne de Piaget, and because I love you, after I break your betrothal, I will go home. Because you deserve better than what I can give you here." He took a pair of very deep breaths. "Because I have to go home or risk setting in motion things that will ruin more lives than just ours."

"What things?"

"If I told you, you would think I'd lost all my wits." He paused for quite a long time. "I honestly don't think I could stand to see that look on your face."

She wanted to protest. She was, as it happened, very good at protesting. But she knew, in a way that made her feel quite ill, that there was no point in arguing. Whatever else he might have been talking about, he had one thing aright. It wasn't just her happiness she had to think on, it was her children's, her parents', Zachary's. She would, if she wed him, be forced to choose between love and duty, which would leave her very poor indeed.

Though she suspected she would have walked away from all her gold if Zachary had been willing to wed her.

She wasn't sure how much longer she stood there in his arms. She wasn't sure if he wept or she did. She only knew that she would never again in her life feel such pain or such sublime comfort. She would never forget how his hands felt on her hair, on her face, on her back holding her close. She would never forget how he lifted her face to kiss her, how he told her she was beautiful, how she felt when he said he would never again draw a decent breath without her.

And she would never forget how her heart felt as it broke.

"Sweetheart," he whispered finally against her ear, "we have to go back. A storm is blowing in."

She shook her head. "I don't care."

He held her even more tightly. "I don't, either, but I think you will when you don't have the energy to dance tonight."

She lifted her head and looked at him. "Are we dancing together tonight?"

"Every one," he said seriously. "Every last bloody one."

She took a deep breath. "Zachary—"

He kissed her again, then kissed her cheeks, along the line of her jaw, then her mouth again. Then he looked at her, his eyes very red. "Mary, my love, I'm so sorry."

"Nay," she said, attempting a smile, "don't be. You are doing me a great service by ridding me of a man I don't want. And nay, I'm not talking about you."

"If there were a service I wanted to offer, it would be to offer myself as your constant companion for the rest of our days." He hesitated, then looked at her bleakly. "I would give anything to have the chance to try to convince you that you wanted me."

"There would be no labor involved," she said quietly.

He gathered her close again. "Dance with me tonight, then let me do what I can for you in a pair of days. I won't fail you."

"I never thought you would."

He took a step back, then reached for her hand and turned them back to where her cousins were waiting. She looked down at his fingers laced with hers, long, callused fingers that she'd watched do everything from make a horseshoe to draw things that were as beautiful as anything her uncle Jake could.

And she wished things could be different.

"Zachary?" she said as they grew closer to her cousins.

He only looked at her.

"I love you."

He caught his breath, then stopped still. He turned her to him, then pulled her into his arms. He looked at her for a long moment, then bent his head and kissed her.

He kissed her for quite a while, truth be told.

"Oh, enough!" Jackson bellowed.

Zachary smiled against her mouth. "I think we've pushed him as far as we're going to today."

"He's been very patient."

"I'm sure I'll pay for it later." He smiled gravely at her. "I love you."

She found, to her surprise, that she believed him. And she believed that he thought that what he was doing was for the best.

She had believed what she'd said as well. She would have lived with him in a hovel, with the swine and the cows. She supposed she could have endured much for the pleasure of his arms around her at night.

She would have endured a great deal indeed.

Chapter 17

Zachary felt the sweat dripping down into his eyes, but he hardly dared wipe it away. He wasn't in the forge where he might have set down his hammer and tongs and been confident that whatever pitiful thing he had under construction wouldn't leap up and attack him. He was in Artane's lists with their undisputed master, and he was painfully aware that the slightest slip in concentration would result in being used as a pincushion for Robin of Artane's dullest blade. He didn't want that, for a variety of reasons, the most pressing of which was that he had to somehow get Styrr to the lists the next morning, send him slinking off in shame, then keep Mary by his side until the day had passed and he knew she was safe.

Then he would go.

He leapt aside and avoided Robin's blade only because he caught the glint of it out of the corner of his eye. Robin straightened, then opened his mouth—no doubt to swear quite inventively. Instead, he looked at Zachary in surprise.

"Are you ill?"

Zachary shook his head. "I'm fine, my lord."

"You look green."

"Shadows from the clouds." Better that than admitting what his thoughts had been.

Robin studied him for a moment or two. "You know, it puzzles me greatly to watch you fight as well as you do, yet have you say nothing of where you've trained—or even whence you hail."

"My lord, there are perhaps things that should remain shrouded in mystery."

Robin grunted. "I daresay. Very well, lad, keep your secrets to yourself—I daresay we all do that in one fashion or another—and leave me to scratch my head until it pains me. I'll survive it well enough. And I think you actually might survive your encounter with Styrr."

Zachary took the opportunity to drag his sleeve across his eyes. "I can work harder, if need be."

"For a woman you don't want."

"I never said I didn't want her, my lord."

Robin looked, for the first time, a little green himself. He studied a spot to Zachary's right for quite some time before he spoke again.

"I was too hasty in this betrothal," he said very grimly.

Zachary imagined just what it was costing Mary's father to admit he'd been wrong, though in his defense, he'd had no reason to suspect Styrr of anything untoward. He remained silent, because there was nothing to say. Robin had obviously let a knee-jerk reaction send him down a path he regretted.

"Don't do the same," Robin advised. He looked at Zachary then. "When you have children of your own."

Zachary returned his look. "My lord, we all make mistakes."

"But we often don't ask others to see to rectifying them."

Zachary smiled, knowing exactly what he was getting at. "My lord, it is my pleasure to fight Styrr."

Robin started to speak, then shook his head. "I imagine it is, and I think I can guess the reason. But I'll say no more, lest I say too much. Let's have ourselves a drink, then we'll be back to our business."

Zachary nodded, then followed him over to where Connor's younger brothers stood guarding several bottles of wine. Robin drank, then looked at Theo.

"Any tidings?"

"If they would be useful to you, Uncle," Theo said deferentially, "I understand there was a messenger come for Lord Styrr this morning. We haven't divined his identity, but when we're at liberty to do so, we will of course seek out the particulars and give them to you without delay."

Robin looked at Zachary. "I think I've been misusing their gifts."

"They do have a knack for a certain kind of thing," Zachary agreed. He would have been happy to try to sell Robin further on the benefits of having two such terrifying informants, but he was distracted by Connor sprinting across the lists toward them.

A chill went down Zachary's spine.

Apparently the same sort of thing was giving Robin the shivers. He turned on Connor with almost a snarl.

"What is it?"

Connor's chest was heaving. "We cannot find Mary."

Zachary felt as if he'd just been slugged in the gut. He had to lean over to catch his breath.

"Where have you looked?" Robin demanded.

"The stables, the hall—"

Robin cursed fluently. He looked at Connor. "Go down to the gate and make certain Styrr doesn't flee with her. We'll spread out and start from the inner bailey gate. Where are the rest of the lads?"

"Running about madly."

"I'll see to organizing them," Robin said curtly. "Twins, come with me. Make *haste*, lads."

Zachary straightened and watched them all bolt toward the road, then reached out and took hold of Connor's arm before he could follow them. "Who was supposed to look after Mary?"

"Parsival," Connor said helplessly, "and he had no intentions of letting her out of his sight. She wanted to go to the kitchens to look for something to take to Rex. He followed her to the hall, then paused to attend to something to save my uncle the trouble. When he went to look for her, she wasn't where she said she would be. He found me, we looked for her briefly, then decided we would need aid."

"Did you see the messenger who came for Styrr?"

"Aye, he's from . . ." Connor looked at Zachary in horror. "He's from Meltham."

"Damn it," Zachary said, dragging his hand through his hair.

"You don't think—"

"That he's pushed Styrr into doing something rash?" Zachary asked. "Without a doubt. Let's go find them."

Connor ran with him back across the lists. Zachary stopped at the edge of the cobblestone path and looked over the inner bailey, wondering where Styrr might be and what it was that had possessed Mary to ditch her keeper. The only thing that eased him at all was knowing that it was a day too early to begin worrying. Unless his being in the past had somehow changed things in ways he hadn't anticipated.

"Connor," he said quickly as Connor was starting toward the gate, "stop. What's the date?"

Connor turned. "What does that mean?"

Zachary shook his head impatiently. "I want the date. It's the eleventh, isn't it?"

Connor looked at him in surprise. "Have you gone daft, Zachary, or can you not count? 'Tis the twelfth!"

Zachary staggered. He felt as if he'd just been kicked in the gut, this time by a horse. "But Godric said his cousin is coming on the sixteenth," he managed. "In five day's time."

"The man is a very fine maker of blades, but you should never trust him with numbers," Connor warned. "Why does any of that matter?"

"It doesn't," Zachary said hoarsely. And it didn't. The future was hard on him and he had no choice but to try to outwit it. "You'd better go to the gates. I'll start looking here."

Connor shot him a look of unease, then nodded and ran off. Zachary launched into a stumbling run in the direction of the stables, then an unwholesome thought occurred to him.

If Styrr had poisoned his brother, who was to say he wouldn't try to poison anyone else—*everyone* else—who might get in his way? And unless he carried the stuff on him from habit, where would he go to get more? Zachary looked across the courtyard to the garden there. Next to it sat a little stone house that was reputedly the healer's quarters. He bolted for it, then skidded to a halt twenty paces from it. It made no sense to give away his location when he might possibly be able to overtake someone and stop them before they did the unthinkable. He kept himself out of sight of the open doorway, then flattened himself against the outside wall.

The conversation going on inside was unfortunately all too audible.

"I heard what that messenger said," Mary was saying sharply.

"He said nothing," Styrr dismissed with a snort. "Fanciful imaginings."

"You've beggared your hall and your people until you've nothing left," Mary pressed on. "And if you think I'll give you a bloody *shilling* to pay for your idiocy, you've less wit than I feared."

"You stupid—"

"Go grovel to your friends at court," she spat, "and leave us alone."

"Be silent!" Styrr thundered.

"Don't touch me," Mary said coldly. "If you do, I'll make certain that every last one of Henry's entourage knows what you've been combining here in the north. You won't dare present yourself to the king's lowliest page—"

Zachary had heard more than enough. He jerked the door open and strode into the house.

And then things took a turn he hadn't planned for.

Styrr caught sight of him immediately. Perhaps he'd even been waiting for someone to find Mary and attempt a rescue of some sort. Before Zachary could yank her away, Styrr had grabbed her. Zachary expected a knife across her throat.

He hadn't expected a vial of poison.

Styrr forced it between her lips before Zachary could shout out a warning. Fortunately for Mary, she was stronger than Styrr gave her credit for being. She spat out what he'd managed to get into her, then twisted like a furious cat, clawing Styrr across the face before he could do anything but let go of her. Zachary pulled her behind him, almost sending her sprawling in his haste. Or perhaps that could have been because she was tripping over Artane's healer and the messenger from Meltham, who were both equally still.

Styrr backed up, looked at Zachary wildly, then upended the vial of poison into his own mouth.

Zachary realized his outstretched hands weren't going to be of any use. He watched as Styrr clutched his throat, gasped several times for breath, then fell on top of the bodies already there on the floor.

He didn't move again.

Zachary turned to Mary in time to watch her make exactly

the same motions as Styrr had—only less violently and in slow motion. She put her hands to her throat, then looked at him, wide-eyed.

"My mouth burns."

Zachary pulled her over to a stool and made her sit. He riffled through the healer's things, looking desperately for something useful. Plantain, perhaps. Lobelia, to make her throw up. At the moment, he would have settled for anything.

He stepped over the bodies and sniffed what was on the fire. He dipped a finger, then tasted. It was bitter enough to be plantain, so he drew out a cup and hurried back to Mary's side. She was an unwholesome shade of gray and she wasn't breathing very well. He put the cup in her hands, but she was shaking too badly to drink. He tried to help her, but she couldn't seem to swallow.

He bellowed for help, then turned back to Mary. "Damn you, Maryanne, don't give in," he said fiercely.

She only turned her face away from him and threw up. He turned her back toward him and put the cup to her lips again.

"Drink," he commanded.

She shook her head weakly. "Can't. Can't . . . swallow."

He could hardly believe what was happening. It was like a bad B horror movie, only this was all too real. He shook her when her eyes started to close.

"Mary, drink!"

She looked at him and attempted a smile. She failed and apparently didn't have the strength to try again. She leaned forward and rested her head against his shoulder.

"I love you," she whispered.

He cursed viciously, clutching her to him. Damn it, damn it, damn it to hell, it wasn't too late. Not when he'd been within inches of saving her life. He was *not* going to watch her lose it like this. Not because of his own stupidity. Not because Godric couldn't count higher than his own damned fingers.

"You're going to be just fine," he said hoarsely. "Just fine."

"Nay—"

"Don't," he said fiercely. "Don't give in. You're strong enough to fight this."

She sighed and it sounded a little as if she were sighing out her life. "You would have made a formidable knight."

"I will," he blurted out. "I'll do whatever it takes, just *don't leave me.*"

She only sighed again, more faintly that time.

Zachary looked around frantically in time to watch Robin stumble into the house with a small group of de Piaget cousins right behind him. Robin looked at the carnage, then at Zachary.

"Poison?"

"Styrr's holding the vial. He poisoned Mary as well." His eyes burned unmercifully, but he ignored it. "Someone make me some plantain tea. Hurry!" He turned back to Mary, but she was no longer speaking.

She was hardly breathing.

"Bring her upstairs," Robin said, looking at Styrr with loathing. "I'll not have her in the same chamber with that piece of filth." He was almost as gray as his daughter. He looked behind him, then dragged Thaddeus forward. "Do what Zachary commands, then come to us in her chamber. If you know aught else from your sire, do that. Wake the healer, if he lives still. Parsival, keep Styrr's mother far away from us, if you have any pity in your soul. Zachary, bring my daughter."

Zachary picked Mary up in his arms immediately, then followed Robin from the healer's house.

He didn't allow himself to think at all.

Half an hour later, he knelt at the foot of Mary's bed. Anne chafed her hands and Robin stood against the wall, watching with a very grim expression. Zachary knew most of Mary's cousins were out in the passageway, pacing. Jackson was reportedly keeping vigil in the chapel.

He continued to use what reflexology he knew on her feet. Thaddeus had brought them all manner of teas, but Mary hadn't been conscious enough to drink them and he hadn't dared try to force them down her throat.

He cursed himself silently. He should have seen it coming. He should have slept outside her door. He should have demanded that she come to the lists with him that morning even though he hadn't because he'd known she would be more comfortable sitting by her mother's fire. He should have done a dozen things he hadn't thought to do and now he wouldn't have a chance to since Mary would die because he'd been stupid enough to think he had his history down.

He blinked, but he still couldn't see her. He wasn't particularly eager to add anything to his already doomed list, but perhaps *eliminate arrogance about all things paranormal* should have a special place there. He'd marched around in a time period not his own with a sort of abandon that should have shocked him. Even with as cavalierly as he and Jamie popped through the ages, they had at least attempted to leave as little trace of their passing as possible. He should have taken his own advice. He'd been training with Robin de Piaget, for pity's sake. That wasn't exactly in keeping with his policy to lie low and do as little as possible. And where had it led him?

To watching a woman he loved continue on a relentless course toward death.

Even with all the things Patrick had taught him about medieval herbs and their uses, he'd been unable to do anything. It was tragic that he hadn't known where he was going or what he would be doing. He might have been able to bring with him some species of modern med—

He froze. Modern medicine.

He felt his mouth fall open. If he could find a way to get Mary back home to a hospital, perhaps he could save her. All he had to do was get to a time gate.

Unfortunately, the nearest working gate was two weeks away on foot. Even on horseback, it would take him four or five days of hard riding.

Unless Anne's solar had changed its mind about its usefulness.

He bowed his head for several minutes, wondering if it might be possible to find the impossible within reach. He pushed himself to his feet, then made Robin and Anne a low bow.

"If you'll excuse me," he said quietly. "I'll return."

Anne looked up and nodded, her face full of grief. Robin didn't look up; he merely stared at Mary in silence. Zachary looked at her once more, then left her chamber. He walked past the cousins there without speaking to them, then continued on until he was standing in front of Anne's solar. He opened the door, then stood in the doorway.

Nothing.

He walked inside, then turned and walked back out. He did it several times and felt nothing each time. He paused with his hands on the door frame, then swore.

And then he realized he wasn't alone.

He looked up to find Robin of Artane standing in the passageway, watching him silently. Zachary was just too tired to come up with a good reason for what he was doing, so he settled for a partial truth.

"I'm losing my mind."

Robin only lifted one eyebrow briefly.

Zachary opened his mouth and words he hadn't intended to speak came tumbling out.

"My lord, I think I can save her."

Robin was silent for a moment or two, then he gestured to the solar behind him. Zachary turned and walked inside, then waited until Robin had shut the door before he spoke.

"My lord," he began, wondering how in the hell he was going to say anything he needed to and not sound like a raving lunatic, "I know where Mary might have a chance of being healed."

Robin leaned back against the door. "Do you?"

"I do." He wished he'd managed to get Robin to leave his sword outside, but he imagined Mary's father didn't need a sword to do damage with. He would just have to take his chances. "The only problem is, I would have to take her home with me."

"And where would home be, Zachary?"

"The Year of Our Lord 2006," Zachary said.

Robin didn't blink, didn't flinch, didn't reach for his sword. He merely stood there, apparently digesting what he was hearing. Zachary wondered if he might possibly master that completely unreadable look by the time he reached Robin's age. Probably not; it was that good.

"Explain," Robin said without any inflection at all in his voice.

Zachary attempted a smile, but he failed. "As impossible as it sounds, there are doorways scattered all over England and Scotland. Doorways through time. On one side of a doorway, or a spot on the ground, or a ring in the grass, is one century. Step through the exact spot at the right moment and you'll find yourself in another century."

"Interesting," Robin said very quietly.

"Disconcerting," Zachary said, taking a deep breath, "especially when you aren't expecting it. I found myself using one of these doorways a fortnight ago. I was in this chamber, only in the year 2006. I stepped out into the passageway and back to your year of 1258. When I realized what had happened and turned to get back to my time, I found the doorway—the gate through time, rather—closed."

"Proof?" Robin asked.

"My clothes," Zachary said without hesitation. "Though perhaps you didn't see them."

"I saw them."

"And?"

Robin pursed his lips. "They were odd, I'll grant you that. So, if you are from—when was it?"

"2006."

"Aye, then," Robin said. "Then why didn't you go back right away?"

"I've been trying," Zachary said frankly. "I tried another pair of gates, one between here and Raventhorpe and another to the north of Seakirk."

"I'll give you Seakirk," Robin said with the faintest of shudders. "Odd things happen there." He rubbed his hands over his face and shook his head. "If I were to believe this madness you spout, am I also to believe your healers in this 2006 of yours can heal my daughter?"

"My lord, I don't think we have any other choice."

Robin's mask slipped a little and Zachary saw the slightest hint of what the day was costing the man.

"But perhaps by morning—" Robin said finally.

If only that was the extent of it. Zachary wished heartily for something very strong to drink, but since he didn't have it and wouldn't have dared indulge even if he had, he supposed he was fresh out of ways to numb himself. He took a deep breath.

"My lord, there is more."

Robin went completely still. "Is there?"

Zachary nodded. "When I was in this very chamber, I read a book that contained a history of your family. All your children, and your grandchildren, and all their descendants. I saw the death dates of quite a few people, but one stuck out to me, though I didn't understand why. I didn't even understand who it was at the time because the name given there is not the name the woman goes by here."

Robin walked across the room and collapsed into a chair. "Maryanne."

Zachary nodded slowly.

"You know the date of her death."

"Yes."

"When?"

"April 12, 1258."

Robin put his face in his hands. A low moan escaped him, the first sound of grief that he'd made yet. He was silent for a handful of moments, though his breathing was very ragged. He finally looked up, his face haggard. "Why didn't you tell me sooner?"

Zachary shifted uncomfortably. "To what end? To change the past is to alter the future with disastrous results." Damn it, why couldn't he get James MacLeod's voice out of his head? "That is why I left in such haste when I asked you for a horse. I realized who Mary was and what her fate was. I thought I had no choice but to leave her to it."

Robin looked at him, his eyes bloodshot. "Yet you returned."

"How could I not?" Zachary asked. "I love her."

He heard the words come out of his mouth and wondered if they were yet another in a long list of things he shouldn't have said.

Robin, however, only looked at him with pity. "I believe you do, lad."

"And since I couldn't simply blurt out what I knew," Zachary said, casting about for something else to say to keep from showing the devastation he felt, "I thought that if I could get her safely past today that she would be free to live out her life as she saw fit. Only I misunderstood the date and thought today was the eleventh." He forwent any discussions of Julian calendars or Gregorian calendars or anything else that would only have given Robin a reason to draw his sword.

Robin rubbed his hands over his face. "Have you done this often?" he asked flatly. "This traveling through time?"

"More than I would like."

Robin looked at him for several minutes in silence, then he cleared his throat. "You're certain this doorway here won't work?"

"Positive. My only hope is a place near Falconberg."

"Too far."

"I agree, but I don't have any other choice."

Robin looked off into the distance for several very long minutes in silence, then turned back. "Perhaps you do."

Zachary felt a stillness descend in the room, a stillness full of secrets and things left unsaid and knowledge that shouldn't have been had. He looked at Mary's father to find the man looking back at him with a glance that was full of things he shouldn't have known.

"What are you saying?" Zachary asked weakly.

"I understand there is a particular place near my hall," Robin said slowly. "Full of magic. I have no experience with it myself, but I've heard strange tales told of it." He paused. "I've heard that ofttimes a soul will just walk over the ground there, then disappear. My brother Montgomery swears he saw it happen once, though he's convinced 'tis a gate to Faery." He paused. "You might have a different opinion."

"Where?"

He pushed himself to his feet. "I'll show you."

Twenty minutes later, Zachary was standing in front of a gate that he could see shimmering in the air in front of him. He was stunned to realize how close it was to Artane and wondered, absently, why he hadn't seen it before. Then again, he'd never had occasion to wander away from the village in that direction.

He looked at Mary's father. "This will work."

Robin only nodded once. "We'll wait until dark, then."

Zachary would have preferred to leave immediately, but he could see that it wouldn't do for him to carry Mary out of the keep and disappear with her. He walked with Robin back to the hall, then went with Artane's lord to Mary's chamber. He sat in a corner and watched as Robin spoke with Anne. He bowed his head so he wouldn't have to watch Mary's mother weep. Listening to her was enough.

In time, Robin called Mary's cousins in. He told them that he thought she wouldn't last the night. He bid them say their good-byes, for Robin suspected they would need to bury her before morning. Zachary listened with only half an ear to the excuses Robin gave. None of them made any particular sense to him, but the lads seemed to accept them all easily enough. Zachary exchanged several manly embraces with men he had come to feel a very brotherly affection for. Even Jackson hugged him briefly without a blade in his hands.

He waited with Robin and Anne until the hall settled down for the night, though he died a bit with every moment that passed. There wasn't anything he could do to hurry the setting of the sun, and he wasn't going to hasten a parting that he was sure would break Robin's and Anne's hearts both. He studiously avoided thinking about the fact that he would have Mary when her parents would not.

If she lived.

When the time came, he went downstairs and saddled Robin's and Anne's horses for them and waited for them in the courtyard. Anne took Mary before her on her horse and covered her with her cloak. Zachary took her reins and led her horse for her. Robin rode ahead, then had a quiet word with the gate guard. The portcullis was raised, then lowered behind them.

Zachary felt a terrible need for haste, but he couldn't bring himself to hurry Mary's parents along. He watched the landscape as he walked, trying to visualize it in the twenty-first century. With any luck, he would land close to a phone, then he would make a call and get Mary to a hospital.

He stopped when he felt the tingle of that very large X in front of him. Robin swung down off his horse, then held up his arms for Mary. Zachary helped Anne down, then tucked her hand under his arm as he walked with her closer to the gate. He stopped, then looked at Mary's parents. The moon came out from behind a cloud and shone down on them.

"You shouldn't come any closer," Zachary said quietly.

Robin cradled Mary close. Anne was weeping softly. She turned to her husband and put her arms around both him and her daughter. They stood there together for many long minutes. Zachary bowed his head, to give them as much privacy as possible.

And he prayed he wasn't making yet another colossal miscalculation.

He supposed there was nothing else to be done. He could leave Mary in the past and she would most certainly die, or he could take her to the future and hope to heaven that someone would be able to reverse the damage the poison had done.

Anne kissed her daughter once more, then turned and looked at him.

"You won't leave her."

"Nay, my lady," he managed, "I won't."

Robin took a deep breath, then stepped forward and carefully put Mary into Zachary's arms. He put his hand on Zachary's shoulder.

"Take care of her."

"I will, my lord," Zachary said gravely. "She will not lack for whatever I can provide."

Robin put his arm around his wife's shoulders. "Then be off with you. Have a care with the both of you."

Zachary nodded. He backed up, holding Mary in his arms. He continued to back up until he found himself standing in the center of the gate. And once he was there, he focused on the proper year. He watched as Robin and Anne shimmered in front of him.

And then they disappeared.

Chapter 18

Theophilus de Piaget stood in the great hall after sunrise and contemplated things that intrigued him.

He watched his aunt and uncle mourn the death of their daughter. He listened to an interesting tale about Robin having dug a grave for her during the night—which he had threatened to do the evening before—because he feared that what she had was contagious and might infect the entire keep. Both Robin and Anne looked grief-stricken enough for that to have been the case.

Theo looked about him at the household, most of whom wept openly. He watched his cousins and brothers who were equally as devastated. For himself, he felt as if someone had cut his heart out of his chest. He loved Mary easily as much as he loved his own sisters. She had been his best mate save his brother, and he had happily remained near her at Artane when he surely could have gone home with his parents.

He could hardly bear the thought of life without her.

He imagined that, in spite of the quickness and secret nature of their courtship, Zachary Smith felt the same way.

He watched his uncle finish his speech to his household, then retreat with his wife upstairs where they could grieve in private. His brothers and cousins also left the great hall to find a place to shed their tears in private. The servants left as well, to go about their duties with heavy hearts.

But Theophilus de Piaget only stood in the shadows and contemplated things that intrigued him.

Because he had eavesdropped on his uncle when he and Zachary had been discussing how to counteract the poison Mary had ingested.

He had also been at that very strange spot in the ground the night before and he'd seen Zachary take Mary in his arms and disappear with her.

It was strange.

Very strange, indeed.

Chapter 19

*Z*achary walked along the road quickly. Artane sat on the bluff in the distance like an enormous bird of prey. He was fairly certain that wasn't the medieval version of it, for which he was most grateful. He had no idea what the local time was, but it had to have been very late. He could only hope he'd landed in the right year. There was light still pouring from the last in a set of row houses in front of him, which made him feel slightly better.

He wished he felt as confident about Mary's odds of surviving something he hadn't been able to stop.

He stepped over the low front fence and walked up to the doorway, then managed to ring the bell with his elbow. He waited impatiently, but the door opened soon enough. The porch light went on at the same time.

An older man stood there. He took one look at Zachary, then called back over his shoulder.

"Doris, we've another one!"

Zachary supposed they got all kinds, but he wasn't going to ask for details. He cleared his throat.

"I'm in a bit of a tight spot," he said apologetically, the modern English feeling strange on his tongue. "If I could use your phone?"

The man looked at him, then at Mary. He stepped back. "You can lay her on the sofa in the parlor. The phone's right there."

Zachary thanked him profusely, then followed him into the front room. He laid Mary down, then sat down on the edge of the couch and considered. He supposed he could have taken her straight to Artane and hoped for the best with whatever doc Gideon could dredge up, but he was dealing with medieval poison, not a modern ailment, and that poison was going to require more than just a visit from a local general practitioner.

It was why he also rejected the thought of an international call to his dad in Seattle. Robert Smith was a fabulous pediatrician, but Zachary suspected his dad wasn't going to be much help with something concocted almost eight hundred years in the past.

He picked up the phone and dialed someone a bit closer to home. It rang on the other end half a dozen times before someone picked up.

"This had better be an emergency."

"It is," Zachary said hoarsely.

"Oh, Zach," Robert Cameron said, sounding very surprised. "You're home."

Zachary closed his eyes, feeling an overwhelming sense of relief rush through him. "What's the date?"

"Still the twelfth of April, but not for much longer."

Zachary took a deep breath. "I need help. Can you send a helicopter to Artane? Actually, no, not to the keep. I'll be in a field to the northwest. I don't have a flashlight, though, or a phone."

"Don't fash yourself over that," Cameron said without hesitation. "I'll send Peter down with the pilot. He'll find you. What else do you need?"

Zachary was enormously grateful for a brother-in-law who was willing to offer help without asking any questions first.

"I have someone with me who's been poisoned," he said, falling back into Gaelic out of habit. "I have no idea what the poison was, or if she'll live. I think I should try the docs in Inverness."

"Can I offer a piece of advice?" Cameron said slowly.

"If you hurry."

"Take her to Moraig's. They won't know what to do with her in Inverness and then you'll have to explain all sorts of things about her condition I'm imagining you won't want to."

Zachary looked at Mary, pale and cold. "But I can't do this by myself. It's far beyond any skill I have."

"I'll call Patrick and have him waiting for you. I'll bring Sunny as well."

Sunshine Cameron was eight months pregnant and probably needed more rest than that, but Zachary couldn't bring himself to argue. With Patrick and Sunny both working on her, surely Mary would survive.

Surely.

Zachary let out his breath slowly. "Thank you, Cam."

"Anything for a brother. We'll see you at Moraig's."

Zachary hung up with a deep sigh, then set the phone on the floor. He smoothed Mary's hair back from her face and fought the urge to panic. He had failed to keep her safe in medieval England, but with any luck, he wouldn't fail as spectacularly in the future.

He took her hand and brought it to his mouth. *A cold and drowsy humor . . .* The words ran through his head over and over again. He wished he'd been a better herbalist. He wished he'd bothered to make certain of the dates. He wished a dozen things that he couldn't go back and change.

He knew how that would turn out.

He could only hope that Patrick and Sunny could see to what he hadn't been skilled enough even to attempt.

"Your lady friend's ill?"

Zachary looked up at the man standing in the doorway of his front room and simply nodded.

"Reenactment society?"

"Yes," Zachary managed. "The food wasn't good."

"'Tis England, lad. What do you expect?"

"Don't you live here, too?"

The man lifted an eyebrow. "I was speaking of my own kitchen, as it happens, but I'd best not say that too loudly. I try to eat at the pub as much as possible." He studied Zachary for another moment or two. "What's coming for you?"

"A helicopter."

"Oy, but that's a fair sight better than the last bloke. He only had a limousine."

Zachary blinked. "The last bloke?"

"Come through last year, no, maybe a pair of years back.

Kilchurn was his name, I think." He looked at Zachary. "What silly buggers ye are."

Zachary felt his mouth fall open. Kilchurn? He opened his mouth to ask for further details, then shook his head. It wasn't possible. Maybe the name was a common one. Or maybe he'd just been under too much stress lately and he was really starting to lose his mind.

"Get you something to drink?" the man asked.

Zachary shook his head. He didn't think he would manage anything strong. Actually, he wasn't sure he would manage anything at all.

He took both Mary's hands in his own and bowed his head. He hoped the helicopter would hurry.

It was almost four in the morning by the time the pilot set down near the woods surrounding Moraig MacLeod's house. Zachary thanked the man for the ride, then quickly carried Mary, wrapped in a blanket, through the woods to Moraig's crooked little cottage. Cameron was right. It wasn't just that the woods were full of magic and the air full of a hint of spring; it was that there was something profoundly healing about the entire place.

The door opened and light spilled out onto the ground as Zachary walked up the path. Patrick stood back and said nothing as Zachary carried Mary inside. He laid her on the bed, then straightened. He would have wrung his hands, but he didn't want to give the impression that he wasn't completely confident that Patrick and Sunny could work miracles.

Patrick pulled up a stool and sat down next to the bed. He checked Mary's pulse, lifted her eyelids and looked into her eyes, then simply took her hand in his and held it.

"Details?"

"She was poisoned. I'm not sure by what."

Patrick looked up. "Medieval poison?"

"She's mid-thirteenth century," Zachary said, shoving his hands in his pockets only to find he still didn't have any pockets. "She spit out most of it, which is probably the only reason she isn't dead. She was unconscious within fifteen minutes. That was this morning. Well, yesterday morning—"

"And you waited this long before you did something?" Patrick asked incredulously.

"It's complicated," Zachary growled. He took a deep breath. "Sorry. I would have come sooner, but I had to convince her parents to let me bring her forward, and I had to hope for a gate that worked since all the ones I'd tried hadn't. It wasn't exactly like hopping on a plane, Pat."

Patrick smiled briefly. "I know how that goes. So, she fell unconscious and then what?"

"She continued to fade." He supposed there would be time later to tell Patrick the entire story, including Styrr's actions and his own knowledge of her death date. "No convulsions. Just unconsciousness. I tried plantain tea, but she couldn't keep it down." He drew up a stool and sat down next to Mary's head. "What can I do?"

"Pray." Patrick pulled his phone out of his pocket and handed it to Zachary. "Call Cameron and let him know you're here. Sunny insisted."

Zachary did, apologizing as he did so for the lateness of the hour. He hung up, then handed the phone back to his brother-in-law. It was profoundly weird to have been in the Middle Ages that morning and now find himself in a house that belonged still in the Middle Ages but boasted several things that were most definitely of a current vintage.

It was no wonder he shook his head a lot.

Patrick set his phone down on the floor, then rubbed his hands together. "We'll do what we can, you and I, until they arrive. We can try tea, but I'm not sure we'll get your lady here to swallow it. We may have to settle for poultices and time."

"Time?"

Patrick shot him a look. "I can't counter what I don't know, Zach, and medieval poisons were generally fatal. Time may be the only thing we have—time to wait out the damage done. But I will do what I can."

Zachary swallowed, hard. "Please do."

"Who is she?"

"Maryanne de Piaget."

Patrick blinked. "One of Gideon's ancestors?"

"Her father is—was—Robin, the second lord of Artane."

Patrick let out a low whistle. "Well, you don't mess about, do you?" He smiled. "Shall I strip her, or shall you?"

"We'll wait for Sunny," Zachary said without hesitation. "If you do it, I'll kill you. If I do it, Mary will kill me."

"Then we'll wait. But we'll take off her boots now."

Zachary did so without hesitation. He sat next to his love while Patrick put the finishing touches on a detoxifying concoction in the kitchen. It smelled reasonably good, which was a bonus. He held her hand and bowed his head.

And he prayed.

It was the beginning of a very long day. Sunny and Cameron came more quickly than he'd expected, which meant they had likely already been on their way. Together they stripped Mary and put her in shorts and a T-shirt that Sunny had brought along. Zachary half expected Mary to wake up and express her dismay over the skimpiness of her clothing.

But she didn't. She only lay there, her dark hair coming free of her braid, her face so pale that every freckle across her nose was visible from three feet away.

Zachary paced until he couldn't any longer, then he finally simply leaned against the wall. Sunny was working on Mary's feet and Patrick was brewing up something else they were going to soak cloths in and put over as much of Mary as they could.

By sunset, Patrick and Sunny both had stepped outside for a breath of fresh air. Zachary was sitting on a stool near Mary's bed. He stroked the hair back from her face and tried to avoid thinking very black thoughts.

They were the same thoughts he'd been avoiding all day. The irony was, he now had her in a time where they could have been together, yet she was so close to dying that he could feel it in the air. He wondered what other fiendish things Fate had in store for either of them.

He decided that it was probably better not to know.

He looked at Cameron, who was sitting in a chair near the fire, simply watching silently. Now, there was a man who had seen enough death over the course of his life to probably think he'd seen enough. Zachary wanted to ask Cameron's opinion, but he couldn't bring himself to. He could only look at Mary and feel absolutely helpless.

"Care to talk?"

Zachary looked at Cameron. "Honestly, I'm not sure I would even know where to begin."

"That she's still breathing is a good sign," he offered.

"Do you think so?"

"It depends on what the poison was, of course, but most things I saw acted very quickly. Within minutes. Either she has the constitution of a horse, or she spat out most of it. Or it wasn't very well made."

Zachary nodded, though he wasn't sure which of the alternatives was the most palatable. He imagined that if Geoffrey of Styrr had been the one making the potions, what Mary had ingested was quite potent. He supposed the truth was she was simply very strong.

The front door opened. He looked up, searching Sunny's face, then Patrick's for any sign of impending disasters. Sunny walked over and put her hand on his head.

"I'm going to go to Patrick's and sleep for a bit," she said with a weary smile. "Then I'll come back and spell him. I promise we won't leave your lady unattended."

Zachary nodded. That didn't sound as if they expected her to die, though he wasn't sure how they would have broken that news to him if they had.

Cameron gathered up his wife and wrapped her in a coat before he ushered her out of the house and pulled the door to quietly behind her.

Zachary looked at Patrick. "What now?"

Patrick sat down on the stool near Mary's feet. "In truth?"

Zachary closed his eyes briefly before he could stop himself. "I'm not sure I can take the truth right now, Pat, if you don't mind." He had passed exhausted sometime during the previous night. He knew tears were running down his cheeks but he didn't even have the energy to stop them. "I haven't had her very long. I honestly never thought I would have her at all. The thought of losing her is just more than I can bring myself to face right now."

"Then don't," Patrick said quietly. "Just take off your boots and lie down with her." He smiled faintly. "Never underestimate the power of another heartbeat next to yours."

"Hippocrates?"

"Moraig MacLeod. Midwife, healer, herbalist, and clan witch. She knew of what she spoke."

Zachary nodded, then heaved himself to his feet. He wished quite desperately for a shower, or a shave, or even a toothbrush. He supposed the last wasn't beyond reach. He found one in the bathroom, used it, then came back into the great room and took off his boots. He crawled over Mary and did his best to fold himself into a space that was made for a woman of about five foot two, not a man who was six foot three trying to hold the woman he loved. He did the best he could, then closed his eyes.

"Thanks, Pat."

"You're welcome. And just so you know, Jamie is worried about you."

"Is he?" Zachary asked in surprise.

"Only now, of course. He didn't worry before."

"Your brother is a hard-hearted bastard."

Patrick laughed for the first time that day. "Such disrespect for your laird who only has your best interests at heart."

"Pat?"

"Aye?"

"Shut up."

Patrick laughed again quietly, then stood over the bed and helped Zachary turn Mary gently so she was lying on her side with her back to his chest. Zachary put his arm around her and paused. He looked up at his brother-in-law.

"I don't know what I'll do if I lose her."

"Don't think about that," Patrick said gravely. "Just keep her close to your heart. She'll know you're there."

Zachary nodded and put his arm around her waist. He felt for her hand and laced his fingers with hers. Her hands were cold and her skin clammy. There had been no change in her over the past twenty-four hours.

He supposed that the status quo was better than the alternative.

He closed his eyes and prayed for a miracle.

Chapter 20

M^{ary} dreamed.

Or, at least, she thought she had dreamed. Her dreams had been foul ones full of pain and things that tore at her skin, loud noises she had never heard before, and the world rocking uncontrollably underneath her. Every bit of her ached abominably, as if she'd not only been thrown from a horse, she'd been stomped on as well, only to thereafter eat bad fish that had left her retching in the garderobe for the whole of the night.

She didn't move. She simply breathed in and out, carefully so as not to disturb the fragile truce she was having with her poor, abused form. She didn't even attempt to open her eyes. She merely lay still and tried to determine where she was and what had happened to her.

The latter was easier than the first. She remembered watching Geoffrey of Styrr walk down the steps from her father's hall and come to an abrupt halt at the sight of a messenger. The look on Styrr's face had been enough to convince her there was good reason to discover why he looked so horrified. The healer's house hadn't seemed a very private place to hold such a conference, though Master Ranulf's protests had been silenced quite abruptly.

That had seemed odd at the time.

She had hovered outside the door and listened to a man she'd discovered was Ilbert of Meltham's messenger. If that hadn't been intriguing enough, the tales of Styrr's wagering and imbibing and other sorts of debaucheries that she'd only half understood certainly had been.

Threats had flown from both sides, ending in a gurgling sound. It hadn't been difficult to surmise that someone had met his end at Master Ranulf's hearth. She had burst into the small hall, indignant, before she'd thought better of it.

Styrr had looked at her with murder in his eyes.

She had managed to keep him at bay with words alone for a bit, but she'd known it wouldn't last. If Zachary hadn't come when he had, she wasn't sure what would have happened to her. She might have died.

She remembered Zachary making her sit, then feeling the horrifying sensation of not being able to breathe. She remembered hearing him shout at her.

And then her nightmares had begun.

She fought them at present for longer than she wanted to before she managed to push them back where she need not look at them. Then all she could do was lie there with her eyes closed and struggle to breathe. Not only was it difficult to do so, it hurt.

She remembered Styrr trying to force something into her mouth, something that smelled faintly of that scent he often carried with him. Poison, assuredly. She didn't suppose she had drunk much, else she most certainly would have been dead. Perhaps she lay in the healer's house, though she couldn't imagine Master Ranulf having a bed as soft as the one she was lying on.

She frowned as other puzzles presented themselves. She could hear the fire occasionally cracking and popping in the hearth near where she lay. The air was full of the smell of herbs, as it was in Artane's healer's house, but she was convinced she had never felt it so warm there. But if she wasn't inside Artane and she wasn't in the healer's house, where was she?

And why was there an arm over her waist and someone breathing against the back of her neck?

She opened her eyes and struggled to see what sort of chamber she found herself in. There were cloaks hanging on the wall by a door, the barest hint of morning light visible through a window in that door, shelves on the wall stacked with things that belonged in a kitchen. There was also a man she didn't recognize sitting in a chair near the fire. His legs were stretched out in front of him, his feet crossed at the ankles, and his eyes were closed. She didn't think he slept, though. Then again, she wasn't seeing very clearly and the only real light in the chamber was given off by the fire, so she was likely judging amiss.

Perhaps the more important thing was to determine who it was who lay behind her with his arm around her waist and his fingers laced with hers.

Could it be Zachary?

She almost hoped not. If her father realized where they were, he would kill him. Actually, he would kill them both.

She tried to speak, but it came out as a croak. She heard the man near the fire stir. That man behind her sat up with a gasp, then groaned before he leaned over her.

"Mary?"

'Twas Zachary. She sighed slightly in relief only to have him move again and send her world spinning.

"Please," she managed.

"Please what, sweetheart?" he asked, his voice catching.

"Please stop moving."

He laughed, though it sounded quite a bit like a sob. He very gingerly crawled over her, then dropped to his knees next to her bed. He took her hands and bent his head over them. She wasn't sure that those weren't his tears falling on her skin. She had to close her eyes, not because she didn't want to look at him, but because she couldn't bear to watch the other man in the chamber move toward them.

She listened to the scrape of a stool, then heard someone settle down onto it. She felt a warm hand come to rest very gently against her forehead.

"No fever."

Zachary made another unwholesome noise. "I think I might lose it very soon."

Mary couldn't bring herself to ask him what he stood to lose. He and his companion were speaking in Gaelic, and she was the first to admit that whilst hers was as good as it could have been for not having lived in Scotland, she was still missing the odd word here and there.

She listened to them speak in hushed tones, as if she had been very ill and they feared to disturb her. They considered briefly teas and sleep and whether or not the fire was hot enough or needed more wood. She remained still until she thought she could open her eyes with any success. She managed it, finally, and strove to see only one of Zachary.

"Did I sleep?" she managed.

He smiled. "Four days' worth. Give or take a few hours." He spoke in French. Somehow, it was very soothing to her ears. "How do you feel?"

"Terrible. You look terrible as well."

"Thank you. I haven't slept very well. Not until I was sure . . ." He took a deep breath. "I just haven't slept well recently."

"Did you think I would die?"

He exchanged a look with the other man, then turned back to her and nodded.

She blinked. He looked as if he'd narrowly avoided something that would have grieved him past his ability to bear it. She wondered if that thing might have been her death.

She looked at the other man, who didn't resemble Zachary in the slightest, though he was very handsome himself. He held her hand in his for a moment or two, frowned as if he considered something about what he found on her wrist, then he put her hand back in Zachary's,

"You, my lady," he said in eminently functional French, "are either very strong, very fortunate, or both."

"I feel very fortunate," she said, wishing she sounded a bit stronger. She looked up at him, then attempted to use her rather unpracticed Gaelic. "Who are you?"

"Patrick," he said easily. "Zachary's brother-in-law—" He looked at her in surprise. "I didn't realize you could speak my tongue. Zachary said nothing of it."

"I didn't know she could," Zachary said. He laughed a little uneasily. "I'm now wondering how many things I said that I'll need to apologize for."

Mary would have shaken her head, but she had a fairly good idea of where that would lead. "A good warrior never reveals all his strengths," she managed.

"Nor all the tongues he knows, apparently," Patrick said with a smile. He rose with a groan. "Zach, I think I need to sleep in a bed for a few hours. I'll leave a note for Sunny to come when she wakes. Don't let your lady rush off and poach any of Jamie's horses quite yet."

Mary would have smiled at that, but she was too tired. She listened to Zachary speak quietly to his brother-in-law as he walked with him across the floor, but she couldn't make out what he was saying. It was effort enough to simply close her eyes to keep the chamber from spinning. She heard Zachary close the door, then cross the chamber to sit down on the stool next to her bed. She would have thanked him for his care of her when she felt his hand cover hers, but in truth it was all she could do to simply draw air into her parched throat.

"What can I fetch you?" Zachary asked quietly in French. "Something to drink?"

She opened her eyes and focused on him with an effort. "Aye," she croaked. "Thank you."

"I'll return."

She watched him go, but he disappeared above her head so she settled for looking about what she assumed was less of a bedchamber and more of a small house. She considered again where she might be. Not Artane's healer's house, nor any other chamber inside her father's keep. She had never been inside Styrr Hall, but she couldn't imagine that either Zachary or her father would have allowed her to be taken there, not after what Geoffrey had done to her. She wasn't at Wyckham. She supposed Zachary might have attempted to carry her to Seakirk Abbey.

But if that were the case, why had his brother-in-law been there?

She would have considered that further, but Zachary had come to sit next to her bed again, a cup in his hand. The expression on his face was one of such relief, it almost brought tears to her eyes. He leaned forward and slipped his hand under her head.

"Let me help you."

She drank, though it burned her throat like fire. She didn't protest when Zachary laid her head gently against her pillow and set the cup on the floor. He looked at her, but his expression was less relieved than it was something else.

Hesitant.

She wondered if he was giving thought to the best way to tell her that now she was out of all danger of dying, he would be on his way. She wondered where she was. And she wondered why her father wasn't standing over Zachary's back with a dagger in his hand, waiting for the perfect moment to repay him for having shared a bed with his only daughter—never mind that she'd been senseless for the duration of that sharing. She opened her mouth to at least find the answer to the easier of those questions, only words came out she hadn't intended.

"Are you leaving me?"

He looked startled. "Nay. Of course not."

She had to blink back tears. Truly, she felt very ill. That was the only reason her form was betraying her so thoroughly. She squeezed his hand as best she could, then took the deepest breath she could manage.

"Where are we?"

He took her hand in both his own. "Mary, there are answers you need, ones you deserve, but I think you should wait a day or two before you have them. If I could offer an opinion."

She might have protested had he not offered his opinion so gently or looked so earnest whilst doing it. She truly wasn't one to shy away from difficult things, but she didn't think she had the strength to face things she would rather have let lie. Perhaps he had it aright. She shifted slightly on the bed.

Then she realized that she wasn't wearing any clothing.

Perhaps that wasn't entirely true, but what she *was* wearing couldn't possibly have counted for anything decent. She clutched the sheets to her chin with the hand Zachary wasn't holding and looked at him in horror.

"How did I become so unclad?"

"My sister-in-law Sunshine did the honors," he said quickly. "We thought you might be more comfortable that way. Well, that and she and Patrick were covering you in all sorts of poultices and things to draw out the poison and they couldn't do that over your clothes."

"Your sister-in-law," she repeated.

"Aye."

More of his kin she didn't expect to find. She knew she wouldn't rest until she had at least one answer.

"Where are we?" she asked again, when she thought she could manage the whole question on a single breath.

Zachary shifted. "Maryanne—"

"I must know."

He took a deep breath, then sighed. "Scotland."

She choked. It was terribly painful to cough, but cough she did until Zachary had pounded on her back a handful of times and she had regained control of herself. She accepted another sip of some species of healing tea, then lay back and struggled to breathe. "Scotland?"

"The Highlands."

"How—"

"There is a very logical—" He paused and took another deep breath. "There is a logical enough explanation for why we're both here, but it requires more explanation than I could give now or you could, I suspect, bear to listen to. I will tell you that you're in a little house on MacLeod soil. It is a good place to heal, even if it did belong to the laird's witch in years past."

"I don't believe in witches," she said without hesitation.

"Neither do I," he said with a grave smile, "but I believe in several other things. Your ability to heal from something that should have killed you is first on that list. The rest is something we should talk about tomorrow—"

A knock sounded on the door, interrupting him. He looked pathetically relieved as he rose.

"That'll be my sister-in-law Sunshine. She's come to tend you."

Mary thought she just might be grateful for that as well. She had a few needs to take care of that she most certainly wasn't going to ask Zachary to help her with.

She watched him hurry across the chamber and considered what he'd told her. Scotland. Difficult to believe, though she couldn't deny what her eyes were seeing. She was in a place she'd never been before, a house that was small but filled to the brim with all manner of luxuries. If this was Zachary's home, then perhaps her father and cousins had misjudged him. No simple lad, be he mason or smith, could have managed such a place.

More curious still was how he'd managed to bring her all the way to Scotland without her having known it, especially given that he'd said she'd slept for only a handful of days.

She wished she'd had Theo and Sam there at her elbow to be about their usual business of ferreting out all the details she required and reporting them to her with breathless excitement. And unless Zachary would send for either of the lads—or both—she would have to rely on herself. At least the twins would find those answers very interesting when next they met.

She could only hope that would be soon.

Chapter 21

Zachary walked across Moraig's little great room and considered the narrowness of his escape. He was going to need to give Mary the entire truth, but he wanted to do so when the shock of it wouldn't kill her. He might have a day's reprieve, but he doubted he would have any longer than that. He dragged his hands through his grimy hair and went to open the door.

Three women stood there, dressed in medieval gowns and bearing baskets of herbs and green things. He leaned against the door frame and smiled in spite of himself.

"And just who are you three supposed to be?" he asked lazily. "Flora, Fauna, and Merryweather?"

"I'm pregnant, not fat, which you know," Sunny said archly. "Now, get out of the way before I sit on you."

Zachary stood to one side and allowed his sister and two sisters-in-law inside. Elizabeth and Madelyn made for the kitchen, taking Sunny's burden with them. Sunny walked over to the bed. Zachary caught her by the elbow before she tried to sit on the stool and fetched a chair for her instead. He helped her down and had a smile as his reward.

"I'm about to pop."

He smiled. "I'm going to keep my mouth shut about that."

"Yeah, since you already called me a fat fairy, maybe you

should." She turned to Mary and reached out to smooth her hair back from her face. "You're awake."

"Thankfully."

Sunny smiled happily and began to do her herbalist thing. Zachary took a brief moment to appreciate Sunny's command of medieval Norman French, polished no doubt by her husband, who had learned it from a friar during his youth, then smiled at Mary before he left Sunny to her work. He walked over to the kitchen and leaned against the counter while his sister and Madelyn sorted out what they'd brought. Madelyn looked up at him.

"Surviving?"

He attempted a confident smile. "For the moment. I think the ride will soon be leaving the gate, though."

"Well, don't look at me for any help. Patrick was already wearing jeans when I met him."

"Thanks for the thought anyway, Madelyn."

She smiled and patted him on the back as she walked away. "You'll manage," she threw over her shoulder.

He could only hope. He went to stand next to his sister for moral support. She pulled things out of her basket for a minute or two, then looked up at him.

"Have you talked to Pat?" she asked quietly. "Or Cameron?"

"Vast amounts to both while Mary slept. They said that in the end time would do what was needful."

"Jamie would agree."

"Jamie is the last one to be offering advice," Zachary said with a snort. "I was there, if you remember, when your husband was making his initial terrifying assault on modern life, so I know exactly what he would tell me. I was also there for the roller-coaster ride that was William de Piaget." He shook his head slowly. "I wish I had a nickel for every time that guy tried to electrocute himself."

"But you didn't have quite as much invested in those transitions, did you?"

He rubbed his hands over his face. "Beth, stop peering into my head, would you? It's really unsettling."

She reached up and ruffled his hair. "You're an open book, Zach. So, on the same subject, do you have a plan?"

And just how the hell was he supposed to answer that? He

had taken a woman, without her permission, hundreds of years out of her time, all because he hadn't wanted to see her lose her life. Her life was saved, but now she was without her parents, her brothers, and her cousins whom she adored. He'd plunked her down in a time where she couldn't speak what most of the country spoke and where she wouldn't recognize any of the clothes, most of the food, and all of the music.

Oh, and he wasn't sure, once she got to thinking about it, that she would want to stay with him for any other reason than he was what was familiar and safe.

He looked at his sister. "My life is hell."

"And hers?"

"Oh, I'm responsible for that hell, too."

Elizabeth put her arms around him and hugged him tightly. She leaned up and kissed him on the cheek, then pulled away. "She'll forgive you. I always forgave you for the crappy things you did to me."

"I never did anything crappy to you."

She shot him a look. "You and your bratty friends tied me to a clothes pole when I was eight and left me there to roast in the sun."

"It was Seattle. We left you there to rot in the rain. And, if you'll remember, you were more than willing to be the maiden in distress. Besides, I was only six. How secure could the knots have possibly been?"

"Very, Mr. Boy Scout. I almost wet my pants before I got someone to untie me."

"I apologize. Again." He hesitated, then leaned back against the counter with a sigh. "I think this is slightly more serious. I hope I didn't make an enormous mistake."

"You didn't have any other choice," Elizabeth said seriously. "She'll understand why you did what you did once she realizes what the alternative was. Besides, it isn't as if she'll be the only medieval expat in the family. We'll make her feel welcome."

"Assuming she'll want to stay with me."

Elizabeth lifted her eyebrows briefly. "Afraid she'll only want you because she feels obligated to?"

"You know, you could beat around the bush for a while and spare my feelings," he said darkly.

She pointed in the direction of the front door. "Go for a

walk and clear your head. Let Mary find her way for a bit, then see where you both stand. You know, it's possible that you might find you don't like her here nearly as much as you did there."

He blinked, then watched his sister smile.

"I imagine she'll have the same reaction to the same thought. Go for a walk. We'll take care of your love."

Zachary found himself helped out the front door before Mary was helped out of bed. He went because he was pushed and because she was a very modest woman with medieval sensibilities. Now, if he'd been the one parading around in his altogether, she probably wouldn't have thought anything of it. But the reverse was definitely not the case.

He walked around for a few minutes, then decided that it was late enough in the morning that he could certainly make a couple of phone calls. There was one soul in particular that he wanted to catch before that soul got busy with his business of making buckets of money. He dialed the cell Cameron had loaned him and only had to wade through three secretaries before his intended victim picked up. Apparently quite reluctantly.

"Zachary," Gideon de Piaget said uneasily. "How lovely. You're calling from Scotland, I assume?"

"Why, yes, I am, you lying git," Zachary said pleasantly. "Now, help me with something I don't think I understood a couple of weeks ago. There is no paranormal activity at Artane, was that it?"

"And to my knowledge, that's true. And you shouldn't call your boss a git."

"You're not my boss."

"Your money source, then."

"You're not going to want to give me any money after I punch you. Then again, I'm going to punch you so hard that the change will come rattling out of your trouser pockets, so maybe I'll have your money after all."

Gideon laughed, more easily that time. "I see you survived your adventures."

"No thanks to you!"

"And how was I supposed to know what was going to happen?" Gideon asked. "You're the expert on time traveling. I just listen to everyone's stories and shake my head in disbelief.

Ghosts I can believe, but time travel? It's complete bollocks. But so I don't wind up making the same unintentional trip, where is that gate?"

"In the solar doorway. And you should really have a better lock on the stuff inside that room. Actually, I'm thinking you should just rope that whole wing off. It's a minefield."

"I'll keep that in mind," Gideon said. "Now, to move on to less uncomfortable topics, when are you headed south again?"

"In a few days. I've had a little interruption."

"So Cameron intimated when I called to check on your, er, status, though he was unwilling to divulge the particulars. You have him properly cowed, apparently."

Zachary snorted. "I could only hope. As for the particulars, I made a friend and she hasn't been well."

"Ah," Gideon said knowingly. "*That* sort of delay."

"Yes, *that* sort of delay. It may take this friend a bit to get back on her feet and I don't want to rush her. I'll take the train down next week if I can still borrow your car."

"Zach, go buy another car. You have money."

Zachary sighed. "I'm cheap."

"You're frugal. It's a Scottish trait. But you can still afford a car."

"All right," Zachary grumbled, "I'll go get my own damn car and be down there in a week. And Gideon, sorry about the panic."

"Oh, we didn't panic," Gideon said easily. "I called Jamie when we realized you'd gone missing, and he told me what had probably happened. He said not to give you another thought, so I didn't."

"Nice."

Gideon only laughed. "If it eases you any, he seems to have complete confidence in you. I should consider that high praise."

Zachary smiled and rubbed the back of his neck. "I do. So, what else happened while I was hobnobbing with your ancestors? Did you put the contractors off for me?"

"No, they've been busily doing what you wanted them to. I popped over occasionally to see to things whilst you were gone, but you can pay for those efforts."

"I'll just bill it all back to you since it was your bloody doorway that sent me on this adventure in the first place!"

Gideon laughed again. "I'll never win this fight, I can see that. Very well, I won't complain as long as you divulge all details of your journey when you've time. I'm in London for the week, but Megan and I can meet you at the old pile of stones next weekend. If you like."

"I'd like. And I should probably warn you that Robin de Piaget would not like to have his ancestral home referred to as an 'old pile of stones,' so you'd better be careful what you say. You wouldn't want to have to apologize for the slight over blades with him, believe me."

Gideon was silent for a long moment. "I think I might need an early lunch. A liquid one, preferably."

"Save your liver for your father's schnapps. I'll see you in a week."

"I'll drink to that. Cheers."

Zachary hung up and continued to pace for a while. It wasn't warm—it was still April, after all—but it was thankfully not raining for a change. He supposed that was just a matter of time. There was something to be said, though, for knowing that a hot fire and a decent shower awaited inside.

As well as a woman that he hadn't dared dream might be his.

He still wasn't sure he dared dream it. He had very vivid memories of Jamie's adjustment from fourteenth-century laird to twentieth-century nobleman. Talk about a roller coaster. He hadn't known Jamie's brother, Patrick, during his transition, nor had he watched Sunshine's husband, Cameron, make that adjustment. He'd had experience with a few others, though, given how many times he'd answered Jamie's door and found someone of a different vintage standing there. He'd gotten to the point where he'd been forced to have rules. No swords down toilets, no blades poked into electrical sockets, and no random phone calls. And no clandestine invasions into his junk-food stashes. Those had served him well for several years.

But, as his sister had said, he'd never had quite the vested interest in a successful transition that he did at present.

That he was even worrying about the like should probably be enough to leave him wearing a permanently perplexed expression. His father certainly had that look down. His dad was another one that Elizabeth had been forced to make excuse phone calls to over the years. He hadn't thought to ask her what she'd told their father about his current, unexplained absence, but he imagined their dad hadn't bought it any more fully than he had any of the others.

He would need to call his parents and check in. After he'd made sure Mary wasn't going to lose it.

Moraig's front door opened a little sooner than he would have liked, truth be told. Sunshine came out with Madelyn; they shook their heads slowly, both of them wearing very serious expressions. Zachary waited until Elizabeth came out before he dared ask any questions.

"And?" was the best he could do on short notice.

"I think," Elizabeth said, pulling the door to behind her, "that you're not going to have an easy afternoon."

"It was the bathroom that did it, wasn't it?"

"The mirror."

Zachary blew out his breath. "What did she say?"

"She threw up."

Zachary would have smiled, but he was too sick at heart to. "And then?"

"An impressive string of somethings in what I'm assuming was medieval Norman French. Sunny didn't translate, but she and Madelyn exchanged knowing glances." She looked up at him. "This can't come as a surprise."

"What, when she was born, or that I fell for a girl just slightly out of my league?" he asked grimly.

"Either. And while we're discussing this whole thing, what did your gate look like?"

He shot her a warning look. "It was a door and don't say anything else."

She only laughed, leaned up and kissed his cheek, then walked toward the path that led down the meadow to her husband's ancestral home. Zachary watched her go for far longer than he should have.

Because he was something of a coward, apparently.

He finally turned and faced the doorway. There was no time like the present to explain the present. If nothing else, Mary could tell him to get lost sooner rather than later and then he wouldn't have to wonder how she felt any longer.

He walked inside the little house, then shut the door softly behind him. Mary was sitting in front of the fire. He was surprised to see her out of bed, though he knew he shouldn't have been. As Cameron had noted, she had the constitution of a horse. And she was stubborn. He hoped those two traits would serve her well.

He walked over to her slowly. She was dressed again in her medieval clothing and wearing her boots. Her hands were comfortably free of anything sharp, though, which should have been reassuring. They were clasped together so tightly in her lap that her knuckles were white, which wasn't. He pulled up a stool in front of her and sat down before he slowly lifted his head to see what he would be facing.

She didn't look good. She was not only very pale, she looked as if she'd just had a terrible shock.

He had a pretty good idea about what that shock had been.

He was tempted to reach for her hands and hold them, but he wasn't sure if he should try that given that he was responsible for her distress. He realized he'd pulled a sheathed dagger from his boot only because he watched his hands put it on her knees.

"Am I to use this on you?" she croaked, putting her hands over his knife.

"You might want to." He cleared his throat. "I think," he began slowly, "that before you start with your questions, I should perhaps ask you one or two of my own."

"Why?"

"Let me ask them, then you'll see why." He looked down at his dirk for a moment or two, then back up at her. "If you thought you had a choice between dying and living, what would you choose?"

"Life," she said without hesitation.

"If it meant leaving Artane?"

"Life, still."

"Leaving your parents?"

She looked at him searchingly. "Why do you ask that?"

"Because," he said slowly, then he had to take a deep breath. "Because I made choices for you. Choices that cannot be undone. I'm afraid they may be ones you won't care for."

"To save my life?"

He nodded solemnly.

She considered for a moment or two, then sat back, as if she pushed herself away from the topic at hand. She trailed her fingers over the hilt of his dagger. "Where was this fashioned?"

"Scotland," he said quietly.

"I see."

And so did he. She wasn't making a firm retreat; she was regrouping for another assault.

"And someone made this blade specifically for you?" she asked.

He nodded. "I'm very particular about my weapons. Not that you would know it judging by what I created at Artane."

She almost smiled. "As you said, you are not a smith, though Master Godric was happy enough with your efforts." She studied him for a moment or two. "You are a puzzle, Zachary Smith. I think I would like the answers to you."

"I'll give them to you, but they are not easy answers."

"Have they aught to do with this blade?"

He nodded because he supposed that was as good a place as any to start. There was nothing like a little context to really put time traveling into perspective. He could hardly believe he was about to do the like for the woman sitting in front of him, a woman who was hundreds of years out of her time without any hope of ever seeing her family again. Unfortunately, he had no choice.

He took a deep breath and dove in. "A very skilled blacksmith in Edinburgh made that dirk for me," he said. "Actually, he made the pair of daggers I always wear. His grandson, whom I encountered in the same forge fifty years later, made me the Claymore I keep in my brother-in-law Jamie's hall. One of his descendants still makes blades in Edinburgh and I visit him periodically just to see what he has on the fire. He doesn't know the history of these dirks, though. I think the truth would be too much for him to bear."

She blinked in surprise. "How is it possible to know so many generations of men?"

"It's possible," he said seriously, "because it is possible to move from century to century—through gates that lead from one time to another. As if you'd walked from a chamber out into a passageway, for example."

She pushed herself so hard against the back of her chair that she would have tipped it if it hadn't been so well balanced. She stared at him in horror. "You're mad."

He looked at her with as much earnestness as he could muster. "I know this is difficult to believe. I wouldn't have believed it either if I hadn't lived through it myself."

She wasn't buying what he was selling. She looked over her shoulder as if she calculated the distance between her and the front door so she could make a break for it before he said anything else.

"Mary," he said quickly, "have I ever hurt you?"

She looked back at him in surprise. "Of course not."

"Lied to you?"

She let out her breath slowly and seemed to relax a bit. "I can't say that you've been overly forthcoming about your past or where you intended to go in the . . . future." She stopped abruptly. "Is this why?"

He nodded gingerly.

She considered for a moment or two in silence, then began to frown. "Go on, though I'm not sure I'll believe you."

He almost smiled. The woman was, as he had noted many times in the past, formidable.

"I won't lie to you, if that makes it all any more palatable. You see, almost a month ago, I had come to Artane—"

"My father's keep?"

"Your father's keep, aye, but as it stands in the Year of Our Lord's Grace 2006. I had come from London to do work for the second son of the current lord of Artane and was a guest in his house. I was poking around in a chamber that had been your mother's solar when I walked through a doorway and found myself in the year 1258." He paused, but she wasn't either running or drawing his dagger so he assumed he was safe to continue. "There are these gates from one century to another scattered all over England and Scotland. One of them apparently lies in your mother's solar door."

Her frown deepened. "More."

He had to close his eyes briefly. He'd heard her father say that in precisely that way for days. More energy, more skill, more devotion to the blade. *More*, until there was no more to give, then yet *more* dredged up from places inside himself he hadn't known existed. He imagined Mary was, in her own way, having to do the same thing at the moment.

He thought he might have to excuse himself eventually and fall apart where she wouldn't have to watch.

"All right, more," he agreed. "For good or ill, this isn't the first time I've traveled to a different time. My brother-in-law Jamie and I have been many places over the past several years, trying to keep ourselves out of events that didn't pertain to us. That's the reason I had to come home as quickly as possible. Actually, partly because I had a life here, but mostly because I couldn't interfere in *your* life there. Inserting myself into your world would have been like taking, well, a piece of fabric and inserting a thread where it didn't belong. It might not have mattered immediately, but in time the thread would have added so much that it would have ruined the pattern."

He listened to Jamie's standard time-travel lecture coming out of his own mouth and thought he should perhaps go over to the wall and bang his head against it until good sense returned. What next? Was he going to start quoting his father soon? He could just imagine the football analogies that his dad would have applied to his current situation. *Don't call a time-out, son, just drop back and go for the Hail Mary. Whatever you do, don't punt.*

His dad, he was quite sure, had never been facing a medieval noblewoman who had been dragged out of her life and plunked down in a cottage whose entirety was just slightly bigger than her former bedroom.

"That is why you stopped by my mother's door so often?" Mary asked quietly.

Zachary dragged his mind back to the matter at hand. "Aye," he said, "though it didn't seem to want to open for me again. I wasn't worried. There are many gates and fortunately Jamie knows them all."

Well, that wasn't exactly true. Jamie knew the ones he'd already used, which were more numerous than Elizabeth had any idea about. He was also firmly convinced there were always more to be found, but that was another topic for another day.

"So," Mary said slowly, "when you said you were going home, what you were doing in truth was looking for another of these gates?"

He nodded.

"Why did you leave so abruptly the last time?"

That was the question he didn't particularly want to answer, but he supposed it was the most important one.

"Because," he said seriously, "I had remembered something I'd read in the solar of the Artane in the future." He had to pause until he thought he could spit out the next part without emotion. "I remembered that I knew the death date of one of Artane's early women."

"Who?"

"Maryanne."

She blanched. She looked at him, then shook her head. "Impossible."

"I thought so, too, at first, but—"

"That's when you borrowed a horse from my father and fled?" she managed. "Instead of telling me?"

"I *couldn't* tell you. I was caught between watching you die and knowing that I couldn't change history by preventing your death. Changing the past changes the future. If I had tried to save your life and you had lived out the rest of your life having children where you weren't supposed to, watching grandchildren come where there had been none before—" He broke off and had to take a steadying breath. "I couldn't stay and watch something happen to you, but I couldn't stay to stop it."

"So you ran."

"I ran."

"But you returned."

He smiled, though he supposed it had been a rather sick one. "For all the good it did. Styrr succeeded in poisoning you, just as you'd feared, and I spent the day watching you fade." He paused until he thought he could manage the rest. "I knew there was only one hope to save your life. I told your father what I planned. He and your mother agreed it was worth the risk, since remaining in 1258 would mean certain death for you." He paused. "And so, I brought you to my time."

"The Year of Our Lord's Grace 2006."

He nodded.

"And I can't go back."

He looked at her hands because he couldn't look at her face. "You could try, I suppose, but I can guarantee the experience will be terrible. You would either arrive before you died, in which case there would be two of you wandering around where there should be only one, or you would arrive after they had buried you, they would think you were a witch, and probably burn you and your parents both."

She put her face in her hands.

He didn't dare touch her, but he did take his knife back and

put it in his boot. He wished desperately for something soothing to say, but there was nothing. Mary would either come to
grips with what he'd done, or she wouldn't. He would have
given anything to have helped her, but there was only so much
he could do. She would have to do the rest.

He could only hope she wouldn't hate him after she'd managed it.

Time passed.

Finally, she dropped her hands into her lap. But she didn't
look at him. She was taking deep breaths, as if she wanted to
avoid making untoward noises.

"Do you want to rest a little?" he asked, finally.

She nodded.

He helped her up, then walked her over to Moraig's bed to
lie down. He hesitated, then sat down in the chair Sunny had
drawn up beside the bed. He watched Mary close her eyes.

He wasn't sure she slept.

He knew he didn't hold out any hope for it himself anytime
soon.

Chapter 22

Mary sat up on her bed, ignoring the desire to lie back down and remain there for the whole of the day. It wasn't as if she would have managed to sleep anyway. Her mind was so full of impossible things that she divided her time between either catching her breath or trying to keep from weeping.

And she never wept.

Well, she'd wept in Zachary's arms on the shore, and she'd been powerfully tempted the day before, but that wasn't her usual manner of conducting her life. She certainly had no intention of displaying such a weakness again.

Though she supposed she might have been entitled to such a display, given the events of the previous day.

She had managed to pass through yesterday's afternoon by feigning sleep. She'd spent the evening in the company of the women of Zachary's family whilst he hovered at the edge of their talk, silent and grim. His sisters, by marriage or not, had fed her, bathed her, then put her to bed in something called flannel jammies. She found them to be marvelously soft and quite comfortable, with the added benefit of not being skirts so she might have hopped on a horse and ridden off if she'd cared to.

'Twas possible she had slept occasionally during the night,

but she was quite sure Zachary hadn't. He had lain down on the floor next to her bed, but every time she'd leaned over to peer down at him, his eyes had been open.

She knew he grieved for her.

She had woken a few minutes ago to find him gone, though she supposed he hadn't gone far. He felt responsible for her. He was that sort of man. A lovely, chivalrous, responsible sort of man.

She looked to her right at the fire he had no doubt made for her comfort and thought about what he'd said to her the day before.

The Future?

It seemed nothing more than something a minstrel would have set to music with the hope that his lord wouldn't find it so ridiculous that no supper would be forthcoming after the song. But why would Zachary lie to her?

He wouldn't because he hadn't ever lied to her in the past and could have no reason to begin the practice presently. She had called him mad, but he'd looked in full possession of his wits.

Perhaps she should have considered more seriously before how strange his clothing had been, and how lacking in modern-day skills he'd been. Or how little like a peasant he'd appeared. Or how strangely he had pronounced so many words and how quickly he'd learned how to say them properly. A highly educated, very well-fashioned, exceptionally handsome smith who couldn't shoe a horse, had fighting abilities her cousins salivated over, and couldn't wait to be somewhere he hadn't been willing to talk about.

She supposed 'twas possible that everything he'd said had been the truth, but she could scarce believe it. The Year of Our Lord's Grace 2006?

And she was now there with no way to return home.

She pushed herself to her feet, away from thoughts that were too uncomfortable to face. She gained the hearth, but had to lean there until the floor stopped heaving beneath her feet and she was certain she could remain upright. She thought she might attempt to cross the floor to the kitchens. Perhaps she would investigate less troubling things for the moment and see if a distraction didn't soothe her.

There were bowls and platters and cups that were made of a glass so fine, she hardly dared touch them. She did anyway and was surprised at their chill. She touched everything else, including the cold, smooth box of a very strange green color. She didn't open anything though, not knowing how it might react to being invaded.

She left the kitchens and staggered to the garderobe. She caught her balance on the wall and suddenly the chamber was filled with light. She would have gasped if she hadn't been so winded. She looked at the wall and saw some sort of small, flat box under her hand. There seemed to be a moveable bit of some sort of something on it. She took her courage in hand and pushed on the upper half of it.

The lights were extinguished. She pushed down and the lights lit themselves again.

Magic, or Future marvel?

She supposed it could be nothing but the latter. By the time she had satisfied herself with that miracle, she felt ready to take on other things. The waterfall from the polished steel spout she had already seen, as well as the polished mirror that had frightened her so badly the day before. She was also accustomed to the seat that served as a very luxurious and tidy chamber pot. It was a vast improvement over her father's garderobe, that much she could say.

She had to sit on the edge of the bathing tub for a moment and rest. Thinking on her parents was still an ache in her chest that she wasn't sure she would ever find a way to assuage.

Her parents and the lads, as well. No matter how daft they had driven her, she would miss Jackson and Thaddeus and Connor. And the little twins. And perhaps Parsival most of all, Frenchman though he might have been. To think she would never see them again . . .

She decided abruptly that 'twas best she not think on it. Not yet. Not until she'd had a chance to find her balance for a bit.

She looked up at the window in the ceiling above her. It seemed a strange place for it, but Sunshine had told her that Zachary had put it in. Indeed, he had designed the entire chamber she was in currently. *The most luxurious surroundings a witch could possibly wish for,* Sunny had said with a deep smile, as if she was terribly fond of Zachary. The window had been put in the ceiling to give light to a place that might have otherwise been too covered in shadows.

Much as Zachary had done when he had walked into her life

unannounced and shown her how much more lovely her life could be with him than with Geoffrey of Styrr.

The life that, inexplicably, she now had.

She considered Zachary's actions a bit more. Now that she looked at them knowing who he was and when he came from, she could understand why he had done what he had. She could see why he had been so anxious to return home and why he had made such an effort not to change the events that had transpired in the keep.

And likely why he hadn't done damage to Styrr in the courtyard that day when Styrr had been trying to belittle him.

Of course, there was the wound to Jackson's pride to consider, but perhaps that couldn't have been helped. Indeed, she supposed it might have done her cousin a bit of good to be humbled by someone besides her father or Kendrick.

She could now also understand why Zachary hadn't been willing to stay even after she'd asked. How could he have, when his home had been so very far away? At least he had held her as if he never wanted to let her go. Perhaps he hadn't wanted to let her go. The fact that he'd troubled himself to endure her father's instruction in the lists to ensure that she wasn't forced to wed Styrr said something about at least his sense of duty toward her, didn't it?

Because I want her for myself.

His words in her father's solar came back to her as if he'd just spoken them aloud. That hadn't been possible then. But now things were different. She was in his time and had no one to turn to but him.

Was it possible he merely felt a sense of obligation where she was concerned?

She climbed to her feet and went to fetch her clothes that Elizabeth had left sitting on a little stool near the wall before she thought on that, either. She dressed, then had to sit again until her head stopped spinning. She finally rose, swayed, then forced her legs to steady themselves beneath her. She had no more time for thinking. The Future, *her* future was upon her and she could do nothing but rise to the challenge of meeting it.

She studiously ignored the fact that she almost collapsed twice before she gained the front door to the cottage.

She looked at the cloaks hanging there by that door and chose a likely one. It fit strangely, but she made do. It fastened in the front with tiny little metal teeth, but mastering it would take time and she had no more time to spare, so she made do there as well.

She walked outside and stopped just under the eaves of the house. It took only a moment for her to find Zachary. He was standing under one of the mighty trees that flanked the path that she could see wound off through the woods. If she hadn't known better, she would have thought him a statue. He was so desperately handsome and so terribly solemn that she half wondered if he had been overcome by all that he carried on his shoulders. She couldn't say she had reacted very well the day before to the tidings he'd given her, though she imagined he hadn't expected anything else.

He was wearing the clothing her sire had given him. It occurred to her suddenly that he was doing so for her comfort, not his own.

By the saints, he was a man without peer.

She leaned back against the side of the house and simply drank in the sight of him. His sister and sisters-in-law loved him; that was obvious. They had sung his praises without hesitation, something she had been willing to listen to without reservation. It had made her wonder, with a rather unpleasant feeling actually, if she might be looking in a direction she shouldn't. She had asked Sunshine casually if Zachary had many women chasing after him.

Dozens, Sunshine had said without hesitation. *But none he's ever loved.*

Mary looked down at her hands. Well, at least she'd bathed away most of the stable leavings from under her fingernails. She'd also washed her hair. And she was the daughter of Robin de Piaget.

Not that that meant much in 2006, likely.

She realized that Zachary was looking at her. She smiled. Or, she attempted to smile, rather. She didn't think it had gone very well. He pushed away from his tree and walked up the path toward her. She forgot, from time to time, how tall he was, or how broad through the shoulders. It wasn't that she wasn't accustomed to well-built men. She was just very unaccustomed to one making her feel very fragile and delicate. And in need of a great amount of chivalry.

"Maryanne," he said gravely. "How are you?"

She was tempted to blurt out the truth, that she was terrified and wanted nothing more than to throw herself in his arms and hide there until she felt more herself. But she was her father's daughter and he would have found such a lack of courage—even given the difficulties of her situation—to be unacceptable. She put her shoulders back and lifted her chin.

"I'm ready to assault this new world." She swayed as she said it, but Zachary didn't seem to notice.

Then again, he very casually reached out and put his hand on her arm to steady her, so perhaps he noticed more than he let on.

"Then it's fortunate that Jamie brought a horse for you this morning."

"Did he?" she asked, feeling pleased. That was indeed something solid and familiar. "Does it need breaking?"

"It needs to be put out to pasture," Zachary said dryly, "but Jamie didn't intend it to be an insult. He thought you might like to ride in a few days and that a gentler mount might suit your still-healing condition."

"But I'm ready today."

He released her arm and she swayed again. She tried to take hold of herself and will her form to shake off the lingering malaise, but she was disappointed to find that wishes were, as her aunt Jennifer was wont to say, not fishes.

She frowned thoughtfully. Her aunt had had several very odd sayings. Spoken in a rather garbled echo of the peasant's English. She hadn't thought much about them at the time, but she began to wonder about them now. In fact, she found there were several things she wondered about.

Odd that those things seemed to center themselves around her uncle Nicholas's trunk, the innards of which she, Theo, and Samuel had only had a single brief glimpse. They'd managed to finger a pair of very magical-looking gray boxes, admire strings of a marvelous stuff attached to those boxes, and turn the pages of a handful of manuscripts in a language neither she nor the twins had had the time to decipher.

They had also managed a look at a map marking several strange and very mysterious locales before they'd been forced to bolt from the solar and feign business in another part of the keep. She had been, at the time, far too old to engage in such investigations, but it had been Theo and Samuel to goad her into it, so perhaps she could be forgiven. They had been convinced for a time afterward that Nicholas was a warlock, but perhaps they could have been forgiven for that as well.

"I think, Maryanne, that you should go back inside—"

"Nay," she said quickly, focusing on Zachary, "I am well. I need air."

He frowned, but she returned the frown. She even managed to get her arms folded over her chest, lest he think that she might be less fierce than she should have been.

He studied her gravely for a moment or two, then carefully reached out and tucked a lock of hair behind her ear. He smiled at her, but his smile faded rather quickly.

She shook her head before he could begin what she was certain would be a conversation about things that were difficult. If she'd spoken about any of it, she would have broken her own vow and begun to weep. As it was, she could still scarce restrain herself from throwing herself into his arms and begging him to hold her and keep her safe.

'Twas appalling, truly.

He smiled slightly, as if he understood what she hadn't said. "All right," he said softly, "we'll go. Let me bank the fire first."

She leaned against the door frame as he did so, then walked with him around the house. There was a very small but adequate stall there, a stall inhabited by the largest horse she'd ever seen. Zachary put reins on him, then backed him out of the stall. The beast looked as if he would have liked nothing better than to pass the coming hour grazing, but he didn't argue when Zachary boosted her up onto his back. Zachary paused, then handed her the reins.

"Mary—"

"Zachary, please," she interrupted quickly. "Please just let us take this poor beast and give him a bit of exercise. The rest will still be awaiting us later."

Some of the tension seemed to go out of him. "You're probably right."

She waited, but he made no move. "Are you not riding with me?"

"I'm waiting for you to go find a useful tree stump. I don't think I can get myself up onto this old lad's back without help."

She did so, then soon found herself with Zachary's arms around her.

"You steer," he said. "I'll nap."

She wondered at first if he held on to her so tightly because he truly intended to sleep and didn't want to fall off, but she knew he was an excellent rider. She was tempted to believe that he truly *wanted* to have his arms around her, but that seemed a complicated way to do what he simply could have done any time he cared to.

Unless he thought he couldn't.

She didn't dare broach the subject with him. There she was, hundreds of years out of her own time, in a land where she had no kin, no gold, nothing but what she was wearing, and she was left with no choice but to rely on the kindness of a man who owed her nothing at all.

A bit like his situation in her time, actually.

"You're distracted."

She looked over her shoulder at him. "I'll try not to lose us."

"I wouldn't worry about that given that Galloping Gus is in charge."

She laughed a little in spite of herself. "Is that his name?"

"I'm sure he wore it well a decade ago." He pointed to his left. "Jamie's is down the meadow. You'll see the castle soon enough. Well, you'll see it eventually. I think we could probably walk there on our own faster than Gus will take us, but maybe we'll try that tomorrow. Wake me when we arrive."

"You aren't going to sleep in truth, are you?"

He rested his chin on her shoulder. "Will you let me fall off if I do?"

"Nay," she said quietly.

He tightened his arms around her briefly. "Then I'll close my eyes for a bit. Let me know if you don't feel well and I'll keep *you* from falling off."

Mary nodded and clicked at Gus, because she wouldn't be unhappy to see a proper castle, but mostly because she was in Zachary's arms—after a fashion—and she had no desire to give him a reason to release her.

As time passed, she realized how much she had to thank James MacLeod for. With every enormous but weary footfall of the horse, she felt more herself. Seeing a perfectly lovely castle in the distance was even more reassuring. The day was lovely, Zachary's arms were comforting, and if she didn't think about it, her heart didn't hurt her as much as it had the night before. There were things about her future that weren't settled, but she could wait. Perhaps it was enough to simply survive the day.

Half an hour later, they were riding into the courtyard of a grim-looking Scottish castle. She brought Gus to a halt, then looked up at the fortress in front of her. And as she looked, something occurred to her that she hadn't considered until that moment.

That map she and the twins had seen had been signed by a James MacLeod.

She was now sitting in front of the ancestral home of a James MacLeod.

She thought back to the little red dots that had been scattered over Scotland, for the most part, but a few in England as well. There had been a large dot near Falconberg and an equally substantial one placed near Artane. She wondered why her uncle Nicholas would have had such a map in his possession, a map made by a man named James MacLeod who was lord of the keep she was sitting in front of at present.

"Zachary?"

"Aye?"

"Does your brother-in-law make maps?"

"Jamie? Aye, he dabbles in it." He swung down off Gus, then looked up at her. "Why do you ask?"

"Because I think I saw one of his maps in my uncle Nicholas's trunk."

He smiled faintly. "I wouldn't be surprised."

"Wouldn't you?" she asked, feeling very surprised indeed. "How would it have gotten there, do you suppose?"

"I imagine it was a wedding present for your aunt."

She felt her mouth fall open. "I beg your pardon?"

"Let me tell you when you're less likely to bolt."

He held up his hands for her. She allowed him to help her down off her horse because, she realized with a start, she was growing accustomed to the little bits of chivalry he seemed to offer without any thought. She didn't protest as he saw her seated on the steps leading up to Jamie's great hall. She didn't question him as he removed Gus's bridle and sent him off with a friendly pat on the rump. She waited as he sat down next to her, then merely watched him as he watched Gus wander off a handful of paces to give attention to a particularly lush patch of edibles. He finally sighed and looked at her.

"This won't be easy, either."

"I'm prepared for the worst."

He smiled, the same sort of affectionate smile she would have had from any number of cousins. It was particularly cheering.

"I imagine you probably are. As for the other, you could say that we have an interesting genealogy here in Scotland." He clasped his hands round his knee and frowned, as if he prepared to proffer something of great import. "As it happens, Jamie is wed to my sister, Elizabeth, which you already know. Jamie's great-granddaughter—"

"Is he *that* old?" she asked in surprise.

"He was born in 1278."

"Oh," she managed, though there was little sound to the word.

"I won't give you all the particulars of *that* tale now," he offered with a quick smile, "simply because I'm certain Jamie would enjoy telling you all about it when you can stomach it. Suffice it to say that Jamie's great-granddaughter Iolanthe married Thomas McKinnon. Thomas has a younger sister, Victoria, who married a Scot, and a yet younger sister, Megan, who married, well, I'll tell you who she married later. His youngest sister is named—"

"Jennifer?" she interrupted in surprise.

"Jennifer," he agreed. "She walked through a time gate near Ledenham Abbey—a gate that was subsequently destroyed—and found herself falling in love and marrying the lord of Wyckham."

She blinked. "My *aunt* is from the Future?"

He nodded with a faint smile.

"And you didn't say anything?" she asked incredulously. She didn't wait for an answer, for she could imagine what it would be and how much it would have to do with not poking holes in the fabric of time. "Does my uncle know? Do my *cousins* know?" She would have pushed herself to her feet and begun to pace, but she didn't think she would manage it. She turned to face him. "No wonder there were so many strange and marvelous things in his trunk."

"Did Theo and Sam find the key?" he asked with twinkling eyes.

"Of course. After my brother Kendrick showed them where to look." She frowned at him. "Now you will tell me that you know her, won't you?"

"I met her briefly when she came to visit Jamie," he conceded. "She was very lovely and very talented. I heard her play a time or two. But then I imagine you have, too."

Mary looked out over Jamie's courtyard. "I can scarce believe it."

"There are many things in this world that defy belief."

She considered the complete improbability of it for several minutes, then looked at Zachary again. "I think she is happy with her life."

He hesitated, then reached out and smoothed his hand over her hair, just once. "I imagine there were times that were difficult for her, given that she was living in a day not her own. But maybe having someone to love made the difference."

He started to say something else, then jumped up with a curse.

"Gus is headed for Beth's petunias. I won't live to see dinner if I don't stop him. And there is Jamie coming from the lists. Hang on and I'll introduce you." He put his hand on her head briefly, then strode off to rescue his sister's flowers.

Mary watched him go and thought about things she hadn't before. About maps, and trunks, and men who adored their wives who hadn't been born in their century.

Perhaps more things were possible than she'd believed before.

Several hours later, she was sitting in Moraig MacLeod's little house. The fire was burning brightly, she'd had an entire mugful of hot cocoa—something Madelyn said she shouldn't admit to Sunshine—and Zachary Smith was reading her *The Canterbury Tales* in the appropriate vernacular.

She set her cup on the floor and looked back over her first full day in the Future. She had been showered with things that made her feel as if she hadn't lost very much. She'd had a horse to ride, good conversation, and now an evening with entertainment she could understand.

And it was all Zachary's doing.

She watched him as he read until the pucker between his eyebrows became fierce enough to indicate serious pains in his head. She took the book away and finished the current tale herself. The letters were fashioned strangely, but it didn't take long to learn to make them out. The tales were surely the most amusing thing she'd heard in quite some time.

She looked up finally to find Zachary watching her. He was resting his elbow on the arm of the chair and his chin on his fist. His expression was one she'd seen before. It was the look men wore when they came to her father wanting his sword skill but supposing they wouldn't make it past his gates to even ask for it.

She wondered what it was Zachary wanted.

"Did you not care for the tale?" she asked.

"It was delightful. I was just watching you and pondering imponderables."

"And what would those be?"

He smiled again, a slightly bemused smile. "I was thinking that it was very strange to be sitting next to the most beautiful woman I've ever seen while she reads a book that was written a hundred years after she was born but seven hundred years before *I* was born."

"Am I that?" she asked in surprise.

"That old?" he asked.

She started to gape at him, but realized he was teasing her. "That beautiful, you lout."

He smiled. "Aye, you are." He continued to watch her, but his smile faded. "How are you, Maryanne?"

She knew what he was asking, and had to take a deep breath before she spoke. "Better than this morning."

He didn't reach for her hand and she couldn't bring herself to reach for his. She wanted to tell him that a life with him was far preferable to death, but if he couldn't remember she'd been willing to trade her horses for chickens and swine, then . . . well, perhaps he wasn't sure how he felt about her now they were in his time.

And she couldn't bring herself to ask him for the truth of it.

A bell ringing made her jump. Zachary stood up and reached for something sitting on the mantel. He smiled at her briefly.

"Excuse me."

She watched him put something to his ear and begin a conversation in a language that sounded a bit like the peasant's English, only this was spoken with a much different cadence. It sounded, as it happened, quite a bit like those strange sayings her aunt was wont to mutter to herself when she thought no one was listening.

Hells bells. You'd better do it in a New York minute, buster. Nicky, do the Future-speak thing again.

Mary paused. Future-speak?

She looked at Zachary, who was having a very earnest conversation with a little flat box pressed to his ear. She was tempted to think he'd just lost all his wits, but she was now in the Future and she supposed conversations with no one in particular might just be the usual business.

Zachary sighed and pushed something on that little box, then held it in both his hands and looked at her.

"I'm afraid I have a little problem," he said slowly. "I need to go to England in the morning. I don't want to leave you here by yourself, but I'm not sure you're ready to travel that far yet."

She blinked. "England? Will you ride the whole way?"

"In a manner of speaking." He paused, then looked at her seriously. "I don't want to leave."

She hardly dared hope he was speaking of more than just his upcoming journey. "I don't want you to go."

He dragged his hand through his hair, then set his little box up on the mantel. He walked over and squatted down in front of her. He hesitated, then reached for her hands. "I want you to have time, Maryanne," he said seriously, "before you have to make any decisions."

She was tempted to tell him that her decisions were made, but she supposed there would be time enough for that in the future. So she only nodded solemnly.

He bent his head and kissed her hands. "Let me get a few things organized, then I'll make you another mug of Sunny's tea before bed."

She nodded and watched him as he paced in front of the fire while speaking again into that little box of his. Perhaps a bit of time alone would do her a goodly service. She would take the time to heal, ride Gus, who had been generous enough to carry them back to Moraig's, and see what of Zachary's world she could master.

Many things could happen in a handful of days, as she could readily attest.

Chapter 23

Zachary stood just inside Moraig's small house early the next morning and wondered if he were making an enormous mistake. Mary was better than she had been the day before, but still far from whole. He'd arranged for two of his three fairy godsisters to sit with her in shifts, and he supposed she wouldn't do herself in with only Moraig's to explore, but still he was uneasy. She might run afoul of any number of deadly future marvels or, heaven help him, step over Moraig's threshold and find herself in a century she didn't recognize, armed with nothing but her beautiful face and her ability to take any horse and ride it like the wind.

Unfortunately, he didn't have much choice but to leave her to her own devices for a bit. Apparently the workers at Wyckham's little cottage were convinced they'd been overrun by ghosts and had gone on strike. Gideon was in London and of no help—not that it was his job to handle that sort of thing anyway. Obviously he was going to have to babysit the site himself for a few days until any untoward visitors had been warned off. He actually suspected the offender was Hugh McKinnon, wanting to try his hand at a few interesting-looking power tools, but he didn't have any proof. Yet.

He looked at Mary seriously. "I think you would be better off staying with Jamie and Elizabeth," he said, again.

"I will be well," she insisted, also not for the first time. "You left me a winter's worth of wood chopped by the side of the house, food enough to feed a score of souls, and a very large horse to ride off on should it be required. What else do I need?"

Me, he almost said, but he refrained. They could have that conversation, if she was willing to have that conversation, when he returned. He hesitated, then cast all caution to the wind. He reached out and pulled her into his arms. He tried to hold her gently, but he thought he might have heard something pop. He buried his face in her waterfall of dark hair and tried not to shudder. If something happened to her . . . well, it didn't bear thinking on.

"You have my cell number," he said.

"Aye."

"And you remember how to use the phone Jamie loaned you."

"Aye."

"And you won't set yourself on fire—"

She laughed. "Zachary, I think I can manage the wonders of your Future for a handful of days."

He pulled back only far enough to look at her. "There might be ghosts."

"I'll ignore them."

"Lock the door. Always."

She looked up at him. "Are you truly this concerned about me?"

He closed his eyes and pulled her close again. He was trying very hard not to push her, not to put pressure on her, not to leave her feeling obligated to have any feelings for him. That was difficult because he was, in reality, her only lifeline in the future. Even the people who surrounded her were there because of him.

He sighed deeply. "Aye, I am truly this concerned about you. Please be careful and please, *please* don't lose yourself."

"Would you search for me?"

"As long as it took, through every century necessary."

"And I would wait for you, as long as it took."

He held her in silence for another handful of minutes, then

pulled away. He put on his coat, slung his backpack over his shoulder, then opened the door and took her hand. He walked outside with her—then came to an abrupt halt. He'd intended to hike to Patrick's and pick up his brother-in-law's little runabout to take to Artane. But now he realized that he wasn't going to have to.

There, in front of him, sat a brand-spanking-new, jet-black Range Rover.

He handed Mary his backpack almost without thinking, then walked over to the car in a daze. The keys were in the door.

He backed up until he was standing next to Mary again.

"What is this?" she asked.

"Something I think I'm going to kill someone for," he said, after he'd taken a deep, cleansing breath.

She looked up at him in surprise. "Why?"

"Because I don't like charity."

She lifted her eyebrows briefly, then went inside for her shoes. Zachary smiled at the picture she soon made in a pair of Madelyn's MacLeod-dress-plaid pajamas and medieval boots, then he began speculating on potential offenders.

Patrick wouldn't have dropped a car on his front stoop if he'd had a sword to his throat. Jamie was a reasonable suspect, but even he had heard enough protests over the years to know not to offer compensation where there was no labor involved first. That left only one person, someone who certainly should have known better. He cursed, then dialed. The phone only rang twice.

"Cameron," came the answer in a brisk, businesslike tone.

"Would you like to tell me, my lord, why it is you forgot one of your cars in front of my doorway this morning?"

"I didn't forget anything," Cameron said smoothly. "I knew exactly what I was doing when I plunked down my hard-earned sterling for that lovely beast, then paid yet more of my hard-earned sterling to one of my greedy cousins so he would put it in your name and deliver it to your current roost."

Zachary blew out his breath in frustration. "Damn it, Cam, I don't want your charity."

"And I can't afford the face of the Cameron/Artane Trust driving around in something that's going to pollute work sites."

Zachary growled before he could stop himself. "I'll buy my own car, thank you very much."

"I'm not asking you to wear a suit, now am I? I'm just asking you to look like a filthy rich architect so I won't have clients calling me and asking if you're trustworthy."

"Have you had clients call you?" Zachary asked in surprise.

"None but that Michael Smythe-Gordon, but he's a nutter, not a client. I'm proactively avoiding anything from anyone else. And you will notice that I didn't buy you a Ferrari."

Zachary dragged his hand through his hair. "I'll pay you back."

"You'll pay me back by splashing my name all over the glorious projects you're taking away from the Lambeth Group. That's enough."

Zachary almost smiled. "What did Garrett ever do to you?"

"He made me raise your fee so high I can hardly put fuel in my Gulfstream, that's what he did," Cameron grumbled. "We haggled over it for a solid fortnight before he was willing to let you go. You know he was going to offer you a partnership, don't you?"

"No," Zachary said, stunned, "I didn't."

"You would have had to wear a suit."

"I think I'll stick with you."

"I thought you might. And if this makes it more palatable for you, consider the car your fee for designing the leisure center last year when you really didn't have time."

"I've already been paid for that."

"Bollocks," Cameron said with a snort. "You did it for the price of a decent meal. Take the car, Zach, and be grateful that your lady will now be safe when you travel. You could also consider getting on the road very soon. I think you have projects to see to."

"I'm heading south this morning."

"Comfortably, I should think. You're welcome."

Zachary smiled. "Thank you. And I do own a suit, you know."

"I'll believe that when I see it," Cameron said. "Hope you have money for petrol. I don't think Derrick filled it up for you. I'm assuming he left you the keys."

"He was on his best behavior, apparently."

Cameron only laughed. "I daresay. Watch out for overzealous traffic officers. I'm not responsible for your points when

Hamish Fergusson deigns to hop out from behind whatever bush he's currently claiming. Cheers."

Zachary hung up and sighed deeply. He picked up his gear and went to put it in the back of something he could have afforded for himself but never would have bought. It would have put too hefty a dent in his savings. But given that he was saving for a very specific thing, perhaps the car was a blessing in disguise.

And Cameron did have a point. He had designed a project for Cameron and Jamie the year before and he'd done it for dinner at the pub. Perhaps things shook out the way they were supposed to in the end.

He could hope.

He walked around to the front of the car to find Mary peering into the headlights. He leaned against the fender and looked at her.

"Well?"

"Does it go fast?"

"Very."

She straightened. "Then you'll be back that much sooner."

She sounded like that was a good thing. He looked at her for a moment in silence, then reached out and gathered her into his arms.

"I'll call you tonight when I get to Artane."

She nodded.

He paused, then took her face in his hands. He kissed her on each cheek, as close to her mouth as he dared. He lifted his head and looked at her, but her eyes were closed and she had definitely trembled. He hugged her once more, then forced himself to pull away.

"Go back inside if you would, love, and let me make sure you get into the right century."

She nodded, then walked back unsteadily to Moraig's doorway. She stepped over the threshold, then turned to face him.

"Content?"

Well, he would have been if he'd been walking back inside the house with her, but since he couldn't, he would content himself with seeing the proper century still lurking inside Moraig's house. He looked at her for another long moment, then walked around the car and got in. He spared a brief moment to enjoy the new-car smell, then backed up.

He waved, had a wave in return, and drove off down the bumpy road past Patrick and Madelyn's hall, past the turnoff to Jamie's, all the way to where the private road hooked into the main road that wound through the village. And he hoped again he wasn't making a terrible mistake. He had a sick sort of feeling in his gut, as if he were proceeding down a path that was lined by unpleasant things that he couldn't see yet, but would sooner than he cared for.

He took a deep breath, chalked the unease up to lack of sleep, and concentrated on getting himself to England in one piece.

It should have been a pleasant trip south. The Range Rover was a dream to drive compared to anything else he'd owned over the past ten years, and he had work in front of him that he knew he would be able to do quickly and well. Mary had a cell phone and Elizabeth and Madelyn to look after her. As long as nothing untoward happened to her, she would be fine.

He couldn't help worrying about what those untoward things might be. He hadn't talked Robin of Artane into letting him bring his only daughter forward just so she could electrocute herself on a toaster.

He was halfway to Edinburgh from Inverness when his phone rang. He picked up immediately, fearing the worst.

"What?"

Gideon de Piaget laughed. "Aren't you the professional one today?"

"I was expecting someone else," Zachary said with an uncomfortable laugh. "Sorry. Hello, Lord Gideon. What may I do to serve you today, my lord?"

"That's better," Gideon said, sounding as if he were suppressing the impulse to purr. "I do so enjoy being deferred to as often as possible."

"I'm hanging up now."

Gideon laughed. "Don't until I wring a favor out of you. I'm running a little late out of London and I was wondering if you'd be willing to drop by Seakirk on your way to Artane and pick up papers Seakirk signed for me. Things to do with the cottage, you know."

"I'd love to." Anything he could do to butter up the lord of

Seakirk so he could potentially relieve the man of one of his properties, he would happily do.

"All right, then. I'll see you tonight at home, will I?"

"I'll be there with bells on."

"Oh, I hope not," Gideon said with a laugh as he hung up.

Zachary spared a thought for the fact that he was making a trip in a day that would have taken him two weeks on horseback in a different century.

The twenty-first century did have its advantages.

Four hours later, he was pulling up to Seakirk's outer gates. The portcullis was raised, but he didn't see anyone manning it. He continued on up the way to a set of more conventional wrought-iron gates that swung in just as effortlessly.

Spooky.

But he wasn't bothered by spooky, so he simply continued on his way, pulling to a stop in what looked like a likely spot. He got out of the car, stretched, and wished he'd stopped more than just once along the way. But he hadn't and there was no taking it back now. He limped up to the front door.

It was opened by a white-haired butler of substantial years who looked so crisp, Zachary stood a little straighter in self-defense.

"I'm Zachary Smith," Zachary said. "I'm here on an errand from Lord Blythwood to pick up papers from the earl."

"Of course you are, Master Smith," the butler intoned. "We've been expecting you."

Zachary ignored the shiver that went down his spine. Somehow, he felt as if he were about to be the main course at an otherworldly banquet of some sort. He took a deep breath. "I didn't catch your name . . ."

"'Tis Worthington, sir," the butler said. He stood back and gestured for Zachary to come inside. "Follow me, if you will."

Zachary didn't dare not. He followed the butler across a fabulously well-preserved great hall and back to stairs that led up to another floor. Everything looked so original, Zachary had to check in repeatedly to make sure he was in the right century. Either the Earl of Seakirk had more money than the Queen, or he was an absolute pain in the backside about his restorations.

Zachary liked that already about him, being something of a perfectionist himself.

Worthington paused in front of a door, then opened it and indicated that Zachary should go inside.

"Is this a family room?" Zachary asked in surprise.

"It is His Lordship's private solar," Worthington conceded.

"Isn't he hesitant to let complete strangers into it?"

"We have an excellent alarm system, sir."

Zachary studied him in silence for a minute. "Ghosts?"

Worthington almost smiled. "I've heard about you."

"I shudder to ask."

"I imagine you do," Worthington said, unperturbed. "You might enjoy the gallery to your left. A very fine collection of medieval weapons."

"Really?"

"Really," Worthington said in a perfect imitation of an American accent. He waited for Zachary to enter the solar, then pulled the door shut.

Zachary was momentarily tempted by the very comfortable-looking sofa, the remote, and the enormous flat screen dominating one wall, but he resisted admirably. There were other treasures to be admired first.

He walked over to an open doorway and found that Worthington hadn't exaggerated. There was indeed an amazing collection of medieval gear inside. He paused at the doorway, then shrugged and walked inside. Ghosts would no doubt tattle on him if he touched anything he wasn't supposed to, so he put his hands in his pockets and contented himself with the thought of just looking.

Or at least he did until he took three steps into the gallery.

There was an enormous portrait hanging over a very lovely eighteenth-century mahogany rolltop desk. Zachary stared up at it and felt for something to sit down on. There was nothing, so he sat down very hard on the floor.

It was Robin and Anne. And their children. Those were apparently Robin's sons. He was certain that was Robin's daughter. It was so startling to see a portrait of Mary with her family that he simply couldn't take it in. He sat there and gaped.

Why was that portrait hanging in the lord of Seakirk's private study?

"Worthington said I had company."

Zachary scrambled to his feet, then turned—

And came face-to-face with Robin de Piaget.

It actually took him a moment to realize it wasn't Robin he was looking at, though the man standing in front of him couldn't have looked any more like him if he'd *been* him. Well, except for his eyes. He had Anne's eyes.

"Your Lordship," Zachary managed. "I'm, um . . ."

"Zachary Smith, if reports are to believed," Seakirk said with a bit of a smirk. "Architect extraordinaire, if those same reports are correct."

"I do my best to please," Zachary said, putting his hand on Seakirk's desk to keep himself upright. He wished mightily for another turn on the floor. He was starting to feel as if that floor were pitching under his feet.

Why was Mary's picture above Seakirk's desk? More to the point, why did Seakirk look so much like Robin de Piaget?

"Yank or Scot? I can't place your accent."

"Yank," Zachary managed. "Transplanted ten years ago."

Seakirk grunted. "You look like you've just seen a ghost. And based on what I've heard, you've seen more than your share."

Zachary smiled, though it felt very strained. "Scotland is full of magic."

"So is England, I daresay."

Zachary imagined that Seakirk had seen his share of magic, but he couldn't for the life of him determine how or when. He just knew that he was positive he was looking at a man who should have died hundreds of years ago.

Kendrick de Piaget.

"Do you need a drink?" Seakirk asked suddenly.

Zachary shook his head sharply. "Sorry. I've been traveling recently. It's, um, jet lag." *Yeah, about eight hundred years' worth and believe it or not, your sister has it, too.* "If I could just get those papers Lord Blythwood left for you to sign, I'll get out of your hair."

Seakirk shot him a puzzled look, then shrugged and went to rummage around in his desk.

"That's a beautiful portrait," Zachary said, because he just couldn't keep his mouth shut.

A perennial problem, apparently.

"My family," Kendrick said absently. He produced papers, then handed them off.

Zachary took them gratefully, then followed Seakirk even more gratefully out of his solar and down the stairs.

"Oh, Kendrick, there you are!"

Zachary looked across the hall to find a woman coming out of another part of the castle. She walked across the floor and came over to lean up and kiss the lord of Seakirk briefly.

"Addy wants a ride on your horse. I told her she would have to convince you." She paused. "I didn't realize you had business."

Kendrick shook his head. "We're finished. Gen, this is Zachary Smith."

Genevieve de Piaget smiled and held out her hand. "I'm Kendrick's wife, Genevieve. You're the head of CAT, aren't you? We're thrilled with your plans for the cottage, by the way."

"That's wonderful," Zachary managed.

"I used to do restoration myself in the States," Genevieve continued, "so I was prepared to be critical. Gideon showed us your portfolio, though, and we were completely wowed. You're an American as well, aren't you?"

Zachary nodded, though he thought if he didn't get out of their hall, he might open his mouth and say something to Genevieve he shouldn't. He suspected it might be anything from, *What in the hell are you doing married to a man who died—and yes I saw it in Artane's Big Fabulous Book of Genealogy—almost eight hundred years ago?* to, *Do you realize that I have your husband's sister hidden away in Scotland and I'm beginning to think she should stay there?*

"You know," Genevieve said, slipping her hand into her husband's, "we should see what Mr. Smith can do with Wyckham. Actually, Kendrick, you should just sell it to him." She smiled. "I can tell just by looking at what he's done that he has a serious case of castle fever."

If they only knew.

"I'll see how the cottage finishes up," Kendrick said with a frown, "then we'll see how well he grovels."

Genevieve laughed. Zachary tried to laugh as well, but all he could do was eye the closest exit and wonder if it would be rude to just make a break for it.

"We'll discuss it later, Zachary," Kendrick said. "I believe I have a date with my daughter in the stables. Why she loves horses so, I can't fathom. I think 'tis best to humor her, though. You never know that she won't grow up to be a brilliant ~sewoman at some point."

Zachary nodded, because he couldn't do anything else. Yes, she would probably grow up to be a brilliant horsewoman, just like her aunt. Only she would have far more freedom than her aunt had ever enjoyed.

Only now her aunt had all the freedom in the world to do what she liked with whatever poor nag he might be able to afford for her. Assuming she was interested in his buying her a poor nag. And that had as its prerequisite her wanting to have anything at all to do with him.

He had to get out of Seakirk before he started babbling.

He shook hands all around, then walked with Kendrick to the door. He was extremely happy to get into his car that would most certainly get him out the gates without trouble and drive away.

And he wondered just what else Fate was going to throw at him that day.

It was sunset before he paused at the ticket booth near Artane's front gates. He had straightened out his crew at the cottage, verified for himself that there were no ghosts, and discovered that all sightings had been reported by a stranger no one seemed to know. A very corporeal stranger. Zachary supposed he would do well to dig a little deeper there, but not that evening. He had business with one Gideon de Piaget, second son of the current earl of Artane.

He paid the granny in the ticket booth her ten pounds without question even though the castle wasn't open for visitors and she actually had to put down her knitting to demand her fee. He slung his bag over his shoulder and walked up the way, trying not to allow his memories of medieval Artane to layer themselves over the current castle.

He had, he would readily admit, seen too much.

Gideon was waiting for him in the courtyard, just as Robin had been more than once. Zachary stumbled, took a firmer grip on both his imagination and his gear, then continued on the way.

"You made good time," Gideon said with a smile. "And I see no smoke billowing up from down the way. An improvement, wouldn't you say?"

Zachary opened his mouth to comment on that, or the weather, or the granny down the way who was going to beggar him before summer, but instead out came words he hadn't intended.

"How well do you know Kendrick of Seakirk?"

Gideon blinked in surprise. Then he shifted.

Zachary immediately sensed a guilty conscience.

"What do you mean?" Gideon hedged.

"I mean how well do you know him? How long have you known him? Did you grow up playing cricket together? Hang out in Nobility Club together? Go to University together? What?"

"Er, we've done, um, business together—"

"Who is he?"

Gideon opened his mouth, no doubt to hedge a bit more, then he shut that mouth and considered. "You frighten me."

"I have a finely attuned BS meter. It's pegged right now."

Gideon smiled sickly. "Let's go inside and I'll tell you what you want to know. Mostly," he added not entirely under his breath.

"I just want one answer," Zachary said, "and I think it's probably better to have it out here so I don't bleed all over your father's floor when I faint and crack my head open."

Gideon turned back. "All right."

"Is he a de Piaget?"

"Very distant cousin." He paused. "Of a sort."

Zachary pursed his lips at the lie. "What about his family?"

Gideon shrugged. "He loves his wife dearly and you'll never meet a man prouder of his children—"

"Not his current family. His other family. The one he grew up in. What does he say about them?"

"Megan and Genevieve have probably talked more than we have about that sort of thing." Gideon shot him a pleading look. "You know, feelings and that sort of rot that make us of the male persuasion very uncomfortable."

"Are his parents still alive," Zachary pressed, "or . . . ?"

"I'm fairly sure it's *or*. I don't know about his siblings."

Zachary hated to make Gideon squirm—he was squirming quite badly now—but he had to have answers.

"Did he have only brothers, or a different combination?"

Gideon laughed uneasily. "What next, Zach? You're making the Inquisition seem mild."

"Just that last question, please," Zachary said seriously. "Did he have only brothers, or not?"

"Two brothers and a sister." Gideon shot him a perplexed look. "I don't know why you're so fixed on this, but I'll tell you all I know. It seems the sister died of consumption whilst Kendrick was off doing, ah, whatever it was he did. He came home to find her gone. He took it very hard, apparently. Megan says he rarely discusses it even with his wife. Too painful."

Zachary could only imagine. And from that little bit right there he knew that Robin had kept to his decision to say nothing about the truth, not even to his other children. Zachary thanked Gideon kindly for the information, then followed him, grateful for the time to wipe any expression off his face. If Kendrick had suffered greatly because he'd thought his sister was dead, odds were he wasn't going to be all that thrilled when he realized that Zachary was directly responsible, albeit not by choice, for the agony he'd gone through.

He went upstairs to wash for supper. He shut his bedroom door, then reached for his phone. He should have called earlier, but he hadn't been able to. He wasn't sure if he should just blurt out what he'd seen, or tell her in person.

He also wasn't at all sure he wanted to deal with the fallout from it quite yet.

She picked up on the third ring. "Aye?" she said hesitantly.

"Maryanne?"

"Zachary," she said, sounding equal parts relieved and happy. "You're safe, then."

"Safe and sound," he said, lying back on the bed and staring up at the canopy overhead. "What did you do today?"

"I took three showers and spent the rest of the afternoon learning to play poker with your nephew Ian, whose Gaelic is flawless."

Zachary smiled and felt the tension ease from him. "He's his father's son, true. Did you lose?"

"Badly at first, but I broke even."

He realized, with a start, that he wasn't in the room he'd been in before.

He was in Mary's room.

Yet another thing to add to the list of very weird things that went on in his life.

He pushed that aside and allowed himself the very great pleasure of listening to her spout a combination of Scottishisms and Jennifer's Americanisms with equal abandon. As he did so, he knew only two things.

He loved Maryanne de Piaget so much it hurt.

And Kendrick de Piaget was going to kill him when he found out.

Chapter 24

Mary looked at herself in the mirror of a Benmore Castle loo and supposed she should have been appalled by what she was seeing. She was wearing jeans that were scandalously revealing, a marginally discreet shirt that reached down past the top of those jeans, and a pair of little slippers in black that wouldn't have held up for one trip through her father's stables. She had met with the approval of her trio of keepers, though, so perhaps she had little to complain about. Indeed, she had them to thank for many things over the past four days.

She had been uncomfortable spending any coin but her own, but Elizabeth had dismissed her concerns with a negligent wave and many tales about Jamie trying to force an inheritance of some sort on Zachary and Zachary's flat refusals. If Mary spent a bit of what Jamie had tried to give away, Jamie would only congratulate her on her good sense. So she had traveled to the nearby village with the women of Zachary's family and subsequently found herself turned into a twenty-first-century miss.

She now had modern clothes and things to go under those modern clothes. She'd had her hair trimmed with scissors instead of a dagger, and her nails attended to in a way that made her hesitate to pick up another pitchfork. She had concentrated on learning as much of modern English as she could and thanked her father silently more than once for his insistence that she put at least as much effort into training her mind as her brothers had.

She had also, over the past few days, spent enjoyable evenings either at Jamie's or Patrick's. She had spoken at length to Jamie and Cameron about their adjustments to things of the Future. She'd fallen in love with all their children. Jamie's sons and Patrick had been perfectly willing to go on very brief explores with her to build her strength, and she had happily held wee girls on her lap in the evening as tales were told in front of the fire.

The greatest gift, however, had been something Elizabeth had brought her the day Zachary had left for England. It was an enormous black book, easily the width and length of her arm completely stretched out, that contained drawings Zachary had made over the course of his travels. They were mostly of buildings, which didn't surprise her, made on whatever scraps of paper he'd had to hand. They were accompanied by notes he'd taken about where he'd gone and lists of souls he'd encountered. Opposite each drawing were things Elizabeth had called photographs. Those had been made also by Zachary, but were present-day images of things he'd seen in the past.

The photographs had been as startling as his drawings, as he was as skilled a photographer as he was an artist, viewing his subjects from a master builder's perspective. The drawings and photographs were full of arches and lines and things that intersected in sensible and logical ways.

She had realized as she had flipped through the pages why Jamie had chosen him to be his companion on travels through the ages. Zachary had been an observer only, content to leave planes and angles meeting where they had been originally designed to meet. She had then understood how much it had cost him to come back to Artane and insert himself into events he'd known he should leave alone.

That said much about his love for her.

She took a deep breath, then blew it out. Perhaps she would go back to Moraig's, build up the fire, then sit with the book again and wander through the ages. It would pass the time until Zachary came home.

She left the garderobe, then went to look for Madelyn. She was sitting at the kitchen table with Hope and Sunshine. Hope was happily chewing on some sort of soft toy. Sunny looked less happy, though she smiled readily enough. Cameron had flown to London for the day and she was no doubt less than comfortable with his being so far away. Mary had been amazed that a man could travel from Scotland to London and back again in a single day and still have daylight to spend afterward.

Future marvels, indeed.

"Would you like lunch?" Madelyn asked.

Mary shook her head. "I think I need to go home—or to Moraig's, rather."

Sunny smiled in understanding. "It is a good place to heal, Mary, and she would have been pleased to see you happily installed there. Why don't we come get you for dinner? Jamie's issued a blanket invitation to go down to the keep."

Mary nodded. "I'd like that."

"Is Zachary coming home soon?"

"He said last night that he thought he could leave in a few days," she said, putting on a smile. "The work is progressing well."

"I'm sure he wishes he were closer," Madelyn offered.

Mary knew the others were merely providing her with an opportunity to burst into tears if she so chose, but she couldn't. She had come to terms with the Future. She just hadn't come to terms with the fact that Zachary hadn't demanded that she wed him as quickly as possible. It was ridiculous to want that so badly, but she couldn't help herself. He had been gone only a few days, but she had missed him.

She smiled at her keepers, then excused herself and left the castle. Madelyn and Sunny had warned her repeatedly to stay on the path. After listening to the stories of Jamie and Zachary disappearing without warning, she had taken the warning to heart.

She continued on in silence. It was odd to have so much time alone if she willed it. She was accustomed to never having a moment's peace to think. Now she could remain inside Moraig MacLeod's simple walls and do nothing but read by the fire and indulge in long, luxurious showers whenever she chose. She had come to love the cozy fire in Moraig's house, the soft furniture, the sturdy lock on the door. She thought of Zachary when she fetched the wood he'd chopped for her, or when she heard her phone ring and knew it was him calling a handful of times a day just to see how she fared. The phone was a marvel, but it couldn't replace what she wanted the most—

She heard the footsteps before she thought to move. She found herself almost ploughed over, but the man running toward her merely reached out a hand and steadied her before he continued on.

"Sorry, Maddy—"

Mary realized, with a start, that it was Zachary. He came to a skidding halt, then turned around and gaped at her.

"Mary?"

The sight of him was like sunshine after a storm. She had forgotten how handsome he was, and how strong, and how familiar and beloved.

She was fairly certain a noise of some sort came out of her, but she couldn't identify it. She ran toward him only to have him meet her halfway. She flung her arms around his neck and felt his arms go around her. He picked her up off the ground and held her so tightly, she couldn't breathe.

"I thought you'd gotten lost," he said hoarsely.

"I was with Madelyn and Sunny," she managed. "I had a makeover."

He laughed, but he didn't release her. He simply held her. She pressed her face against his hair and closed her eyes. And in that moment, she knew she was lost. She had known she missed him, but this was something else entirely. She had missed her brothers and cousins when they'd gone off, and she had welcomed them back happily when they'd returned, but she had never in her life felt such an overwhelming rush of relief.

"I can't let you go," he said finally.

"Please don't."

He laughed again, sounding as relieved as she felt. He let her slide back down to her feet. He continued to hold her close, though, as if he simply couldn't bring himself to release her.

"I didn't think to stop at Benmore," he said. "I went to Moraig's, but when you weren't there . . . well, I panicked."

"I should have left word written somewhere."

"I should have called. I wanted to surprise you." He pulled back far enough to look down at her. "Let's go home."

She smiled up at him. "Aye."

And then that moment, she felt something shift. He smoothed his hand over her hair, then bent his head and kissed her, just to the side of her mouth. Then he kissed the other side of her mouth. Then he smiled down at her.

"Maybe I shouldn't have done that."

"If you say that to me again, I will pull the dirk from your boot and stab you."

He laughed and put his arm around her shoulders. "You're feeling better. Let's go sit in front of the fire and you can tell me all about it."

She walked with him along the path and through the woods to the little house that leaned against a tree and was full of healing. Zachary held her hand tightly as they crossed the threshold. She understood why. Sunny had told her, with an accompanying shiver, just how the doorway had gone awry for her and her husband.

Zachary helped her with her coat, then walked her over to a chair before he took off his own coat and built up the fire. He turned and squatted down in front of her.

"What do you want for lunch?" he asked.

"Anything but bangers and mash."

"You've been eating at Jamie's," he noted. "I don't think Moraig's kitchen would put up with them, though, so you're probably safe here. I'll see what I can find."

"You could sit—"

"I've been sitting for hours. Just rest and I'll see to lunch."

She found that she couldn't. She listened to him rummage about in the kitchen for a handful of minutes before she rose and wandered over to lean against the little wall that separated the kitchen from the great chamber. She looked at Zachary in his jeans and bare feet, with a shirt stretched over his broad shoulders, and wondered what her father had done with Zachary's future clothes when he'd arrived. Had them burned, likely.

Perhaps her father had known what Zachary was.

For herself, all she knew was that she was unreasonably happy to have him almost within arm's reach. She loved the way his dark hair fell into his eyes in time for him to blow it out of his way. She watched him heat soup and remembered how willing he'd been to work in her father's blacksmith's forge. He'd shoveled manure, he'd burned his hands, he'd humored the twins when they'd hounded him endlessly about his past and his lack of French. All because he was just that sort of lovely, responsible man.

She realized suddenly that he was watching her.

"Kind thoughts?" he asked.

"I was just thinking that I've never known a lord's son, not even my relatives, who would have managed what you have."

"It doesn't take much to shovel manure, Mary."

She smiled. "Is there anything you can't do, Zachary?"

He set his stirring spoon aside, then crossed the two steps that separated him from the counter that stood between them. He leaned his hands on it and looked at her seriously. "Exercise self-control."

"I beg your pardon?"

"I want you to have time before I start kissing you senseless from dawn to dusk."

She suppressed the urge to fan herself. "I've had time."

"You need more."

"Are you saying I don't know my own mind?"

He took a deep breath, let it out, then leaned forward and kissed her.

It was only the briefest touch of his lips against hers, but it was all the more devastating for its sweetness.

"Time."

"Nay."

He pulled back. "Let's negotiate after supper. Can I assume Jamie's feeding us?"

"Aye."

"Will you dance with me?"

"I might if you'll stop telling me I don't know my own mind."

He leaned forward and kissed her again, then turned away and began to fuss with his soup. He looked at her once over his shoulder. "After supper. If you'll humor me then."

She thought she might be willing to humor him sooner than that, but she supposed she had all the time in the world for that sort of thing.

She nodded, then went to sit down before her knees gave way.

Several hours later, she was walking back into Moraig's little house, still holding tightly to Zachary's hand when they crossed the threshold. He hung up both their coats, then went to build up the fire, just as he'd done every time they walked into the house. Mary leaned against the wall and watched him work. Jamie had suggested that 'twas far past time she stayed in the keep and let Zachary fend for himself at Moraig's. He'd warned Zachary about the evils of sleeping too close to a woman who had not agreed to have anything serious to do with his sorry self. She hadn't bothered to point out to Jamie that Zachary hadn't asked her to have anything to do with him.

She supposed Jamie might have known that.

Zachary had only ignored his brother-in-law and danced with her every dance Joshua had been able to play.

Jamie had tsk-tsked him very loudly.

She blinked when she realized that Zachary had stood and was now brushing off his hands, watching her as he did so.

She felt a little weak in the knees, truth be told.

He walked over to her, took her hand, then led her to a chair in front of the fire. He sat, then held open his arms. She took a deep breath, then made herself at home on his lap.

"Would your father be appalled?" he asked with a smile.

"My father would kill us."

He pulled her braid forward over her shoulder. "I give you my solemn vow that you will remain unravished." He shot her a quick smile, then began to unbraid her hair. "I think I can cling to the shreds of my self-control well enough for that."

"Unfortunately."

He looked at her in surprise, then laughed. "You've spent too much time with my sister and sisters-in-law."

She swallowed, hard. "I missed you, Zachary."

He put his arms around her and pulled her close. "I missed you, too. And if I start thinking about it, I'll start kissing you. And if I start kissing you, Maryanne . . . well, you have a better opinion of my self-control than I do."

She pulled back and looked at him. "I begged once."

He looked a little stricken. "And it almost killed me not to do what I wanted to do, which was drop to my knees and plead with you to be mine, then wonder how in the hell I was going to convince your father of the same."

"He would have said aye."

He shook his head. "I don't think so. And I couldn't have asked you to then."

And now? she wanted to ask, but she couldn't bring herself to. She had begged once. She wouldn't do it again.

He stared at her for several moments in silence, then met her eyes and smiled. "Do you know you have seven freckles?"

"Six."

"Nope, there are seven. Let me count them for you."

She realized only after he'd pulled her closer that he intended to count them with kisses. She closed her eyes and shivered in spite of herself.

Aye, her father would have killed them both. But he would have killed Zachary very slowly.

He kissed his way across one cheek, over her nose, then finished by attending to the other cheek. She realized she was trembling, but she couldn't stop it. She supposed there was no sense in telling Zachary that he was the first man she'd ever been kissed by. If he didn't know it . . . well, he had to know.

He looked at her again, kissed her very softly, then settled her so she might rest her head on his shoulder. He trailed his hand through her hair, combing it with his fingers. The other arm he kept around her, periodically stroking her back.

"Maryanne?" he said finally.

"Aye?"

He was silent for quite a bit longer, but he didn't stop touching her. "I want you to be sure. I haven't given you any choices about your future so far."

"And if I choose you?"

"You haven't seen what else is available."

She thought he was jesting at first, then she realized he wasn't. She lifted her head and looked at him in surprise. "You're in earnest."

He nodded, though he looked none too happy about it.

"You know, Zachary, 'tis possible to carry chivalry too far."

Half his mouth quirked up. "Is it?"

"My parents had no choice."

He pursed his lips. "Your father adored your mother and she him. Your grandfather's sword in his back was just for show. He told me himself."

"You and my father spoke together often."

"It kept me from weeping while he was grinding me into the dust in the lists."

"What else did you talk about?"

"You. I made impossibly long lists of your virtues."

"You didn't."

"I did. Then I attempted equally long lists of all the things I could do to keep you fed if the occasion arose. He wasn't impressed."

"I imagine he was."

He laughed uneasily. "He wasn't. He said I was a terrible smith, a cheeky stable boy, and a lousy dancer. He did let me bring you with me, so I suppose that says something, though I imagine he didn't think he had much choice." He paused and looked at her seriously. "I want you to come south with me, Maryanne."

"Why?"

He reached up and tucked hair behind one of her ears, then smiled as he met her eyes. "There's something I want you to see. Actually, someone I want you to meet. And after you've met him, if you want me, I will then drop to my knees and be the one to beg."

"Who is this soul?" she asked in surprise.

He shook his head. "Just come with me. We'll see my brother on the way down. He'll get you what you'll need to be legal in the twenty-first century. You'll like his wife, Margaret. She was born in the twelfth century."

She managed a smile. "Is any of your family wed to souls from your own time?"

"My other brothers are," he said. "The rest of us had the good fortune to fall in love elsewhere, I suppose."

She realized what he'd said. Apparently he did, too, though he seemed disinclined to gainsay himself. He only looked at her hair as he fussed with it.

"I told you before that I loved you," he said, not meeting her eyes.

"I thought you'd forgotten."

He looked at her then. "I haven't. But I want you to be sure."

"If you say that one more time, I truly will stab you."

He laughed and pulled her close. "Then come here, wench, and help me find something more constructive to do with my mouth."

"Wench," she muttered in mock offense, then she found that

she had no more breath for speaking. She was heartily glad that she was sitting down, though that didn't ease the chills that ran through her.

"Maryanne?" he murmured against her mouth quite a while later.

She couldn't even open her eyes. She could scarce draw breath. "Aye?" she managed.

"I love you."

She did look at him then. "And I love you."

"Go to bed, woman. Take my dirks with you."

She smiled and kissed him softly. "I've no need of them. I trust you."

He shot her a skeptical look, then laughed uneasily. "I suppose you should." He paused, then pulled her close again. "Just a few more minutes."

"I think I can remain awake."

"Good of you."

It was quite a while later that she crawled unsteadily off his lap. She would go south with him, meet whomever he thought she should, then she would tell him that she had made her decision long ago, on that first day when she watched him stand in her father's courtyard and refuse to humiliate a man who had so richly deserved it.

She put her hands on the arms of his chair, leaned over, then looked in his eyes.

"My mind is made up," she said softly.

"Come south and see."

"I'm in earnest."

He put his hand behind her head, then leaned forward and kissed her. "I will wait," he said, looking at her seriously. "I will wait for as long as it takes, love."

She thought a pair of days might be long enough, but it was obvious he didn't. She only smiled, kissed him again, then went to find her flannel jammies.

Chapter 25

Zachary rubbed the place between his eyes that had begun to pound and wished he'd spent just a little more time on his medieval Norman French. It would have made the past eighteen hours slightly more enjoyable. He had the same sort of headache he'd had for the first few days in Mary's time, a headache brought on not by sword hilts against his skull but by all the unrelenting, rapid-fire medieval Norman French being spoken without pause.

It had been worth it, though, to see Mary happy and relaxed. They had caught up with his brother Alex and his wife in a discreet little bed-and-breakfast in Edinburgh so Alex could then tap his appropriately nefarious contacts to get Mary grounded firmly in the twenty-first century. Zachary hadn't asked any questions and his brother hadn't volunteered any answers. Actually, Zachary hadn't been able to do much besides simply watch Mary and marvel at the changes in her.

Modern life suited her. It had nothing to do with seeing her in jeans and a sweater, or listening to her talk animatedly about this Future marvel or that one. It was just that even with only a small bit of time and space, she had settled more fully into herself somehow. Perhaps that time alone at Moraig's had been good for her in ways he hadn't anticipated.

He watched Mary and Margaret walk ahead of him now, exchanging promises for future meetings where they could discuss the improbabilities of the future and the absolute perfection of Margaret's first biological child. His brother Alex was walking with them and participating in the Norman French conversation with the ease of a man who had been married to a medieval woman for eight years and was raising three adopted children of that same vintage.

Zachary had hoped that Mary would be eased by a morning spent with someone who had grown up in the past, yet had now made a very pleasant life with a modern sort of guy. Well, Margaret was stuck with his brother so maybe she deserved more pity than congratulations, but he'd thought it was impolite to point that out, so he'd kept his mouth shut.

Alex looked over his shoulder at him and lifted one eyebrow in a look that said very clearly that Mary was crazy to lower herself to have anything to do with a man who still preferred Ho Hos to hummus. Zachary had seen the look before so he ignored it.

He couldn't imagine that Mary didn't know exactly how he felt about her. And he supposed he wouldn't have been foolish to believe she felt the same way. He just had the feeling that Kendrick of Seakirk wasn't going to be nearly as happy about the state of affairs of their hearts as his sisters-in-law had been. And he suspected, by the look of him, that Kendrick hadn't slacked off on his swordplay over the years.

Alex dropped back to walk alongside him. "Where will you be?" he asked quietly. "Artane?"

"For the next couple of days, at least."

"I'll get her passport and birth certificate to you there, then." He studied Zachary for a moment, then he took a deep breath and put on his pontificating blowhard attorney expression.

Zachary steeled himself for the worst. His brother, preparing to wax poetic about things he was sure he wouldn't like. It couldn't be good.

"You haven't said as much," Alex said slowly, "but I can't help but assume you're going to Seakirk first."

Zachary felt something someone else might have called dread toy with settling in his stomach. "Why would you think that?"

Alex looked at him blandly. "Because I know who lives there."

Zachary stopped still. "You do?"

"I've done the occasional bit of work for him." Alex laced his fingers together and stretched them out in front of him before he smiled in a particularly enigmatic fashion. "I helped a friend of his out of a legal tangle a couple of years ago. I saw a painting of the earl's family—or his parents and siblings, rather—while I was there."

Zachary choked. He didn't even protest when his brother slapped him several times rather forcefully on the back. "You're kidding."

"I never kid about legal tangles or family portraits."

"Why didn't you tell me before?" Zachary wheezed.

"Tell you what, when?" Alex asked pointedly. "Were we supposed to chat before you hopped back to medieval Artane to then fall hard for a certain medieval miss?"

Zachary looked at his brother narrowly. "Who was the friend with the tangle?"

Alex smirked. "Jake Kilchurn."

Zachary knew he shouldn't have been surprised, but he found he was just the same.

"I helped Jake convert his vast assets into the right tender to buy Robin's sister, Amanda," Alex continued relentlessly, "because you know they don't give away their precious treasures to untitled losers who don't even have a full-time job."

"I had a job before," Zachary growled, "and I have one now." He shook his head in disbelief. "Why do I talk to you?"

"Because I'm family and you have to. As for the other, I didn't tell you because I had no idea you would go and fall for Amanda's niece. I will tell you, though, that those Artane men are mighty reluctant to part with their women to untitled yahoos who don't have a bed of their own."

"You already said that."

"I like to hear myself talk."

Zachary cursed his brother, but it was without the level of venom he would have liked to have used. He was too winded. Alex only laughed—rather more robustly than necessary—as if he were enjoying a particularly delicious joke.

Zachary thought he might have to lean over soon until the stars stopped swirling around his head. "Think Robin knows about any of this? About the time traveling?"

"Of course he knows. Jake told him where—sorry, *when*—he

was from before he used that great big X near Artane to come back here and get the goods."

"Then he knew what I was from the very beginning."

"Unless he'd had a recent blow to the head and lost all his long-term memories, then yes, I would imagine so."

Zachary rubbed his hands over his face. "I need a drink."

"You don't drink. At least not now, though Jamie has a very interesting story about you and a cache of Barbados rum."

"I know that story, though I'm surprised Jamie does because he was the one who spent the night with his head in a fern!" Zachary had to take a deep breath. "My first and only serious brush with demon liquor, thank you very much. Though I'm tempted to have another one very soon."

"I wouldn't until I'd figured out a way to tell Kendrick de Piaget why it is you've been snogging with his sister pretty much constantly for the past week."

"It hasn't been the past week. It's only been the past couple of days."

"I'm sure he'll appreciate the distinction."

Zachary felt a little queasy. "It's the twenty-first century."

"Not at Seakirk it isn't." Alex shook his head slowly. "You're in way over your head, little brother. Call me if you want me to come scrape up the bloody pulp that's left after he finishes with you."

"He's that good?"

Alex only looked at him for a minute in silence, then laughed and walked away. He was still chuckling when he gathered up his wife and baby, bid Mary a fond good-bye, then walked back to the bed-and-breakfast where they'd all been staying. Zachary continued on because he had comfortable leather seats inside his car, and he very much needed a place to sit down.

He was slightly sidetracked by the sight of Maryanne de Piaget waiting for him there by that car. He pulled her into his arms and thought there was no reason not to kiss her a bit while he was at it, just so she would remember that he had adored her before her brother had beaten the absolute crap out of him.

She pulled away, laughing. "I thought your head pained you."

"I'm tougher than I look."

She put her hands on his face and leaned up on her toes to kiss him. "Thank you for this morning. It was a very great gift."

"It was a very great pleasure to watch you natter on in your native tongue."

"You speak it very well."

He could only hope he would have the chance to improve. He opened the door for her and waited for her get in. She stopped him before he started to close the door.

"How does the seat belt work again?"

He leaned over and buckled her in, then stopped when he realized she'd taken hold of the front of his shirt. He perched on the edge of the seat when she moved over to make room for him. He found himself smiling.

"Need help with anything else?"

"Come a little closer and I'll tell you."

Heaven help him, he was in trouble. "What other languages can you say that in?"

"Will I have a kiss for each?"

He took a deep breath and cast caution to the wind. Well, they'd cast caution to the wind already, but there was no point in not continuing on with what was apparently working so well. "A kiss for each?" he managed. "Absolutely."

She smiled. "Then let me see what I know."

It was quite a while later that he pulled away, because she did indeed know quite a few languages. She looked thoroughly kissed and he wasn't sure he was going to be walking very well anytime soon. He looked into her very lovely, very green eyes, then kissed her one last time.

"A walk on the beach?" he suggested.

She smiled. "It sounds lovely."

"I'll keep my hands in my pockets."

"I won't."

He laughed, then forced himself to pull away and shut the door.

It was the beginning of a charmed day. He walked with her along the beach, kissed her almost as often as he dared, and took as many pictures of her as she was willing to sit for. And he suppressed a dozen times the urge to ask her to marry him.

While she was still potentially willing.

He imagined that his stress over possibly destroying that willingness had begun to show by the time they were driving through the village at Seakirk. Mary was very quiet until they drove up to the outer gates.

"Zachary?"

He took a deep breath and looked at her. "What?"

"Why are we here at Seakirk?"

He squeezed her hand that was resting on his leg. "There's just someone I want you to see before you make any serious decisions about your future."

"Zachary," she said quietly, "the decisions are made."

"I mean about marriage."

"I was referring to marriage."

He paused in front of the outer gates, leaned over, and kissed her softly. "No matter what happens here, I just want you to know that I've made my decision, too, and I'm not going to change my mind. I'll understand, though, if you want to."

She blinked. "You will?"

He pulled away. "Of course not. It'll kill me. I'm just trying to be polite."

"Zachary Smith, you're daft."

"I'm beginning to think so, too." He watched the portcullis be raised, then sighed. "Here goes nothing."

More gates opened as if by magic—or paranormal means, which wouldn't have surprised him—and he drove up the way.

"Ever been here?" he asked, because he had to say something to keep from shouting.

"Seakirk?" she asked in surprise. "Saints, nay. Matilda Buchanan is—was—a witch. And even if that could be doubted, it was a well-known fact that her lover Richard was a warlock. Ask anyone who knew either of them."

Zachary thought he just might have that chance very soon, especially considering he'd pried out of Megan de Piaget the details that Kendrick of Artane had been slain by Richard of York, cursed by Matilda of Seakirk, then lived as a ghost in the very keep in front of them for almost eight hundred years.

"Zachary, you're very nervous."

"I'm not nervous." And he wasn't. He was thirty-one, for pity's sake, far too old to feel like a seventh grader being hauled into the principal's office. He looked for a few quick excuses as to why he'd been doing things the principal might have disapproved of, but he wasn't sure those excuses would fly in his current circumstances.

In his defense, he hadn't known Kendrick was Mary's brother when he'd brought her back from the Middle Ages. Of course, he hadn't said anything when he'd figured it out, which was definitely a point against him. He also hadn't gone to get her right away and delivered her to Kendrick's door right away, nor had he avoided kissing her senseless until he'd delivered her to Kendrick's door and asked the man if he could. His conversation with his brother came back to him suddenly with unwholesome clarity.

It's the twenty-first century.

Not at Seakirk it isn't.

Zachary had the feeling that truer words had never been spoken.

He pulled to a stop in the courtyard, then got out of the car before he was tempted to kiss Mary again. He walked around to her side and opened the door. He reached in and unbuckled her, then stopped and looked at her.

"I love you," he said gravely.

She put her hand behind his head and leaned forward to kiss him. "Don't leave me."

"I don't think I should even touch you here."

She blanched. "Zachary—"

He kissed her again very quickly, then stepped back. He helped her out of the car, then released her hand. She took hold of the back of his jacket and held on. When he balked, she stuck her chin out and silently dared him to say aught. He shut her door, then sighed deeply. He held out his hand and waited for her to put hers in it. His doom was probably already sealed; there was no sense in not putting all the nails into his coffin.

He walked up the stairs with her, then knocked on the door. Mary was trembling. He looked at her in surprise.

"What is it?"

"You're frightening me."

He put his arm around her and pulled her close. "I'm not sure how to tell you this—"

"Ah, nay, not that sort of business," she warned.

"There is someone inside whom you will know."

"From the Future?" she whispered.

"Nay, love, from the past." He took a deep breath and started to elaborate, but the door opened before he could.

"Oh, Master Smith," Worthington said in his perfectly cultured butler's voice.

Then he did a double take.

Zachary understood completely. He smiled politely. "Is His Lordship in?"

Worthington only nodded silently, his eyes absolutely enormous. He looked at Mary for another moment or two, then shut the door in their faces.

Zachary shot Mary a smile. "He's usually better than that. I think you overwhelmed him."

She scowled. "We're here to meet some titled fool?"

"Well—"

The door was wrenched open suddenly. "What the hell'd you do to my . . . butler . . ."

Zachary wished he'd had the whole thing on video; it would have made it much easier to see everything he wanted to. He supposed he could have watched Kendrick gape and listened to Mary gasp and he would have known all he needed to. He did manage to glance at Mary briefly. She looked as if she'd seen a ghost.

Appropriate, actually.

Kendrick stumbled backward, then leaned over for a moment or two, taking deep, even breaths.

"Kendrick, what is . . . it . . ."

Zachary watched Genevieve wind down in much the same way her husband had. She stared at Mary in astonishment, then turned that same look on him.

"Who . . . ?"

Zachary only smiled very faintly. He stepped away from Mary and waited for her to make the first move.

She didn't have to. Kendrick straightened, reached out, then yanked his sister into his hall and into his arms. And then he lost it. Zachary looked away politely as the good lord of Seakirk fell apart. Until he realized Mary wasn't weeping, that is. He found that she was looking at him over her shoulder, her expression full of confusion and dismay. He attempted a smile.

He imagined he had failed.

Mary turned back and held on to her brother, who was completely undone.

"There's a story here," Genevieve said faintly.

Zachary nodded, but he didn't offer any details. He wasn't sure that Kendrick could handle any details at the moment.

But it took the good lord of Seakirk less time than Zachary expected to pull himself together. He sucked in a deep breath, then held his sister away from him.

"You're supposed to be dead," he said in disbelief.

"'Tis complicated."

"Explain it now, then."

Zachary watched her wave in his general direction. He suppressed the urge to duck behind Worthington for protection.

"I met Zachary in the past," she said faintly. "Styrr poisoned me and Zachary saved me by bringing me to the Future."

Zachary wondered absently if every medieval expat would say the word so it sounded capitalized, or if he was just used to thinking of it that way for them.

"He brought you to the future," Kendrick repeated incredulously. "When?"

"Well over a se'nnight ago, perhaps," Mary said. She looked over her shoulder then. "When was it, Zachary?"

"About then," Zachary said carefully.

The change in Kendrick's mood was expected, but unsettling nonetheless. He set his sister aside and folded his arms over his chest.

"You've had her that long and you didn't tell me," he said flatly.

"I didn't know about you, my lord," Zachary said reasonably. "Not until last week."

"You should have told me last week then!"

Zachary nodded slowly. "I could have—"

"You *should* have!" Kendrick bellowed.

"My lord—"

"And you," Kendrick said, whirling on Mary. His voice was quavering badly. "Why didn't you call? I assume you had access to a telephone, or did he keep you captive in some hovel?"

Mary looked at him in surprise. "What are you talking about?"

Zachary cleared his throat. "I didn't tell her, my lord, because I thought—"

"You *thought*," Kendrick echoed incredulously.

"I *thought*," Zachary continued pointedly, "that since she

had been very ill, another shock to her system might be one thing too many."

"*Merde,*" Kendrick snarled.

"Kendrick," Genevieve ventured, "perhaps we should—"

"How dare you keep my sister from me," Kendrick continued on furiously. "And don't try to convince me that it was for your lofty, altruistic reasons!"

Zachary took a deep breath. He couldn't look at Mary, because he wasn't sure he could bear to witness her expression. On the off chance that she shared her brother's fury.

"My reasons *were* altruistic," he said evenly. "For the most part. And for the rest, yes, you're right. I didn't bring her back to England the moment I knew who you were and what she was to you because I had this nagging suspicion that once you saw her, you were going to remind her that she's an earl's sister and I'm a peasant and then we would be back where we were almost eight hundred years ago."

"You're bloody well right about that last bit," Kendrick said hotly. "My sister is a woman of rank and station and she will not *date* an untitled, barely-squeaking-along working sod, much less do anything else with you."

"I'm not barely squeaking along—"

"My sister will not work down at the local Tesco so you can make ends meet!"

"I make half a million bloody pounds a year for the Trust—"

"A job you have yet to start!"

Zachary was very happy Kendrick didn't have a sword, though he wasn't sure why. He had the feeling that Kendrick could do an equal amount of damage with his bare hands. He took another deep breath. "I make enough to provide for her. And no, I don't have a title, but this, Your Lordship, is the twenty-first century. I didn't have what was required in the thirteenth, but things have changed here."

"Of course they haven't!"

"When I brought her home, I had no idea you were alive," Zachary continued, struggling to keep his tone even. "And I thought that I just might stand the chance of having that Lamborghini."

Kendrick blinked. "That what?"

"Something so far out of my reach that I could only stare at it stupidly," Zachary said grimly, "and wonder what it might feel like under my hands."

Kendrick gaped at him for a moment, then he did what Zachary knew he should have expected from the first.

He punched him full in the face.

Zachary stumbled backward, tripped over the threshold, then did what he always did when in those sorts of situations: he admired a set of very well-preserved stairs as he rolled down them. He decided he would find something especially nice to give Patrick MacLeod for Christmas that year in gratitude for all the injuries he'd avoided by having taken his brother-in-law's Roll Your Way to No Broken Bones survival course.

He landed flat on his back in the courtyard, winded. It took him a moment before he dared open his eyes, and when he did, he wished he hadn't.

Michael Smythe-Gordon was standing over him, smirking.

Perfect.

"Yet another triumph to add to your résumé," Viscount Franbury sneered.

Zachary crawled to his feet. He had to lean against his car, though, which didn't make him happy. "Michael," he said as calmly as he could manage. "What a surprise."

"It shouldn't come as one," Franbury said. "I believe I made mention of my plan to ruin you."

"I thought you were bluffing."

Franbury drew around himself centuries of fine breeding. "You'll find, my naive friend, that I never bluff. But by all means, continue on with your peaceful existence. It won't last long." He looked up the stairs. "It won't last much longer at all."

Zachary watched Franbury ascend Seakirk's fine stairs and knock briskly on the front door. He could imagine a few reasons why Franbury would want to have a little tête-à-tête with Kendrick de Piaget and none of them were good. He wasn't above hoping that Kendrick would treat Michael to the same sort of send-off he had just experienced himself, so he decided he would stick around long enough to see the show.

Kendrick jerked open the door and looked out, then scowled. "And who are you?"

"Michael Smythe-Gordon. Viscount Franbury, if you'd rather. I believe we have an appointment?"

•

"Viscount," Kendrick said, shooting Zachary a glare. "Well, that's the type of lad I'm interested in, always. One with a *title*."

Zachary could have sworn he heard swearing going on inside before Kendrick managed to get Michael in and the door shut, but he wasn't sure if it was that or he was hallucinating. He walked around to the back of his car and pulled out Mary's bag. He took it with him and braved the stairs again.

He was ready for Kendrick's fist and managed to duck out of the way.

"I have your sister's things!" he managed before Kendrick took a second swing.

Kendrick ripped the bag out of his hands, then gave him another shove. Zachary managed to spin and make it down the stairs without rolling and without killing himself. He landed rather heavily on one leg, then turned and looked back up at the door. Kendrick was glaring at him.

"Don't come back."

"That's for Mary to decide."

"I will decide for her!" Kendrick bellowed just before he slammed the door shut a final time.

Zachary went to lean against the side of his car. He stood there for several minutes, just watching the front door. He realized quite a crowd was gathering in the direction of what had been a garden minutes before but now looked quite a bit like medieval lists—some impressive paranormal activity, truly. He realized with equal certainty that the souls he was looking at were most definitely not mortal. He paid them no heed, not even when one of them, a burly brute dressed all in black, ran at him and plunged a sword into his chest.

Zachary only yawned. "You missed."

The ghost drew himself up. "I most certainly did not!"

"Nay, he didn't," offered another ghost who hastened over. "Colin of Berkhamshire never misses."

Zachary looked at the small gaggle of medieval knights who had suddenly gathered around their offended leader. "Look, I appreciate the effort you're making on my behalf, but I've got too much on my mind to really give you the attention you deserve."

Colin of Berkhamshire withdrew his sword from Zachary's chest and resheathed it. He folded his massive arms over his equally beefy chest. "We've heard about you."

"I imagine you have," Zachary said wearily. He couldn't bring himself to ask if the rumors had been good ones or bad ones. He considered asking the shades if they'd done any haunting in a southerly direction in the past week, but decided against that as well. It had probably been Franbury, carrying on with his quest to be as big a pain in the arse as possible. He looked up at the very shut door for another moment or two, cocked an ear to listen for continuing shouting, then sighed and turned away.

Mary had a phone and she knew how to use it. There was nothing else to be done.

Of course he wasn't going to give up that easily, but he was certainly going to give her some room to spend enough time with her brother to at least put her heart at ease.

He climbed into his car and turned toward the gates.

*C*hapter 26

*G*enevieve de Piaget stood at the doorway of her husband's castle and watched as two paths diverged. The one her husband was taking led to the lists, which didn't surprise her. The one her sister-in-law—a woman she'd never thought to ever encounter this side of the grave—was taking led toward the stables. Genevieve chose the one of a less-equine nature, because she was fairly sure it would, as Frost would have said, make all the difference.

It was going to be Kendrick's job to find his way down that other road.

It had been a very interesting couple of hours, what with the arrival of a woman who she had assumed had been dead for centuries, the ejection out the front door of that woman's would-be suitor, and yet another man added to the mix in the person of Michael Smythe-Gordon, who apparently had more vindictiveness than sense.

Kendrick had listened to the Viscount Franbury only long enough to realize he was a small-minded fool who was only being polite in order to dig up paranormal dirt on Zachary Smith. He'd thrown Franbury out the front door, citing lack of time for such a ridiculous conversation.

Too close to home, no doubt.

There had then ensued another round of shouting, tears, and conversations in the vintage French that Genevieve had been very relieved she'd taken the trouble to learn. Trouble had begun to brew when Kendrick had told Mary how she was going to conduct her affairs from then on. When he'd frisked her and confiscated her mobile phone, the discussions had deteriorated rapidly into threats and curses.

Genevieve had watched her five boys watching the goings-on with openmouthed astonishment.

Mary had turned to her and demanded directions to the stables. She hadn't dared not give them. Kendrick had stomped off after his sister, but apparently thought better of following her, hence the diverging paths. Genevieve had followed at a distance because her husband had wept and he rarely wept. She had to see if there was anything left of him.

She walked around the castle and through gardens that were a perfect front for the very medieval-looking lists in the back. Her husband used that bit of ground regularly for its intended purposes. He lured their sons out there just as regularly, which wasn't an effort, given that they were just as driven as he was.

It was in the genes, apparently.

Today, though, the lists weren't being used for training with the sword or the schooling of horses. They were empty except for a man sitting on a bench pushed up against a wall. Genevieve walked over to that bench and sat down. She looked at her husband.

"Are you possessed?" she asked bluntly.

He shot her a dark look. "Nay, 'tis just me. The horse's arse you wed."

"What happened to you?"

"I think I became my father."

Genevieve laughed in spite of herself, then leaned back against the wall and began to rub her hand over his back. "I imagine you didn't see this one coming."

He was silent for a very long time, then he turned to look at her. His eyes were very red. "I was on the Continent when she died. I came back to find her gone almost two years and my parents well past their grief. I hardly had time to grieve before the whole business with Seakirk came to the fore. And then . . . well, you know what happened then." He paused. "I loved my sister deeply."

"She is a lot like you."

"Trouble?"

"Well," Genevieve said, trying not to smile, "I wasn't going to say that, but since you did, I'll agree. She certainly isn't shy about expressing her opinion."

"Heard her, did you?"

"Kendrick, everyone in the village probably heard her. I don't think you're going to find her to be very tractable."

He sighed and dragged his hands through his hair. "I don't want that Smith character taking her away before I've had a chance to have her to myself for a bit." He paused. "A few months. Maybe longer."

"She loves him."

"She can love him all she likes—from a distance. I am her nearest living relative and I will decide if and when she's to have anything to do with him."

Genevieve cleared her throat carefully. "You know, husband, those are pretty potent juices you're stewing yourself in."

He only scowled.

"She can use the phone, you know."

"I took hers away."

"She'll find another."

"I forbade her!"

"I imagine she'll ignore you when she's finished cleaning your stables."

Kendrick scowled a bit more. "'Tis a good place for her. She loves horses."

"She loves him more."

"How do you know?"

"I just do."

He slapped his hands on his knees and pushed himself to his feet. "I'm going to go remind her who is in charge."

"Good luck."

He shot her a dark look before he stomped off, cursing.

Genevieve watched another pair of paths meet and then diverge. The eldest of her triplet sons, Robin, exchanged a brief word with his father, then continued on toward her. He sat down and stared off over the lists for quite some time, just as his father had done, then he turned to look at her.

"My aunt?"

She nodded solemnly.

"Mum, you have a bit of explaining to do."

"Going to draw your sword and motivate me if I refuse?"

He only gave her an arch look so reminiscent of his father that she laughed. What a delightful life she had, a life that was colored with so many things that didn't find themselves in the current century.

Just as Zachary Smith's would be, if he had the chance.

She stood up and waited for her eldest to do the same. Robin offered her his arm as he'd seen his father do countless times. She took his arm, sighed at the fact that she was going to be looking up at him sooner than she wanted to be, then nodded toward the castle.

"Let's make the big circle, Robin."

"Will the tale be a long one?"

"Yes, son. It will be." *Almost eight hundred years' worth,* she added to herself. But he was his father's son, and he had spent his life getting into things he should have stayed out of. She didn't imagine much would come as a surprise to him. She had great hopes that her conversation would go well.

She didn't hold out the same hope for her husband.

Chapter 27

Zachary pulled into Artane's car park an hour before sun-set. He turned his car off, then sat back and looked at the sea in front of him. It should have been soothing, but somehow it wasn't. He couldn't blame the ocean for that. Pretending to work while waiting for a phone call from a particular woman wasn't exactly conducive to a stress-free afternoon.

He hadn't dared call Mary himself yet, so he'd tried to keep occupied with his own business. He'd popped by Wyckham to make sure his workers were still unhaunted, then continued on to Artane. At least he could crash in comfortable surroundings while he nursed his bruises and wished he had somehow man-aged to handle things a bit better. Though he wasn't sure what he could have done differently. For better or worse he was again meddling in things he shouldn't have been, and he couldn't go back and change what was done.

Damn it, he was really going to have to be done with all things paranormal. And sooner rather than later.

He started toward the castle, then stopped and looked behind him. There was a white van parked on the other side of the car park. He stared at it, watching as a man opened the back doors and pulled out a professional-looking video camera. Wonderful. That was all he needed, to have to wade through someone making some sort of documentary about well-preserved medieval castles while he was trying to just get in and out of the gates.

He ignored the cameraman and walked up to the gates. He flipped the granny at the ticket window a twenty-pound note, then continued on his way only to find himself chased down and hugged.

"It wasn't much," he said, narrowly avoiding being impaled by one of the knitting needles she obviously didn't remember she'd tucked into her granny bun. "Mrs. . . ."

"Gladstone," she said, giving him a sweet smile. She put a guidebook into his hands. "You'd best have one of these, dearie, before they're all gone."

Zachary smiled faintly. "Having a run on them, Mrs. Gladstone?"

"Some annoying bloke's been trying to have a discount on me stock," she said, beginning to frown. "Franbury, or some such high-sounding name. And him not even willing to pay His Lordship's very reasonable entrance fee!"

"Shocking," Zachary said seriously.

Franbury again? Would he never manage to get rid of the man? Zachary thanked Mrs. Gladstone again for her generosity, wished her a good evening, then continued on his way.

He wondered if he might get inside the keep as easily. He had the feeling Gideon and Kendrick knew each other far better than they'd let on. It wouldn't have surprised him to have found the door barred and his pink slip pinned to the outside.

Instead, he found Gideon's wife, Megan, sitting on the stairs enjoying a little peace and quiet. He stopped a handful of steps below her and attempted a smile.

"Lady Blythwood."

"You've been busy today."

"Kendrick called."

"Nope, Genevieve."

"I imagine the result was the same."

Megan only moved over so he could sit next to her. He set his backpack down and did just that. He rubbed his hands over his face for good measure, but it didn't help him find clarity.

"Do you want my take on this?" Megan asked.

He smiled at her wearily. "I'm all ears."

"Then I'll fill them full of things you won't get anywhere else. Don't blame yourself for any of it. You just took him by surprise.

If he showed any sort of unmanly emotion—which, given how much he loved his sister, I imagine he did—then he had to go a pretty long way the other direction to make up for it."

Zachary pointed to his eye, which he could fortunately still see out of, but which would be sporting a very serious bruise come morning.

"See?" Megan said pointedly. "He wouldn't have done that in the course of a normal day. He's actually remarkably laid back considering who he is. Give him some time. He'll cool off and see reason eventually."

"I wish I shared your optimism," he said with a sigh. "He doesn't even think I can support her."

"Then he has no idea how much you're making with the Trust."

"Too much?" he asked, wincing.

"Oh, definitely not. Robert Cameron thinks you're a bargain. I think you'll be getting a ridiculous raise next year, so brace yourself." She reached over and patted his arm. "Cam thinks the world of you. Just so you know, he said if you weren't in charge of our little restoration trust, he and his checkbook didn't come out to play."

Zachary considered. "I don't suppose a letter of recommendation or two would soften Kendrick's heart."

"No," Megan said with a laugh, "I don't imagine so, but time will. And I put in a good word for you with Gen, which I'm sure she'll pass on at the appropriate moment." She put her hands on her knees and rose. "I think there's chocolate truffle cake in the fridge, if you're interested. It'll make you feel better."

"It won't solve things, but it might be a good start."

"Then go put your stuff away, then meet me in the kitchen."

Zachary picked up his backpack and started to follow her. He stopped, then reached down to pick up the guidebook he'd left sitting next to him. On the cover was Artane in all its glory, still perched on the edge of the sea like a dragon from some fantasy illustrator's imagination. The keep was a magnificent place, full of enormous amounts of history, home to generations of remarkable people.

He could attest to that personally.

He ran upstairs to dump his backpack in the guest room, then checked his phone. There were no calls, but he hadn't expected any. Mary either had her hands full with her brother or was thinking up ways to inflict on Kendrick a little payback for the pain and suffering she'd experienced. Either way, he wasn't ready to interrupt.

He stood in the middle of the room—Mary's room—and wondered if he hadn't made a terrible mistake. Well, several of them. Maybe Kendrick was right and money didn't matter, but a title did. Maybe Mary deserved things he couldn't give her. Maybe he should have walked away the moment he first realized that he loved her.

Not the Lamborghini kind of love. This was let-me-look-at-you-over-the-breakfast-table-for-the-rest-of-my-life-and-that-won't-be-long-enough kind of love. It was let's-have-ten-kids-and-a-dog-and-you'll-still-be-the-love-of-my-life kind of love.

It was an I-can't-catch-my-breath-when-I-look-at-you kind of love.

It was the kind of love that not even chocolate—even chocolate truffle cake from Artane's spectacular chef—was going to ever come close to being a substitute for.

A n hour later he found himself pacing the length and breadth of Artane's great hall. He'd left his phone upstairs so he wouldn't be tempted to either call Mary or torment himself with the fact that she hadn't called him. She was probably having a fabulous afternoon spent catching up with a brother she obviously loved very much. He envisioned her indulging in happy conversation in front of the fire, surrounded by her family.

He supposed he might have had the same thing by joining Gideon and Megan in Gideon's father's solar, but he couldn't bring himself to. He was restless for many reasons he just didn't have the stomach to think about. If Mary hadn't called by the time he was ready to call it a day, he would just call her. The worst she could do was hang up on him.

He stopped in front of the lord's table, leaned back against it, then looked out over the great hall. He could remember quite vividly dancing with one Mary de Piaget in that hall on several occasions. He wondered, absently, if there might be grooves in the stone from where other dancers over the years had done the same thing.

He sighed and looked down the length of the lord's table. Perhaps there were just as many marks there from generations of diners. He reached for the guidebook he'd forgotten he'd left behind and thumbed through it idly. There were the obligatory pictures of Artane through the ages, first in artists' sketches, then in grainy photographs. Some enterprising soul had then begun to discuss the more notable lords of Artane, beginning with Rhys, and his son, Robin—

Zachary froze.

There, reproduced in lovely sepia tones, were the plans for the kennels he'd done for Robin.

He almost dropped the book in surprise. He hadn't thought twice about it, hadn't even considered that a simple drawing of kennels might survive the ages and wind up in a book that Artane's current lord sold to tourists.

He turned the page to see if there were any details provided along with the drawing only to come face-to-face with Maryanne de Piaget herself.

He did drop the book then. He picked it back up with shaking hands and struggled to find the particular page he'd been looking at. Yes, that was most definitely her face. Not only was it her face, she was identified in a little italicized caption on the facing page.

The daughter of Robin de Piaget, Maryanne, who died tragically at the age of twenty-seven.

His mouth felt very dry all of a sudden. It was entirely possible that she could escape notice. It wasn't unheard of for descendants to have not only the same name but bear a startling likeness to their ancestors. She could easily explain away any untoward comparisons that someone might make. He could help her. Hell, any number of his in-laws could do that for her.

He tossed the guidebook back onto the table and began to pace around the great hall, feeling slightly frantic. Something else occurred to him and he strode over to the table and snatched up the guidebook. He flipped to the appropriate page and felt dread settle into the pit of his stomach. There in the corner of each drawing was something he hadn't given a second's thought to in 1258.

Zachary William Smith, AIA, RIBA.

Something Franbury would have easily been able to match to any number of plans—and their revisions—that Zachary had made for him during the whole of January and February.

I'll see you ruined.

Franbury's words were like a sharp pain in his head that rapidly became relentless pounding. It wasn't possible that Franbury had made the connection . . . but it wasn't impossible, either.

He leaned back against the table again and studied the ceiling of the great hall. Franbury had called Cameron to make trouble. He'd tracked Kendrick down and was obviously trying to stir up something there.

But surely not even Franbury could wrap his mind around such a ridiculous thought that Zachary could have drawn something that pertained to a woman who should have died hundreds of years ago.

At least he wouldn't have until he'd seen Mary standing in Kendrick of Seakirk's hall. No wonder he looked at her with such astonishment.

"Zach, old man, what is it?"

Zachary looked at Gideon, who was standing five feet away, watching him with alarm. He said nothing, he merely shoved the guidebook at Gideon. Gideon looked, studied, then paled.

"A bit dodgy, that."

"You haven't heard from Franbury, have you?"

"Endlessly," Gideon said, still looking slightly green. "I only took his call once, though. He's an absolute nutter."

"What did he want?"

"He wanted particulars about you," Gideon said slowly. "And he was curious about any sort of paranormal activity here at Artane. Oh, and he wanted to know when you might be lodging here next."

Zachary was happy to be leaning against the table. "What do you know about the white van in the car park?"

Gideon shook his head slowly. "Nothing, but I suppose we could go find out, if you like."

Zachary nodded, though he wasn't at all eager to see what was going on outside the gates. But since he couldn't fight what he didn't know, he had no choice. He left the guidebook behind on the table and walked with Gideon across the hall and out the front door. He experienced a brief feeling of the past layering itself over the future, but the cars in the courtyard staved that off well enough.

Mrs. Gladstone had obviously left her post for the night, leaving them free to continue on their way down into the car park.

Zachary felt more unsettled with every step he took in that direction, as if something unseen were dogging his footsteps.

Or as if he'd walked those same steps in some other time.

He swore, but it didn't help him any. He strode across the gravel with Gideon, then stopped next to the passenger side of the van. He peered inside, but there was no one there. There were, however, copious amounts of recording equipment.

Gideon handed him a flashlight. Zachary turned it on then shined the light inside the front of the van, looking for anything useful. He was somehow not at all surprised to see a folder there with Franbury's name scribbled prominently on the front.

And next to it was a guidebook.

Artane's guidebook.

"What are you going to do?" Gideon asked grimly.

"I'm working on it."

"Might we work on it inside?"

Zachary nodded. He backed away from the van, clicked off the flashlight, then handed it to Gideon. He started back toward the keep with Gideon at his side. The moon was out, fortunately, and the sky happily devoid of anything that might have gotten in its way. Zachary walked past the ticket booth, then paused at the gate for Gideon to open it. He waited until Gideon had locked the gate behind him before he continued on along the cobblestone road that led up to the castle itself. It was only once he'd reached the stairs leading to the great hall that he trusted himself to speak.

"Got a spare key?" he asked.

"For the hall or for the gate?"

"The gate. Actually, if you'll just give me ten minutes, I won't need to borrow one."

Gideon's mouth fell open. "What are you going to do?"

"Don't ask."

Gideon caught him by the arm before he could start up the steps. "And if your, er, girlfriend calls?"

"I won't be gone long."

"And if she arrives and wants to know where you won't be gone long to?"

Zachary looked at him seriously. "Show her the guidebook. She'll understand."

Gideon released him slowly. He said nothing else, but Zachary supposed there was nothing else to be said. He ran up the steps and went inside the hall. He was very grateful he'd brought his medieval gear along with him. He'd done so on a whim, thinking that it might make Mary more comfortable somehow if they could dress up and pretend seven and a half centuries hadn't passed since the last time she'd seen her home.

He'd never thought he would need it for a more critical bit of business.

Chapter 28

Mary dragged her sleeve across her face, set her pitchfork aside, and rebraided her hair. She was tempted to sit down on a strangely fashioned squared bale of hay, but that would have perhaps given the appearance of weakness. Never mind that she'd sat often enough over the past few hours. She'd found an added reserve of strength—and anger—and she knew exactly how to make best use of both.

Kendrick's stables were spectacular, which earned him a positive mark or two in her book. He, however, was a horse's arse, which removed those marks before anyone could have noticed that they'd been there in the first place.

She had already finished with one side of the aisle, so she turned to the other. She removed one of his mounts, tied it up out in the aisle, then set to cleaning the stall with a vengeance. She was furious, but even after almost three hours of having the peace to decide, she wasn't sure with whom.

She had first thought Zachary should be the recipient of all her anger. He had known, the bloody lout had *known* that her brother was alive and he hadn't called her immediately to let her know. Instead, he had allowed her to languish in the rain in bloody *Scotland* before he'd managed to drag her sorry self back to the right side of the border where he could present her to an actual relative who might have wanted to see her a bit sooner.

She cursed as she narrowly missed stabbing herself in the foot with the pitchfork.

She paused and blew stray strands of hair out of her eyes. She had already taken off her sweater but she now stripped off another layer, tossed it onto the hay with her sweater, then set to work in jeans and a T-shirt.

Jeans and a T-shirt that she had listened to Zachary insist that Elizabeth take his gold for.

In time, she returned the gelding to his home, then began work on another stall. By the time that was finished and yet another begun, she felt some of the fog of anger recede.

The truth was, Zachary couldn't have given her the tidings over the phone. She was quite sure learning who Kendrick was had come as an equal shock to him. Indeed, she wasn't certain she wasn't still in a like state. She hadn't had the entire tale, but she'd readily seen that her brother was now the father of six. He'd bellowed something at her about curses and shades and centuries, but she'd honestly been too distracted to pay any of it any heed. There was a tale there, and one she would have at her earliest opportunity—*after* she'd rid herself of the desire to kill him.

Nay, Zachary couldn't have told her any of that over the phone.

And the truth of it was, he'd needed to be about his labors. Hadn't he returned to Scotland far more quickly than he'd intended to? And hadn't he then brought her immediately to England? And hadn't he insisted that she not decide if she wanted him or not until she'd had the chance to meet someone in particular?

She'd just never imagined that someone would be her brother.

She put the steed back in his stall and stood there for a moment, cursing under her breath. Nay, she wasn't going to kill Zachary, she was going to kill Kendrick. 'Twas difficult to believe she had actually forgotten just how autocratic he could be. He was stubborn, and overbearing, and far too much like their father for her taste. She snorted. Ridding her of her mobile phone. Telling her that her jeans were too tight. Commenting on the cut of her jib.

She wasn't quite sure what that last one meant, but the criticism had been implied easily enough.

Nay, she was now finished with opinionated men telling her what she would and would not do. After all, she was now a twenty-first-century woman. She had freedoms. And rights. And other things she was certain she would discover if she could manage a bloody quarter hour without having to listen to her brother go on and on.

She realized, in a startling flash, that she wouldn't have had those thoughts occur to her if Zachary hadn't let her season in that lovely cottage in the woods for those few brief days. It also might not have occurred to her if she hadn't spent a goodly part of those four days either in the company of his sisters, who were very much like her aunts, or by herself where she'd had the chance to simply sit and think.

She took a firmer grip on the pitchfork. She was going to tell her brother she loved him, thank him for a lovely handful of hours in his stables, then she was going to go back inside, find someone else's phone, then call Zachary so he could come and fetch her.

She turned, then froze.

Kendrick was standing just inside his stables. He looked so much like their father, she doubted for a moment where she was. Or when, rather. She looked down at herself, just to be certain she was still wearing jeans—ones that were too tight, apparently—then let out her breath slowly. Proper century, but wrong location.

She leaned the pitchfork against a stall door and folded her arms over her chest in her father's favorite pose of intimidation.

"I'm going to call him," she announced.

Kendrick's expression darkened. "Nay, you aren't."

She wished she'd had a dagger, but since she didn't, she settled for the pitchfork. She reached out and rested her hand on it casually. "Get out of my way or I'll stab you."

"You wouldn't."

"I would."

"You wee stubborn wench."

"You great overbearing lout," she said through gritted teeth. "I am no longer a child, Kendrick, I am a woman full grown and I have made my choice."

"Father would be appalled."

She pursed her lips and decided that she had no alternative but to deal with her brother as she always had. She would ignore him unless he got in her way, then she would run him over with a horse. She'd done it before, with great success. She returned the pitchfork to its home, then gathered up her sweater and shirt and walked past her brother.

Or tried to, rather.

He caught her by the arm.

She made the mistake of looking up at him. He looked absolutely devastated. She cursed him, but that didn't change the fact that by the time she'd put her gear on a bale of hay and put her arms around her brother, she was as near to weeping as she ever came. He was making unmanly noises of grief as well, so perhaps it didn't matter.

"I missed you," he said finally. "Not that you had much chance to miss me."

She pulled back and looked up at him with a smile. "I haven't seen you in a year, you heartless oaf. You could have come home more often instead of wreaking havoc all over the Continent with Royce and that terrifying Saracen of yours."

"We didn't wreak havoc, we made mischief. And buckets of gold."

"Mercenary."

He smiled, the sunny smile that she had to admit she had loved since the first time she could remember having seen it. Kendrick was a horse's arse, as she had pointed out to his edification more than once, but he was also a most loyal and devoted brother.

And she wasn't terribly unhappy to know she would have him and her love both in the same century.

He sighed deeply and put his arm around her shoulders. "Fetch your gear, Mary, and we'll go have something to eat."

"I'm calling Zachary first."

"Tell him we're meeting in the lists before I decide if you might date him. I have standards, you know."

"We're past this dating business of yours, Kendrick, and he trained with Father, so I imagine you won't intimidate him."

Kendrick snorted. "Trained? Rather Father no doubt destroyed him every morning before breaking his fast just for sport. How long was he darkening our door?"

"A fortnight, at least."

He shot her a look. "You can't fall in love in a fortnight, Mary."

"I think I fell in love with him the first time he, unlike the rest of you oafs, actually plied a little chivalry on me."

Kendrick snorted. "You're a romantic."

"How long did it take you to fall in love with Genevieve?"

"Before or after I tried to murder her?"

Mary started to ask, then thought better of it and shut her mouth. She imagined she would have the entire tale at some point, but she wasn't sure she could stomach it at present. She leaned her head against her brother's shoulder and walked with him back to his hall.

Half an hour later, she was feeling her way down into a chair. Not because it was comfortable, but because her knees wouldn't hold her up. She looked at her brother in shock.

"He must be mistaken."

Kendrick shook his head. "Gideon says Zachary has gone on a little, ah, errand. He's not sure when he'll be back."

"You're lying," she said promptly. "What did he really say?"

"Can't tell," Kendrick said, shaking the phone. "Sometimes these things don't work as well as they should."

Mary glared at him. "If you don't tell me what I want to know, I'll insist your wife do it for me. And I'll have one of your sons make certain she's translated it aright. Don't tell me they cannot."

Kendrick sighed, then spoke for another moment or two into the phone, his expression becoming more serious with each bit of listening. He finally ended the conversation and looked at her. "Gideon admits that Zachary went off on an errand of a particular nature. I won't speculate as to that nature, but I imagine we'll want to go to Artane. Just so you'll be there when he returns."

She was heartily glad to be sitting down. "He couldn't have intended to use a gate through time."

"I—"

"He wouldn't have." She looked up at him. "'Tis perilous, which he knows full well. He told me during our travels here that he had once tried to right a wrong across the seas in what he called the Colonies. He scarce escaped with his life. He wouldn't be foolish enough to try it now."

Kendrick's expression had become very grim indeed. "He must have had good reason, then."

She pushed herself to her feet, swayed once, then steadied herself. "Whatever the reason, he'll need aid."

"Well, *you* certainly can't go save him."

She glared at him. "Don't start this again."

He scowled. "What has possessed you to be so difficult? Not that you weren't before, but you have taken it to new and unpleasant heights here today."

"'Tis the jeans."

He pursed his lips. "They are merely a symptom of a disease you were born with, I'm afraid." He turned away. "Very well, I'll take you to Artane, where you will await this fool who has likely gone off to find you a wooing gift from another century. I'll beat sense into him when he returns."

She didn't argue the point. She watched him disappear only after telling Worthington to help Genevieve collect the children and their things and put them in the car. He returned soon enough with a bag slung over one shoulder and a sword in his other hand.

"Let's be off, sister."

Mary followed him out of the keep in time to watch Worthington put her suitcase in the back of Kendrick's car. It looked as if it would go very fast indeed, which likely would have pleased her at another time. Now, she only cared inasmuch as it would carry her home that much more swiftly.

Kendrick drove out of the castle gates and through the village at a very sedate pace, but soon left that idea behind.

"Sorry," he said, shooting her a look.

She would have smiled if she hadn't been so terrified that Zachary would never find his way back to her. "I don't mind the speed."

"I imagine you don't." He shook his head. "I think, Mary, that you were meant to be in this modern century."

"I daresay you have that aright."

He glanced at her briefly. "I'll unbend far enough to tell you that I've heard this Smith character is fairly canny. Gideon, our

nephew several generations removed, speaks very highly of
him. Though I imagine you could tell me more tales than I could
tell you."

"Not now."

"Nay, sister, not now. After I've humiliated him in the lists,
perhaps."

"Kendrick, you are a horse's arse."

He squeezed her hand briefly, then concentrated on the
road.

They walked into Artane at sunset. She wasn't sure what she
had expected, but she was so distraught that nothing made much
of an impression. She knew she met the current lord of Artane
and his lady wife. She knew she eventually listened to Kendrick's children tumble into the hall with the abandon that bespoke familiarity with the place. She met Megan de Piaget, who
so strongly resembled a younger version of her sister Jennifer
that Mary found herself rendered speechless. When she found
her tongue, she promised to give Megan all manner of tales
about Jennifer and her children. But later, after she thought she
could breathe again.

She asked and was given leave to wander the keep at will.
She nodded her thanks, then walked to the back of the hall and
up steps that were so grooved and worn, she could hardly believe they belonged to her father's keep. That alone was evidence of the centuries she had leapt over to reach a place where
jeans were available.

She walked down the passageway and stopped at the doorway to her mother's solar. She put her hand on the wood, then
she pushed the door open. The chamber was full of things she
could see shadows of, but she didn't suppose she cared to find
out what they were in truth.

She took a deep breath and continued on until she reached
her own bedchamber. She opened the door and realized she
had no idea how to light the room.

"Light switch on your left."

She shrieked in spite of herself, then spun around to find
Kendrick leaning against the opposite wall of the passageway.

"How long have you been following me?" she asked breathlessly.

"Long enough."

He pushed himself away from the wall and reached around her to turn on more of those magical Future lights. She turned around and looked inside her chamber.

Zachary's clothes were tossed over the back of a chair and his backpack was sitting on the floor nearby. Mary walked into the chamber and sank down onto the bed. She looked to her left. Zachary's keys were sitting on a low table there, as if he'd simply put them down for a moment, fully intending to come back and fetch them. She stared at them for several moments in silence, then looked up at her brother.

"I don't understand why he did this."

Kendrick handed her a manuscript. "Read through that and I imagine you will."

Mary accepted the book and turned the pages slowly. Obviously Kendrick didn't know Zachary as well as she did. He wouldn't have risked not only his life but her parents' lives as well simply because of something he'd read in a—

She froze.

There in front of her was one of the drawings he'd done for her father's kennels. She ran her fingers over the page, marveling at the clarity of the . . . well, she couldn't call it a drawing. It was some sort of photograph, similar to the ones she'd seen in Zachary's book. She looked up at Kendrick.

"Why does this matter?"

"It matters first because he signed the bloody plans. And for what I imagine truly caused him concern, turn the page."

She did and came face-to-face with herself. She stared at her own face there and shook her head. Indeed, she shook her head several times. 'Twas unusual, perhaps, but surely not of such import that he would have felt the need to return to the past to do . . . what? He might have liked to look at her, but surely no one else would.

And then she realized that wasn't exactly true.

"Franbury," she breathed. She looked at her brother. "That bloody oaf who came to your hall today. What did he want again? I didn't understand half of what he said."

"He was quite interested," Kendrick began sourly, "in whatever paranormal activities I might have heard associated with a certain Zachary William Smith, architect. Paranormal as in ghosts, time travel, magic. The sort of thing that we, as it happens, both have quite a bit of experience with. The sort of thing any number of souls would no doubt be happy to discuss with irritating government busybodies."

She felt a shiver go down her spine. "And would the current king send us to that new Tower he built in London?"

"The Tower is now old, the king is a queen, but aye, you have the rest of it aright."

She swallowed with difficulty. "Then Zachary is risking his life to save us."

"Oh, his own arse is being saved as well," Kendrick muttered, "but aye, I imagine we figure into his thinking quite prominently."

"You mean, *I* do. You, he would likely happily see sent to the gallows."

Her brother smiled faintly, then came to sit next to her on the bed. "Likely so, and I imagine I deserve it. I'll go easy on him when I meet him in the lists upon his return. Just for you."

"You're not meeting him in the lists."

"And you're not traipsing back through time to aid him."

"Of course not," she said. "Why would I?"

He shot her a look, then stood. "Let's go find supper. That will pass the time pleasantly. Before you know it, I'll be happily humiliating your would-be beau in the lists with my sword held between my teeth. Truly something not to be missed. But supper first."

Mary nodded and rose as well. Aye, she would first find supper, then she would go look for other things. There had been many things in her mother's solar, things that might be of a rather old vintage. Perhaps even things from Wyckham, things that might once have been contained in her uncle Nicholas's trunk.

Maps were, as many in her family could attest, very useful things indeed.

Chapter 29

Zachary made his way up at twilight to what he hoped was the medieval incarnation of Artane's gates. He had no way of knowing the exact date, which bothered him just as much as it should have. He easily could have come too early in time, in which case trying to fix the problem of his signature on two pieces of parchment was going to be useless. He might have arrived years too late when someone else was lord and wouldn't be so willing to let him do what he had to. Worse still would be arriving in the middle of his last stay where he would have to avoid not only everyone he knew in the keep, but himself as well.

He knew how that ended up.

He usually had more of a plan than simply hoping for the best, but he hadn't had much time to come up with anything better. He had to get inside the keep one way or another. It was probably too much to hope for that it would be easy.

He realized suddenly that he wasn't the only one out for a little walk. He knew this because he found himself in the way of two men bolting up the road toward the keep from the village and couldn't get out of their way fast enough to avoid landing in a pile with them.

Thaddeus and Parsival, as it happened.

Thaddeus's mouth fell open. "Merciful saints above, what are *you* doing here? I thought—" He shut his mouth suddenly, then looked at Parsival. "I mean to say, *we* thought—"

"Thad, don't attempt speech," Parsival said with a sigh, heaving himself up to his knees. He looked at Zachary. "You have taken a very great risk, *mon ami*. There are those in the keep who firmly believe that you—" He took a deep breath. "I'll let you speculate on what they believe. You are free, of course, to rid us of the exertions of such speculation."

Zachary sat up and put his hand against the spot on his back that had connected with a particularly unyielding cobblestone. "I can't explain anything in any way that would satisfy you— either of you. I can only ask that for friendship's sake, and for whatever love you bore your cousin, that you help me get inside the keep. Into Robin's solar."

Parsival studied him for a moment or two, then heaved himself to his feet and extended a hand to pull Zachary to his. "Keep your face covered. We'll see you inside."

"Thank you," Zachary said, feeling vastly relieved.

"You made my cousin happy for the last few days of her life. Consider it my thanks for that."

Zachary nodded. He ignored the fact that Thaddeus was still gaping at him as if he'd seen a ghost. Or at least he did until Parsival slapped his cousin smartly on the back of the head. Thaddeus shut his mouth, pulled his hood over his head, and dropped back to bring up the rear.

Zachary kept his own hood around his face, ruthlessly tamped down his nerves as Parsival made excuses for bringing in a new friend at the side gate, then continued to try to look as inconspicuous as possible as they made their way up to the keep.

He would have given much to have had Mrs. Gladstone chasing him, demanding her very reasonable fee that was going to beggar him come fall.

Parsival led Zachary not to the keep, but to the healer's house. Zachary wasn't at all thrilled to be making another visit there, but he imagined Parsival was trying to keep him from being stared at by everyone eating dinner inside. Apparently the healer had died earlier in the week from the aftereffects of poison. Zachary didn't ask for any details, nor did he want to know how Styrr's mother had handled the news of her son's perfidy. He simply sat with Parsival in that cold, unwelcoming little room where Styrr had tried to poison Mary, in the dark, until Thaddeus went on a little reconnaissance mission and announced that the hall was being put to bed for the night.

Zachary followed Mary's cousins into the keep, keeping himself well in the shadows and praying he would actually get to Robin's solar without being discovered. He had to. Mary's future, and his, and a family tree full of others depended on it. He would have liked to have believed that Michael Smythe-Gordon didn't have the stomach for a long, very public airing of MacLeod and de Piaget dirty laundry, but he knew better. The irritation of having to look at zinnias had apparently been enough to convince him to do quite a few nasty things.

Parsival paused at Robin's solar door, then opened it without knocking. There was a sternly voiced complaint from inside, but Parsival begged sincere pardon, then looked at Zachary.

"'Tis up to you now, *mon ami*," he said quietly.

"Keep my secret," Zachary asked, just as quietly.

"But of course."

Zachary pushed past him and walked into Robin's solar, then shut the door behind him. He supposed the only reason Robin didn't release the dagger he had in his hand was that he realized into whose chest he was about to fling it.

Robin's knees buckled and he sat abruptly. "Don't tell me—"

Zachary shoved his hood back off his head. "She is well, my lord."

Robin put his hand over his mouth and closed his eyes for a moment or two before he cleared his throat roughly.

"She survived, then."

"It was difficult for her, but aye, my lord, she did."

"Then what in the bloody hell are you doing here?" Robin asked weakly.

Zachary started to sit, then hesitated. "May I?"

Robin waved him on to a chair. "By all means."

Zachary took off his cloak, sat down, and enjoyed his first decent breath of the night. "I had to come, my lord, because of something I did here."

"Difficult to believe," Robin said with apparently as much of a snort as he could muster, "considering how little trouble you were."

Zachary smiled briefly. "I apologize for continuing the

tradition. This has to do with the plans I drew for your kennels and the portrait of Mary. I signed them without thinking and someone in my time has, I fear, seen them and connected me to them." He paused. "I fear he has less-than-pleasant intentions."

"Afraid he'll ruin your reputation?" Robin asked lightly.

"I honestly couldn't care less about myself. But it isn't only the drawings of your kennels he's seen. If he somehow realizes who Mary is and—"

Robin apparently didn't need to hear any more conjecture. He cursed, then fetched sheaves of parchment from his trunk. He laid them on his table, then sat heavily.

"I'll be sorry to lose them, but I can see the danger in keeping them. Will you cast them into the fire, or shall I?"

Zachary shook his head. "I think merely removing my mark will be enough. If you don't mind?"

"If you're certain," Robin said slowly.

Zachary smiled briefly. "This will be sufficient."

"Then be about it, lad."

Zachary pulled a charcoal pencil and a paper stump out of his boot and set to work. He would have preferred to simply erase his name and the qualifications after it, but he didn't dare attempt it considering what he'd used to draw with in the first place. It would just leave a smudge that would look even more out of place than his very modern signature.

Instead, he took each sheaf and carefully drew flora, fauna, or other vegetation to obscure his name. Mary's portrait was more difficult, but there he only had to conceal his initials. He stuck his tools back into his boot—Robin's boot, actually—then looked over the drawings again to make certain he'd done a thorough job.

He slid the drawings across Robin's table. "Enough, do you think?"

Robin studied them carefully, then sat back and nodded. "Unpleasant lads you have in that 2006 of yours, apparently."

"Some things are constant through the years, my lord. The soul in question is nothing more than a man of no character making up for it with a very big mouth."

"Aye, well, we have those in my day as well. I suppose we could spend the evening discussing—"

A knock sounded suddenly and a man entered before Zachary managed to do anything but turn his back to the door.

"Ah, Rob, you're not alone. Sorry."

"Stay," Robin said, rising and walking over to shut the door. "Come have a seat with us, brother, and meet the man who completely humiliated your eldest with his bare hands alone."

Zachary rose and turned, then felt his mouth fall open as he came face-to-face with none other than Jake Kilchurn. If Robin's words hadn't already told him as much, the fact that Jake looked exactly like his son would have.

"My lord," he stammered.

"My sister's husband, Jackson Alexander Kilchurn the Fourth," Robin said mildly. "If you want to know where Jackson the Fifth comes by his arrogance, witness this man. A larger pain in the arse I do not know."

Jake walked over to a chair in front of the fire and collapsed into it. "That is the thanks I have for taking your sister off your hands all those years ago." He looked up with a smile. "So, this is the lad who made off with your daughter."

"So it would seem," Robin agreed.

"I know his brother," Jake said.

In perfect English.

"Somehow," Robin said, in the same tongue, "that just doesn't surprise me."

Zachary choked. He was grateful for the chair pushed his way so he could sit and the cup shoved into his hands so he could drink. He finally regained his breath without any help from either of the other two there. He actually couldn't see either of them until he could breathe and his eyes stopped watering. He gaped first at Robin, then at Jake.

"I need a drink," he managed.

"You have one," Jake said with a smirk, "so drink it down, Zachary, then tell me who's won the World Series for the past couple of years."

"You're an American," Zachary managed.

"Married to a Brit," Jake agreed. "Thanks to Jamie's coin dealer and that big red X you've been using. I'm surprised Alex didn't tell you as much."

Zachary found himself with his head between his knees, mostly because Robin's hand was holding it there. He finally waved his love's father off and managed to straighten. He looked at Robin.

"Then you did know."

"Of course I knew," he said with a snort, reverting back to his mother tongue. "Who do you think burned your clothes so *you* didn't burn at the stake?"

"Why didn't you tell me?"

"Because it sounds daft," Robin said promptly. "And because of what I told you before: irony." He shot Jake a look before he continued. "I had of course been privy to the impossible romances of my brother Nicholas and my sister Amanda with their respective spouses and I was fully convinced I had thereby endured all a man might reasonably be expected to suffer, leaving me thereafter free from any such brushes with travelers not from my own time."

"Your first mistake," Jake said mildly. "You didn't suffer nearly as much as you think you did."

Robin shot his brother-in-law a look, then turned back to Zachary. "I shepherded my eldest son through a tempestuous but perfectly reasonable courtship with the lass over the border and had my youngest provide for his own happiness without my having to do anything at all. I had given up on my second son mending his womanizing ways, but assumed he would eventually find a very patient woman to wed and do so without undue fuss."

"Leaving Mary only for you to provide with marital bliss," Jake said with a smile.

"Only to then watch her pull a Future lad out of my dungeon and stand over him like an avenging angel." Robin scowled. "And, damn me if she didn't then go and fall in love with him!"

"Ironic," Jake agreed.

"As I said." Robin looked at Zachary. "Take my advice: keep your head down, make my gel happy, and don't make any rash statements of the sort that Fate might take note of. You'll regret it if you do otherwise."

Zachary nodded and decided to keep his lists to himself.

"I'm assuming Mary will have you," Robin said.

Zachary wasn't quite sure where to even begin to talk about any of that.

Apparently Robin saw something in his face that gave away things he hadn't intended. Mary's father began to frown.

"Have you run afoul of a few nit-picking relations who don't know you as well as I do?" he demanded.

Zachary supposed it would be best to just follow Robin's advice and keep his mouth shut. He settled for a solemn nod.

Robin finished his wine, considered something for a moment or two, then rose and went to sit at his table. He wrote something down, then affixed his seal to the bottom of the page. He resumed his seat in front of the fire and handed Zachary the sheet of parchment.

I, Robin of Artane, do hereby grant my wholehearted permission for my daughter to marry Zachary Smith, a man worthy of her in every respect. Such is my will concerning my daughter and is not to be gainsaid.

Zachary looked at Robin. "Wholehearted?"

Robin shrugged with a half smile. "I'm not holding the date of your birth against you."

Zachary had to clear his throat a time or two before he could say anything else. "Thank you, my lord. This is more than I hoped for."

"You'd best see to her well," Robin said sternly. "I imagine I'll come haunt you otherwise."

Given the quite likely possibility of that, Zachary thought it best to agree right off. "I will do my best to never do anything that will necessitate any nighttime hauntings from you, my lord."

"I imagine you won't." Robin took an unsteady breath. "If I didn't feel as if my guts were being ripped out right now, my lad, I might be able to enjoy the fact that she'll be running roughshod over someone else besides me for a change."

"I'm sorry, my lord," Zachary said quietly. "I can't imagine it."

"You'll have a daughter someday, Zachary, and then you'll understand. I give you my permission to make any potential suitors muck out your stables right off—just to see which ones are too proud to humor you."

Zachary smiled in spite of himself. "Was that your test?"

"Aye, and you were the only one to pass it."

"If I'd known what the prize was, I would have shoveled harder."

Robin laughed a little more easily that time. "I daresay." He pushed himself to his feet and walked to his door. "I'm going to go fetch my Anne. She'll want to see you."

Zachary stood and waited for Robin to leave before he resumed his seat and looked at Jake. "I have to admit I'm a little surprised we didn't meet before."

"I think you were working in Devon while I was stumbling

through Jamie's medieval survival course. I'm not sure where you were when Alex was getting me out of a few nasty legal snarls."

Zachary studied Jake thoughtfully. "Do your children know?"

"I haven't said anything to them," Jake said with a half smile, "but I'm one for thinking that there are some secrets that should remain secrets."

"Even from your children."

Jake shrugged. "What would it serve them to know? For better or worse, this is their time. It's best they just be satisfied with it. Of course, I'm deeply suspicious of those bloody twins of Nick's. It wouldn't surprise me to learn they know all sorts of things they shouldn't. I'd be even less surprised to find they've talked to my kids about those very things. So, to answer your first question, yes. I imagine some of my children know. I'm just waiting for the day they catch me napping and trot off to use one of Jamie's gates."

"I've often wondered if it would be better to try to destroy all the gates. Or at least wall off that big one I just used."

Jake shook his head. "You might as well spray paint a big X on the ground. Trust me, those monstrous boys of Nick's would make a beeline for it. I'm not sure they won't anyway."

"Heaven help us all," Zachary said with feeling.

"It's a terrifying thought," Jake agreed. He studied Zachary for a moment or two. "I'm assuming you've shown Mary what lurks at Seakirk."

Zachary pointed to his no-doubt rapidly blackening eye.

Jake grinned wickedly. "He's been a terror since the moment he was born."

"Why do I get the feeling part of that is your fault?"

"I owed him. He put me through hell in the future, which left me no choice but to repay him handsomely in the past."

"I sense a vicious circle in there somewhere."

Jake only laughed. "I imagine so. Did Mary let him push her around?"

"I'm not entirely sure. I heard quite a bit of shouting after I rolled down his front stairs, but I didn't stick around to find out who was saying what." He sipped his wine and gathered a few more thoughts together. "I'm assuming you haven't said anything to anyone here about what happened to him?"

"No, but I will tell Robin after the fact. Kendrick said Genevieve was worth seven hundred and fifty years of haunting and I believe him. I'm afraid, though, that my being here has already changed things. Kendrick told me that all of his family was at Artane when he was killed, but I'm fairly sure Nicholas and his family will be in France that time of year thanks to his having wed Jennifer. I had actually planned to take Amanda and our younger ones to Italy just to be away from the madness and I'm pretty sure that isn't how Kendrick remembers things. I suppose we'll just see how it all turns out in the end." He smiled. "Jamie would have quite a bit to say about it, wouldn't he?"

"I could give you his don't-change-the-past lectures verbatim."

"I imagine you could," Jake agreed, "and I imagine you could give me an equal number of instances when he's ignored his own rules."

"He never likes to stand in the way of true love," Zachary agreed.

"Naturally." He studied Zachary for a moment in silence. "Will it bother you to give it up?"

"The time traveling?" Zachary asked in surprise. He shook his head. "Not when my alternative is staying at home with that tomboy who's sent me in circles since the moment I met her."

Jake laughed. "How many pairs of jeans does she already own?"

"I'm not sure, but I'm sure I should be afraid."

"I imagine you should," Jake agreed. "And here comes my own tomboy who would probably be very jealous of your lady's wardrobe."

Zachary stood as Robin ushered in his wife and another dark-haired beauty who Zachary assumed was Robin's sister, Amanda. She gave him an assessing look before she walked over and sat on her husband's lap. Zachary turned to Anne and made her a low bow.

"My lady."

She took his hands and squeezed them. "How fares my Maryanne?" she asked, her green eyes very bloodshot.

"She is well, my lady."

She nodded, took a deep breath, then turned and took a bundle from her husband. She laid it on the table, then unwrapped it and shook out a green dress covered with exquisite embroidery.

"I made this for her over the past few days." She looked at Zachary quickly. "I thought it was only foolishness, for I didn't expect to see you again, but now I'm pleased to find it was useful after all." She paused. "'Tis a wedding gown."

"It's lovely," Zachary said honestly.

"There is a tunic to match," Anne added. "For you."

Zachary could only hope he'd have the chance to wear it. He had to clear his throat several times before he thought he could speak without his voice breaking. "Thank you, my lady."

She folded the dress back up very carefully, smoothed her hand over it a final time, then went to sit in the chair her husband held for her.

Zachary waited until Robin was seated in front of the fire, then took his own seat and had another cup of wine. He was tired, but there were times when weariness had to be ignored. He had tales and discussions to commit to memory so he could repeat them for Mary.

He briefly considered his own memories of gates going awry, then pushed the thoughts aside. The gate would work because he would give it no choice. And he would studiously avoid asking Jake if he'd ever tried it and found it unresponsive.

There were just some things that were better not to know ahead of time.

H_e walked to the stables well before dawn, because Robin had insisted he take Mary's horses to her. Robin and Jake had discussed the merits of adding equine bloodlines where they didn't belong, but Zachary hadn't had the heart to refuse the request. He left Robin to guard the entrance, then continued on silently, hoping he wouldn't wake the stable lads. He realized, as he saw the cluster of souls in front of Rex's stall, that the exercise had been futile.

He was somehow very unsurprised to find that the whole crew was there: Connor, Thaddeus, Parsival, and the little twins. Well, and Jackson the Fifth as well, standing to one side, glaring.

And all was right with the world, apparently.

He opened his mouth to attempt a dodge of some kind, but saw immediately that there was no point. They were all looking at him knowingly. Parsival shrugged with a rueful smile. Jackson, however, didn't join in that smiling.

"For someone who reportedly died unexpectedly almost a fortnight ago," he said shortly, "you're looking very well."

"Ah," Zachary began slowly.

"Don't bother with excuses, *mon ami*," Parsival said pleasantly. "We know it all already."

"Aye," Connor said with a yawn. "Strange happenings in this part of the world."

"Not to mention in our own families," Thaddeus said with a grin that was very reminiscent of his father's.

"Do any of your parents know you know?" Zachary asked politely. "Or your siblings?"

Theo's eyes were very wide. "Do you think we would tell them?"

"Do you think we would tell *you*?" Samuel added. "Of course, seeing the business of this sort of traveling with our own eyes adds a certain *je ne sais quoi* to our secret knowledge—"

"Oh, shut up, Sam," Connor said shortly. He looked at Zachary. "You see now what I must endure."

Zachary sent Connor a look of pity, then turned back to the twins. "I'm not going to give you any more details than you have already. And I will appreciate it, of course, if you'll keep to yourselves anything you know—or think you know."

"You don't need a pair of squires?" Samuel asked.

Theo leaned close to his brother and put on his best smile.

That was more unsettling than it probably should have been.

"Nay," Zachary said, trying to put just the right amount of regret into his tone, "but I'm sure there will be plenty of lords in your future who will be fighting themselves to have you come work for them."

Samuel and Theo exchanged a look that would have given their father gray hairs if he'd seen it. Connor slung an arm around each twin and cleared his throat pointedly.

"I'll see to them."

Zachary hoped he would manage it. He shook hands all around and thanked each of them for their aid. He turned to Jackson last.

"I will take care of her," he said gravely. "I give you my word on that."

"You'd damned well better," Jackson growled. He glared at Zachary, hesitated, then cursed. He reached behind him and pulled a sheathed sword out of Rex's now-empty stall.

Zachary half expected Jackson to draw it and use it. Instead, he merely handed it over, hilt first. Zachary took it, feeling a little off balance.

"What's this?"

"Uncle and I had it made for you."

Zachary felt his eyebrows go up of their own accord. "Did you think I would return?"

Jackson pursed his lips. "I just had a feeling. A very unpleasant feeling, if you must know, but a feeling just the same." He nodded to the sword. "We've had Godric's cousin working on that blade for a solid se'nnight. He remade it three times before my uncle was satisfied with it."

"Are you satisfied with it?" Zachary asked, because he couldn't help himself.

"I was merely hoping you would trip and impale yourself on it, so I didn't much care how it was fashioned."

"Oh, Jack," Thaddeus said with a deep sigh, "just stop, would you?"

Jackson shot his brother a glare, then looked at Zachary. "I don't like this."

"I imagine you don't," Zachary said quietly, "but there is no going back now. I *will* take care of her."

"Not that I'll have means to verify that," Jackson said darkly.

"Oh, I don't know about that," Thaddeus said.

"Shut up, Thad."

Zachary stepped out of the potential line of fire, accepted reins for two horses, then took a final look at the lads standing there in a huddle. He would have to draw them when he got home, so Mary would have them at least on paper. He nodded a final time, then headed toward the courtyard. He looked at Robin, who had been joined by Jake.

"I'm ready."

"And if the gate isn't," Jake said easily, "you can always stay and work in Robin's stables. A life truly to look forward to."

Zachary shot him a look. "Or I could come work in yours and continue the discussion I just had with your sons a moment ago."

Jake grunted. "You'd better hope that gate works, laddie, because I *will* make your life hell while you shovel out my stalls."

Zachary laughed a little, because he had to make light of that possibility, though he had no intention of remaining behind.

The life he had to look forward to was on the other side of a gate that *was* going to work for him. He wasn't going to give it any choice.

If the gate guards thought anything of Robin's command that the portcullis be raised, they said nothing. Zachary kept his head down and walked with Jake as he and Robin led the horses down the path.

It took less time than he expected to reach the right spot in the grass. The sky was just beginning to lighten in the east and the gate shimmered there as if it had been covered with dew. Zachary took a deep breath and looked at Robin.

"Thank you, my lord," he said quietly. "For all your many kindnesses."

Robin waved his words aside. "'Twas nothing, son. Take care of my girl. Name a child after me."

Zachary didn't dare mention that Kendrick had apparently already done that. He exchanged a brief look with Jake, then smiled at Robin and nodded. He took the reins of both horses, bid Robin a final good-bye, then paused. He frowned at the sight of a cluster of cousins standing there in the distance, but he supposed there was nothing to be done about that. He turned and walked forward until he was standing on the gate itself.

And then events took a turn he hadn't anticipated.

Chapter 30

Mary stood in the middle of a field near Artane and stared at the air that shimmered in front of her. She had seen a great many things over the course of her life—more particularly in the past se'nnight of it—but she had never seen anything like what she found in front of her.

A time gate just where James MacLeod's map said it would find itself.

She hadn't found her uncle Nicholas's map—well, she had, but not all of it. She'd been looking through things in her mother's solar and stumbled upon the book Zachary had told her of, the one that contained the history of her family. It had been interesting, truly, but not what she'd been looking for. She had started to turn away only to see something out of the corner of her eye.

Part of a sheaf of parchment that had seemingly been tucked under that very heavy book of history.

She had lifted the book and found a fragment of the map she had seen before at Wyckham. It had been brittle with age and very faded, but still eminently useful. It had taken a bit of study, but she'd finally decided upon the spot she thought it indicated. She had made a production of going to her rest the night before, forced herself to sleep for a bit, then risen well before dawn and slipped out of the keep. She had narrowly avoided an encounter with that insufferable oaf Franbury, then hurried on her way to what she had determined was the proper locale.

Obviously she had reached it, if the magic that hung in the air before her was any indication.

She watched now in astonishment as things began to take shape on the spot before her. She first saw the outline of horses, then a man standing between them, holding their reins. Merciful saints above, 'twas Zachary.

She started forward but he shook his head sharply.

"Don't," he called, his voice faint even in the stillness of the morning. "I'll come to you."

She started to compliment him on his good sense when she realized that he wasn't all she could see. She looked over his shoulder and felt her mouth fall open.

Her father stood there. Her uncle Jake stood to his right and her cousins stood in a group behind her uncle. She would have thought them nothing more than shadows from her dreams, but she could see all too clearly the looks of astonishment they wore. She imagined her expression matched theirs perfectly.

And then she couldn't see any of them very well for the tears that sprang suddenly to her eyes.

She dragged her sleeve across her burning eyes and wished that was all that vexed her. There was a buzzing sound as well, something that rent the air and throbbed in her ears. She looked up in time to see some horrible bird of prey that approached relentlessly. She would have screamed, but she was too distracted by the sound of her horses doing the same.

The bird flew over her and continued on its way whilst her horses bolted, jerking Zachary off his feet. He lost the reins, but that wasn't what terrified her so. He began to fade, as if he'd been a specter who had appeared only long enough to show her what she stood to lose. She leapt forward just as a flurry of cousins also threw themselves into the shimmering bit of air in front of her. Zachary was hauled to his feet and shoved forward.

Mary stopped and looked over Zachary's head. Her father was still standing there, doing his best no doubt to mask an expression of grief she wouldn't have wanted to see. He lifted his hand in farewell.

Then he disappeared.

She had no time to think on that, for Zachary lost his footing and slammed into her with all his weight and bore her back to the ground. Predictably, she lost her breath.

He heaved himself up onto his hands and knees, then crawled to one side and pulled her up and into his arms. He wrapped his arms around her so tightly, he stole what little air she managed to suck in.

"Are you hurt?" he demanded.

She attempted speech, but all she could manage was a squeak.

He laughed a little and eased his hold on her. "I'm so sorry," he said, sounding a little winded himself. "I seem to do this to you more often than I should."

She threw her arms around his neck and clung to him with all her strength. "Fool."

"I see I didn't wind you completely."

"I've enough breath for calling you a dozen names," she wheezed.

"Call me anything you care to," he said, "just stay close enough to do so."

She pressed her face against his hair and suppressed the urge to burst into tears for any number of reasons, beginning with having seen her father not twenty paces from her and ending with realizing how close she had come to watching Zachary disappear. He could have gone missing in any number of centuries and the saints only knew if he would have found his way out. She wondered if the cousin who had aided him would suffer that fate.

She sincerely hoped not.

"I love you," she managed when she'd caught most of her breath. "Even if you did just attempt to crush me."

He pulled back far enough to smile at her. "I love you and I apologize." He took her face in his hands, then hesitated. "Do I dare kiss you, or are you liable to blacken my other eye?"

She pursed her lips, then leaned forward and kissed him. "Ignore my brother. I do most of the time."

He smoothed her hair out of her eyes. "I'm sorry I didn't find a better way to tell you about him. I honestly didn't have a clue who he was until the day I drove down from Scotland."

"Nay," she said, shaking her head, "you could have done nothing differently. I'm sorry I didn't save you his tender ministrations and that it took so long for my temper to cool. I did threaten him when he tried to stop me from calling you, but by the time I managed to have my mobile back from him, you didn't answer." She paused. "We feared the worst until we arrived and realized why you'd done what you had."

"I had no choice," he said quietly. "Franbury would have made our lives hell otherwise. I'm not certain that he still won't try, but he'll find it more difficult now." He paused, then looked at her carefully. "It was your father's idea to send along your horses, if you're curious. As a wedding gift."

She reached up and brushed his hair out of his eyes, then smiled. "Do you come along with them?"

He chewed on his words for a moment or two. "Would you be interested if I did?"

"Is that a proposal?"

He took her face in his hands, then very carefully leaned forward and kissed her. "No. Not until I clean up a bit and have a nap so I can do something more original than fall to my knees and beg you to be mine."

"I would settle for that."

He smiled, a sweet smile that left her smiling in return. "I would at least like to fall there with some grace. Let's go find your horses, then I'll look for an appropriate place to kneel." He pushed himself to his feet, then reached down to pull her to hers. "Do we run after them, or try to find help?"

"Neither." She whistled, heard answering whinnies, then whistled again. Within minutes, both Bella and Rex were trotting toward her. She caught Rex and left Zachary to snatch up Bella's reins. She looked at him around Rex's nose.

"Thank you."

"Your father loves you deeply," he said softly.

She had to take a deep breath, but she managed a smile. "I think he saw me."

"I imagine he did. It will ease his heart to know for himself that you're well and whole." He reached for her hand. "Let's go settle your horses, then we'll settle ourselves and I'll tell you about the conversations I had last night."

She nodded and made her way with him through a village that was certainly less horse friendly than it had been in her father's day, but not completely past managing.

In time, she walked with Zachary up the strangely covered road that led to the outer gates of the castle. And who should be coming out those gates but her brother, dressed in jeans and carrying his sheathed sword propped up against his shoulder. He stopped and leaned against the wall to wait for them.

Mary frowned at him once she was sure she was close enough that he could see her expression clearly.

"Go put your sword away," she said loudly. "You've no need of it."

"You haven't seen what lies in wait for that lad who wants to date you." He looked at Zachary. "You don't mind if I stay to watch, do you?"

Zachary sighed deeply. "Will I enjoy the next hour as much as you will?"

"You might, if you could see out of that black eye you're sporting. Where'd you get it?"

"Kendrick," Mary warned.

Kendrick only laughed a bit. "We'll discuss those particulars later. Do my own perfectly functioning eyes deceive me, or is that Rex you have there?"

"It is, but don't plan on riding him anytime soon," she said. "It won't go any better for you than it did the last time."

Kendrick laughed briefly. "I'd forgotten that." He looked at Zachary. "Life is very strange."

Mary supposed there was no use in commenting on that. She concentrated instead on James MacLeod and Robert Cameron, who were walking out of the gates. They shook hands with Kendrick, heaped what they obviously considered an appropriate amount of brotherly teasing upon Zachary's head, then they turned to admire her horseflesh. Jamie smiled.

"We'll take your spectacular horses for you, lady, if you will. I fear 'twas our flying over them this morning that caused them to bolt."

Mary was tempted to ask for details, but perhaps there would be time enough for that later. She handed Rex off to Cameron, then watched Jamie wait for Zachary to remove a sword from Bella's saddle before he led her off as well.

Kendrick looked with interest at Zachary's blade. "Where did you come by that?"

"Your father had it made for me. Jackson helped a bit, though

I understand his only concern was that it be sharp enough that I might possibly fall on it by mistake and die."

"That sounds like Jack," Kendrick said without hesitation. "Am I to understand he wasn't too fond of you?"

"I don't think he liked the fact that I love your sister."

"His good sense was legendary."

"Kendrick," Mary said in exasperation, "stop it."

"Jackson would want me to carry on in his stead," Kendrick said solemnly. He looked at Zachary. "I will, however, leave off long enough for you to see to that piece of mischief being combined at the ticket window. Mary, take his sword. He won't need it."

Zachary handed her his sword, then smiled briefly. "I'll return."

"I know," she said quietly.

He shot Kendrick a look, then bent his head and kissed her quickly on the cheek. "I won't tell you what to do, but I think it might be wise to stay out of Franbury's sights if you can."

She nodded, and watched him walk away unsteadily. She doubted that he'd slept much the night before if he'd been with her family.

She turned to her brother. "I'll expect you to protect him if need be."

"He'll manage—"

"Aye, with you there to help him, he will." She took him by the arm and pulled him along with her. "Let's be off."

She walked up the path from the outer gates, suppressing a shiver as she did so. 'Twas difficult to believe that a month earlier, she had been walking through those gates knowing that her future—or her doom, rather—lay with Geoffrey of Styrr. She wouldn't have dreamed that she might have something else, or be walking up those gates in a time so far removed from her own.

She stopped just behind Zachary, who had jerked back suddenly to avoid being struck by a manuscript that had been flung out of the guard chamber to her left. It was followed rapidly by another and another until there was quite a pile of them lying at Zachary's feet.

He bent and picked up one of the manuscripts. Mary could see 'twas one of the guidebooks. Zachary's hands trembled as he held it, though she supposed that was from weariness, not from any weakness on his part. He looked over his shoulder at her.

"Want to look with me?"

"Nay, I'll look for you." She moved to stand at his side, then took the book from him.

She turned the pages until she reached the drawings he had made of her father's kennels. She looked closely, but she couldn't see his name written there as she'd seen it the night before. Zachary put his arm around her shoulders only to have Kendrick flick it off. Mary glared at her brother and pulled Zachary's arm back around her. She held the book up for him.

"I daresay the photograph has changed, but I cannot read the English. What does it say?"

"It says," he began with a smile, "that this is an example of how advanced society was at Artane in the Middle Ages. The buildings were quite obviously superior to anything found anywhere else in England at the time."

"Someone is flattering my father," she said.

"I imagine someone is."

Mary turned the page and saw herself there. She looked up at Zachary.

"And this?"

He tightened his arm around her shoulders briefly. "I couldn't bring myself to ask your father to destroy that, and I imagine he wouldn't have done so anyway. Though I suppose if he had given his word, he would have."

"He was a man of his word," Kendrick agreed, "no matter the personal cost."

Mary watched her love look at her brother briefly. "I imagine we have a few interesting things to discuss at some point, my lord."

"If I leave you alive to do so," Kendrick said with a yawn.

Zachary sighed lightly, then looked at Mary again. "I think Franbury might think you resemble the woman in that sketch, but he'll have no signature now to connect either you or me to the past. We'll be safe enough. But I'm not sure Gideon's gatekeeper will be if I don't rescue her. If you'll excuse me, I'll go make certain of it."

Mary waved him on to his business. He walked over to the guard chamber to no doubt try to stem the tide of books rushing out onto the cobblestones. He was soon joined by Gideon, who protested loudly the destruction of his father's property.

"This should be interesting," Kendrick murmured.

She looked up at her brother. "Just so you know: if he hadn't returned, I would have gone after him."

He pursed his lips and refrained from comment.

"And if you hurt him today, I will repay you for it."

"You might try."

She pointed up the way. "Remember who I now have in the stables and how badly it pained you the last time he pitched you onto your sorry arse. He'll do that again, then he'll trample you because I'll tell him to."

Kendrick shifted uncomfortably. "Very well, I'll leave something of your love. And I'll do you the favor of telling you what that fool Franbury is now shouting, though I imagine you can guess well enough without my aid."

He had that aright. Franbury came rushing out of the guard chamber suddenly, his hands wrapped around his head to protect it, bellowing things he was sure were curses.

The granny who apparently kept watch over her domain was clouting him with some sort of heavy purse. Mary watched in astonishment as she then plucked a long stick out of that purse and brandished it.

"A Future weapon?" she whispered to her brother.

"Knitting needle. She's obviously been pushed a bit too far." He smiled for a bit longer, then his smile faded. He ceased with any pretense of not caring about the outcome of what was transpiring in front of them.

She had no less interest in it. Franbury had managed to escape the granny with her needle and had now turned on Zachary, shouting until his face was a most unattractive shade of red. Zachary only stood there with his arms folded over his chest, apparently waiting for Franbury to shout himself out. The whole scene reminded her sharply of that morning with Styrr in her father's courtyard.

Kendrick looked back over his shoulder suddenly, then snorted.

"Cameras. Unsurprising."

"What?" She looked behind her to find a man standing there with a black box of sorts on his shoulder.

"'Tis a video camera. It captures what you see in front of

you, then replays it for later consumption. Truly one of modern man's most marvelous inventions. I can't imagine our good viscount is going to be pleased at having his antics so captured, though."

Indeed Franbury was not. He realized he was being watched and shouted at the man now standing next to her to cease with what he was doing. Once the man lowered his box, Franbury swung at Zachary. Zachary only ducked and left the viscount stumbling from having overbalanced himself. Franbury straightened and spat out a slew of things Mary was certain weren't complimentary.

He then turned on Gideon, whose expression would have caused a lesser man—or a more intelligent one, perhaps—to take a step backward.

"My nephew," Kendrick said proudly, elbowing her in the ribs. "I taught him that look."

"I imagine you did."

Franbury and Gideon spoke for several minutes, though she supposed it couldn't have been called a conversation. Franbury shouted and Gideon simply stood there, now wearing a look of utter contempt.

"Franbury's convinced Gideon has changed the guidebooks," Kendrick said with a smirk. "He can't quite remember what it was about them that intrigued him so before, but he knows there was something important because he's brought a bloody cameraman to document it. He's certain we're hiding something inside the keep."

"Gideon won't allow him inside, will he?"

Kendrick shrugged casually. "If he thinks it will occupy Franbury's time well, I suppose he might. I understand that there are several keeps scattered throughout England which boast paranormal elements that a man such as Michael Smythe-Gordon might find interesting. Not that *I* would know anything about that, of course."

Mary smiled before she could stop herself. "I daresay you have quite a few things going on at Seakirk, as it has always been a dodgy place. But Artane?"

"One never knows. We'll have to see what turns up in the next hour or so. Don't go throw yourself at that lad over there in the meantime, though, until I've finished with him."

She handed him his sword instead of clouting him over the

head with it because she was her father's daughter and she knew the value of steel. And she would most certainly throw herself at her love—but perhaps later, when he wouldn't yawn his way through it. She watched him talking to Gideon, then looked up at her brother, who resembled her father so much it was startling, and felt her heart ache a bit. She sighed and slipped her arm through his.

"I saw Father this morning," she said quietly.

His look of shock was almost rewarding enough to ease her slightly.

"You jest," he said faintly.

She shook her head slowly. "Zachary was in the middle of that doorway through time and Father was on the other side." She paused. "I wish he could have seen you, to know you are well and happy."

Kendrick took a deep breath. "He knows."

"How?" she asked in surprise.

"Jake told him."

"Jake?" she echoed. "Our uncle Jake? And how would he know to do that?"

"Because I told him to when I saw him a pair of years ago here in the Future."

She leaned heavily on him. "I need a nap."

"Not with that lad over there you don't."

"Kendrick, leave him be. He's had enough for one day."

"Not if he wants you, he hasn't."

She started to remind her brother of the equine danger he would face if he pushed her too far, but he took a figurative step backward before she could.

"Very well," he conceded. "I'll allow him a brief rest."

"I'll oversee his taking of it myself."

"Mary!"

She walked away, smiling, because she couldn't keep herself from it. Her love and her brother in the same century. It was truly so much more than she'd dared hope for and so much more than she deserved.

Zachary was standing on the path in front of her, listening to Gideon with half an ear, but watching her. She thought of all the times she had watched him in her father's time, wishing that things would be different and she might have him in truth.

Zachary turned, leaving Gideon standing there, still talking. He met her halfway, then opened his arms.

She walked into his embrace, put her arms around him, and closed her eyes. She wished, briefly, that she'd known about her aunt Jennifer—or apparently her uncle Jake, for that matter—so she might have asked them how they had made such wonderful lives in times not their own, then she decided they had likely known what she had discovered.

Someone to love made all the difference.

Chapter 31

Zachary held Mary not nearly as long as he would have liked, though likely far longer than her brother wanted him to. He looked over her head to find Kendrick standing ten feet away, patting his sword meaningfully.

"Mary?"

"Hmmm?"

"I think your brother has plans."

"You should have some, too," she advised, "and they should include killing him quickly to rid us of the annoyance of his presence. Please."

He laughed briefly. "I think you would miss him, so I'll forbear. I also imagine we could escape not only him, but this entire collection of in-laws and future in-laws if we tried hard enough. Let me finish up here, satisfy your brother briefly, then we'll attempt it."

She released him as reluctantly as he could have wished for, then handed his sword to Gideon and helped him gather up the rest of the guidebooks. He carried them all back into the ticket booth and stacked them for Mrs. Gladstone.

She of the voracious till was sitting in her padded chair busily picking up dropped stitches. She glanced up at him. "That bloke fair ruined me Fair Isle work and I will *not* forget the insult."

"I'm sure Lord Gideon will see him appropriately chastised," Zachary offered.

Mrs. Gladstone pursed her lips. "I certainly hope so." She glanced out her window. "I see the Earl of Seakirk has a sword. And so do ye, apparently. Going to use them soon?"

Zachary laughed a little uneasily. "Mrs. Gladstone, why would you think that?"

"Lad, you live in the north long enough and you see it all." She looked over her bifocals at him. "I'd charge ye the normal entrance, but I note ye've no pockets."

"I'll pay double the next time."

"See that ye do." She pulled a teal blue metal four-millimeter out of her bun and pointed it at him. "Ye don't want to meet this in the dark, I daresay."

Zachary nodded gravely, left Mrs. Gladstone to her Fair Isle, then walked up the way with Mary, collecting a following as he did so. It felt slightly surreal to find himself in the company of medieval men and one very lovely woman who were all dressed in jeans while he was the only one dressed in medieval gear and possessing a birthdate that fell within the past hundred years.

So much for no more paranormal activities.

He paused at the edge of what had once been Artane's lists and was now a wide swath of green grass and looked first at Jamie and Cameron.

"Why are you here?"

"We came this morning," Jamie said with a bored look, "just to see what Lord Gideon had on the fire."

"Don't listen to him," Cameron said dryly. "He was actually worried enough about you that he forced me to fly him down before breakfast."

"How did you know anything at all?" Zachary asked in surprise.

"Gideon called him last night," Cameron said. "Apparently he thought you'd gone off rashly."

"Can you blame me?" Zachary asked. "Leave it to Franbury to find what he shouldn't."

Jamie laughed briefly. "Zach, what does that lad have against you?"

"Zinnias," Zachary said distinctly, "but don't make me give you the details now. I'm not sure how far Franbury's been digging. I think he got lucky with the guidebook, but now he has nothing more to go on."

"Just vague impressions of memories that were there yesterday but are there no longer," Jamie said in satisfaction. "I'm going to go home and make further study of this phenomenon." He paused. "It might require quite a bit of research to do properly."

Zachary winced. His poor sister.

"But for now, let us leave the fool to his speculations," Jamie said. "He won't find anything here and we'll make certain he finds nothing anywhere else. Now we have a morning of fine sport to look forward to. Lady Mary, shall we go find ourselves a seat where we might be comfortable whilst watching the spectacle? I taught Zachary everything he knows about swords, you know. Anything underhanded he knows he learned from my brother, who is not the purist I am."

"Tell me more," Mary asked, walking off with Jamie and looking more interested than she should have. "My father was a swordsman, you know."

"I've heard tell of his prowess. One of my sincerest regrets is that I have not encountered him."

Zachary watched Jamie and Mary walk off, then he looked at Cameron. "Yet."

Cameron shook his head and smiled. "No century is safe, no lists are sacred."

"Heaven help Robin of Artane."

"I imagine he'll agree, in time." Cameron studied him. "You look exhausted. Sleep any last night?"

Zachary shook his head. "I was too busy hobnobbing with medieval legends. I'll sleep later."

"If Seakirk leaves anything of you."

"Are you helping?"

Cameron laughed and clapped him on the shoulder. "Likely not, though I will thank you for putting Franbury off the scent. I wouldn't worry about anything else. As for myself, I'm going to go find somewhere to sit as well. Just looking at you is making me weary."

Zachary sighed deeply and watched his brother-in-law walk off. He turned and followed Kendrick out into what was apparently going to serve for the lists that morning.

He yawned and rubbed his hand over his face before he

could stop himself. He wasn't unused to going without sleep to meet a deadline, but he was the first to admit it had been a pretty unusual month. Even the last week had been tough. He'd driven from Scotland to Artane three times, been more worried about how a certain medieval woman might feel about him than he wanted to admit, and he'd just spent the past sixteen hours hopping over eight centuries and back to fix something he should have seen coming in the first place.

And now his future comfort at Seakirk's dinner table rested on how he fared against Robin of Artane's son, a son who he had the feeling had been just as driven in his day as Robin had been.

Kendrick threw away the sheath to his sword, then stood there facing him with his sword bared and a look of challenge on his face.

Zachary yawned again, because he couldn't help it.

Jamie laughed.

Zachary shot his brother-in-law a look of warning, then unsheathed his sword. Unfortunately he had to yawn again before he could use it.

"Oh, by the saints," Kendrick said in disgust, "are you going to sleep through this entire exercise?"

"I might."

Kendrick's look darkened. "I don't suppose you spoke to my father about any of this, did you?"

Zachary would have preferred to satisfy Kendrick on his own merits, but he supposed Robin hadn't given him that particular piece of paper just to have him keep it in his boot. He resheathed his sword, then pulled the letter out and handed it to Kendrick.

Kendrick read, then pursed his lips. "Very well, my father has spoken and I won't gainsay him. You may have her freely, but it will be at a time of *my* choosing."

"It will not," Mary said loudly. She walked out into the lists. "I can decide for myself when I'll wed him. I do *not* need your aid in this endeavor. And let me see that missive."

Kendrick handed it to her with a grunt. Zachary watched Mary read it, then turn to him.

"Did you tell him that I loved you?"

Zachary shook his head with a smile. "I told him that I

loved you, which he already knew. I told him that I hoped for the rest."

"Well, then?"

He walked over to her, handed her suddenly spluttering brother his sword, then pulled her into his arms. "Let me ask you when we have some privacy," he whispered in her ear. "A walk along the beach in a bit?"

She tightened her arms around him briefly. "Aye. But I need to go tend my horses first."

He laughed. "Of course you do. I'll go beg a crust of bread from Lord Edward's cook, then come find you."

She nodded, leaned up to kiss him quickly, then turned and ran toward the stables. Zachary watched her go, then realized he'd been joined in that effort by her brother. He looked at Kendrick.

"My lord?"

Kendrick handed him back his sword. "Sadly enough, I don't dare gainsay my father, though I *will* meet you in the lists before you wed her. In six months or so."

Zachary felt his mouth fall open.

Kendrick laughed at him, clapped him on the shoulder, then walked away. "Gideon, lad, where's breakfast? I don't know about any of you, but it's been a very taxing morning for me so far and I need something strengthening before we go searching for that idiot Franbury. I wonder what he's gotten into this time that Zachary will need to go rectify in a different century?"

Zachary didn't want to find out, but he followed after the others readily enough because food was involved.

And then he fully intended to go look for the woman who was grooming her father's wedding presents to her so he could finally have some privacy with her.

He picked up a guidebook that some distracted soul had left lying on the front steps leading up to the great hall, flipped through the pages, and looked again at the changed drawings. The trip hadn't been without its dangers, especially the end of it. If he hadn't been hauled to his feet and shoved through the gate, heaven only knew where he would have landed.

He wondered what had happened to whoever had pushed him.

It was tempting to speculate, but he resisted. He would investigate later, when he could see straight. He walked over to the lord's table, set his sword down, and wondered if it would be impolite to simply stretch out and have a nap right there. He might have, but he was suddenly distracted by the howls of pure terror coming from the direction of the kitchens. Someone had obviously been busy.

He leaned against the table and watched as Franbury and his camera guy came tearing out of the passageway. They were screaming as if they'd looked into the very pit of hell and seen something there that they really hadn't wanted to. Franbury was absolutely white as a sheet and his cameraman looked no less terrified. Gideon did the second man the favor of reaching out and plucking the camera from his hands as he bolted by. Cameron held open the front door to apparently save Franbury and his friend the trouble.

Their screeches faded into the distance.

Zachary could hardly wait to see what had inspired such an abrupt departure.

Ambrose, Hugh, and Fulbert came strolling out of the passageway without haste, chatting amicably. Well, perhaps amicably wasn't the right word to use. On closer inspection, Zachary saw that Fulbert and Hugh were arguing about something. Maybe there were niceties that had been failed to be observed in the haunting just perpetrated. Zachary wasn't sure he wanted to know the details.

John Drummond, laird of the clan Drummond during some as-yet-undetermined century—Hugh could have told him, no doubt—came striding out behind the trio. He was covered in blood, maggots, and other gruesome substances. He was also scratching his head. With a hand that wasn't attached to the other arm.

"I say," Gideon managed faintly. "That is a bit much, don't you think?"

The Drummond put himself back together, cleaned up with a snap of his fingers, then sauntered over to the table. He looked at Zachary archly until Zachary made him a low bow.

"My laird," Zachary said deferentially. "I can tell I have you to thank for that very fine rescue."

"You do," the Drummond said without hesitation. "My bit's done, but I will come back for the wedding."

"Where are you off to now?" Jamie asked politely.

The Drummond turned to him. "I'm off to haunt a few of my brother's descendants. They've been living quite richly on *my* gold all these years and I've been itching for an excuse to point out the error of their ways."

"All descendants of noble ancestors aren't necessarily guilty of nefarious deeds," Kendrick offered.

The Drummond looked at him. "I've heard about you."

"I imagine you have," Kendrick said mildly.

The Drummond grunted, then looked at Zachary. "I suppose I can't leave without giving you a bit of a thank-you as well."

"Me?" Zachary asked in surprise. "Why?"

John Drummond pursed his lips, considered, then looked at Jamie briefly before he turned back to Zachary. "I didn't tell you before, but I wanted to thank you for your efforts to save that little American lass." He paused. "You know the one."

Zachary was quite happy to be leaning against the table. He knew exactly who the Drummond was talking about. He could only nod, mute.

"She was one of my descendants," Laird Drummond said gruffly. "I could do nothing for her, of course, save watch and fret." He cleared his throat. "I aided you today because you're my kin. But I want you to know I'm also grateful for what you tried to do for a gel you didn't know." He shot Kendrick a look. "Keep that in mind when you're vexing my grandson here. I'm not afeared of those pantywaists you have guarding your keep. I *will* come haunt you with a vengeance if you treat him ill."

Kendrick didn't look particularly intimidated, but he did make the Drummond a small bow. "I will do no more than a brother would do."

"That's what I'm afraid of."

Zachary watched the Drummond stride across the hall to join his other undead cohorts. He nodded to the collection of medieval and not-so-medieval nobility gathered at the lord's table before he changed his mind about breakfast and instead took his own path across the hall. He was happy to leave the others to the dissecting of not only the morning's events but Franbury's camcorder.

He loped down the stairs and walked to the stables. Perhaps the location wasn't exactly the same, but the building more than made up for it in its sheer splendor. Gideon hadn't been exaggerating when he said his father was keen on horses.

He walked down the aisle until he found Rex. He leaned against the stall door and watched Mary groom her horse. She was just as careful and thorough as she had been almost eight hundred years earlier. Some things didn't change.

She finished, allowed him to open the door for her, then went to put away her brushes. He shut the stall door, then leaned against it and waited for her to return.

"Will he adjust, do you think?" he asked as she stopped next to him.

"Rex?" she asked. "Aye, easily. Good feed and a little brushing do wonders, apparently."

He turned her to him and looped his arms around her waist. "And you? How are you?"

"Zachary, the century doesn't matter as long as I have you."

"Mary, you're about to convince me that you love me."

"I do." She hugged him briefly. "But I don't think you're going to be awake much longer to contemplate that. Let's go nap in the hayloft."

"And wake up with your brother's pitchfork in my gut?" he asked with a laugh. "Not a chance. We'll take the Range Rover to the beach and nap there where he can't find us."

She smiled at him. "Happily. But I have to show you something first."

He soon found himself sitting on a bale of hay, watching her go inside the stall next to Bella. He shouldn't have been so happy to be off his feet, but he found he was. It had been a very, very long night and day.

He enjoyed his rest for about thirty seconds until he saw Mary struggling to carry four saddlebags of a medieval make. He set them down on the floor, then sat down next to her and frowned in surprise.

"Did your father send along rocks?"

"Didn't you look?"

He shook his head. "I was too preoccupied with getting back to the right year."

She heaved one of the bags up and dropped it on his lap. "Then look now."

He opened it gingerly and found it full of a collection of

rough drawstring bags. Mary took one and spilled part of its contents into her hand.

The gold sparkled dimly in the light from the windows.

"What's this?" he asked in astonishment.

"My dowry."

"How do you know?"

She pulled a slip of parchment from the back pocket of her jeans. "My father said as much. Three are mine, one is yours."

He wouldn't have been any more surprised if Robin had appeared at the door and said as much. "But why?"

"Because my father said you deserved it," she said softly. "You were willing to shovel manure for me."

He put his hand to the back of her head, then leaned over and kissed her softly. "You were reward enough."

She smiled, hugged him briefly, then pulled away. "How much is it worth in your day? Our day, I should say."

Zachary shrugged helplessly. "I have no idea."

She fingered the coins in her hand for a moment. "Could I buy Moraig's house with this?"

"A thousand times over and still have enough left to splurge on a few hot showers," he said with a smile. "But you don't want to live in Scotland, do you?"

She shrugged, though she didn't look particularly casual. "I just want to live with you. The location doesn't matter."

But it mattered to him. Visions of Wyckham floated in front of him. In the summer surrounded by rolling hills and flower-strewn meadows, in the winter surrounded by snow-covered hills and winding country lanes, at sunset, when the plastered walls turned to gold, or pink, or purple.

Mary put the gold back in the pouch, then put it back in the saddlebag.

"You know, this is all yours now," she said, looking at him with a grave smile.

"Of course it isn't," he said without hesitation.

"Of course, it is. That's what a dowry is for, after all. So a man can keep his knights and horses fed and make certain his roof doesn't leak. I think my father sent along extra so my horses wouldn't beggar you."

Zachary shook his head. "Mary, I can't take this."

She brushed the bangs out of his eyes, then leaned forward

and kissed him. "Don't force me to drag you out to the lists and best you there."

"I think you just might today," he said. He put his arms around her and held her close for a moment or two in silence, then pulled away. "Let's talk about it later. All I want now is to escape with you before your brother decides we need a chaperon."

"I'll distract him whilst you find a place for this."

He was happy to let her try. He hauled into the keep saddlebags that were heavy enough that he couldn't believe he hadn't noticed them earlier, and then asked Gideon for a room that actually had a lock on it.

One thing was for certain: he was *not* putting them in Anne's solar.

S_{everal} hours later, he was pulling into Wyckham's suggestion of a car park. He shut off the engine, then leaned back against the seat and looked at what was left of the castle.

Then it occurred to him that Mary hadn't seen it in its current state.

"I'm sorry," he stammered. "I didn't think."

She looked at him, but her expression was full of understanding and not a little pity. "No wonder you couldn't stop looking at the place."

"Well, I was actually trying to distract myself from looking at you, if you want the entire truth," he admitted, "but yes, I was a little overwhelmed."

"Might we go inside?"

"It's your brother's," he said with a faint smile. "I don't think he'll mind."

"Kendrick owns Wyckham now?" she asked in surprise.

Zachary nodded. "I'm not sure when he bought it, but it's definitely his now. The cottage I've been working on is right next to it. We can look at both, if you like."

"Aye, I would."

He opened her door for her, then locked the car and shoved the keys in his pocket. He walked around the courtyard with her, mourning the loss of things he knew had been there in the past. The garden was overrun, the lists empty, the stables but a fond memory. He walked inside the keep with her, but it was just a shell of its former self. He'd already known that, of course, but seeing it all again through Mary's eyes was more difficult than he'd imagined it would be.

"Let's go look at the cottage," he suggested. "At least it has a roof."

She nodded, then walked with him out the gates and around the corner of a wall to the little cottage that butted up against the stone.

It had been a charming place to begin with, true, but he had to admit that the improvements had been good ones. There was a large hearth in the great room, with a pair of bedrooms and a bathroom opening off that main room. The kitchen was in the back, dominated by a bright blue Aga sitting in one corner. It was definitely larger than Moraig's house, but had much of the same charm, only this had been run through a British filter. Every time Zachary walked across the threshold, he felt as if he'd walked back in time fifty years.

Figuratively, of course.

He leaned against a wall and watched Mary wander through the place. She touched wood and stone, ran her fingers over overstuffed furniture and along windowsills, then wandered in and out of the kitchen. She came to a stop in a different doorway.

"What was it like when you first saw it?"

"Bare."

She smiled. "'Tis lovely. Kendrick must be pleased."

"I wish he would be slightly less pleased so he would sell it to me."

"Won't he?"

He shook his head, but smiled just the same. "We'll find something, Mary, and I'll redo it to suit you."

She looked at him seriously. "I would have lived with the swine and the chickens, Zachary."

"I know," he said quietly.

And he did know it. He was also rather relieved that it wouldn't be necessary. He would have been happy to have had the chance to turn Wyckham into the same bit of magnificence Nicholas de Piaget had created for his love, but perhaps there were things in this life that were simply beyond reach.

He was profoundly grateful that Maryanne de Piaget wasn't one of them.

He walked over to her, took her into his arms, then held her close for a moment or two before he looked around for a decent place to kneel.

Chapter 32

M*ary* stood in her mother's solar, not because there was space for her to dress there, but because her mother would have wanted it so. It was, after all, the chamber where brides traditionally dressed for their weddings. She had help in the form of Elizabeth, Madelyn, and Genevieve, who were fussing with her hair, and Sunshine, who was sitting in the most comfortable chair in the chamber, holding off having her child. Mary wasn't sure how she was managing it, though she supposed Sunny knew what she was doing.

Madelyn apparently didn't share her confidence. She looked at her sister with a frown. "The contractions are coming closer together, aren't they?" she demanded.

Sunny was the picture of serenity. "A bit, but the hypnobirthing is helping." She smiled. "It's why we have a helicopter waiting. I have every intention of watching Mary's wedding. I think, though, that I'm going to go home and have this baby this afternoon."

"Sunny!" Madelyn exclaimed.

"Shh," Sunny said with a smile. "You can fly home with us."

"But Patrick—"

"Is *not* going to be my midwife," Sunny said, "no matter

how much I love him. Mrs. Gilmarten has delivered over a
thousand babies and never lost a mother or a child. She's waiting with Madame Gies in the kitchen at home. I'll be fine." She
looked at Mary. "But forgive me if we don't stay for the dancing afterward."

Mary looked at Elizabeth. "Let's hurry."

Elizabeth arranged a circlet of silver over a veil that was so
sheer, Mary could hardly believe it didn't fall apart when
touched.

"You're ready and you're lovely," Elizabeth said, embracing
her carefully. "We'll go ahead to the chapel."

Madelyn and Sunny squeezed her hands and kissed her
cheeks, then left the solar with Elizabeth. Mary looked at Genevieve.

"Are you staying with me?" she asked quietly.

Genevieve linked arms with her. "I am and I would, even if
I hadn't promised Zachary I'd get you safely downstairs. He's
not exactly trusting of that doorway over there, and I can't say
I blame him." She paused. "And if I can say so, I think your
mother would be thrilled with how beautiful you look in that
dress."

"Perhaps she'll be here in spirit," Mary said.

"I imagine so." She smiled and tugged gently. "Let's go before your brother wears a trench in the floor."

Mary nodded and walked with her to the door. She hadn't
wept in the past month, but she found that she was tempted at
present. She wasn't unhappy with her life. She simply missed
her parents and her cousins. Today, especially.

But somehow the thought of the man who was waiting for
her in the chapel eased that more than she would have thought
possible.

She took a deep breath, then crossed the threshold behind
Genevieve. She honestly couldn't tell the century from the
passageway outside the solar, but when she looked back, she
saw the chamber was as they'd left it. She looked at Genevieve, shrugged, then continued on down the passageway
with her.

Kendrick was waiting for her downstairs. He was dressed in
medieval finery. She stopped still when she saw him, simply
because she feared she had taken a wrong turn and landed herself in a century other than her own.

Except Genevieve was there, too.

Kendrick strode forward and caught her by the shoulders. "Are you unwell?"

She shook her head. "Confused."

He drew her hand under his arm to rest in the crook of his elbow. "That will pass, I imagine, though I've no experience with it. Talk to your husband about it this afternoon, for I'm sure he has more tales to tell you than he should." He shot her a look. "Husband. Appalling."

"I love him."

He sighed heavily. "I know. I'm resigned to it. And I'll grant you that he isn't completely without redeeming traits."

"Kendrick, he's trained with you almost every morning for a month."

"Only because he knew I wouldn't let him in the hall door to see you until he had."

Genevieve sighed, then leaned up and kissed her husband quickly. "I'll walk ahead to the chapel. Don't get lost, either of you."

Kendrick smiled at his wife. "I wouldn't dare. We'll be there in a minute."

Mary watched her walk out the hall and down the stairs, then looked up at her brother. "I'm so happy you're here."

He looked at her, his eyes suddenly bright. "I would give you the sort of embrace that flowery sentiment deserves, but I would ruin your hair." He leaned forward and kissed both her cheeks. "I am very glad you're here," he said roughly. "More than I'll own, of course. Now, let's be about this before you reduce me to tears."

She walked with him out of the hall, down the steps, and across the way to the chapel. It was filled to the brim with her family and Zachary's. Most of the guests had no choice but to stand, so she hoped the priest would be about his work before they fainted from the press.

She also hoped the priest wouldn't freak out, as one of Kendrick's sons would have said. Madelyn's parents had conferred with him over the phone as to the Latin to be used, and Lord Edward had prepared him for the fact that this was going to be another in a long line of medieval-style ceremonies that Artane was becoming famous for. Mary had felt better knowing it wouldn't be the first the poor man had celebrated.

And then she caught sight of Zachary and found she couldn't think about the particulars any longer.

He was simply stunning in the tunic her mother had made for him, black hose, and black boots. His brothers stood in a line next to him along with Jamie, Patrick, Jamie's cousin Ian, and Cameron. On her side were Gideon, his father, and all Kendrick's lads. She smiled at the boys, then took a deep breath and concentrated on walking steadily as Kendrick led her to the front of the chapel and put her hand in Zachary's.

She supposed he didn't mind that her eyes were leaking, given that his were doing the same thing.

"I love you," he murmured.

"I love you," she said, blinking furiously. "I only wish I could see you."

He smiled, then squeezed her hand.

"A recounting," Kendrick said solemnly, "of what each will bring to this miraculous union."

Mary shot him a dark look, but found he was entirely in earnest. He nodded at Zachary's father.

"After you, sir."

Mary felt Zachary take a careful breath next to her. She looked up at him, but he only lifted his eyebrows briefly. She knew he was more than a little uncomfortable with what was happening, but Kendrick had been adamant that it was necessary to carry on in a fully medieval fashion so she wouldn't feel slighted.

She understood Zachary's reluctance. He had chosen over the course of his life to be modest about his accomplishments and allow those accomplishments to speak for themselves. Perhaps he didn't have as much gold to his name as Kendrick did—though he would certainly have a staggering amount when he accepted her dowry, which he would do against his will, she was sure—but if she'd found herself either in the wilds of Scotland or another century, there was no one she would rather have had protecting her.

She leaned close. "Buck up."

He looked at her in surprise. "What?"

"You heard me."

He smiled at her briefly, then no doubt suppressed the urge to sigh.

He had to do that last bit several times. His father gave an accounting of his education and funds, then Jamie made a great production of describing an inheritance he'd apparently been trying to give Zachary for years. Patrick gave him all he said he deserved, which was a horse. Cameron very solemnly doubled his salary.

"I'm going to kill them all," Zachary muttered under his breath. "For various reasons."

"Do it later," she advised. "And hold on."

He looked at her, startled. "Why?"

"Kendrick hasn't begun yet."

"Hell," he managed. "Can I sit down during it?"

"You can't and don't swear in church."

He took a deep breath. "All right."

"Meet him in the lists later." Mary turned and watched her brother. He stepped up beside her and looked at the priest.

"Make certain your scribe takes this down correctly," he said imperiously.

The saints pity the poor lad, he didn't dare not.

"My father has dowered my sister with things that I'll keep private so the taxman doesn't take most of them on her way out the door," Kendrick said with a grumble, "but I'll name what I'll see she brings to the union."

Zachary opened his mouth to speak—to protest, no doubt—but Mary squeezed his hand, hard. He muttered instead what she was certain was another curse under his breath.

"In coin, she brings enough for several years of hay, grain, and other particulars suitable to her horse madness," Kendrick began seriously, "as well as enough to see to restoring that wreck she demanded I give her."

Mary looked up at Zachary because she couldn't not watch his reaction.

"Wreck?" he echoed.

She only smiled.

"And along with the wreck," Kendrick continued, "she will bring the title of countess. Her husband will wear the title of earl. Because I was told I had to buy that for him as well," he said not fully under his breath.

Zachary's mouth fell open. "I beg your pardon?"

"Wyckham, lad," Kendrick said with not the slightest trace of a smirk on his face. "Or, I should say, Your Lordship. You didn't think I was going to let my sister live in a tent on the shore, did you?"

"I just want to know where *my* title is," Zachary's father muttered loudly enough for most of the company to hear.

Mary couldn't take her eyes off Zachary. He had expected to be forced to take her gold she knew, but this . . . aye, this was something he hadn't expected. He dragged his free hand through his hair, then looked at Kendrick.

"Why?"

"Because you love my sister."

Mary found her love then looking at her.

"Wyckham?" he managed.

"Because you love *it*," she said softly. "And because Uncle Nicholas would trust you with it, just as my father has trusted you with me. If I might make that comparison."

He shook his head briefly. "How did you manage it?"

She leaned close. "I took Kendrick out in the lists and ran over him with my horse."

A smile tugged at his mouth. "You didn't."

"Actually, I didn't. I used his horse. As for the other, 'twas all because of you, of course. He saw what you did with your brother's keep at Falconberg. And he knew you'd seen the original Wyckham and would care for it properly."

Zachary put his arm around her waist, pressed a kiss against her temple, then reached around her and shook Kendrick's hand. "Thank you, my lord," he said quietly.

"You're welcome, er, my lord." Kendrick rolled his eyes. "I cannot believe my sister has forced that little bit of deference upon me for the rest of your days." He shot Zachary a look. "I suppose I should admit that the cottage is yours as well. 'Twill give you someplace to lay your head until you've finished the keep, though I can't guarantee you won't have visitors from time to time. And if you say this is the best thing that happened to you today, I *will* take you out in the lists and kill you."

Zachary laughed, then reached out to steady the priest. Mary found him then looking down at her.

"It isn't the best thing," he said quietly.

"But 'tis a good thing," she said, just as quietly.

"Only because there are many, many darkened corners there," he said with a smile, "and a fine hall to dance in."

"You sound like my uncle Nicholas."

"He's my inspiration."

Mary understood.

She signed the appropriate document when asked, agreed to the appropriate pledges and promises, then found herself pulled into her husband's arms and kissed very sweetly for her trouble.

"Cam," Sunny whispered gingerly, "we need to go. Mary and Zachary, congratulations."

Cameron patted them both, then leapt across the chapel, swept his wife up into his arms, and strode from the chapel with her. Madelyn ran after her, her daughter in her arms. Patrick clapped a hand on Zachary's shoulder.

"Have a nice life. Mary, best of luck with him."

Mary watched the chapel empty as children piled out to see the helicopter take off and adults left to supervise. Indeed, she was more than happy to simply close her eyes and stand there with her husband's arms around her. In time, she lifted her head and smiled up at him.

"Well?" she asked.

"Alone at last," he said, then he bent his head and kissed her.

"Supper's being prepared," a voice said loudly from the doorway.

Zachary lifted his head and shot her brother an even look. "Beat it."

Kendrick only laughed and walked away.

Mary looked up at Zachary and found she couldn't stop a slightly giddy laugh. "Well?"

"You went house hunting with me for a solid fortnight, Mary-anne Smith."

"I couldn't tell you."

"How long have you known?"

"Since Rex's first night here. I went home with Kendrick and told him what he was going to do."

"You're intimidating."

"There's a lesson there for you, I imagine."

He reached up and lifted off the circlet of silver, then set it aside with her veil. Then he bent his head and kissed the spot just behind her ear.

"Keep you appeased at all times is that lesson, I imagine."

"Don't start that."

He lifted his head and took a deep breath. "I likely shouldn't, should I?"

"Nay, my lord, you shouldn't. But you should come dance with me. And then please let us leave before midnight."

"Midnight?" he echoed incredulously.

She laughed and walked away. "That was a jest, Zachary. Let's go have something to eat." She looked over her shoulder at him. "Are you going to tell me now where we're going on our honeymoon?"

He shook his head with a smile as he caught up to her. "I have my own set of secrets, you know."

"I know most of them."

"Love, you know *all* of them. Except the one concerning our destination tonight, but you'll find out that one eventually."

It was sunset before she found herself in the car with her husband, driving to a place he wouldn't tell her. She realized, after a bit, that she suspected where he might be going. But considering the keep didn't have a roof, she supposed she might be looking at a rather soggy night.

She leaned her head back against the seat and watched Zachary as he drove. He had his fingers curled around one of her hands that rested on his leg, but he was focused on getting them through the rain. She listened to the windscreen wipers, periodically watched the raindrops as they beaded up against the sunroof, but mostly she just watched her husband and marveled that he was hers. Then again, she'd been doing that for most of the afternoon.

It had been a perfect day. Their afternoon had been spent with their families, celebrating, eating, and dancing. She had found herself welcomed easily into his family, without even so much as a flicker of hesitation. His father had looked at her closely a time or two, but she supposed he would find out soon enough what her birthdate was. She supposed she could thank her sister-in-law Margaret for having seasoned them so well for her.

Lord Edward and his wife, Helen, had gone out of their way to make her feel like a daughter. They had been gracious and generous with not only their time but their substance. The celebration was certainly equal to what she would have seen at Artane in her day. The only difference was the water had been drinkable and she'd known she had jeans to look forward to at some point during the evening.

Zachary pulled into Wyckham's car park and turned the car

off. She watched as the last rays of the sun burst suddenly through the clouds and stained the castle a pale gold.

"Beautiful," she breathed.

"Aye, you are."

She realized Zachary was watching her. "You're missing the sunset."

"But looking at my future."

She smiled and leaned over to kiss him. "Thank you for making me a part of it."

"You *are* it," he said. He tucked her hair behind her ear and smiled at her. "Do you mind Wyckham for your honeymoon?"

"Are we camping in the great hall?"

"No, I rented the cottage for five hundred quid a night."

She gaped at him. "Kendrick didn't charge you that."

"He did and he laughed uproariously while he was at it," Zachary said. "I thought it would be as close as we ever got to the place, so I couldn't say no."

"He's a mercenary."

"I think he would agree." He kissed her hand, then smiled at her. "Wait for me and I'll come get you."

"You have before."

"It was the very best doorway I ever stepped through, believe me."

Mary waited until he'd opened her door for her, then she ran with him to the cottage. He opened it, then picked her up in his arms and carried her through the doorway. She sat down on the sofa and watched him make a fire in the hearth. She hadn't allowed herself to think about her life overmuch during the past pair of fortnights, but now that Zachary was safely hers, she indulged in it freely.

It was nothing short of a miracle that at a score and seven she now found herself wed to a man who prized her for who she was and what she loved, a man who was the equal of her brothers and cousins in wit and canniness, a man who hadn't been afraid to pass whatever tests her father had set for him.

And a man who built a very nice fire indeed.

He brushed his hands off, then looked at her from where he knelt next to the hearth. "We could light the stove as well, if you're cold. It's ready to go."

She tilted her head to look at him. "Were you here before?"

"Yesterday," he admitted, "with your brother. He came with

me ostensibly to chop wood, but what happened was he made me not only chop but conjugate all sorts of obscure Norman French verbs while he sat on his sorry arse with his feet up and watched."

She rested her chin on her fists and smiled. "What words did you practice?"

He smiled and walked over to her on his knees. "Very useful ones, actually. After I finished with all the verbs he was interested in—most of them having to do with death and mayhem—I began with *to hold*, then moved fairly quickly on to *to kiss*, followed by *to touch*."

She felt slightly warmer than she should have, no doubt. "And then?"

"And then I asked him for a direct idiomatic translation of *come here, wench, and let me carry you to my bed where I'll keep you captive for at least a fortnight, with brief respites for food and hot showers*."

She laughed in spite of herself. "I'm slightly surprised he didn't come after you for that."

"I was the one with the axe."

She put her arms around his neck and smiled into his very lovely sea-colored eyes. "Let me hear those conjugations you worked so diligently on whilst providing me with fuel for a superior fire."

"Why don't I show you them instead?"

She couldn't have agreed more. He was making serious inroads into doing just that when a draft began to irritate her. She managed to look over to the threshold to find the door ajar.

"Zachary, the door is open."

He looked blearily in that direction, then back at her. He took her hands, kissed both palms in an appallingly lingering fashion, then pushed himself to his feet. "Don't move."

"I'm not sure I can."

He laughed uneasily then walked over to the door, not precisely steady on his feet, either. She could have sworn she saw something standing there just on the other side of the threshold, perhaps a man dressed in a plaid with a long sword hanging at his side. For all she knew, there might have been two or three such men with sharp blades and fierce miens.

He husband shut the door firmly, then bolted it for good measure.

And then he wooed her to his bed in her own language where she found that conjugations of obscure verbs was not the only thing he was very good at.

Several hours later, she watched Zachary by the light of the candle on the nightstand. She supposed he slept, though she wasn't sure she dared. She might have missed an opportunity to watch him, else.

Her father had told her that day in the lists that all he'd wanted for her was the opportunity to be a wife and a mother. She supposed he'd never considered that she might find that sort of happiness hundreds of years away from where he had, one by one, turned away dozens of men who had come to vie for her hand.

Who would have thought that the last one would be the one worth waiting for?

She closed her eyes, because she simply couldn't keep them open any longer. Zachary's arms were still around her, keeping her safe just the same.

Her father would have approved.

Epilogue

Zachary Smith stood on the edge of the great hall, looked up at the perfect Norman arch that spanned from one side to the other, and came to a conclusion.

He was more fortunate than any man had the right to be.

He smoothed down the front of his medieval tunic, then folded his arms over his chest and looked out over the festivities. His guests were celebrating both the finish of Wyckham's remodel and the christening of his firstborn child. He imagined the present company didn't look any different from the original party to celebrate Wyckham's first major remodel and the many christenings to happen there. The guests were dressed in medieval gear, musicians on period instruments entertained the guests, and a steady stream of surprisingly authentic food came from the kitchen to be laid on the lord's table so the dancers could shore up their strength.

The guest list had been varied and extensive. Two of his three brothers were in attendance with their families, all of his brothers-in-law on his side, and a very large contingent from Artane and Seakirk were there as well. Mary's great-great-nephew William had come along with his wife, Julianna, to provide much of the authenticity, given that their business was running reenactment tours. William had, as his clients would admit, a knack for setting just the right medieval sort of tone.

Zachary understood completely.

He watched the dancers swirling in the light from torches and hearthfire and allowed himself a bit of reflection on the past year and a half of his life.

Or, the past seventeen months. The first month of his marriage to Mary de Piaget had been filled with such an abundance of bliss and pleasure that he hadn't been able to tell the days apart. They had happily ensconced themselves in that little cottage outside Wyckham's walls and done little besides attend very diligently to their marriage, less diligently to her horses in the hastily built stable Kendrick had seen to for them, and only in desperation to other necessities such as food.

Bliss, indeed.

He counted himself just as fortunate once their extended honeymoon had been over and Mary had turned out to be just as enthusiastic about the Trust's projects as he was. They had spent months looking for and working on things that suited them both. But they'd also devoted an equal amount of time to restoring Wyckham, especially given that Mary had been particularly determined to see their first child born inside castle walls.

"I'm confused."

Zachary looked next to him to find his father standing there looking, well, confused. "About what, Dad?"

"The vintage of some of these people," Robert Smith said with a perplexed frown. "That William de Piaget is very good at organizing his team, I'll give you that, but I think some of his bench is batting for the other side. The *medieval* side, if you know what I mean."

Zachary didn't dare speculate. "Dad—"

"Son, did I ever ask you what you did with most of your weekends over the past almost twelve years? With that terrifying son-in-law of mine?"

"You didn't," Zachary said with a smile, "so don't start now. You won't like the answers."

"I already know the answers, Zachary," Robert said with a snort. "I'm just thinking it was time you settled down."

"I have. I'm finished with all that paranormal business."

"I hate to say this, son, but never say never."

Zachary shook his head. "Not a chance. Besides, Jamie's been taking Derrick Cameron on his adventures for months now. I have other things to do with my time."

"Well, your bride would be inducement enough to keep on the right side of the field, I imagine." He paused and looked at Mary speculatively. "1250," he announced.

"1231."

"I was close," he said archly. "You'd be surprised what sorts of things you can learn after college." He shot Zachary a look. "Actually, I imagine *you* wouldn't be."

"No," Zachary agreed with a smile, "I don't think I would."

"I've been doing all sorts of medieval research," his father added. "Never know when it might come in handy."

"Dad, quit while you're ahead."

"That's what your mother keeps telling me." He looked over the crowd once more. "I'm telling you, son. There's more of the real thing going on out there than you realize."

"Whatever you say, Dad."

"And a few ghosts, if I'm not mistaken." Robert shivered. "I recognize one of them because I've seen him in my backyard." He looked at Zachary. "He's been sitting in a brown Naugahyde recliner in the middle of my rutabaga patch."

"John Drummond?"

"So your mother says. She talks to him, why I don't know. I just hoe around him and keep my head down."

"Wise."

His father grunted, then walked off, apparently to look for something familiar to eat.

Zachary looked around. Well, his father had it partly right. There were many souls there of a medieval vintage, but they were ones who had been in the future long enough to blend in quite well.

He froze.

He could have sworn he saw a couple of blond heads peeking out from behind a banner . . . he shook his head. Impossible. He was just imagining things. After all, being a new father with the accompanying lack of sleep was enough to make anyone hallucinate now and then.

He looked around the hall and took up again his contemplation of the marvel that had become his life. He had work that he loved, a car that didn't smoke, and a castle he had wanted from the first moment he'd seen it. He had enough money for gas, horse feed, and fixing Wyckham's roof far into his old age. He had a title he could casually point to when in the company of and being hassled by his brother Alex and his brothers-in-law Jamie, Patrick, Cameron, Kendrick, and Gideon.

And while those things were very nice indeed, they couldn't hold a candle to what he valued most.

He looked for the woman who held that place in his life and found her talking to Sunshine Cameron in whatever they had chosen as the language of the day. It could have been anything from medieval Norman French to Latin; he had ceased to be surprised by the tongues his wife had mastered in her youth. He supposed she and Sunny were discussing the delights of their children, though Zachary had to admit he was partial to the two-month-old Mary held cradled close to her heart.

Her Weeness, the lady Anne Smith.

Kendrick had suggested Robinanne, just to make certain the medieval grandparents didn't feel slighted, and his father had suggested Roberta, for obvious reasons. His mother, Mary, had only smiled and agreed that Anne was a very lovely name with a long history attached.

Zachary suspected his mother had spent more time in Artane's solar reading de Piaget genealogy than was good for her.

Zachary leaned back against the wall and allowed himself the pleasure of simply watching his wife. She had once told him that it had bothered her that her mother was the epitome of grace and decorum whereas she had always tramped about in the mud in boots and uncombed hair. He wished he'd had a camera now to add to the collection of photos he'd taken of her that proved that the reality of Maryanne de Piaget Smith was vastly different from what she thought it was.

She was a perfect combination of her father's competitiveness and her mother's graciousness. He had watched her woo crusty Scots so thoroughly that they had relinquished without hesitation structures of historical significance they'd been using as extra garages. He'd watched her match wits with greedy landowners and soothe nervous landlords, winning things that cried out for a bit of tender care. She'd left the reluctant grannies to him, which he supposed had been fitting, given how much success he'd had with Mrs. Gladstone at Artane's ticket booth, who still charged him double whenever he walked through the gates.

Mary, of course, she let in for free.

He smiled to himself. Everywhere Mary went, souls warmed to her beauty and charm. That he understood as well. He spent quite a bit of his time just watching as she assaulted modern life, demanding *more* in a way that her father would have approved of. She demanded more from her horses, more from her black sports car sitting in the garage—the price of which he couldn't think about without wincing a little—more from every moment of every day she drew breath. She was, as he had told her more than once, exhausting.

He was happy to take the occasional nap in order to keep up.

He realized she was walking toward him and he pushed away from the wall, then made her a low bow. "My lady."

"My lord."

He kissed her softly, then frowned. "Where's Anne?"

"With your sister." She smiled up at him. "I thought you might want to dance."

He pulled her into his arms, because he just couldn't help himself. He held her close to his heart and marveled at the fact that he had been so richly blessed with things he hadn't anticipated. All he'd wanted was a simple life with a decent job and a fresh-faced girl next door.

Instead, what he'd gotten was a castle that took his breath away every time he walked inside, a job that left him eagerly anticipating what he would find around the next corner, and a woman who left him speechless every time he looked at her.

"I love you," he murmured.

"What brought that on?"

"I was just thinking about my life," he admitted. "And thinking that it was a bit like Wyckham in the rain."

"Ah, Zachary," she said with a half laugh. "Surely not."

"Oh, it was," he said honestly. He tucked a strand of hair behind her ear and kept her close with his other arm around her waist. "There I was, the grubby peasant just trying to make a living—"

"You were never grubby. And you were never a peasant."

He smiled. "All right, I'll give you not grubby. But I was just tromping around without any direction, hoping that I could someday get out of that rain."

"And then?"

"And then, as I was standing in this imaginary courtyard that looks remarkably like our courtyard, the sun came out and turned the entire place into something out of a fairy tale, an impossibly beautiful fairy tale where the ragged peasant finds himself continually staring in amazement at the lord's daughter he has in his arms."

"A lord's daughter in boots."

"Well, you do have to tend your horses."

She looked up at him seriously. "Am I all that to you, my love?"

He took her face in his hands and kissed her softly. "Maryanne, sweetheart, you are that and more. I don't think I really saw birds or heard bells or noticed roses on the side of the road until—"

"Until you walked into my father's loo?"

He laughed and wrapped his arms around her. "Yes. Until the first time I saw you and had my world grind to a halt. And now it's all just spinning so quickly, all I want to do is sit down and watch, on the off chance I'll miss something."

"You're very poetic tonight, husband."

"You're very inspiring." He pulled back a little and smiled at her. "Which dance shall we do?"

"You promised you'd learn one a year and you're almost out of time for this year," she said.

"I promise I'll learn one tomorrow. Don't make me humiliate myself in front of your brother now."

She put her arms back around him and hugged him tightly. "I won't, but I will thank you for tonight," she whispered. "For all these people and the music and the food, and everything you've done to make me comfortable."

He shook his head. "It's nothing compared to what you've given me, Maryanne."

She pulled away, smiling, and took his hand. "Stop before I start tearing up. Kendrick will make you pay for that."

Zachary knew she had a point, so he went with her and prepared to do his best not to fall on his face in front of his guests. It was one thing to just dance; it was another thing entirely to dance with a woman he loved with an I-can't-catch-my-breath-when-I-look-at-you kind of love.

He had a last look at all the souls around him, mortal or not, then turned his attentions back to the woman he'd longed for but never dreamed he would have.

And he lost his breath. Again.

Happily.

TURN THE PAGE
TO LEARN MORE ABOUT THE MACLEOD
AND DE PIAGET FAMILIES.

family lineage in the books of
Lynn Kurland

Robert

Ian
m: Jane
Fergusson

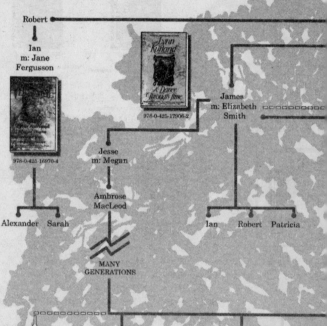

978-0-425-16970-4

978-0-425-17906-2

James
m: Elizabeth
Smith

Jesse
m: Megan

Ambrose
MacLeod

Alexander   Sarah

Ian   Robert   Patricia

MANY
GENERATIONS

Samuel MacLeod
m: Sydney Kincaid

978-0-515-12865-9

Thomas
MacLeod
McKinnon
m: Iolanthe
MacLeod

978-0-425-18197-3

Victoria
MacLeod
McKinnon
m: Connor
MacDougal

978-0-515-14127-6

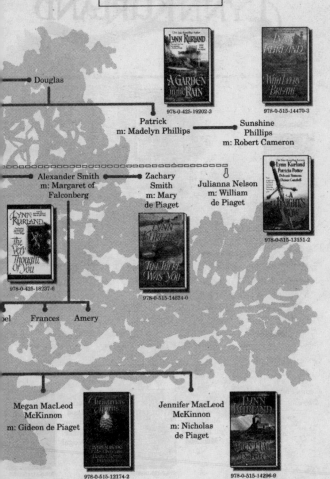

MACLEOD

Douglas

Patrick
m: Madelyn Phillips

978-0-425-19202-3

Sunshine
Phillips
m: Robert Cameron

978-0-515-14470-3

Alexander Smith
m: Margaret of
Falconberg

Zachary
Smith
m: Mary
de Piaget

Julianna Nelson
m: William
de Piaget

978-0-515-13151-2

978-0-425-18237-6

978-0-515-14624-0

bel   Frances   Amery

Megan MacLeod
McKinnon
m: Gideon de Piaget

Jennifer MacLeod
McKinnon
m: Nicholas
de Piaget

978-0-515-12174-2

978-0-515-14296-9

PA-6802

family lineage in the books of
LYNN KURLAND

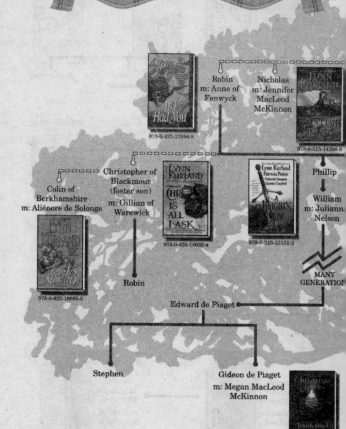

Robin
m: Anne of
Fenwyck

Nicholas
m: Jennifer
MacLeod
McKinnon

978-0-425-17694-8

978-0-515-14296-9

Phillip

Colin of
Berkhamshire
m: Aliénore de Solonge

Christopher of
Blackmour
(foster son)
m: Gillian of
Warewick

978-0-426-18033-4

978-0-515-13151-2

William
m: Juliann
Nelson

MANY
GENERATION

978-0-425-18685-5

Robin

Edward de Piaget

Stephen

Gideon de Piaget
m: Megan MacLeod
McKinnon

978-0-515-12174-2

DE PIAGET

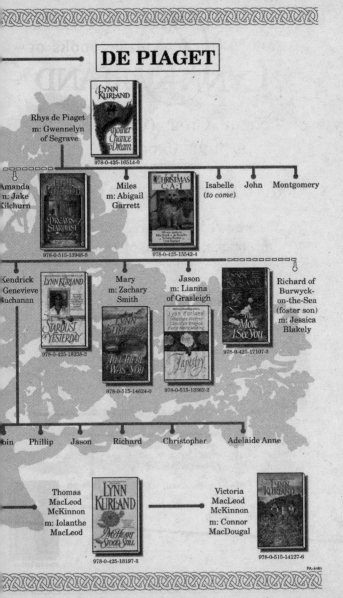

Rhys de Piaget
m: Gwennelyn
of Segrave

Another Chance to Dream
978-0-425-16514-0

Amanda
m: Jake
Kilchurn

Dreams of Stardust
978-0-515-13948-8

Miles
m: Abigail
Garrett

Christmas C·A·T
978-0-425-15542-4

Isabelle
(*to come*)

John

Montgomery

Kendrick
Genevieve
Buchanan

Stardust of Yesterday
978-0-425-18238-3

Mary
m: Zachary
Smith

Till There Was You
978-0-515-14624-0

Jason
m: Lianna
of Grasleigh

Tapestry
978-0-515-13362-2

The More I See You
978-0-425-17107-3

Richard of
Burwyck-
on-the-Sea
(foster son)
m: Jessica
Blakely

bin   Phillip   Jason   Richard   Christopher   Adelaide Anne

Thomas
MacLeod
McKinnon
m: Iolanthe
MacLeod

My Heart Stood Still
978-0-425-18197-3

Victoria
MacLeod
McKinnon
m: Connor
MacDougal

978-0-515-14127-6

PA-4/6b

Penguin Group (USA) Inc.
is proud to present

GREAT READS—GUARANTEED

We are so confident you will love
this book that we are offering a
100% money-back guarantee!

If you are not 100% satisfied with
this publication, Penguin Group (USA) Inc.
will refund your money!
Simply return the book before
July 5, 2009 for a full refund.